Summa Ghost

Chris Nelson

Summa Pacific LLC, San Diego, California

Paperback ISBN: 979-8-9926611-0-1
eBook ISBN: 979-8-9926611-1-8

Links:

    X (formerly Twitter): @SummaGhost
    Instagram: summaghost
    Web: www.SummaGhost.com

Acknowledgments:

    Many thanks to friends and close family who offered
    thoughtful suggestions for improving this book.
    Special thanks to Gerald Shaw for his editorial
    contributions. The author is responsible for any
    remaining errors.

Edition: Wolf 03; November 2025.

For my father, who loved
his family, loved to teach,
and loved to question.

Summa Ghost

Prologue

Advanced Subatomic Beings

This story is science fiction. It takes place in our Milky Way, far from Earth. It starts on a planet named Kodiak, located in the Perseus Arm of the Milky Way. From there, it moves back in time to Summa, a much larger and highly advanced planet in the Sagittarius Arm of the Milky Way.

Our main character is Apollo. On Kodiak, he is a physical human being. On Planet Summa, before Kodiak, his being is a ghost comprised of subatomic matter organized into a sophisticated network of light and energy.

Apollo and all ghosts on Planet Summa are in human form. They are smart, and they experience love, hate, compassion, and ambition. They strive for knowledge, self-worth, power, and progress. They also battle, and as Apollo matures, Summa devolves into a brutal civil war.

The billions of ghosts on Planet Summa are broken into households, but they are all children of one set of parents: Olam and Megantha.

1

Malta's Watch

Present day, on an Earth-like planet named Kodiak in the Perseus Arm of the Milky Way ...

Malta was a purple ghost. Her ghost grays were accented with a shining, purple aura, purple eyes, and lighted, gray, purple hair. She was attractive in a dangerous way, with a sly, cunning look that perfectly matched her personality.

The light of her being pulsed at a calm, even rate as she watched three human boys huddled close to a small campfire. The boys were trying to sleep, and Malta could see they were cold on this chilly forest night. Their sleep looked fitful.

As a ghost, Malta was unaffected by the cold and needed almost no sleep. She was perched in the crook of a stunted pine tree bordering the boys' camp.

The boys were in their late teens, and she knew them well. They knew her, too—or they had—from their past lives as ghosts on a planet named Summa. Now, as humans on Kodiak, they had no memory of her, nor could they see her or sense her presence.

One of the three boys was named Apollo. That was his Summa name. Here, on Kodiak, his parents had named him "Tasunke." Malta knew it meant horse. She also knew that if his parents had known about Apollo's powerful past on Summa, they would have named him "Wolf." The light of

Malta's ghost aura pulsed quicker at her thoughts of Apollo. It always did.

Malta loved Apollo from their time together on Planet Summa. Back then, they were both embroiled in Summa's world war. They fought for opposing armies. At first, they fought against each other. Then they love-fought. Finally, she fought to help Apollo.

Malta looked high above the trees. Intermittent clouds idled in the night sky, leftovers from rain the boys had endured earlier today. The churning warm air of the storm had passed, replaced with heavier, colder, stagnant night air.

Malta's gaze shifted from the sky to Apollo, whose ghost aura she could see in the darkness. Despite the essence of his ghost being thoroughly fused with his human body, the light of his beautiful blue aura emanated from his eyes and the crown of his head.

Malta knew Apollo had little perception of his long history on Summa, or of who he really was. She wished Apollo could see his past and his true self. Even more, she wished Apollo could see her. Despite being so close, he was far, and she missed him terribly. His human eyes could not see her or her aura. They were veiled from so much truth.

Apollo was with his two best friends. One was Tamir, a brilliant boy who, like Apollo, had been a warrior on Planet Summa. Tamir's ghost was green. His Kodiak parents had named him "Oncona." It had something to do with an owl. *Good*, thought Malta. At least that name makes sense, assuming owls are as wise as they look.

Apollo's other friend was named Myke, and his Kodiak name was "Keyah," which was for the earth of Kodiak itself. *Appropriate,* thought Malta. Myke was down-to-earth, direct, and grumpy, like he had been on Summa.

Also, like on Summa, Myke was infinitely devoted to Apollo. Despite his relatively young human age, Myke was a fierce fighter.

One of the boys woke, put wood on the fire, and then slept. Malta knew the boys were tired. They had been traveling for days, tracking a nomadic clan that had come down from forests far up north. The clan had raided several villages in Apollo's area. Apollo's was attacked a week ago. The clan had wisely struck while many men were away on a fall hunting excursion. Teenage girls were taken as captives. One captive was Celti, Apollo's younger sister.

Malta continued her watch over the three boys. They were barely old enough to undertake their current quest. But Malta knew that Apollo was determined to save his sister, and Myke and Tamir would not let him go alone.

Malta had watched as Apollo's mother pleaded with him to stay. The chances of getting Celti back were slim. His mother feared losing her son. *I'll do my best to protect him,* Malta thought. But she knew her abilities to do so, as a ghost, were limited.

Apollo's dark human hair was a mess. His face, hands, and fingernails were dirty from days of hard travel. A muddy smudge had been on his cheek all day. Malta wished she could touch him to clean it off. The dirt contrasted sharply with his piercing blue eyes—the same eyes she had so loved when they were both ghosts on Summa.

Malta knew Apollo's antelope skin coat was too thin for this northward trip. Already, the boys had entered aspen and ash country, the leaves just starting to turn with the fall. But the clan wintered much farther north, in boreal forests thick with pine, spruce, and fir.

Malta wished she could show the boys what she knew. Their worlds and perspectives were so limited. They had no memory of all the science they learned on Summa. Here on Kodiak, the boys' written language was limited. Apollo's reading and writing skills were rudimentary at best. There were almost no books and few written records. It was so primitive!

The night's first moon was rising, and the second, smaller, sister moon would appear in a few hours. Malta knew that the second moon, to Apollo, represented his little sister. "I will find you," she had heard Apollo vow to that small moon and his friends.

Before Apollo had lain down for the night, Malta had watched him do what he did every night. He moved away from the others and went to a clearing to look at the sky. Some leaves on nearby trees were bright yellow, reflecting the moon's light. These leaves made no sound, and the air was still, the ambiance temple-like, as Apollo spoke to the heavens.

Malta knew that Apollo understood there was someone with whom he should converse. Each night, Malta would watch Apollo's interactions with the sky. Sometimes, when Apollo kept his mind still and listened carefully, she could see Sapienti's light wash down and penetrate Apollo's thick skull. Apollo would thank the Sky Spirit for the inspiration. Other times, she watched as Sapienti's light fell on Apollo, but his body was too tired, or his mind too noisy, and the light could do nothing for him. Then there were the nights Sapienti was totally quiet, leaving Apollo to his own determination. *I wouldn't be quiet,* she thought. *If Apollo were trying to speak with me, I would always respond.*

Tonight, as Malta watched the human she loved, she saw him plead with the Sky Spirit to protect his sister. Malta was sure his pleas were heard, and she hoped he would receive guidance.

She moved close to Apollo, her female aura pulsing faster and brighter as she neared him. The male pulse of Apollo's ghost did not change, proof that he had no sense of her close presence. Malta spoke aloud to him, though she knew he could not hear. "I will try to help you," she told him. "I love you, Apollo. I always will. I know who you are and what you did for Planet Summa. You deserve help, and I will try."

2

Wolf Sense

While Apollo and his friends rested, Malta left her crook in the tree near their camp and rose above the forest. She flew ahead to find the clan that had taken Celti. She navigated over thick pines and small meadows, then a canyon with a small river, its waters silver ribbons in the night's light. From her altitude, she soon saw campfires, and she arrived at the clan in minutes, having crossed territory the human boys would need a day to cover on foot.

Malta found Apollo's little sister, Celti. The clan had given her basic bedding for warmth. She was tied up, but it did not appear she was being mistreated. Malta looked at Celti's feet. Her moccasins were wearing out and showed some holes. Celti's feet were tough and could go a long distance, but this was rough terrain, and Malta hoped the clan would give her better footwear. Malta could see that Celti was stuffing grass into her moccasins to plug holes.

Life with a physical body is hard, Malta thought. *I'm glad I'm still a ghost.*

Through the night air, the distant mournful howl of a singular wolf could be heard. Malta watched as Celti bolted straight up out of her bedding.

One of her captors, a large man with a flat nose, looked at her and laughed. "Don't be afraid, little girl. We will eat you before the wolves do." At that, his friends laughed, too.

Malta knew they had mistaken Celti's reaction to the wolf. They thought she was afraid. Little could they know of her gift. "You don't know either, do you, Celti?" Malta remarked to the girl, moving close to her. "But you can feel it. That is for sure."

Celti, of course, as a human, could neither hear nor sense Malta. Celti's focus remained on the night. Malta watched the girl as she sniffed the air. Instinctively, Celti was reaching out for something she did not yet understand.

Celti and Apollo's home on Kodiak was too far south for wolves. There were coyotes, which would be interesting to Celti, an animal lover, but until now, Malta doubted that Celti had ever heard or seen a wolf. Malta knew that Celti's captors would have no clue about the dormant power inside this girl. They were walking her directly into the source. Malta could see that Celti was already plugged in, and her wolf power was switching on. The clan's winter home was full-on wolf country. *Celti's real home,* Malta thought. *She doesn't know it yet. It's Apollo's real home, too. They are brother and sister wolves. Their lives on Summa showed us that.*

Malta knew the clan's raid, albeit seemingly random from the clan's perspective, was far from random. No… the Sky Spirit was the director in this human drama. The wolf aspect was only part of the plot. Another, equally important part, was one of the other girls who had been taken captive. That girl's Summa name was Torith.

Malta knew that Torith and Apollo were meant to be together. Right now, here on Kodiak, they did not know each other, being from widely separated villages. But on Summa, they had fought together and loved each other. The clan's raids were now bringing them together.

Malta had long since put away her jealousy of Torith. Malta's choices were made, as were the consequences. She would love Apollo as a ghost. Torith would love him as a human.

Malta watched Celti and Torith. Already, they seemed to have a natural bond, even though they would have no memory of each other from before. It had only been yesterday that Torith was taken captive.

The flat-nosed man came over to Celti, and Malta saw her bristle. Flat nose looked her over, close and personal. Malta could see the fog from his stinky, warm breath on her, and Malta thought the captor might abuse her. Malta debated attempting a ghost attack on the man, but then she saw Torith move into action. Here on Kodiak, Torith might remember nothing from her full life on Summa, but at her core, she was still Torith, which meant she was a powerhouse.

Malta saw Torith leap to her feet and grab her lower stomach. Then, she started gyrating in pain, moaning, and escalating into outright screams of agony. Torith, lucky or not, was menstruating. Malta knew that, and it was another reason Malta was happy to remain a ghost. The men should have known Torith's condition, but Malta's experience was that men pretend to ignore the world of menstruation. To them, it was a terrifying mystery, and one they deluded themselves into thinking did not exist. Torith used that mentality to her advantage. She reached her tied hands under her coat and came out with a handful of blood. She showed it to the men, who were now terrified. All of them backed away from this bloody witch. Nobody was going to touch her or any of the girls.

Malta saw Torith catch Celti's eye and wink at her, but then Torith continued acting like she was in horrible pain, much worse than she was.

The men were grossed out. They untied Celti so she could help the crazy, bleeding woman. One stood guard with a bow in case Celti ran, but there was no way the men were going anywhere near that mess.

Celti ordered one of the men to give her his blanket. He did. Malta was surprised. It meant the man was going to have a cold night. Celti and Torith's acting skills were strong!

Malta thought it amazing that all these people—Apollo, Tamir, Myke, Celti, and Torith—who had been close to each other on Summa, were now intertwined here on this double-mooned earth. The Sky Spirit, as Apollo called him, definitely had a plan.

Half an hour later, the captives and captors had calmed down, and everybody was trying to sleep. Torith and Celti were buried together in their newly acquired blanket. Malta smiled, seeing the one captor who now had no bedding. *Good for you, you butt-faced pitner,* Malta thought.

Malta launched into the midnight air and headed back to the boys, wondering how they were doing. The second sister moon was starting to peek over the eastern horizon. Apollo would soon wake his team and get them moving. Malta wanted to arrive before Apollo woke. While he slept, she sometimes could feel some of his dreams. With his mental defenses asleep, she could marginally inject herself into his brain. In doing so, she would try to remind him of her, Summa, and all he had been before. Once, she heard Apollo tell Tamir about a dream he'd had. It was a dream about being on another planet and romantically fighting with a purple ghost. Malta knew that was not a dream. It was a faint memory.

As Malta closed in on Apollo's camp, she could see something was wrong. The boys were fast asleep, and a pack of parasite ghosts had surrounded and attacked them. Apollo and Tamir were in distress. Like Malta, the attackers were ghosts who had been banished from Summa for their rebellion. They had lost the war on Summa. But unlike Malta, these ghosts only had one desire, and that was to continue the battle here on Kodiak. Their hatred burned strong, and they relished hammering on Apollo, Tamir, and Myke.

The effects of the attack showed on Apollo and Tamir's faces. Their auras flickered erratically as they struggled in their dreams. Malta knew these boys were too strong to be seriously hurt, and when they awoke, they would shoo away their attackers' negativity. But it angered her that they were being attacked at all. How dare these kutard ghosts assault the man she loved!

As for Myke, the ghosts were attacking him, too. But Malta could only laugh at that. She had been inside Myke's essence at night. Intruders were not welcome. His whole persona screamed, "Get out!" The ghosts trying to stage a coup on Myke's psyche were wasting their time and not having any fun. Myke was a rock.

Malta knew this ghost gang. Their leader was a weasel of a ghost named Lucen. Apollo had fought Lucen on Summa and beaten him badly. Now Lucen was looking for revenge, and Malta would have none of it. Malta attacked the ghost gang with full force. She was no weakling of a fighter, having been a high-ranking commander on Summa in the rebellion army. Some of Lucen's ghosts tried to resist, but Malta slammed them hard.

"Okay, okay," Lucen said. "We're leaving. You're crazy. We're going."

They started to leave, but it was not fast enough for Malta, so she ramped up her attack even more, going after them like the wolverine version of a she-devil banshee.

"Alright!" Lucen pleaded. "We're outta here!" He and his ghosties blasted away in a hurry.

"You leave Apollo alone!" she yelled at them as their auras disappeared over the tree line.

The commotion awakened Apollo, who sat up and tried to clear his head. Tamir was sitting up, too. They looked at each other. "Wild dream," Apollo said, shaking his head.

"Me too," said Tamir.

They looked over at Myke, who had not stirred. "Not him," said Apollo. "Look at that earth baby."

"Yep," said Tamir. "I doubt he's even cold." Tamir started to stand up. "I'm freezing. I need to get moving."

"Sister Moon is starting to show," said Apollo, looking towards the East.

At that point, Apollo and Tamir heard the distant cry of a wolf, north of them, in higher terrain. "I hope we see one of those," Apollo said. "I've heard stories about them."

"Nothing like a yappy coyote," Tamir added. "I talked to a hunter who goes north. He says they hunt in packs, with great skill. They are big, and sometimes they kill humans."

Apollo did not respond. Malta saw him go over and wake the grumpy earth boy. Five minutes later, they were put together and continued tracking north. An hour later, Apollo used his bow to shoot a small deer, which they quickly field-dressed to protect the meat. Unlike usual, they did not have time to use all parts of the deer. It was a shame, for example, to waste the hide. They cut thin strips of some of the best meat, which they cooked over a fire. They were quick, and the process only cost them two hours. The rapid cooking led to charred, tough, dry meat. But at least it was nutrition, and it would keep them going. This morning's kill would feed them for several days. Soon, they were back to tracking the clan.

So much work to keep those bodies working, Malta thought as she watched. *I'm glad I'm a ghost.*

By noon, the boys had found where the clan had camped the night before. Malta watched Apollo search the ground, where he located several stalks of grass tied into small double loops. "She's still alive," he told Tamir, holding up a double loop. "Celti's sign."

Malta saw Apollo pick at some grass that showed dried blood. Apollo smelled the blood. Malta wondered if Apollo could discern the difference in blood types. She was not sure, but she doubted it. Apollo looked worried. Malta wished she could tell Apollo the blood was not Celti's.

The boys continued. They were closing in. Malta heard them talk strategy, but they really did not know what to do. There were only three of them. They knew from the tracks that the clan must have twenty men, all of whom would be seasoned warriors.

Two more days passed. They had moved into higher terrain, with thicker trees and colder weather.

The boys had to take more care where they camped. This took time because they needed some shelter and, ideally, big rocks to reflect heat from their fire. It was too cold to be in the open. They had found a beautiful moose hide cloak on the trail, accidentally dropped by the clan. It was Tamir who spotted it first. He offered it to Apollo, but Apollo refused. Tamir was the skinniest of the three of them.

He needed it the most, but Apollo and Myke needed more clothing, too.

Two days later, Apollo and the boys saw the clan from high ground as it crossed a grass meadow in a small valley a mile ahead. Malta heard the boys trying to decide if one of the captives was Celti. Malta knew Celti was still safe. Torith was, too. One of the other captive girls, however, had fallen very ill. The clan had finally taken most of her clothing and left her. The wolves soon finished her.

The timing of the moons had become less favorable for Apollo and the boys. The moons were coming up later in the night, which meant the boys did not have the light they needed for an early start.

This night, like all others, Apollo went off to speak to the sky. It was dark, and neither moon showed. It was also overcast, and there was no light from the stars. This was a particularly dark flavor of night.

As Apollo spoke to the sky, two things happened at once. Malta knew they were not a coincidence. The first was Sapienti's light coming down from above. Apollo was receiving a strong feed this time. The second was that, right then, a pack of wolves started howling with an intensity Malta had never heard before.

Malta knew where both camps were. From what she could tell, the mad wolf howling was coming from a high point midway between the camps. Apollo certainly heard the ruckus, and Celti would have, too. *That is not by chance,* Malta thought. *The Sky Spirit is playing chess tonight. He is moving his players into position.*

Malta watched as Apollo continued to converse with the Great Spirit while also looking in the direction of the wolves. Then Sapienti's light dissipated. "Thank you," she heard Apollo say. "I understand."

Apollo walked back to his camp, where Myke and Timir were building up the fire. "We're going to have visitors tonight," Apollo said.

"What?"

"Tonight. Visitors."

Myke and Tamir looked at each other, then back at Apollo.

"Who?" Myke asked. "Tell us." Myke's voice was direct.

Apollo held both hands out in front of him as if pushing back. "Look," Apollo said. "You need to believe me. It will be wolves. Two of them. Tonight. Coming here to camp."

Again, Myke and Tamir looked at each other. "Is this a joke?" Tamir asked. "What are you talking about?" Both Myke and Tamir started to chuckle. "Is this your little-boy campfire story?"

Wolves howled again, right at the instant. This time, they were much closer. Apollo pointed toward the sound, showing a knowing look on his face.

Myke and Tamir were not laughing anymore. "That's not funny, Apollo," Tamir said. He sounded nervous. "You are giving me the heebie-jeebies."

Malta was enjoying this. Her brave boys were scared. Normally, she would want to protect them, but Malta knew what the wolves meant. There was no danger, at least not to the boys. It was fun to watch them squirm.

Myke picked up his bow. He also checked the large knife on his hip. It was a beautiful instrument, carved from the antler of an elk. Myke's face said, *I-don't-know-if-you-are-messing-with-me… but… I'm-going-to-be-ready-anyway.*

The blackness of the night would prevent the boys from seeing anything beyond the light of the campfire. Malta shivered, thinking of how vulnerable she would feel as a human in this situation.

"Wait here," Apollo said to his friends. At that, Apollo stepped a few yards from camp. He was visible, the firelight on his back. But everything beyond him was pure darkness.

"He doesn't even have his bow!" Tamir said.

"Put more wood on the fire," Myke said. Tamir was near their woodpile, and he complied.

Apollo stood his ground. The night was quiet. Nothing happened for about ten minutes.

"Are you okay, buddy?" Myke called out.

Apollo held up a hand, signaling silence.

Another ten minutes went by. Then, Apollo went down on both knees, still facing the dark.

Malta knew what was happening, and she wanted to see it from Myke's perspective. She moved over to be near him. She could see Apollo reaching out his hand, and she watched the tension build on Myke and Tamir's faces as they strained to see anything beyond Apollo.

Suddenly, there it was. Terrifying at first. The blue eyes of an enormous wolf, its head gray in color, with the gray interrupted by shards of black. The wolf's muzzle came within inches of Apollo's face. Man and beast were eye to eye. Firelight reflected off the blue in the wolf's eyes. The wolf licked Apollo's nose.

Normally, Malta would have seen the wolf's aura long before the animal was visible to the boys. But to Malta's amazement, the wolf had suppressed its aura on the approach, and only now did the animal release its light. Even more surprising, the blue of the wolf's aura perfectly matched the blue of Apollo's. Also, the light of their auras surged in sync, matching each other's pattern. Without a doubt, Apollo and this wolf belonged together.

A second wolf appeared, equally big. It was brown and gray.

"Apollo's wolves!" Malta exclaimed to herself. His ghost wolves from Planet Summa. Here, now, in the flesh!

3

Planet Summa

Years before, on Planet Summa, in the Milky Way's Sagittarius arm. Apollo and his friends, Tamir and Torith, are ghosts in their early teens ...

Apollo's blue eyes broke away from the screen of his computer and shifted to his friend, Tamir, who was at his workstation on the other side of the classroom. Tamir showed no movement. His ghost being was frozen, his green eyes fixed and forward. Apollo could see that Tamir was in one of his thinking trances. Typical, thought Apollo, who turned back to his computer... his "comm"... keeping his head down to avoid the teacher's roving eye.

Apollo's fingers rapidly moved across the device's input keyboard, entering the words his eager mind formed about today's field trip. His fingers stopped, visible for an instant, only to disappear again in a flurry of motion. Apollo's report was going well, and he would finish soon.

Apollo paused to think. While doing so, his eyes randomly settled on a large globe in the front of the room. The globe's sphere was lit from the inside, and it beautifully represented all of Planet Summa.

Apollo frequently checked on Tamir, who had not typed anything for five minutes.

Frustrating, Apollo thought.

Apollo knew Tamir's lack of movement was not

because Tamir had nothing to say. No, on the contrary, Tamir had too much to say, but the teacher had been clear: this report was only to be three pages. Any more would result in a lower grade. Brevity would be Tamir's greatest challenge.

Once the students' reports were done, they could go home for the day. Apollo did not want to wait long after class for Tamir to finish. Unfortunately, Apollo could see that waiting would be inevitable.

I'm gonna have to wait for him outside, Apollo thought, preferring to be in front of the school while Tamir finished. Apollo entered the last paragraphs of his report, then he did a quick proof and hit submit. His teacher acknowledged the submission by verbally telling Apollo he could go.

Apollo touched the "Away" button on his comm, to which it responded. "Are you sure?" Apollo touched "Yes," and the comm vaporized, uploading its physical self to a regional network server.

Apollo caught Tamir's eye, signaled that he would wait outside, and then glided out of the room. He had to be home in thirty minutes. He could make it in fifteen. Hopefully, Tamir would finish soon so they could talk before Apollo had to go.

While Apollo waited in front of the classroom, others were leaving the school. Most students came out of their classrooms through the doors, as you were supposed to, but a few emerged directly through the walls. As ghosts, they could do that. There was a school rule against it, but enforcement was lax. Punishment rarely consisted of more than a lecture on proper ghost manners.

Apollo saw his friend, Torith, exit her room in a nearby building. She had used the door, and she immediately waved at Apollo and came over to greet him. Her attention made Apollo happy.

"Torith! How are you?"

"Apollo... Hi... !" She seemed to be in a hurry. The aura of her black hair flashed aquas and browns. Her eyes did the same, and her whole being pulsed with energy.

"It's great to see you," Apollo said.

"Thanks," she said. "Hey... I can't stay because I need to rush home."

Apollo had hoped differently. He was disappointed.

"I'm sorry, Apollo," she said.

Apollo could tell she meant it.

"Mom is going to a meeting where that Sughi guy is speaking. Have you heard of him?"

"Yes," Apollo nodded, "I think he's—"

"Yeah, so anyway," she interrupted, "I have to take care of my little brother so she can go."

"Why?" asked Apollo. "Can't she take him? Or can't she be in both places?"

"Yes," she said, "but it's all part of making me re-spon-si-ble." Torith rolled her eyes, clearly unhappy with the idea.

Apollo tried to say more, but she cut him off. "Sorry, A.P., I gotta blast."

Apollo liked Torith. "Okay... well... see you tomorrow or something," he mumbled, trying to show obvious disappointment. But Torith could not have noticed. She was already gone.

Apollo had heard about the guy named "Sughi." Everybody had, and he knew that Sughi's full name was "B. Z. Sughi."

"Come on, Tamir! Hurry up!" Apollo muttered, shaking his head.

Apollo waited another five minutes and was going to leave when Tamir shot out of the classroom.

"It's about time!" exclaimed Apollo, digging at his friend. "I'll bet you were the last one in there."

"No... no, not me. I wasn't last," Tamir responded defensively. "But that report was hard. I could have written a hundred pages about those fish." Tamir then abruptly changed the subject. "Hey, do you want to go surfing at the canyon? I asked Mom this morning, and she said I could go."

"No, that's the problem, I have to be home by four thirty."

"Why?"

"I don't know. Mom sent me a message on my comm."

"Are you in trouble?"

"Naw. Torith said Mom is going to some Sughi meeting. Maybe that's why I need to be home, but ..."

"Sughi meeting?" Tamir's green eyes lit up, and his aura pulsed with interest.

"Yeah, I just saw Torith. She was in a big rush to get home to help."

"Man, I wish I could go to that meeting," said Tamir. "I hear the Z-Man can pump it out. All of Summa is talking about him."

Apollo did not respond. He had little interest in the Z-Man.

Tamir continued, "My oldest brother has been to some of the meetings. He comes home all jazzed."

Apollo looked down and away. He did not want to talk about Sughi, and he switched the subject. "So, what about tomorrow?"

"Tomorrow?"

"Yes... surfing... at the canyon. I can't go today."

Tamir's face went into thinking mode. "Okay," he said. "That should work. I'll check with Mom and call you."

At that instant, a comm materialized in front of Apollo. It was self-suspended at waist height and arm's length. The comm's display was blank except for a call-waiting indicator. Apollo knew he could ask the comm to tell him who was calling, but he was sure it was Mom, so he reached over and touched the screen. His mother's face appeared on the display. She could see him just as he could her.

"Hi, Mom," said Apollo.

Tamir stood off to the side and out of the comm's field of view. He immediately started pulling faces at Apollo, trying to get him to break concentration and laugh. Apollo knew what was happening and forced himself to look straight at the comm.

"Apollo, honey. It's four ten. Will you be home by four thirty, like I asked?"

"Yes, Mom. I'm leaving in just a sec. Why do I have to be home?"

"Reemo—your Mentor—called me this morning. He said he'd like to come by and talk to you. He should be here at five. But I want you home half an hour early to calm down and recharge."

Upon hearing the word "Mentor," Tamir switched his antics from mere face pulling to full-bodied teasing, raising his arms above his head and lowering them towards the ground. Tamir made sweeping, mocking bows as if paying homage to Apollo, like he was some great god or king.

Apollo's eyes wavered briefly from the comm to Tamir, and he struggled to hold a straight face. That was all Mom needed, and immediately, the comm rotated to bring Tamir into view. This caught Tamir in the middle of one of his ridiculous bows.

"Oh... Hello, Tamir," she said. "I see you're having fun." She gave Tamir a knowing smile.

"Good... day... ahh... Mom... Megantha."

Apollo saw Tamir trying to wipe the embarrassment off his face. Tamir's green aura ramped up, showing a strong surge.

"Did you and Apollo have a good time on the field trip today?"

"Yes, Mom, it was great."

Now it was Apollo's turn to pull faces at Tamir, and his favorite made him look something like a duck-billed platypus. He took his two arms and pushed them through the sides of his chest and up his neck so they were inside him and no longer visible. Then he stuck his hands out of his mouth, held them palm-to-palm, and flapped them open and shut so they looked like the bill of the platypus. Then Apollo tried to pull a duck-bill face with his own ghost face. This was impossible, and he made wild facial contortions trying to do so.

Apollo knew his platty act was sure to unseat Tamir. He and Tamir had made quite a scene a few days ago, pulling this same face to the whole class. The class had been studying mammals that swim. The teacher had left the room for a few minutes, and Apollo and Tamir took advantage of the lack of supervision to show off and put on a duck-billed-platty show.

"How deep did they take you, Tamir?" Megantha asked.

Today's field trip was to the ocean to study fish that live deep. They went below ten thousand feet. It was dark down there, and the adults kept them together.

Apollo could see that Tamir did not hear Megantha's

question. Instead, all of Tamir's concentration was on not
bursting out laughing.

"Tamir... Tamir, are you okay?"

Apollo watched as Tamir tried to hold his composure.

"So, did you get to see any of those deep-sea angler
fish?"

The deep-sea angler was probably the best fish they
had seen all day. Apollo remembered them well, and he
knew Tamir did, too. The lighted lures sticking out of their
heads were awesome.

Apollo took advantage of their mother's question to
switch from a platypus face to an angler fish by sticking an
arm out the top of his head, making a fist, and cocking it
towards Tamir while also puffing his cheeks up like a
blowfish.

This was too much, and to Tamir's total humiliation,
he burst out laughing, backing away from the comm and
putting his hands up in defeat.

At Megantha's command, the comm immediately
repositioned for a view of both boys. "All right, boys, so
much for talking to you two."

Apollo raised his fist in a sign of triumph, proud of
his victory over Tamir's self-control.

"I'll see you in a few minutes, Apollo." Her tone
meant she was okay with their silliness, but it also meant that
Apollo had better be home on time.

"Okay, Mom." Apollo was about to send the comm
away when he remembered surfing tomorrow. "Oh, Mom!
Can I go surfing at the canyon tomorrow?"

"Alone?"

"No, with Tamir and Torith?"

This was the first Apollo had said anything to Tamir
about taking Torith. Tamir gave him a look. Apollo knew he

should have said something to Tamir first.

"Yes, of course. But will you two take care of Torith?"

Apollo was surprised by Mom's question. He always thought Torith could take care of herself. But he answered, "Yes, Mom."

"Both of you?"

"Yes," said Tamir. "We will."

"Okay. Have fun tomorrow. And, Apollo, you'd better start home."

"I will, Mom."

Apollo knew the conversation with Mom was finished, and he wanted to quickly tap the comm's screen and send it back to the server, but he forced himself to politely wait the extra few seconds. Etiquette said Mom needed to sign off first.

"Bye, boys," she said, ending their session, and Apollo released the comm.

Tamir jumped in. "Torith? Who said anything about her going?" Tamir was acting upset.

Apollo knew Tamir liked Torith, and it would be fine with him if she came. But Apollo knew Tamir was stinging from Apollo's victory over his self-control. Tamir had to get back at Apollo somehow.

"Oh, come on, T. You know you like Torith. If she can come, you'll be there."

"Yeah, but she'll come for you." It was no secret that Torith favored Apollo over Tamir.

"Well, maybe I can get her to bring a friend. How 'bout that?"

"Whatever," said Tamir, shrugging his shoulders in a vain attempt to hide his interest.

"Alright. I'll work on that. Now… I need to go. I'm

going to be late. See you."

    "Later," said Tamir.

4

Lake Minnick

Apollo had only minutes to cover the forty-mile distance to his home. Between the school and home was a good-sized lake named Lake Minnick. Apollo loved that lake and had spent many hours exploring its shorelines. Sometimes, Tamir or Torith joined him on his lake excursions. It was a wonderful place. Its water was beautifully clear, and one of Apollo's favorite lake activities was to loiter just above the water's surface while watching the freshwater fish below.

Lake Minnick was only part of the journey home. After the lake, the terrain rose sharply into a steep mountain range with tops above the timberline. On the other side of that range was a high valley covered with small lakes, scrawny pines, durable alpine scrub, and scattered rocky knolls. Then, there was a second mountain range. Apollo's home—and Torith's—were about seven miles apart on the far side of the second range.

Normally, it took Apollo fifteen to twenty minutes to get home. If he did not lollygag, he could make it by four-thirty. He left Tamir and rose to altitude, pushing his weightless, subatomic ghost essence through the air. He chose a higher altitude than usual, wanting to avoid any ghost students who were also headed home. Most traffic was down at a few hundred feet off the ground. Apollo went to a thousand.

Soon, he was over Lake Minnick, with the first of the

two mountain ranges rising beyond. A breeze was forming, born of colder, heavier air in the high terrain. It rolled down the steep slopes and swept across the lake, ruffling the water's otherwise glassy surface.

In the middle of Lake Minnick were two islands, one bigger than the other. The best fish were close to the bigger one, and much of that island was covered with pine trees. In the middle of the island was a clearing containing an enormous, round granite rock.

Apollo did not have time to stop and explore the lake, but he glanced briefly down at the larger of the two islands. When doing so, his eye caught something that did not seem right.

Ignore it, he thought. *I'm in a hurry.* He flew on for another ten seconds, now well into crossing the lake.

What was that? He kept going. *Not now. I have to get home!*

He continued for another ten seconds, and then his frontal lobe knocked hard on his conscience. *What did you see?*

Apollo stopped. Recalculating, he decided he had to turn around, go back, and look. "It's going to make me late," he said to himself. He hoped Mom would understand, even if it meant a discourse on time management.

Reversing course and halving his above-ground altitude, he was soon back over the island. He could see several ghosts near the white rock in the middle of the island. One ghost was surrounded by three others. Why surrounded?

He came closer.

Then he realized the person in the middle was Torith. *What's she doing here?* Apollo advanced, wanting a better look. *I thought she had to be home.*

The breeze off the mountain blew a little stronger,

and another wave of ripples textured the lake. Apollo recognized two of the three ghosts surrounding Torith. One was Gammon, an older boy at the school. Apollo knew little about him except that Tamir and others said he was mean and bossy. The other was a friend of Gammon's named Escue. The third person was an older girl Apollo remembered seeing at school, but he did not know her. She had a mysterious look, and her eyes and aura were a deep purple.

Apollo continued his approach, worried for Torith and apprehensive about Gammon and his companions.

Gammon saw Apollo seconds before Apollo arrived. Gammon turned and aggressively faced Apollo. At the same time, he barked orders at Escue and the purple girl, who stayed firmly facing Torith. All of this was not good; worse, Torith looked confused and scared. There were none of the normal shimmers of light in her black hair. Her eyes were dull and colorless. She showed no pulsing aura. She was beaten down. Apollo knew this was bad.

"Get out of here, kid!" shouted Gammon. Apollo was too young and insignificant for Gammon to know or care about his name. "This is our business, and you're not part of it!"

Apollo was intimidated, but he asked the older boy what was happening.

"None of your beeswax, wiffle boy," retorted Gammon, with as much insult as possible.

Apollo had no idea what a "wiffle boy" was, but it could not be a compliment. "I... I want to ask Torith something."

"Yo... fikabean. I don't believe I stuttered. She's talkin' to me right now. And that means she's not gonna be jaw-jacking with you." While aggressively stating this,

Gammon moved within two feet of Apollo, clearly invading his comfort zone. At this short distance, the presence of Gammon and Apollo's ghosts intermixed. They could feel each other's emotions and intensity levels. It was a back-and-forth electricity.

Apollo knew Gammon's ghost could sense its superior power, and the older boy would easily read his fear. But when it came to Torith, he was clear. He would be brave. Steeling himself, he held Gammon's gaze without flinching.

Gammon was weird-looking. Scary, too. The kids at school all knew him for that. He was pale with short black hair and black eyes, contrasting with an extra-light complexion. His aura was there, but it was not a color. It simply existed, and it was hard to describe. The kid was downright spooky. Tamir called him a zombie, saying he doubted Gammon was from Planet Summa. "He was born on the moon," Tamir had said. "A moon baby. He's not really a ghost." Some of the kids at school started calling Gammon Moon Baby, but that was only behind his back. Nobody dared say it to his face.

Gammon's eyes blazed like coal. Apollo tried to shine his eyes, too, forcing power to his blues. Apollo also pushed power to his blue aura, accentuating his surge, hoping to project strength.

But Apollo knew Gammon was too old and strong for him. He could feel this as they stayed toe-to-toe, flailing at each other with their internal voltage. Apollo was losing fast. He could not hold his position. *But I have to protect Torith! What are they doing to her?*

Apollo had been through numerous conversations with Dad and Mom about what was happening right now. Gammon could not make him do anything Apollo had the mental strength to resist.

Mom would always tell him, "You think it's hard now when somebody is trying to force you to do something you don't want to do? Well, it will be much more difficult when you are physical… when you're a Blood. You'll feel that person's power, just like you do now, but they'll also be able to hurt, damage, and break your physical, Blood body. You must learn to be strong, my son, because it's all in preparation for later."

Apollo backed up a couple of feet, trying to put space between himself and Gammon.

"Torith!" he cried out, fear in his voice for her and for Gammon's inevitable reaction at being openly defied. "Are you okay?"

"Apollo!" he heard her call back, fear in her voice, too.

But that was all Apollo heard because Gammon's response was outright ballistic. Gammon lunged at Apollo, yelling and screaming obscenities. "You, pitner! You mealy-mouthed pitner! I told you to leave. Now get out of here!"

Apollo may not have known what a "wiffle boy" was, but he had heard the word "pitner." His family did not use it, and neither did his friends. Mom would punish him severely if she ever heard him say it.

Gammon did not stop there. He lunged again, and this time, he did not stop a foot or two away. Gammon went for Apollo's core, invading the same physical space as Apollo, mixing his ghost with Apollo's, becoming part of him. All over, under, inside, and outside of him. Gammon moved around and through him, projecting intense, painful voltages of hate, blackness, and aggressiveness.

Once again, Apollo was caught off guard. He knew Gammon would be angry, but Apollo never expected this level of attack. He tried to fight back, but the essence of his subatomic ghost did not have the power to match that of Gammon.

Apollo's ghost was an intricately woven network of light, energy, and subatomic matter. These forces coursed through billions of pathways, all interconnected by intelligent hubs called menapses. As Apollo matured, his menapses multiplied, weaving an even denser and more sophisticated web that expanded the strength and reach of his ghostly essence.

In battle or under extreme stress, the menapses served as protectants. If overloaded, they would spark open to sever connections and prevent the spread of damage to the rest of Apollo's ghostly essence—his network.

Gammon's onslaught was a direct attack on Apollo's core. Millions of his menapses were overloading and protectively sparking open. This was painful, and it was breaking Apollo down. He had to stop the damage before he was rendered inert.

Apollo backed off, then moved sideways, up and down. But Gammon was much too fast and experienced. Apollo's willpower and resolve were depleting. Apollo had no choice but to escape. He went into the ground, directly into dense granite rock. To help Torith, he would first need to retreat and regroup.

5

Protect Torith

After going underground, Apollo quickly maneuvered through a random zig-zag pattern to escape Gammon. Gammon tried to follow—Apollo could feel it—but even Gammon's age, strength, and experience were not enough to keep up with the younger boy. Down in this dense rock, he and Apollo only had forward senses of a few feet. They could easily travel at speeds exceeding their vision and sensory capabilities. Luckily for Apollo, this meant he could escape the older and stronger Gammon.

Apollo knew immediately when he had shaken his enemy because the assault on his essence ceased, bringing instant relief and allowing him to think clearly. Now, he had to put distance between himself and Gammon.

Apollo stayed underground and headed in a direction he estimated would take him off the island and under the lake. He tried to make a straight line deeper into the rock. Once he thought he had gone far enough, Apollo started back up, hoping to come up under the lake water. However, distance and direction were hard to judge when transitioning through dense matter such as granite. He was surprised to come across a good-sized tree root, indicating he was nearing the surface of what had to be the island and not the lake itself.

Apollo was about to go back down when he realized the tree was a better option than his original plan. He followed the tree root slowly, looking for the tree's main trunk, which he found with little difficulty.

Apollo stayed inside the tree trunk and tracked it up and up, well above ground level, staying concealed inside, hoping the high vantage point would give him a good look at what was happening. Then he moved his head slowly, from the center of the tree's trunk to the outside, through the thick, rough bark of the massive pine. He looked around, careful to expose as little of himself as possible.

He found himself looking out over the lake. He was in a tree at the edge of the island. Gammon, Torith, and the others were behind him. Apollo went back through the tree and looked out the other side.

There they were. Torith, Escue, the purple girl, and Gammon. Gammon was circling, looking for Apollo while also talking loudly to Torith. "Your boyfriend's a coward, Torith. Did you see how he ran away? We'd never do that. You join us, and we'll stand by you to the end!"

"You're a jerk, Gammon," she said, showing defiance. "You're a lot older than him, and you beat him up."

"Oh, Willey-pooh, Tor, I didn't hurt him. He butted in where he wasn't supposed to. That's rude, and somebody had to set him straight."

Gammon stopped hunting for Apollo and went over to within arm's length of Torith. Seeing this, Apollo quickly transitioned out of the safety of the dense tree, through the thin, physical air, and then immediately into another, larger tree closer to Torith. The mountain breeze pushed on the branches of this mighty tree, and Apollo could feel the trunk stress as it moved back and forth.

He had to be careful because Gammon and the others might see him if he moved too close to the outer edges of the trunk. Keeping his body back, he pushed his head forward, right eye to right ear, exposing only this portion of himself.

"I told you, I have to get home, Gammon. Let me go!"

Apollo knew Gammon could not force her to stay. There was no way to stop her from leaving. So why did she think she could not go? Gammon was not threatening to fight her the way he fought Apollo, was he?

"Look, Torith. We're forming a group, and we need you to be part of it. In the group, we watch out for each other. We protect each other. And the more ghosts who join, the stronger we get."

"Well, if it's so good, why does it have to be a secret?"

"It's not a secret," said Gammon. "But we don't want everybody. We want strong ghosts like you. That's why we're giving you a personal invitation."

That's a dumb way to make an invitation, thought Apollo.

Apollo had heard rumors about a group of kids at school who were in a secret club. They called themselves "Flint." Apollo wondered if Gammon was one of the group's leaders.

Gammon continued, "Torith, our group is a *good* thing. It's not bad. Look at Escue here. He doesn't feel like a beanhead anymore. He's happy. He has self-esteem. He's part of something. You'll be doing good by joining. You'll be helping ghosts like him. We need you, Torith."

Apollo agreed that Escue was a dweeb. He probably needed a group. But Torith did not. For her age, she was a powerful ghost and not one to be bullied.

"Forget it, Gammon. You make me come here when I'm supposed to be home. And now you try to get me to join your freaky club. I'm leavin'!"

And at that, Torith took off, straight up, at full speed.

Apollo wished she had not acted so fast. He was still trying to figure out what was happening, and he wanted more time to summon up the courage to take another beating from Gammon.

Torith did not get far before the three older kids caught her and surrounded her. She continued to push on while also trying to shake them. Apollo could see that her tormentors had moved in tight despite her attempts to evade. They were all in a group, so close that Torith would be overwhelmed by the power of three older, determined ghosts. Apollo had no choice but to blast off and try to help.

Apollo was frightened, but the protectiveness he felt for Torith wrapped his fear in anger. He raced to join an aerial dogfight he expected to lose. He watched Torith turn a hard right, then she jerked left, then up and down, trying to throw off her opponents. She was having no success. She needed help. Apollo would be in the fight soon. He aimed directly for Gammon.

In the split second before impact, Apollo's brain flashed a clear memory of what his mother had told him. "Remember, Apollo. If it gets bad, you can call me, and I'll be there immediately."

When Apollo was a little kid, he used to call his mom all the time. Every little kid did. Something would frighten him, or he needed help, and she would be right there. All he would have to do was make the conscious effort to call her. That deliberate act of calling out to her summoned her every time. It was immediate. It was the same when he called Dad.

Then, as he matured, there were times when he called, and she did not come. If he was at school, he was expected to get help from his teacher or maybe from a friend.

He had to learn to handle things on his own.

Now, Apollo was at an age where everything was reversed. Calling for Mommy's help was a no-no, at least it was at school. If the kids were teasing you, and you called Mom or Dad, you would be teased even more.

Right now, Apollo wanted to call Mom for help. This was an emergency. She would come immediately, and the instant she showed up, the fight with Gammon would end. But Torith had not called her, so Apollo would not either. "I'll take the beating," Apollo growled to himself, psyching himself for the fight. And a "beating" it would be.

Apollo plowed headfirst into Gammon and tore through Escue, trying to explode energy inside them as much as he could. Then he slammed the purple girl. There was something attractive and wild about her that made him want to hit her again, but instead, he stayed mission-focused and hammered Gammon a second time. Apollo could tell Gammon was surprised the "wiffle boy" was back.

"You're dead!" Gammon snarled at Apollo.

Apollo tried to maneuver close to Torith. The light in her was being assaulted. Apollo could feel it. The menapses of her network were breaking down. She was doing her best to resist their power wave, but it was overwhelming. Now that Apollo was there, Gammon's focus diverted primarily to Apollo, leaving Torith to the purple girl and Escue, the dweeb. Torith's odds had become much better. She might be younger, but she was no weakling.

"Come on, Torith," Apollo yelled. "Let them hurt you. You can't stop it. We have to get home!" As soon as Apollo said this, he realized he had found a workable plan. The strategy was to not fight back, not at all. Don't resist! Don't argue! Don't fight! Instead, spend all effort helping Torith go home. Know that it'll hurt. But all that mattered was forward motion. It was the only solution. "Keep going, Torith! Go! Go! Go!"

Apollo felt Gammon's fury. Apollo did not resist. Instead, he concentrated his whole being on going straight to Torith's house, keeping her in tow. "Torith, you can be home in five minutes. Go! Let them hurt you. It doesn't matter. It will be over soon. Just go!"

Apollo could tell that Torith understood because she glued herself to him. The two of them headed straight for her house, no longer taking any evasive action. "Close your mind to everything. Stay strong inside and think of one thing: Go Home!"

Gammon, Escue, and the purple girl were furious at the defiance. They burned Apollo's young soul with their hate, anger, and fierce determination to control. All three inserted themselves into the same space as Apollo and Torith, trying to come between them, slamming their energy networks, blowing their menapses, and destroying their ghost essence. The close proximity of these five battling, intertwined ghosts sent their emotions to a boiling, swirling mass of intensity. For Apollo, it was painful and exhausting. He knew it would be for Torith, too. Hopefully, they could hold out.

Apollo's whole concentration tightened. The pain inside him and the hate being inflicted on the two of them became secondary. He could feel Torith's focus tighten, too, and there was power in their synchrony.

"You pitner!" Gammon was yelling. "You puss-sucking pitner! I'll tell everybody about you, you blue-eyed creep. Everybody will know how you ran away from me today!"

Apollo shut Gammon out as much as he could.

"Torith's mine! You kutard. She would have joined

us if your fat head hadn't shown up. I'm goin' to tell the whole school you're a sissy, you little, white maggot! By the time I'm done, there won't be a word 'kutard' anymore. Instead, they'll all say 'Apollo,' and Apollo will mean kutard, and kutard will mean Apollo. Apollo! Kutard! Apollo! Kutard! Apollo! Kutard! Kutard! Kutard!"

Gammon continued his screaming directly into Apollo's ear, keeping pace as they raced towards Torith's. Apollo knew that being called a kutard was as bad as being called a pitner, if not worse. Again, this was a word he would never say.

Gammon's incessant assault made Apollo wrap himself tighter into a cocoon of determination, focused only on his and Torith's goal. Gammon was breaking Apollo down, but not fast enough to prevent him from getting Torith to her home.

The assault continued until they arrived within a mile of Torith's. Then Gammon snapped orders to Escue and the purple girl, and they left, breaking off their attack and taking their nasty meanness with them. Apollo and Torith were finally free. Exhausted, they moved apart, no longer acting as one. They were too tired to say much.

Torith mumbled a "thank you" as she looked up and caught Apollo's eye.

He could see her gratitude. Apollo told her to go inside, which she did without delay. There was nothing more he could do for her. What she needed most was Mom, who could recharge and heal her.

Apollo needed the same. He debated going in with her. Mom would help him, too. But he knew it was best for him to go to his own home. Mom could help him there. She could be everywhere at the same time.

Apollo asked the network for a comm, and one

quickly downloaded. The little clock icon in one corner said it was 4:45. The nightmare with Gammon had seemed like hours, but it had only lasted minutes. Apollo called Megantha—Mom.

She answered.

"I'm sorry I'm late, Mom," said Apollo, trying to act normal despite his turmoil and fatigue. "Torith was attacked. I helped her."

Apollo could see his mother looking him over. He knew she could read him perfectly. Her face showed concern.

"Do you want me to call the Mentor and have him come some other time? He's supposed to see you in fifteen minutes."

"Mom... I don't know... I don't feel very good right now."

Apollo looked down at the ground, finding it hard to face the comm's monitor. The relief of being rid of Gammon and the comfort of now talking to Mom melted him.

"Apollo," she called to him softly. "Look at me, sweetie."

Apollo met his mother's eyes. "Do you want me to come get you and bring you home?"

"Mom..." his voice cracked. "Mom, I... I need to come to you... on my own." Apollo tried to maintain his composure. "I got Torith to her home, and now I need to get myself home."

"Apollo," she said soothingly. "I love you, and I'm proud of you. See you in a minute, my little wombat." Then, she abruptly killed the connection, and the comm went blank.

Apollo was grateful she had turned off the connection. He sent the comm back to the server. Then he gathered himself, summoning his last reserves of energy, and he started for home. It was not far. Only four minutes. Four exhausting minutes. He made it.

6

Mom

Apollo badly needed to heal and recharge, and he was relieved to find himself in the spacious entryway of his home.

The floor of this part of the house was finished with deep black tile. The tile was spotless, well-polished, and embedded with chips of jade-colored rock. Above him, the ceiling was ten times his height, and it arched upwards to a large, round skylight made of seamless, thick glass. It was late in the day, and the light coming through this spectacularly shaped glass cast a faint, orange hue on the off-white walls of the ceiling and entryway.

To his right was a curved, brightly lit hallway leading to his room and those of several of his house brothers and sisters. To his left was another hallway. This one was straight and had the same black tile as the entryway. This hallway was wide and long, leading to an enormous living room. One side of the living room had west-facing, floor-to-ceiling windows that overlooked a valley below.

Apollo looked down the long hallway to the living room. Light coming through that room's large windows reflected off the spotless, black tile. Apollo did not notice the tile or its reflection because he saw his mother instead. The light from the living room behind her framed her, and she stood there, waiting for him, arms outstretched.

In his fight with Gammon, Apollo had been forced to

harden his psyche against Gammon's attacks. He had formed a protective shell around himself. Seeing his mom there, smiling and waiting, meant there was no longer any need for any defense. His whole frame went limp. The fight was over. Now, his challenge was to go to his mother. The boy had zero energy. He stalled and could not move forward. The distance between him and Megantha seemed insurmountable.

Apollo knew his mother could easily come to him, but he also knew she would do what was best for him. She wanted him to go to her.

Their eyes met. Even from this distance, Apollo could detect the endless colors in hers. Like her eyes, her aura was powerful and all-colored. She projected a majestic white, consisting of an endless color spectrum.

Apollo knew her penetrating eyes saw everything; they saw exactly how tired he felt at this instant. "Come to me, Apollo," she said. "I'm very proud of what you did today."

Apollo remained still, his head low and his ghost frame limp. Zero energy meant zero movement. He wanted to go to her, but he could not. She was too far. Along one side of the entryway was a long, thin table carved from solid granite, the same type of granite found at Lake Minnick. In the middle of this table was a single, potted orange tree, no taller than Apollo. Apollo struggled for a few seconds, digging deep inside himself for enough energy to move the few feet to the small tree.

Once at the tree, Apollo reached and touched it. Despite the tree's small size, its physical weight and mass were hundreds of thousands of times more than Apollo's infinitely fine, subatomic ghost. Touching the orange tree, Apollo drew from its internal electrical current, and soon his ghost frame harvested enough energy that he could move towards his mother. He started down the hallway in her direction.

"I am with Torith," she said. Her voice was clear and even-toned, despite her being at the end of the hall. She could do this: talk softly and calmly to Apollo from two feet away—or ten—or a hundred. It was one of the many things she could do. Her voice was immune to distance.

Apollo continued towards her.

"Without you, Torith does not think she could have withstood Gammon and his friends."

Apollo knew he had done well, but hearing her confirmation was sweet. Finally, he made it to her, and she took him into her arms, squeezing him tight. Immediately, Apollo felt her love and power flow through him. The charge he had received from the orange tree was tiny compared to the full-bodied, all-encompassing radiation her physical presence gave him. Gone was the hurt and pain from the fight with Gammon.

Mom took Apollo, and they sat on a plush, off-white sofa that spanned one wall of the spacious living room. When his mother sat down, the sofa absorbed her weight, the full-bodied pillows compressing and rustling as they reacted to the force exerted upon them. Apollo's ghost, on the other hand, caused no reaction in the physical pillows. Instead, he partially transitioned into one of them as he sat beside his mom, her right arm firmly around his shoulders while she held his hands in her left.

"Apollo," she said, "let's not talk for a few minutes. We'll sit here. You can rest." Apollo was happy about that. All he wanted right now was to be in her presence. She could read his thoughts if she chose to, and they could talk about them later.

Megantha shifted her weight, jostling Apollo. She

reached up and rubbed her hand through his hair and along one cheek. Apollo liked this. He liked how she could actually touch him. He could not transition through her like he could through ghosts and the other physical matter in his world. He was made up of the same refined physical matter she was. The difference was density. She was infinitely denser than Apollo. She was so dense that she could move physical things like the couch, rocks, or trees. She could do the same to ghosts like Apollo, Torith, or Tamir. She could physically lay hold of Apollo and prevent him from going somewhere, or she could hug and comfort him like she was doing now.

One time, Apollo watched his mother pick up flat, round stones and throw them so they skipped across Lake Minnick. She told him that when he was a physical person—a Blood—he would be able to do the same. For some reason, that manifestation of physical power held more sway on Apollo than the endless other examples Mom, Dad, and all of Apollo's teachers had ever given him. When he told Mom about it, she responded, "Little boys are little boys. They like to throw things. It's hardwired."

Apollo could vaguely sense the temperatures of physical things, but only if he concentrated on them. More evident to him was the amount of electrical current found in various types of matter. Physical rocks, water, and dirt had some electricity. Plants and trees had more.

Planet Summa's animals—including its fish and insects—were mostly ghosts like Apollo and his friends, destined to become Bloods on earths someday. But Summa also had some Blood animals: physical creatures brimming with electricity. Apollo's infinitely fine, subatomic structure could quickly recharge from contact with any Blood animal, fish, or insect. Something as small as a Blood ant had infinitely more mass than Apollo's ghost.

The Blood animals on Summa, despite being physical, were not like Apollo's mother. Apollo could transition through a Blood animal, but not through his mother. She was impenetrable. She was solid. Apollo could positively feel the warmth of her touch. He could sense the texture of her hand when it caressed his cheek. There was a powerful aura surrounding her that permeated through him. All of this made being in her presence a powerful experience. When he had done well, that experience was pure excellence. When he disappointed her, her presence was unbearable.

After a long silence, Megantha spoke to her son. "You know, Apollo. I would have come to help you if you had asked."

"I know," the boy answered, "but I did not want to be a baby."

"Hmmm...," was her response, and she squeezed him a little. "Well... that's part of growing up. Knowing when to ask for help and when to do it alone."

"But Mom, the kids would have made fun of me."

"You are right, but did you think about Torith?"

Apollo didn't understand. "Mom, I was trying to help her."

"Yes. And you did great. You stood up to an older and stronger boy. I'm very proud of you for that. But you and Torith had to endure a lot of pain to fight Gammon. Maybe you should have spared her that pain and called me to stop it."

Apollo now began to understand.

"Can you see how your fear of being ridiculed meant your friend had to go through more hurt than necessary?"

Apollo wanted to tell her that Torith could have

called her, too. But he also understood his mother's point. "So... Mom... you're saying I should have called you because that way Torith wouldn't get hurt... and that's the best thing even if people make fun of me?"

"Look at me, son." Megantha gently took him by the chin and turned his face toward hers. "Sometimes, there is not a right way to do things. Today, what you did was perfectly fine. And I'm so proud of you, I can hardly stand it."

As she spoke to him, close, face-to-face, Apollo locked his eyes onto hers, mesmerized by their palette of endless colors superimposed on a piercing diamond background.

"I want you to learn as much as possible from what happened today. It was not wrong for you not to call me."

Apollo and his mother talked more, and then they sat silently for a few more minutes. Next, she asked him another question. "So, Gammon goes to your school, right?"

"Yes," he answered, wishing she had not brought it up. It was a problem he did not want to think about right now.

"Are you worried about what he might do to you?"

Suddenly, the comfort of his mother's arms was not so comforting. He shifted, still beside her as they sat on the sofa. Apollo knew the problem with Gammon was not over because Gammon would surely want revenge for what Apollo did today.

"Mom," he said, "I don't want to talk about it... okay?"

"That's fine, my little wombat." She ran the back of her fingers down his cheek. "But remember, nobody can make you do something wrong. Not even Gammon and his friends. Do you understand?"

"Yes," he responded humbly, nodding and looking down towards the floor.

"Good. And remember, if you think you can't stand up to Gammon, call me... or Dad... or your old brother, Dramos. Get some help."

Apollo mumbled something bordering more on a grunt than a clear-cut yes. He could imagine how hard it would be to call for her in front of his friends or schoolmates. It would be so embarrassing.

Apollo did not want to talk about this anymore. He knew Mom was right, but everything about the inevitable future conflicts with Gammon was distasteful. He had been through enough Gammonism for one day. The easiest thing to do was to agree with her. "Okay, Mom. If it gets really bad with Gammon, I'll call for help."

Megantha smiled at Apollo and hugged him.

"Mom, I don't understand why you and Dad let people be so mean—like Gammon was today. Why don't you tell Gammon to bug off?"

"Well, son, how about if you talk with your father about that? When was the last time you talked with him?"

"Yesterd—no... the day before." Apollo had always been told he should talk to Dad at least once daily, if not more. So, his answer caused some guilt.

"You know, you're old enough now that he isn't going to always come to you. Sometimes you have to ask."

Apollo was well aware of this. He had been taught this concept since he was very young. It was all part of preparing him for the test. The big test. Life as a Blood, where he would live in another place, away from his parents. A place where he would need to reach out to his father for help, and where that help would seem distant and hard to obtain.

Olam—his father—used to come and see him all the time. He would come multiple times a day, sometimes many times, if something was wrong. He would hold Apollo and talk to him. Sometimes, they would play. But in the last several years, he stopped showing up as much. In moments of selfishness that could be called pouting, Apollo was angry with his father for this. Apollo would try to convince himself that Olam did not care for him like he used to. But Apollo knew in his heart this was not true. Whenever he asked for his father, Olam came. Sometimes, not right away, but he always came. Apollo knew it was he, Apollo, who had pulled away, not his father.

Apollo felt Megantha give him one last hug, and then she stood up, releasing her hold on him. "I think you should go ask for him now, son. Two days is too long."

Apollo's physical batteries were recharged. Emotional recovery would take more time, but he was well on his way to that, too. She had washed away the pain and blackness. Apollo left the couch and started across the living room.

"Oh, Apollo. About the Mentor who was supposed to see you today. I told him you'd had a little problem at school and that you could not meet with him. He said he wanted to come tomorrow, Thursday."

"Tomorrow? But, Mom, I—"

"I know, son," she broke in. "You're going surfing tomorrow. Right? With Tamir and Torith?"

"Yes. Tamir for sure. Torith is a maybe."

"Right. I asked your Mentor to come on Friday, after school, at five, like he was planning to do today. That's okay, isn't it?"

"Yes… great," Apollo answered, happy she had not interfered with the surfing. Apollo knew his Mentor wanted to talk about Apollo's progress in the Puissance—the Power—and Mom would definitely think the Puissance was more important than surfing. He was surprised Megantha had not scheduled the Mentor for tomorrow. "Thanks, Mom."

Apollo headed off to his room. He left the living room, moved down the hall, and passed through the spacious entryway with the glass dome and the little orange tree. Then he turned and entered the curved hallway, which led to his room and those of several other brothers and sisters.

The first belonged to Dramos, Apollo's older brother. Dramos was good to Apollo. He did not tease much, and he had taught Apollo how to surf the canyon. Apollo wanted to tell him about Gammon. He imagined Dramos putting a serious hurt on Gammon and his gang. But Dramos was not home yet. He would still be at school, where his schedule was demanding. Also, Dramos was advancing well in the Puissance, which often kept him away from home. Apollo admired his older brother, and he knew Mom and Dad were proud of him.

Next to Dramos' room was that of his sister, Celestine. She was older than Apollo but younger than Dramos. She preferred to be called "Celti." She was the oldest girl still living at home. Apollo knew she'd be sympathetic if he told her about Gammon. Celti's real interest, however, was animals. Playing animal games with her was the way to her heart. Apollo liked being with her. He had gladly played the parts of her pet dog, cat, monkey, squirrel, tigerfish, and many other animals.

Apollo's was next to Celestine's, followed by those of his younger brother, Jank, and his younger sister, Natilia.

Apollo arrived at the doorway to his room. Mom had designed the house so all the kids' rooms had doors. However, since Apollo and his brothers and sisters were ghosts, their physical composition was too fine to manually open or close physical doors. To solve this, each door frame had a small electronic panel with a red and green button. Red for "closed" and green for "open." These buttons were touch-sensitive, like the screen or keyboard of a comm. Their sensitivity was set to respond to the tiny electrical signature of a ghost.

Arriving at his room, Apollo found the door open, as he had left it this morning. He touched the red button on the panel, and the door shut behind him as he entered the room. Then he asked for a comm. He was going to call Tamir and tell him about Gammon. He would need Tamir's emotional support in the days ahead, especially if Gammon or his friends gave him a hard time at school.

The comm materialized, and Apollo started to call Tamir. But then he stopped, remembering his mother's words. Two days was too long to go without talking to Dad. Apollo knew his mom was right. Apollo wondered why he had waited this long.

7

Dad

Apollo directed his mind towards his father, calling for him. He consciously and deliberately made the mental effort to reach out and ask to speak with him. On the surface, the process of contacting his father appeared very similar to that of asking for a comm. But in actuality, it was very different. When he called for a comm, his request was granted by the master server, which was merely a machine. Area sensors fed the request to the server, which initiated steps to physically download a comm. But when he called for Olam, his Dad, the link was directly to him, and that link had no connectivity limits. There was no intermediary server or downloading process.

After Apollo made the call, the response was instantaneous. Dad was immediately in Apollo's room. "Apollo, my good son," he said, standing in front of the boy, his arms outstretched. "Come to me."

Apollo stepped forward and was embraced. His father radiated the same warmth and power as Megantha. "I've missed you, Apollo."

"I know, Dad," said Apollo. "I missed you, too. I'm sorry I haven't called more."

His father's eyes and aura were like his mother's. They were rich, piercing, and diamond white. They radiated all colors at once. Apollo could see blue, orange, yellow, and green simultaneously. The only word for it was white, yet it was anything but. He remembered from science class that equal amounts of red, green, and blue light combine to create white. His father's eyes and aura shifted those ratios constantly, creating infinite color variations within the white.

"So... my son. You had a little run-in with Gammon today." There was a slight chuckle in his voice.

"Yeah, Dad. I don't understand why he's so mean."

Olam held Apollo out at arm's length, his hands on Apollo's shoulders, maintaining a steady eye-to-eye. "And you want me to stop him... right?"

"Well... he's your son."

"And your brother."

"Yes. But not a house brother. Not like Dramos or Jank."

"But still your brother."

"A jerk of a brother, Dad. He attacked Torith and me. It hurt!"

Olam did not respond immediately, and Apollo sensed the pause was for his benefit, to give him time to think about what he was saying.

"I mean... Dad... did you talk to him?"

Apollo saw his father smile. It was a knowing smile. "Well, son, as a matter of fact, I'm talking with him right now."

Apollo knew his Dad could be in endless places at once... like Mom. Apollo had grown up knowing this, and he had always taken it for granted. But it was impossible to understand. "You say that, but do you really mean right now?"

"Well, by right now, I mean right now from your perspective."

"But Dad, you're here with me."

"Right, and I'm there with Gammon."

Apollo shook his head. "I know... but how?"

"Apollo, it's only from your level of understanding that I am here with you and there with him, all at the same time. There is only one of me, and I can only be in one place at any time."

"Right, so... ?" Apollo shook his head. "That only makes it more confusing." He paused, processing. "Are you talking with other ghosts too? Right now?"

"You mean, other than you and Gammon?"

"Of course, son. Thousands of them. Both ghosts and Bloods."

Apollo had not thought about the Bloods. "Thousands? All right now?"

"Remember, by right now, we're talking about your perspective. Right?"

"Uh-huh... I guess."

"Then that's right. For example, in the last of your seconds, I talked to 118,435 of my children, including you."

Apollo cocked his head sideways, and his mouth dropped open. "Dad, that's impossible." He had a blank look on his face. "You can't... I mean... How?" Then his blank look changed to one of amazement. "That's incredible!"

"Let me ask you a question, son."

"Okay."

"Do you think I would have so many children that I would not have time to talk with them like we're talking now?"

Apollo had to admit this did not seem logical.

"You have no idea how much I love you. It would defeat everything I want to accomplish if I became too busy to see you. That would not be happiness for me. It would be an ultimate heartbreak and frustration if my children called for me and I did not have time for them."

This reasoning was very comforting to Apollo, even if it did nothing to explain how his father could do this.

"Of course, if they don't call for me, then that is a different problem."

Apollo knew this was a mild reprimand. But his father was smiling, and the scolding was sweet. "I know, Dad. Like I told you, I'll call more."

"Great! Now, you've had some astronomy classes?"

"Yes." Apollo wondered where this was going.

"We're in the Milky Way galaxy, right?"

"Yes."

"What arm?"

"Sag… Sagittarius."

"Good. Good. And can you tell me how many stars are in our galaxy?"

Apollo did not know the number. "Millions?"

Olam pointed his finger upward.

"Billions?" said Apollo.

"Billions is close enough. Do you think I've been to all those stars?"

Apollo was going to say yes, but then thought about it more and answered, "Probably any of them where you needed to go."

"Excellent. Why would I need to go?"

"Not the stars. The planets around those stars. The planets with life."

"Yes, good," said Olam. "Any planet or star… or moon… where there is a reason for me to go."

Apollo nodded yes.

"Are you comfortable with that idea? That I've been to all those places?"

"Yep." Apollo shook his head up and down.

"Alright. Which is easier for you to believe: that I've

been to all those stars and planets or that I can talk to
118,000 of my children at once?"

"The stars," said Apollo.

"How far apart are those stars?"

"Light years. Five, ten, a hundred, thousands?"

"Good. Let's say I need to go to one that is a hundred
light-years away. How long does it take for me to get there?"

"I don't know," said Apollo. "Five minutes?"

"Son, for me, five minutes is an eternity. I can do it
instantly. It does not take me any time to travel between
them."

Apollo's brain was starting to hurt. "Dad, that's hard
to understand." Apollo was frustrated.

"I know, son. Here's a way to look at it that might
help: It takes me no time to go from one place to another.
None at all. So, to keep it simple, if it takes me no time to go
from you to Gammon and back and forth, then, to you, it's as
if I never left."

Apollo thought about this. "I kind of understand
that."

"So, if it takes me no time to go somewhere, then I
can be in an infinite number of places, all at the same time."

"I wish my brain were like Tamir's," said Apollo.
"He'd probably understand better than I can."

"Tamir's a great boy," said Olam. "But so are you.
For now, you might find it easier to think of me as being able
to move very fast. So fast that I can be many places in a split
second, even if those places are light-years apart."

"That's fast, Dad," responded Apollo, laughing.
"Really fast!"

Everything about Apollo's father was incredible.
They spent the next forty-five minutes talking. His father
joked with him about the angler fish and platypus face he

and Tamir liked to pull. He even did one himself, and he actually did look like an angler, with the little, lighted ball coming off the front of his head.

They talked a lot about the problem with Gammon. Olam would not tell Apollo what he was saying to Gammon. Apollo hoped it was a reprimand. But he did let Apollo know he was proud of the strength Apollo showed today. "You stood up for what was right." Olam also said he would not stop Gammon if he chose to continue hurting people. Instead, he emphasized the importance of Apollo's proper response to Gammon's actions.

"But Dad. Why was Gammon so crazy today about Torith joining his group? And what is the group about anyway?"

Olam explained that ghosts find power in groups. "It's like you and Tamir," he said. "When you're with him, you feel more powerful, right?"

Apollo agreed.

"You have to decide whether or not you think Gammon's group is good or bad."

"I don't want anything to do with that idiot."

Olam gave Apollo a disapproving look.

"I'm sorry, Dad." Apollo knew he should not talk that way. "But I already know his group can't be good."

"And how do you know that?"

"Because he was forcing Torith to join, even though she did not want to. And he started fighting me when I tried to help her. You would never do that with the Puissance. Even though the Puissance is right, you would not make us be part of it. Right?"

"That's true, Apollo."

After Olam's earlier amusing fish act, the two of them had stood apart and moved casually around the room as they talked. But now, Olam moved towards his son and embraced him again. "The good guys never force anyone to join them. Never."

Olam released his embrace but kept one arm around Apollo's shoulder. "You know, son, if you were younger, I would tell you if Gammon's group is a good thing or a bad one. But I know you can figure it out on your own, so I'm not going to tell you."

"Well, Dad, like I said, I don't think it's good."

"Okay, but keep thinking about it. You don't know anything about it. All you know is that he hurt you, and he tried to force Torith. But maybe he thought it was good, even if he went about it wrong."

Apollo had not thought about this.

"Apollo, you're going to find times when ghosts are trying to do the right thing, but go about it the wrong way. Does that make sense?"

"Yeah."

"And sometimes they are doing the wrong thing, but how they do it makes it look right."

Apollo churned on that.

"And on occasion, they're wrong, but they think they're right, and they have a lot of good reasons why they think that way."

"Daaad?" said Apollo, putting his hands up to his head, shaking it with a slightly dumb look, making it clear the advice was coming too fast.

Olam laughed lightly. "That was a lot of juice. Do you know what I said?"

Apollo thought he could figure it out if he had time to absorb and think about it. "Well... I think you're saying I must figure out what's right."

"Good. And lots of times, things that look right are

not."

"And it can be the other way around, too?"

"Exactly."

"Okay... okay, I can see that," said Apollo, stalling for time while his mental gears caught up. "But I thought you would always tell me what's right, as long as I ask."

"No."

"No? But that's—"

"Not what you've been taught?"

"Yeah."

"Let's put it this way: I won't always give you an immediate answer on what's right. There are going to be more and more times when I want you to figure it out for yourself. Once you've worked at it and think you've got it, come to me, and we'll talk about it."

At this, Apollo sighed and said, "Getting old is hard, Dad."

"Oh? So now you think you are old?" Olam was teasing.

"Older than before," Apollo countered. "To Jank and Natilia, I'm old."

"Good one, Apollo. Perspective is important."

The two of them chatted for a few more minutes, and then Olam said goodbye, his final words being, "Let's talk again soon. I love you."

8

Home

Apollo felt complete after his father's visit, and he waited almost half an hour before calling Tamir on the comm. They talked about Gammon, Torith, and surfing.

Next, he tried to talk to Torith, but Mom answered. She said Torith was still upset, and it was best she not take any calls this evening. "Torith can go surfing with you tomorrow after school, if she feels up to it. She can decide tomorrow."

Apollo left his room and went to the living room. Dramos was home. Mom was there, too. She and Dramos were discussing a project he was doing for school. Celti was home, over by the large floor-to-ceiling windows, her nose stuck in a comm. Apollo assumed she was reading a book about animals.

Natilia and Jank were not there, which was unusual for this time of day. They normally did not want to miss anything.

Apollo mumbled greetings to Dramos and Celti, then asked, "Where are the Pups?"

Dramos had been the first to suggest the name "Pups." It fit because Jank and Natilia always played or fought together, and they were quite a bit younger.

Mom explained that the Pups had quarreled. She had sent them to their rooms.

"Hey, A.P.," said Dramos, turning away from Mom

to talk to him. "A little bird told me you had quite a day."

Apollo wondered how Dramos knew unless Mom told him. He looked at her, but she held her hands up with the unmistakable gestures of "not me."

Dramos continued, "I stopped by Torith's house on my way home. To see Super Jack."

Super Jack was everyone's nickname for Torith's older brother, Jackson. He and Dramos were friends.

Celti perked up, and she asked, "What's going on? What are you two talking about?"

Dramos turned to her. "Well, Celts, A.P. here had a rumble today. With a kid named Gammon."

Celestine's face adopted a look of concern. "Apollo... are you okay?"

Apollo said something to her about being alright and turned his attention back to Dramos.

"You should've called me on the comm," Dramos said. "I would have come to help. Super Jack, too."

Apollo had not considered this during the fight because it would not have worked. "Your school is too far from Lake Minnick."

"Yes, but Super Jack was home. He could have helped. You should have called. He's mad about what happened. So am I."

Apollo was happy to hear that. Super Jack, or Dramos, could easily put the hurt on Gammon.

Dramos and Celti wanted to hear the whole story. Then Natilia and Jank came in, with Jank proudly announcing that he was out of Mom Jail! Apollo had to tell them the story, too. Their version was pared down.

The story fired Jank up, especially when he saw that Dramos wanted revenge. The little boy announced, "Let's go fight him now!" Jank hurried over to a large standing floor lamp in one corner of the room. He started attacking the lamp as if it were Gammon. Jank flailed himself at it and transitioned in and out of it, much as Gammon had done to Apollo. While doing this, Jank yelled, "Dramos, you, me, and Apollo... let's go get him!" followed by, "Take that, Gammon-head. And that! And that! And that!"

At first, Mom started reprimanding Jank, but soon Natilia was caught up in Jank's enthusiasm. She started fighting the lamp, too. The two had pent-up frustration from their earlier tiff, and the lamp became a perfect outlet. They zoomed around the room like the young pups they were, going from Celti by the big windows to the lamp across the room, speeding back and forth, burning photons.

The Pups' mock battle quickly turned into a game rather than a fight, and Megantha and the three oldest became amused with the Pups' antics. Natilia was so young she still could not pronounce all her words, and one of the things she had a hard time saying correctly was the sound "th," like in the word "that." She tried to mimic Jank's "take that," but when she said it, it came out, "Take wrat! Take wrat! Gammon-head!"

"That's right, Nati," called Dramos. "You tell 'em! Take wrat, you dirty rat!"

The play on words made Megantha laugh, and it put an end to any teaching moment.

With Mom laughing, the Pups were pumped up even more, racing all over the house, entertaining the rest of the family. This went on until they were exhausted, which was perfect for Mom, who later had little difficulty coaxing them to their rooms for a night's rest and recharge.

Just before midnight, and before Mom put the Pups down, Father visited the family for about an hour. Unlike his earlier, more purposeful visit with Apollo, this one was relaxed and casual. He talked with Celti about the book she was reading, and he and Dramos spoke about his school project. He played with the Pups. At one point, he, Apollo, and Dramos put on a silly canyon surfing demonstration. For Apollo, it was a perfect ending to a long day.

9

Pancake Boy

The next day at school, Apollo kept a watchful eye out for Gammon. There was nothing to prevent Gammon from coming to Apollo's side of the school, where the younger student classes were located. Generally, the kids Gammon's age stayed on their side of the grounds, not wanting much to do with the younger ones. They only came over when they had to pick up a brother or sister on their way home, or sometimes there was a favorite teacher they wanted to visit. Apollo's teacher, named MM, was that way. His students often came back to see him.

Torith's classroom was right on the imaginary border between the big kids and little kids' sides of the school. Apollo was worried Gammon would try to approach her. Gammon may have singled her out because she was close to his territory. He may have seen how she was a "take-charge" type of girl. Maybe Gammon was thinking that if he brought her into his group, a bunch of her friends would follow.

This morning's first hours of class were not dull. The subject was math, but MM never taught straight math. Instead, he made it real. He taught formulas related to mass and circumference and, in turn, related those to gravitational fields and density. The students had to calculate how much a hundred-pound frog would weigh on different planets and stars, with MM supplying density and circumference information about each of these planetary objects.

Apollo found that the frog would weigh anywhere from one pound to a million pounds, depending on the planetary body on which it resided.

As the class worked through these examples, MM pointed out that, in the future, when the students moved from being ghosts on Planet Summa to physical beings on earths somewhere in the Milky Way, weight and mass would rule their lives.

Tamir's hand went up. MM called on him, and Tamir asked, "If some of us go to a planet with a lot of mass, and others go to a low-mass planet, will our Blood bodies be different?"

"Good question, Tamir. Let's talk about it. Let's say your physical world is half the mass of Apollo's. And let's say you weigh one hundred and twenty pounds. How much would you weigh in Apollo's world?"

"Two-hundred-and-forty pounds."

"Correct. Now, for a harder question: What are some implications of being in a world where you weigh one hundred and twenty pounds versus one where you weigh two hundred and forty?"

Nobody said anything. Apollo saw that Tamir had raised his hand. MM signaled him to put it down. Others needed to answer.

There was a girl in the class named Rachael whom Apollo did not know well. She was smart, but she was quiet most of the time.

"How about you, Rachael?" MM asked. "What do you think?"

"Well," she said, thinking. "It would affect how we are built. If Tamir is on the one-hundred-and-twenty-pound world, he'll be skinny, like he is now."

Tamir tried to catch Rachael's eye. "Hey," he said,

faking offense.

Rachael continued, "And Apollo, in his two-hundred-and-forty-pound world… he'll be short and squatty."

It was Apollo's turn. "Hey!"

"Excellent, Rachael," MM said. "People in the two-hundred-and-forty-pound world will have to have much more muscular legs than those in the one-hundred-and-twenty-pound world." MM let that sink in. "So, Rachael… let me ask you another question. Apollo and Tamir are good friends, right? What if Tamir gets in a spaceship and travels from his one-hundred-and-twenty-pound world to Apollo's two-hundred-and-forty pounder?"

Rachael mulled it over and then said, "I think Tamir would turn flat like a pancake!" The whole class laughed.

Tamir feigned more offense. Apollo added to Rachael's teasing. "A pancake with platypus lips!" The class laughed at that, too.

"So, class," MM asked, "do you think we're going to worlds with drastically different masses, meaning significantly different gravitational pulls? Or do you think all the worlds we go to will have similar mass and pull?"

Tamir's hand went up.

"Ah-ah-ah," interrupted MM before Tamir could say anything. "No questions. We're going to make this a homework assignment. I want three pages on this issue. No more than three pages," he emphasized, looking at Tamir. "If you think we're going to be Bloods in worlds with very different gravitational pulls, or vice versa, then I want you to say so. And I want you to explain two things: First, tell me why you have chosen your position. And second, tell me about its effects on your Blood or physical body."

Rachael's hand went up. "Can we ask Olam?"

"Rachael," answered MM, "you can always ask

Olam... or Megantha... anything. And if they tell you the answer, we want to hear it!"

MM told them to check their comms if they had questions about the assignment. "It's due in two days!" Then, MM dismissed the class for a fifteen-minute break.

As the students filed out of the classroom, politely using the doorway rather than going through the walls, Apollo and Tamir jostled their way through the others, trying to get close to Rachael. "So, Tamir," said Apollo, louder than needed, "that Rachael girl... she probably thinks you'd look good all flat."

Rachael was next to a girl who was her friend. The two of them looked at each other, and Rachael said, "Pancake boy!" She said it loud and deliberately, clearly teasing Tamir. The girls laughed, and others did, too.

Before Tamir could make a comeback, the girls had left the building and were gone.

Once out of the building, Tamir wanted to go after Rachael, but Apollo stopped him. "We need to check on Torith. Let's see if she's out of class."

Apollo could see Tamir was keeping a watch out for Rachael as they headed towards Torith's classroom building. Apollo was also doing a "watch," but his was for Gammon.

At Torith's building, the boys made their way to her classroom. Her class was also on a break, and Apollo quickly recognized Torith's black, light-streaked hair. She was facing away from them in an animated conversation with two other girls.

"Torith!" Apollo called.

She did not react and continued the full-motion conversation with her friends. "Torith!" Apollo called louder.

Torith turned. Catching sight of Apollo, she put her

friends on hold and rushed over.

"Apollo... Hi... and Tamir! How are you?"

"Okay," answered Apollo. Then, gesturing towards Tamir, Apollo added, "Pancake boy is doing okay, too."

Torith's face showed confusion over the "pancake boy" comment.

Apollo went on, "Have you seen Gammon today?"

"Yes," Torith said. "He was staring at me this morning. But it was from the other side of the playground."

"Creepy," Tamir said, his green eyes darkening.

"Torith," Apollo asked, "I tried to call you last night, but Mom said no."

Torith nodded.

"Also, Tamir knows what happened." Apollo was gesturing towards Tamir. "I explained it to him."

Torith seemed relieved. Just then, Torith's teacher returned and said they were starting class. Tamir and Apollo needed to leave, and they began to go.

"Oh... what about surfing, Torith? We're going after school. Do you want to come?"

Torith gave them a thumbs-up, and they rushed out of her classroom and back to theirs. Given yesterday's trauma, Apollo was surprised Torith agreed to go with them. *Strong girl*, he thought.

Back in class, Apollo suggested they ask "pancake girl" if she wanted to go surfing, too. Tamir seemed very interested in that. But asking her was another matter.

"I'll do it," Apollo said. "But I'm going to tell her it was your idea."

Tamir did not resist that plan, and later in the day, during a class break, Apollo managed to pull Rachael aside.

"I can't, Apollo," she said, offering no further explanation. "But I wish I could go with you guys. Please ask me again, okay?"

Apollo agreed.

"And... your friend, Tamir. We were teasing him. You know that?"

"I'll tell him, Rachael. But you should, too. He would like that."

Throughout the rest of the school day, Tamir and Rachael did not volley anymore. However, Apollo saw them share several curious stares.

Late in the classroom day, MM allotted some time for class members to discuss the earth gravity assignment. He split the class into four groups. Apollo snuck over to Tamir's group. Tamir and several others started debating the topic. Some of them thought the earths would all be the same mass. Others said it did not matter. "So, what if some Bloods are squatty pancakes and others are bean poles?"

After school, Tamir and Apollo went straight over and found Torith. She said she still had not had any problems with Gammon today.

"What about that Escue, kid? Or the purple girl?" Apollo asked.

"Nothing," Torith said. "But I heard more about Flint."

Tamir perked up, and the green in his aura heightened.

"One of my friends has an older brother in it. They say Gammon started it, but it is a B. Z. Sughi group."

"B. Z. Sughi!" exclaimed Tamir with surprise. "Really?"

"Yes," said Torith. "That's what he said. It's supposed to be a group where everybody helps each other."

"Helps beat up other kids?" Apollo asked sarcastically, the blue in his eyes showing cold. "Force people?"

They talked some more, and then Tamir reminded them they were going surfing.

Apollo agreed and announced, "Let's go ride some waves!" At this, Apollo shot up into the air and came down in a dive right for them, veering away just over their heads and shooting out at an angle, spreading his arms and legs to catch the imaginary wave. "Yeah-hoo!"

This was enough for the three friends to forget about Flint, Gammon, and all the drama of the past two days. They took off in the direction of the canyon, traveling at near full speed. The race to the surf zone was on, and they looked forward to riding some powerful canyon waves.

10

Surfing

Thirteen miles upriver from Lake Minnick, the Tungsten River flowed through a deep canyon with steep granite walls. The waters ran faster and faster in an increasingly narrow canyon until they shot out over a two-thousand-foot waterfall and slammed into a churning catch pool below. From there, the Tungsten River reformed and continued its progress toward Lake Minnick.

On a sunny day, the Tungsten River was slate blue, contrasting with the white granite of the canyon walls. On a cloudy day, the waters turned a metallic gray.

Hundreds of thousands of years ago, there had been no falls here. Then, Summa's crust broke along a fault line that passed directly through the canyon. Over the millennia, the lower side dropped thousands of feet. The fault line ran down and backward, away from the top of the falls. This meant that once the water went over the falls, the rock dropped away and behind it, allowing the water an unobstructed free fall. Much of the water met terminal velocity before it hit the bottom.

The upper canyon was straight and deep. At the bottom of the falls, the canyon S-turned sharply before straightening out and continuing onto the lake. In the S-turn, the canyon was narrow like above, but beyond this turn, the canyon widened and mellowed.

The falls were officially named Granite Falls, but

everybody knew them as "The Falls." The fault line and the falls were imposing geological features, and it was not long before they came into Apollo's airborne view.

He could see that the water was flowing full and strong. Apollo pushed hard, planning to arrive at the top of the falls ahead of Torith and Tamir. But then he changed plans and dove to enter the canyon below the falls. He aimed for the river below the S-turn. This meant he'd no longer beat Torith and Tamir. He did not care. He wanted to feel the booming power of the water's impact. The sound waves coming off the impact zone were strong, and they continued through the S-turn and down the canyon.

Apollo wanted to transition against these sound waves, sensing where they had the most force, where they formed the best for sound surfing, and which ones would take him the farthest.

He looked behind and above and saw that Torith and Tamir were staying high, headed for the top of the falls. But then Tamir changed course and followed Apollo. Apollo knew why. Tamir, too, would want to scope out the waves before his first run.

Apollo stopped racing and waited for Tamir to catch up. Then, they swooped in low above the river and worked their way into the bottom of the S-turn. The sound waves were strong now, slowing their progress, and the waves' force magnified exponentially as the two friends came out of the first half of the S-turn and started into the second. Once out of the last turn, they were directly in line with the sound waves coming off the impact zone, channeled directly to them by the steep canyon walls.

Approaching the falls, their efforts to move upstream became more focused. Tamir worked his way back and forth, up and down, above the churning river, feeling for the pathway with the best sound currents. Apollo watched his friend while he did the same. Soon, they were near the base of the falls. Clouds of mist swirled around them, cutting their visibility by half. There was permanent moss on the rocks on both sides of the canyon.

Suddenly, two surfers shot past them and on down towards the S-turn. They were going fast, but not nearly as fast as Apollo and Tamir could go. They had not caught the best waves. Apollo and Tamir looked at each other and shook their heads. Tamir gave a thumbs-down sign, and Apollo responded with the same. *Posers*, thought Apollo.

Apollo backed away from the falls and then blasted straight up out of the mist towards Torith. He lost track of Tamir, who was still below.

As Apollo approached the top, he could see Torith waiting. She was also waving and pointing to the canyon below. She said something, but the roar of the falls garbled her words. Apollo came closer. Her face was hyped up.

"Did you see those surfers?" she asked excitedly.

"Yes. They were lame... slow."

"Did you see who they were?"

Apollo had not. "Maybe Tamir did. He's still down there."

Torith was all abuzz. Even in the sun, her aura showed, and her eyes flashed. "The girl. Did you recognize her?"

"No."

"Apollo, she's the purple girl who was with Gammon yesterday!"

Apollo remembered seeing some purple on one of the surfers. "Tory... did she see you?"

"No."

"Good, then come on. We don't want her to see you

now... at least not yet."

The two surfers from below were starting back up. Soon, they would be close enough for the purple girl to recognize them. Apollo knew he, Torith, and Tamir had to get out of there to talk strategy.

Tamir had just arrived, but Apollo had no time to explain.

"We gotta go, Tamir. Come on!" cried Apollo. "We'll talk at the bottom. Let's go!"

Apollo could see a confused look on Tamir's face. He motioned downward to Tamir, and then he took off straight down the falls, hoping Torith and Tamir would follow.

Usually, Apollo liked to gather internal forces and concentrate before his first ride of the day. That was part of the ritual, the enjoyment. But now that he was screaming straight down towards the impact pool, the thrill inside him ramped up immediately. Regardless of the distraction of enemy surfers, he was determined to make this ride as good as any other.

He maneuvered quickly into the central mass of water, which he could feel accelerating faster and faster. This was the easy part. Stay in the main flow and do not become caught anywhere on its perimeter where the water was breaking up and becoming mist from air friction.

Soon, this inner core reached terminal velocity. It was thrilling to be free-falling inside this massive column of water. There was tremendous power, and there was also near silence. Sound, time, and motion stopped. It was surreal. Even if Apollo did not catch a sound wave at the bottom of the falls, this part of the ride made each surf a gift.

Catching a sound wave required much more speed than the water's terminal velocity. Once the free-falling water hit maximum speed, Apollo jumped into the stream of falling air dragged down by the waterfall. This air was traveling nearly as fast as the water itself. Apollo blasted down this air channel, resulting in a speed much greater than he could generate on his own. Branches of water were separating from the central core, any one of which would slow Apollo's speed. He had to maneuver around these water branches while staying in the fast-moving air. If all went well, he would have tremendous speed at the bottom.

The water thundered as it impacted the bottom of the falls. This generated booming sound waves, and Apollo's goal was to ride the surface tension of the biggest of these waves, traveling at the speed of sound. Successfully catching a sound wave was a fantastic and wild ride for any ghost.

At the bottom of the falls, Apollo shot out from the water core, now screaming horizontally along the pool's surface. He pushed his speed to the max and spread himself out like a sail to catch a sound wave. The first waves were too small. They passed through him. Then, a powerful set blasted his way. He caught one of the first waves. Now, he was a ghost rocket. The ride was on!

His challenge was to hang onto this speed for as long as possible. The wave was rushing him directly into the canyon wall at the first part of the S-curve. The first turn was left, and Apollo moved left on the wave for a better angle. This is where the reconnaissance he and Tamir had done on the way up would pay off. Apollo had to jump to a different sound wave to make this left turn. He made the switch, continuing in the S turn. Now the right turn was coming up. His execution was perfect, and his speed continued.

Up ahead, to the far right, was a huge rock sticking out of the canyon wall. It was nicknamed the Android. If he oversteered, he'd be blown into that rock, and his ride would be over. Fighting to hold the correct angle, Apollo stayed right, but not too right. At the last second, he pushed hard left and cleared the Android by only a few feet. He shot into the open canyon beyond the S-curve, his wave and speed soon petering out from the diminished sound waves.

It had been a perfect run. Apollo turned around just in time to see Torith plow into the Android. Getting that far was still a good run, and she had nothing to be ashamed of.

He knew what Torith was going through right now. When you slammed into the rock, you had to sit tight for a minute and gather your bearings. It was often hard to figure out how to move out of the rock. Half of that rock was attached to the main wall, and if you headed that direction, you'd be wandering around in the mountain for minutes or more, trying to find your way out. The best option was to try to go sideways back towards the river. To do that, you had to wait and carefully listen through the rock for vibrations from the powerful falls. These you followed to the river for a quick exit.

Apollo kept his eye on the Android, and Torith soon transitioned out. He saw her look around, and Apollo waved his arms for her attention. She saw him and moved his way.

Apollo continued to watch the end of the S-curve, hoping Tamir would emerge. But even when Torith caught up to him, there was no Tamir. "Where is he? Do you think he followed us?"

Torith was looking for Tamir, too.

While she was looking, Apollo teased, "So, how's Android today?"

"Hey," she said, in mocked defensiveness, flashing her aqua brown eyes, "I had a good run!"

Torith then switched to a more serious tone. "What are we gonna do? I don't want to run into that girl."

"I know," he answered. "It's a problem. But there are three of us and only two of them. Do you know who the other guy is?"

"I don't even know if it's a guy," she answered. "We jumped out of there too fast."

Apollo continued to watch for Tamir, who finally appeared at the last bend of the S-turn. He was transitioning at a normal speed, much slower than surfing speed. This meant he had not caught a wave, or maybe he'd been pushed into a canyon wall before coming into view. Tamir came straight for them, apparently having spotted them.

Apollo was worried the other two surfers would also appear and perhaps try to approach. So, even before Tamir had caught up to them, Apollo told Torith they needed to move. "Let's go to Flathead," he told her, pointing down the river.

Apollo and Torith started towards Flathead. Apollo looked back and motioned to Tamir to follow. Apollo knew Tamir would be irritated by this treatment.

Going down the canyon, Flathead was on the left, with the river passing to its right. This was a plateau about eighty feet above the river. There was a steep rock face from Flathead down to the water. Across the river from the plateau, the terrain was much less dramatic. There were some large boulders near the water, and then the land had a few trees and rose gently to rolling hills, beyond which were actual mountains.

Flathead was covered with pine trees, thick enough to offer ample concealment. Apollo took Torith into the trees, ensuring Tamir saw where they were going. Tamir caught up, and the three of them worked into an area where the thickness of the trees muffled the light and sounds of the outside world. This part of the forest was like a wilderness temple decorated with a thick carpeting of pine needles.

"What's with you guys?" demanded Tamir, too loud for the quiet setting, unable to hide his frustration. "You took off without me... and then you don't wait!"

"Tammiirr!" said Apollo, getting right in his friend's face for emphasis. "Do you know who those surfers are?"

"No."

"One of them is the girl who attacked Torith yesterday. She's Gammon's friend!"

The lights come on in Tamir's brain. Suddenly, it all made sense. "Oohhh!" he responded, shaking his head up and down.

"Did they see you, Tamir?"

"No... no... I mean... they saw me, but they don't know who I am. I jumped right after you two did."

"She might know who you are," said Torith. "Do you know who was with the girl?"

"No," said Tamir. "I know it was a guy—not a girl—but I don't know who."

"Escue?"

"No, no. Not that weirdo," Tamir said. "I know who Escue is."

"Hmmm...," went Apollo. "So, what should we do?"

"I want to talk to her," Torith answered. This was a switch from what she had said earlier.

"Really?" asked Tamir. "After what they did to you?"

"What if Gammon shows up?" Apollo asked.

"Then we leave," Torith said. "He's too much of a jerk."

"What about the other guy? What if he tries to fight?" Tamir asked.

"Then we fight, too," Apollo said. "Us three against two." Apollo had a determined look on his face. "And if more of them show up, I'm calling Mom. We're not going to let them beat us up again."

"So... ?" Tamir had a quizzical look, and Apollo could tell his friend's brain was churning. "We're just trying to learn more about Flint, right?"

Torith and Apollo nodded.

"And we want to know why they're being so mean?"

"Yep," said Apollo.

"Okay," said Tamir. "Alright... I guess... well... count me in. I want to talk to her, too. If their stupid Flint group has something to do with B. Z. Sughi, I'm interested."

Now that they had a plan, the three of them shot out of the Flathead Forest and beelined towards the top of the falls. Transitioning over Android, Apollo could see two ghosts down in the S-turn about halfway through it. If they were surfers, they had not done well. The two ghosts also started heading for the top of the falls. Apollo and his friends would arrive there first, but not by much.

The view from the top of the falls was an incredible display of gravity. Apollo knew that concept would dominate his life when he was a Blood. But as a ghost, he was mostly immune to its forces. He could go straight up almost as fast as he could down. In the future, when he was a Blood, he would have mass. If he jumped off the falls, the impact would kill him. He would be too heavy to ride sound waves, although theoretically, he could ride water waves, which sounded fun.

Apollo, Tamir, and Torith gathered at the top of the falls and waited for the girl and her companion. The two figures they had seen in the S-curve below were rising, and Apollo and Torith soon recognized the purple girl from yesterday. The boy with her was not Escue. He was older—more the age of the purple girl—and they did not know who he was.

The purple girl recognized Apollo and Torith and slowed, apparently considering her options. Then she advanced, as an older child would, confident in their age difference. She and her friend joined Apollo's group at the surf jumping-off point.

Tamir broke the ice. "So, Tory, is that her?" Tamir said it loud enough for everybody to hear.

Before Torith responded, the girl spoke. "Hi, Torith. I hope you're okay from yesterday. You too, Apollo." There was no mockery or insincerity in her voice. She was not attacking in any way. This surprised Apollo, who was geared up for a fight.

"Is he part of your group, too?" asked Apollo, his blues intense and making little effort to hide his hostility.

The boy with the girl looked confused.

"No," she said. Then, turning to the boy, she quickly explained, "They want to know if you're with Gammon." Turning back to Apollo, she said, "He's somebody I'm working on. The group would be good for him, just like it would be for you, Torith."

The older purple girl continued to display no aggressiveness, defensiveness, or hostility. Her voice was calm and friendly, and she was intoxicatingly self-confident.

"What's your name?" asked Apollo.

"Malta," she answered. "And this is Brian."

Malta's aura showed purple, as did her eyes. To Apollo, her demeanor was captivating.

Torith stepped forward, closer to Malta. "Did you wail on Brian like you did me?"

"Of course not. Brian is a friend."

"Well, Torith," said Tamir sarcastically, "What does that make you?"

Malta did not react to Tamir's jab. Instead, to Torith, she said, "We think it's important for you to join us. We felt stronger about it after we fought with you yesterday."

"Oh, yes," said Tamir, with sarcasm. "You have to fight someone to really know them." Tamir made a puking sound. "That's horse caca!"

"How do you expect anybody to join you if you attack them?" asked Apollo. "All you're going to do is make a bunch of ghosts hate you. There's no way Torith or any of us will ever join you because of that."

"Do you even know what we're about?" she asked, still calm. "If you knew—"

"I know you have a stupid name," interrupted Tamir, still willing to confront.

"What... you mean mine?" she asked, surprised.

"Nooo!" they said in unison. "Not Malta. Flint!"

"Ohhh," she said with a laugh and exaggerated relief. "Flint!"

"It's too wanna-be," said Tamir. "Like you're trying too hard."

"Is your name Tamir?" she asked with some hesitation, unsure she was right.

"How do you know that?" Tamir's hackles were up.

"Well," she said, pausing for effect. "I know it because I've made it my business to know a lot about your friend, Torith."

Malta looked at Torith while Apollo looked at both girls, back and forth. Malta was definitely in control, which made Apollo nervous. His threat-seeking radar was buzzing.

"Why?" asked Tamir.

Malta responded to the question by continuing to look straight at Torith. "Because you, Tory, are my project. You need to be part of us, and it's my job to make it happen.

The only way I can do that is to get to know everything about you."

"Yeah, right," Torith said. "And you think I'm going to want anything to do with you after yesterday."

"Yesterday was yesterday," said Malta. "There were some good reasons why we attacked you the way we did. Hopefully, someday, you'll be part of us and understand, and then we'll explain why we acted the way we did."

Malta's calm and reassuring demeanor was fascinating and mysterious. But Apollo did not like the way she called Torith "Tory." It was too familiar for somebody who did not know her well.

"So, what is Flatu-Flint anyway?" asked Tamir. Apollo stifled a laugh.

Malta took a deeper-than-normal pause before answering. It looked like Tamir had finally struck a nerve. "Flint," she said with emphasis, facing Torith but glancing at Tamir, "is the name for our group that studies and follows B. Z. Sughi."

"Sughi's supposed to be a good guy!" said Tamir. "I doubt he told you to attack my friends."

"He says that sometimes you must force people to do the right thing. It's for their own good, just like Mom forced us to do things when we were little."

"So that's what you guys are all about, forcing ghosts to do things?" It was Torith who asked this question, cocking her head sideways and raising an eyebrow to show disbelief.

"No," said Malta. "We don't force ghosts to do what we think is right. You and I already know what's right. Olam and Megantha, our teachers, our Mentors, and a lot of others have taught us that."

"Huh?" quipped Tamir.

Malta continued, "We're not in the business of

determining what is right. Instead, we push people to do what they already know is right."

Apollo thought Malta and her Flint group were way off. He could tell Tamir thought so, too. There was more talk, and then Malta surprised Apollo by abruptly dropping the discussion and instead complimenting Torith on her surfing. Malta said it was her first day at the canyon, and she hoped Torith would teach her how to surf.

Apollo did not believe anything Malta said, and it surprised him when Torith agreed to show her some techniques. Apollo mumbled objections. He knew Torith heard them, but she ignored them.

Apollo and Tamir's eyes locked as they both shook their heads in frustration. *Why is Torith agreeing to help her?*

Torith took Malta and started her girls' surf school. Apollo and Tamir were not happy with that, and they moved away, wanting distance from the nonsense. Brian was alone and cut out of any grouping. Apollo made no effort to include him. "Come on, Pancake Boy," Apollo said, "let's ride," and he and Tamir took off down the falls.

Apollo and Tamir surfed together for over an hour, doing their best to monitor Malta and Torith for any problems, but not wanting direct involvement. The boys stayed entirely away from Brian. Torith then came over and finished her surfing day with Apollo and Tamir. They asked her why she would help Malta. "She beat you up yesterday," said Apollo. "Why would you want anything to do with her?"

"I had to show that I'm not afraid of her," Torith said. "Don't you see, guys? She tries to be in charge. Yes, she's older, but I'm not going to run away."

Apollo had to agree that Torith's approach was not

all bad.

The three of them had no more contact with Malta and Brian the rest of the day. Later, they started home, and near Lake Minnick, they split up to go to their separate houses.

"See ya later, Pancake Boy," Apollo said. "You too, Tor."

Alone now, Apollo was left with his thoughts as he finished his trip home. He wondered about Torith and Malta. *They're so different. Both are strong and beautiful. Purple Malta is dangerous, and she's trouble. Torith is stubborn and not afraid of anything.* It was a lot for his little boy brain to process.

11

The Puissance

The next day, after school, Apollo rushed home to prepare for his meeting with the Mentor. This was the meeting he was supposed to have had two days ago, but his fight with Gammon made that impossible. The Mentor was slated to arrive at five o'clock. Like before, Mom wanted him home early to calm down and put himself in the right frame of mind.

"Remember," she had told him last night, "the Puissance is the ultimate power. It's Olam's power and mine."

Apollo knew this. The Mentor's job was to work with Apollo and help him learn about the power. It was the Mentor who would say when Apollo was ready for advancement.

Apollo arrived home well before four-thirty. The Pups, Jank and Natilia, were home, but his older brother, Dramos, and his older sister, Celti, were not. No doubt they were at school.

Apollo paused in the home's large entryway and looked up at the glass dome in the ceiling. Then he went down the hall towards the living room. Mom was there, and he hugged her. He talked with the Pups and teased them for a while, unwinding from his time at school.

Today, little Jank had managed to coach home a very bewildered ghost leopard shark. This confused animal insisted on transitioning above water rather than in the ocean, where it belonged. Mom explained to Jank that when the shark was a Blood, it would not be able to make the same mistake it was making now. "With fins, he won't go very far on land... and he has gills, which means his Blood body will die trying to remove oxygen from the air. He needs to be in water."

Jank insisted on keeping "LeRoy," the shark, as a pet. "I already have a name for him and everything, Mom," Jank pleaded. "Look, he's happy here. He likes me!"

There was no question about the shark's affection for Jank. It followed the boy everywhere in the house. Apollo had seen animals become out of sync with their natural environment. Ghost fish on land was the most common example, but he had seen a ghost bird and a ghost deer underwater in Lake Minnick. Once, he saw a lizard and a sea turtle high on a snowy mountain. But he had never seen one of these confused animals treat a human ghost the way this ghost shark was treating Jank. LeRoy was acting like Jank was his mother.

"You can keep LeRoy overnight," said Megantha. "And tomorrow, you and Natilia can come with me, and we'll take LeRoy back to the ocean. He'll be happier there."

Soon, it was five o'clock, and a house chime sounded to indicate the presence of Apollo's Mentor.

Apollo went to greet him.

"Apollo! My friend!" said the Mentor, a huge smile on his face. "Your humble servant is here to teach you!"

"Mentor Reemo!" responded Apollo a little stiffly. He always felt uncomfortable when Reemo called himself Apollo's servant. "Please... come in."

Reemo came into the home. Megantha arrived at the entryway, and Reemo greeted her, too. "Hello, Mom," he said, treating her with warmth and respect.

She gave Reemo a hug, and the two of them talked briefly about what he was doing and his current work as a Mentor. "It's keeping me busy," he told her. "Right now, I have almost fifty SunStars."

"And how is my Apollo doing?" she asked him.

Reemo turned to look at Apollo and gave him a smile. "I'm proud of him. He's progressing well."

Apollo waited patiently while they continued to talk. Then his mother left, and Apollo and Reemo went into a room off the far side of the living room. This was a study room, and it was meant to be a quiet place.

Reemo asked about Dramos. This did not surprise Apollo, who was extremely proud of his older brother. For his age, Dramos was progressing unusually fast in the Puissance.

"You are, too, Apollo," Reemo said. "Your brother is an incredible person, but so are you."

Apollo appreciated the compliment, and he knew he was advancing well, albeit nothing like Dramos.

After some instruction, Reemo started asking Apollo about the four levels in the Puissance. Apollo was on the student or apprentice level, making him a SunStar. Reemo was a Mentor, and the next level up was Forza, followed by the highest level, Quasar. Mom and Dad were Quasars.

"Who else is a Quasar?" Reemo asked.

This was easy stuff for Apollo and almost beneath him. But Apollo respected Reemo and was willing to tolerate the rudimentary questioning. "Diamond is one," Apollo answered. "Sapienti is the other."

"Anymore?"

Apollo wondered if this was a trick question. "Hmmm... no... no, just the four of them."

Apollo did not know where Reemo was going with this, but the simple questioning allowed Apollo's mind to wander, and it settled on B. Z. Sughi.

"Can you tell me the differences between Mentors, Forzas, and Quasars?"

Apollo did not answer but instead asked, "What about Sughi? B. Z. Sughi? Is he a Mentor like you, Reemo?"

"Oh, no," said Reemo, shaking his head negatively. "No way," he added with some disgust in his voice.

Apollo perked right up at Reemo's apparent dislike for Sughi. Apollo asked to hear more. "You mean... he's only a SunStar apprentice... like me? I thought for sure he'd be a Mentor. He's so popular."

"Yes," Reemo said with emphasis. "An apprentice. Only an apprentice."

Apollo was amazed. "But... how... I mean... Sughi is famous." Apollo shook his head. *Only a SunStar!* Apollo thought. "But... his Mentor... doesn't he want to promote Sughi?"

"B. Z.'s Mentor won't recommend him. He says Sughi is not ready. Sughi has been a SunStar for a long time."

"Uh-huh," said Apollo.

Reemo continued, "The Mentors... we meet every so often. In the meetings, this issue has come up several times. We've asked Orion—that's Sughi's Mentor—why he won't recommend him for advancement. Orion says B. Z. isn't ready. He won't elaborate. Some of the Mentors are upset over it."

Apollo was surprised to hear there would be disagreement among the Mentors.

Reemo continued, "Some Mentors are angry. We had a big argument about it during our last Mentor meeting. A bunch of the Mentors were banding together and saying that Orion is wrong, and they practically demanded that Sughi be recommended for advancement."

"What do you think?" asked Apollo.

Reemo looked up and around, then said, "Look, if Orion thinks Sughi is not ready, I must trust that Orion is right. But other people are unhappy with that position."

"Unhappy? Mad?"

"Yes. That huge argument during our last meeting… I've never seen anything like it."

Apollo didn't get it. "Why doesn't somebody ask Olam? Or one of the Forzas?"

"When we ask, Olam says it's Orion's decision, but Olam gives no other reasoning. The Forzas won't either."

Apollo wished Tamir were here to hear this. Tamir would have better questions. "What would you do if Sughi were your apprentice?"

"I honestly don't know, Apollo," Reemo said, his smile gone. "For now, I support Orion. My only complaint is that Orion should be telling us more. Many ghosts are upset, and maybe if he gave more explanation, they wouldn't be."

"Yes, but what about privacy?" Apollo asked.

"Good point, Apollo," Reemo said.

Apollo and Reemo did not speak for nearly a full minute, both lost in their thoughts. Then Apollo asked, "So if Sughi is not being advanced, then I guess you don't think people should be following him?"

"I don't, Apollo. Something's not right there. B. Z. is the most natural leader I know. He's dynamic. He is very likable, and people want to follow him."

"But?"

"Sughi says he has a plan that will make it so everybody passes the test when they are Bloods. Some ghosts say it's the most loving way. Nobody will fail."

"By forcing people to do the right thing… right?" Apollo asked. "That girl, Malta, was saying something about that."

"Yes. He presents it as if we all work together and help each other. The strong help the weak. One for all. And… in the end… everybody crosses the finish line. He says that's what we must do if we love each other."

"But is that really a test?" Apollo asked.

"Maybe the test is mostly for the strong. To see how far they'll go to help the weak?"

"Yes," answered Apollo. "But forcing people?"

"I know," Reemo answered, looking frustrated. "Like you, I wish we had better answers. It's beginning to tear people apart."

12

Hungry, Tired, Clueless

Later that night, Apollo talked with his older brother, Dramos, about Malta, Gammon, and B. Z. Sughi. "It seems like they want to boss people around, Apollo told him. "They want to force ghosts to do things, supposedly for their own good."

Dramos said he'd had government classes at the university. There was a lot of discussion about control systems we might have to live under when we are Bloods on faraway planets. "Governments are going to force us to do all kinds of things," he said. "Like now, but worse."

"So, does that mean you think Malta and Gammon are doing the right thing? Trying to force people?" Apollo asked.

"No way. They have no authority."

Apollo agreed.

"The whole rules thing is hard, Apollo. Rules matter here on Summa. But when we live on Blood earths, rules and governments will matter more. Nobody is starving here, but some of us will be there. Freezing and sick, too. Here, we don't need shelter, but there, we will. And to make things even more difficult, when we're Bloods, we won't remember anything about Summa. We're going to need rules.

None of this was new to Apollo, and he had been over it with friends and teachers before. But he liked being with Dramos. Hashing over the common with him was quality time.

Apollo and Dramos had gone outside, up onto the roof of the house, to talk. To the west, the day's light was almost gone. Only a little purple remained.

"It's going to be tough when we are Bloods," Apollo said.

"Yep," Dramos answered. "We'll be hungry, tired, and clueless."

"What if we're starving and have to feed our kids?" Apollo asked. "Do you think we'll steal food?"

"I guess if things are really bad," Dramos answered. "But you know, Mom and Dad want us to succeed. They're not setting us up to fail. I have to think that most of us will do fine as long as we do our best."

"I know," Apollo said. Then, with sarcasm, he continued, "Dad says many of us will shine like the sun." Apollo accentuated the word sun with hand gestures that drew a big circle.

Dramos shrugged. "I'm sure Dad's right. There will be lots of bad, but a lot of good, too. I mean, we'll be hungry, and because of that, it will feel fantastic to eat. When we're hot, we can swim in the ocean."

"No flying around like we can now," Apollo said with a dejected tone. Then he perked up and said, 'But I know one thing that will feel good."

Dramos looked over.

"To beat up mean kids like Gammon."

Dramos smiled. "I hear you, brother. Fight for the right! Nothing like it. Maybe when we are Bloods, we'll be soldiers… for the good guys, of course!"

A ghost sagehen flew by, awkward in flight as it circled them once. Then, it headed towards nearby trees, and the forest swallowed its aura.

Dramos tracked the bird and commented, "That will be food. Especially if it flies as badly as that one."

More silence followed as each pondered their futures.

"You and I are strong, Apollo. We're going to do well as Bloods. I think Dad is right. We'll be like the sun. Strong and helping others. That is what you and I do. No way our families will starve. We won't let that happen. Your friends, too. Tamir and Torith are going to rock it. Look how awesome they are now."

Apollo hoped Dramas was right.

"As for that Moon Baby, Gammon, and his purple witch, Malta… who knows? They're strong, too. But they seem like takers and manipulators to me. Hopefully, guys like you and I will put them in their place."

13

Feral Cats

The next day, after school, Tamir, Apollo, and Torith were talking before going home. Tamir was telling Torith about the assignment he and Apollo had turned in to their teacher, MM, earlier in the day. This was the one about how different earths might have different gravitational pulls, causing differences in the physical Blood bodies of Summa Ghosts living on those planets.

Apollo and Torith were also teasing Tamir about the girl named Rachael. Tamir and Rachael had not had any banter after Tamir's exchange with her a few days ago. But today in class, after the students had handed in their assignments, MM asked his students to indicate by show of hands who had taken what position on the gravity thing. First, he wanted to see who thought ghosts would be sent as physical Bloods to different worlds with big differences in gravity. Only two students took that position. One was Tamir, which did not surprise anyone, and the other was Rachael, which seemed unusual. MM asked her why. She responded, "Well, at least Pancake Boy and I agree on something." The class laughed. Her timing and delivery were perfect. She had scored again.

While Apollo, Torith, and Tamir were talking, they had not noticed that Gammon and the purple girl, Malta, were approaching from behind. Gammon surprised them by saying, "Hello, Torith. Nice to see you."

Apollo saw Torith whirl around. She looked startled, and Apollo was surprised, too. Apollo watched Torith quickly compose herself as she made a show of obviously ignoring Gammon. "Hi, Malta," Torith said.

"Hi, Torith," Malta answered. "Can we talk to you? Just the two of us?"

"Don't do it," said Tamir.

"Stay out of this, pot-digger," snapped Gammon. "Same for you, Apollo. We're not going to hurt her."

"Pot-digger? Is that some Flat-u-Flint insult?" quipped Tamir, returning fire.

Apollo laughed nervously at Tamir's comment despite the seriousness of the moment. Then, he maneuvered protectively between Tamir and Gammon. Apollo faced Torith. "Tor, let's talk. The three of us for a minute, okay?"

At first, Torith looked like she was going to agree. But then she changed her mind and said, "You know, I don't think we need to do that. Instead, let's talk, the four of us." Looking around Apollo at Gammon, she added, "The four of us, meaning everybody but you... pot-digger."

Now it was Tamir's turn to laugh, but that did not last long because, on close approach, there were four more kids, all of them Gammon's age. One of them was Brian, the boy who had been with Malta surfing in the canyon two days ago.

"Heads up, Apollo," Tamir warned. "They have reinforcements!"

Apollo recognized Brian and saw the dweeb of a boy named Escue, who had been with Gammon and Malta during the first attack. The other two were a boy and a girl, neither of whom Apollo knew.

The arrival of reinforcements changed everything. There was no more time for verbal banter. "Torith, we need to leave!" Apollo commanded. "Come on!"

Apollo saw a hint of panic on Torith's face. He could not blame her. Six older kids were attacking. Apollo sprang by her side. "Remember last time!" he said, close to her face, locking his blues with her aqua browns. "We stick right together. You with me!" Then, looking over at Tamir, "You too, T! Both of you, stay with me! Keep it tight!"

Apollo took off, slow at first, giving Torith and Tamir time to catch him and form up. Then they accelerated full blast, heading for Apollo's home. Gammon, Malta, Brian, Escue, and the other two pursued, gaining fast.

Apollo was scared but focused. He had been in this situation before, and he had won. "No matter what, stay with me!" he ordered his best friends. He sensed their fear. Apollo could only hope Torith and Tamir would comply with his commands.

It did not take long for the six older ones to be on them. Gammon immediately attacked Apollo, moving around and through him, forcing his will upon Apollo, tearing at his network and breaking down his connective menapses. For Apollo, the pain and damage were progressively debilitating.

Apollo knew his friends were being subjected to the same. Because everyone was so close, they were all fighting each other. Apollo kept yelling at Torith and Tamir to stay close to him. This meant all nine ghosts were in a swirling mass of conflict as Apollo tried to lead them toward home.

Having somebody tear right inside you, forcing themselves on you, is surreal. You are still you, but you also want to become the person who invaded you. You know what you think, but you also strongly feel the emotions of that other person. You are one, but you are also two or more people, depending on how many have invaded. When the invader tries to force you to do something, it's hard not to comply, especially when the invader is as determined and vicious as Gammon.

Apollo could see that Torith and Tamir were sticking right with him. They were letting him lead, which confirmed to Apollo that it was up to him to get them out of this mess. Gammon's attack made him sick and clouded his thoughts. Apollo struggled to concentrate, attempting rational thought through the storm of hate. He knew the most dangerous thing he could do right now would be to stop. That would give the six attackers time to break them down. He had to push on as best he could towards his home.

By now, they were over Lake Minnick. Gammon attacked relentlessly, and he was winning. The older attackers were too strong. The sanctuary of home was too far away, but Apollo kept speeding forward, dragging Torith and Tamir with him.

Apollo tried to sense Torith's strength. But there was no way to talk with her. All Apollo knew was that he was overwhelmed. His friends had to be, also. The six enemies were yelling and forcing themselves on them. The offensive words of "pitner" and "kutard" showered like hot sparks. Apollo was smothered with pain, hate, and bitterness.

You have to protect Torith! He ordered himself. *Protect her!*

But it was all too strong and too fast.

After they passed Lake Minnick, Apollo knew this had to end. He could not go on, and he doubted Torith and Tamir could either. He had to call for Mom. He would be ridiculed. But he would do it to protect his friends. He had to, for their sakes. Mostly, he did not want Torith to suffer anymore, regardless of any consequences to him.

Apollo called for Megantha.

Boom! She was there as soon as he called. The fighting stopped immediately.

Megantha snatched Gammon and Malta by the backs of their necks, wrangling them like feral cats. She commanded that the other four attackers go home. "Now!"

Brian, Escue, and the other two scattered.

Gammon looked surprised, and he locked eyes with Apollo. Apollo knew this was Gammon's way of saying there would be payback.

Gammon tried to wriggle free, and Megantha clamped down hard. Gammon winced and stopped resisting.

Then Megantha flipped Gammon around to face her, switching her grip to his shoulder. "Stop this, son!" she ordered. "No more!"

Gammon said nothing, but he showed a strong look of defiance. A vicious stream was in his eyes, and Apollo could see he was angry. Gammon's colorless aura palpitated furiously.

Megantha then spun Malta around, ordering her to stay put, which she did, showing no resistance. Apollo was amazed to see no look of anger or defiance on her face as she stared into her mother's eyes. Malta's purple aura surged powerfully, but it was an even, controlled surge. In the back of his mind, Apollo had to acknowledge that Malta was an incredible specimen, despite the bad in her.

Apollo could see that both Torith and Tamir appeared exhausted, and they looked relieved that the fight was over. But Apollo also saw that neither thanked Megantha for coming, nor did they thank Apollo for calling her. He understood. He had called Mom! Everybody at school would hear about it. He would be ridiculed for weeks! Tamir and Torith would be ridiculed, too!

Apollo tried to explain himself. "Look, Tamir, I

didn't want them to keep beating on us. They're the bad guys! We're not. And they won't stop!"

Tamir looked down and mumbled something about agreeing with him. But he was noncommittal, and Apollo was embarrassed.

Torith said, "It's okay, Apollo. It's alright."

Torith was patronizing him, and that did not help.

Apollo's eyes scanned low. "I wanted to protect you, Torith."

Megantha spoke up. "Gammon, why don't you explain what you're trying to accomplish through these attacks?" And then, turning to Malta, "You too, Malta. You know you're not supposed to fight like that. So why?"

Gammon was defiant. "It's for their good. They won't listen. Torith could help a lot of ghosts if she joined us."

Megantha sighed. "Gammon, you can't force ghosts to do things, even if you think you're right."

"That's not true," bantered Gammon. "You force kids to go to school. You force them to be quiet. You force them to rest at night. What do you mean we can't force ghosts? You force them all the time."

"I don't want you forcing me to do anything, Gammon!" Torith retorted. "I don't need you telling me how to be good. Especially not you!"

"It's not about you, Tory. It's about all the ghosts you could help. You're strong, like Malta. If you join, you'll help many people, and your friends will join too."

Then Malta spoke. "Apollo, I had to be convinced, too. At first, I thought Flint was wrong. But it's not, and it's worth fighting for."

"Worth beating us up?"

"Yes, Apollo, worth beating you up. Someday—if

Torith joins us—she'll thank us."

"Dream on, Malta," injected Torith. "You were nice when we surfed. But you've attacked me twice. You're two-faced. You'll do anything to get your way. You're not my friend. Stay away from me."

Malta started to say something, but Torith turned to Megantha and cut Malta off by asking, "Mom, I want to go home. May I leave?"

"Sure, Torith. But we'll talk more about this later. Okay?"

"Yes." Torith glanced at Apollo and waved a hand at Tamir. Then she left, keeping her back toward Gammon and Malta, making an obvious point to ignore them.

"We want to leave too," said Gammon.

"Will you apologize?"

"No," said Gammon. "I won't because I did the right thing."

Megantha shook her head in disappointment.

Apollo was amazed that Gammon did not melt at the sight of their mother's sadness.

Megantha turned to Apollo and said, "I'm sorry this happened today. And, Apollo, I'm sorry about last time, too."

Apollo nodded his head in acknowledgment.

Megantha continued, "Apollo, you need to know that even though Gammon will be punished for what he did today, I won't monitor everything he does. That means he might attack you or Torith again. Do you understand?"

"Yes," said Apollo.

"What a pot-diggin' Flat-u-Flint," said Tamir under his breath, provoking a smile from Apollo.

"Gammon has a certain amount of agency commensurate with his age."

Gammon sneered in defiance. "I'm right, Mom. You know it. And as for you... Apollo... you Mamma's Boy... you'll pay for today. Flint's here to stay. You have no idea how strong we're going to be."

"Enough!" commanded Megantha. She tightened her grip on him and then snapped him to his home.

Megantha, Apollo, Malta, and Tamir looked at each other. There was an awkward silence. Then Megantha spoke. "Is there anything you want to say, Malta?"

Malta's demeanor and level of respect were totally different than Gammon's, as was her tone of voice. She made no effort to move away from Megantha, and she switched to a pussy cat personality, the total opposite of the savage feline she had been a minute ago. "Mom," she said, looking Megantha firmly in the eye. "I know you think I did the wrong thing today. I'm sure you think the things we are trying to accomplish with Flint are wrong."

"Flint is not all wrong," said Megantha. "But the way you're going about it is out of line."

"I know you think that," said Malta. "We've talked about it."

"A lot of good that did," threw in Tamir.

Megantha gave Tamir a look that meant "be quiet." Malta, on the other hand, never let her eyes waver from Megantha's.

"Well, Malta," said Megantha, "I can see that I'm not going to change your mind, at least not today. So why don't you go home? Alright?"

"Yes, Mom," said Malta, with a slight bow. "Goodbye, Apollo," she said while leaving.

Apollo instinctively responded with a "goodbye," although, after saying it, he wished he hadn't.

They watched her leave, and then Megantha turned to

Tamir and asked, "Tamir, I know you're very interested in B. Z. Sughi."

Tamir nodded.

"So, why don't you want any part of Flint?"

"I can't believe Sughi wants people beat up who won't join him. I don't think Gammon is legit. He's just sayin' Flint is a Sughi group to get ghosts to join him. Flint is a stupid group with a stupid name that makes Gammon feel powerful."

Apollo noticed that his mother did not agree with or disagree with Tamir. This was so unlike her. Why were his parents so insistent on not voicing an opinion on a group that was obviously wrong?

"One more thing, Tamir," said Megantha. "Do you think Apollo did the right thing to call me?"

"Mom, don't ask him that," complained Apollo. "I know he's embarrassed by it. We're gonna be made fun of at school tomorrow."

Both Apollo and Megantha looked at Tamir, who did not want to meet either of them in the eyes. Finally, looking down at the ground, Tamir said, "I think we could have fought longer, Apollo."

Apollo was devastated by this remark. "Even Torith?" he asked.

"I don't know," said Tamir, shaking his head. "But I know I could have lasted longer."

After this, Apollo and Megantha went home, and so did Tamir. For the rest of the evening, Apollo fretted over what Tamir had said. He had taken upon himself the responsibility of trying to lead them out of trouble. When he thought it was getting too rough, he had called Mom, making it clear he was the Mamma's Boy, not Tamir or Torith. He tried to do the right thing in a difficult and confusing situation. Now, after what Tamir said, he was afraid he had made the wrong choice.

He needed to talk about it some more, but he did not want to talk to Mom or Dad. He wanted the opinion of somebody who saw things more from his perspective. He considered calling Reemo, but he mostly wanted Dramos. Apollo called him.

Dramos answered Apollo's call right away. He spoke softly, saying he was in the university library. "I'll be home in an hour," he said. "We can talk then."

And talk they did. Apollo explained the whole thing with Gammon, repeating his description of the attack at Lake Minnick a few days ago, followed by meeting Malta surfing, and now today's gang attack by Gammon and the older kids.

Through all this, Apollo could see anger rising in Dramos' face. Apollo asked, "Do you think I did the right thing by calling Mom?"

Dramos was silent for a few moments. Then he said, "You know, Apollo, I don't know. Only you can know."

"But I wasn't sure how strong Tamir and Torith were. I was afraid they were losing it."

"I get it," said Dramos. "All you wanted to do was protect them."

"Yes!"

Dramos thought. "Then I think you made the right choice, Apollo. But… you may have been wrong about your friends. It sounds like they are stronger than you thought."

Apollo could see Dramos' point. Unfortunately, it only complicated his feelings about his decision.

Then Dramos added, "So you made your choice. Now, you live with it. Right or wrong, Gammon will spread it to everybody that you're a *fraidy-cat* Momma's Boy."

Apollo hung his head. "I know."

"And it looks like Tamir will be less than solid in standing up for you on this one. Especially if he thought he could have fought longer."

"Torith, too," said Apollo. "I was mostly trying to protect her. If she really could have fought longer, then I messed up."

Apollo and Dramos were silent, mulling it over. Then, Apollo asked, "So what do I do?"

Dramos looked up and then refocused on Apollo. "You own it, Apollo. You one hundred percent own it. Don't make excuses. Don't give explanations. Be a rock about it. Own it."

14

Weird Brian

At that moment, Apollo and Dramos heard the chime from the front door. Somebody had come to the house. It was late in the day and too late for visits. Apollo and Dramos had been talking in the study off to one side of the living room. This was the same study where Apollo had met with Reemo. They came out into the living room. Mom and the Pups were there, playing. She looked up and said, "Apollo, you should answer the door. The person is here to see you."

Now Apollo was on guard. Mom rarely told them in advance who was at the door. She always knew, but she usually let them answer it without telling them.

"Who?" asked Apollo.

"Just go, son. You'll be surprised."

Apollo started down the hallway. "Oh, and Dramos, you go with him," said Mom.

Now Apollo was doubly on guard, and from his eye contact with Dramos, he knew his older brother was, too.

The boys continued down the hallway, together now. The Pups tried to go, but Mom stopped them. "No, no," she said. "You two stay here. It's private business."

Apollo touched the keypad next to the door, and it opened. To Apollo's surprise, Brian was there. This was the same Brian who had been part of today's attack.

Apollo stepped back, and Dramos moved up even with him. Brian still had not said anything, but there was a pained look on his face.

"W... what are you doing here?" asked Apollo, as unfriendly as he could muster.

"Apollo, I'm not here to fight. I want to talk. Please... can I come in?"

"This is Brian. He helped Gammon and Malta attack us today," Apollo said to Dramos.

Upon hearing this, Dramos stepped in front of Apollo and took control. "Maybe I should fight you, *boy*. That way, you'll know what it's like to be bullied by somebody older."

Brian did not move or retaliate in any way. Then, very softly, he said to both of them, "I've come to apologize."

Apollo was taken aback with surprise.

"Did Torith call you?" Brian asked.

"Torith? No... why?"

"Because I already apologized to her. And I asked her not to call you before I got here."

"She didn't call... right, A.P.?" asked Dramos.

"Right."

Dramos continued, "I still think I should put some hurt on you for beating up my little brother. How do we know this isn't another Flint trick?" Then, looking at Apollo, Dramos repeated, "Flint trick," with a smirk.

Apollo laughed and added, "If Tamir were here, he'd call it a Flat-u-Flint trick."

Brian laughed nervously. Dramos liked the comment, too. The tension was easing.

"Tell you what," said Dramos. "You say you've already been to Torith's. Let's see what she has to say. Then maybe we'll let you in."

"Fine... fine," said Brian, backing up and away from the door. "I'll wait."

Dramos shut the front door, leaving Brian outside.

Apollo understood this was a power move on Dramos' part, but even so, it made him uncomfortable to treat Brian like that, especially if Brian was sincere.

Dramos asked for a comm, and then he called Torith.

Torith answered immediately. It was apparent she had been waiting for the call. "Did he show up yet?" she asked anxiously.

"Brian?"

"Yes... yes!" she said impatiently. "Have you talked to him?"

"No," said Dramos. "We wanted to talk to you first."

"Look, you guys," she said. "Hear him out. Brian is weird, but he's sincere."

Dramos and Apollo let Brian in. They marched him down the hall, through the living room, and into the study.

While in the living room, Megantha said, "Thank you for coming, Brian. I'm proud of you, son."

Upon hearing that, Apollo and Dramos knew Brian would tell the truth. But Dramos kept up his I'm-older-and-tougher-than-you-act... for show. "Okay, Brian. Let's have it."

Brian sighed, then started, "Apollo, I'm not strong like you, and I don't have friends, at least not good ones. I'm a follower, and I know it—"

Dramos cut him off. "Look, Brian. We're looking for an apology, not a sympathy plea."

"I know... I know," said Brian, bobbing his head. "Please hear me out. I'm trying to explain."

Dramos said nothing but gave him a look that said, "Well, get on with it."

But instead of talking, Brian just hovered there, a little wide-eyed, his head still bobbing, and looking nervous.

"Well?" said Dramos, impatiently.

"That Malta... she's amazing," said Brian. "I've always liked her and wished she were my friend. When she started paying attention to me, I decided to do whatever she wanted. I didn't care. I wanted her to like me so much."

Apollo understood the attraction.

"You're pathetic," said Dramos.

Brian paused before answering. Then, his head bobbing up and down in the affirmative, he said, "Yes, you're right. I am pathetic. I compromised a lot to be with her."

"You know," said Dramos, "when you're a Blood, females like Malta will eat you alive. Right now, all you want is her company. But your Blood will want a lot more, if you know what I mean. You'll crave her so bad that you'll do anything to get her.

Brian half-smiled. "I don't know how I'll handle being a Blood. I am terrible as a ghost. But... look... all I know is that what we did today was wrong. Apollo, I'm sorry. I won't do it again."

"What if Malta makes you?"

Brian again became frozen in the mouth and stopped talking. Apollo was annoyed at his quirky communication traits, and he was sure it was driving Dramos nuts.

Then, shaking his head, Brian responded, "It will be hard when Malta asks me to do something. I like her so much! I'll have to stay away from her... and Gammon."

"But will they let you? Aren't you part of their group?"

"I am. And that's a problem. If I desert..." Brian paused, annoyingly. "If I desert, they'll hound me. I have to sit next to them in class. I deal with them every day. A lot of people don't like Gammon, but he's bossy, and they listen to him. He'll call me a traitor. He'll hate me."

"He hates me, too," said Apollo.

"Tell us about Flint," asked Dramos. "I still don't understand what it's trying to accomplish. Is it really a group started by Sughi? The Flash?"

"The Flash?" asked Brian.

"B. Z. Sughi... The Flash... all the same person," said Dramos, showing impatience.

Apollo had not heard the term Flash for Sughi, so he could see why Brian didn't know it either.

"Gammon's Mentor is a big believer in Sughi," Brian explained.

"But how can that guy be a Mentor if he tells ghosts to follow Sughi and not Olam?"

"Oh... no... no. That's not it at all. That Mentor isn't saying not to follow Olam. He's saying that Olam wants all his children to pass the Blood test, and Sughi has a plan to make sure it happens."

"But Olam told me it's not a test unless we can fail it," said Apollo. "He disagrees that people should be forced to do the right thing."

"I know, and Gammon and all the guys in Flint are cautious about never saying they are against Olam. Instead, they say they want to do everything to make sure people don't fail the Blood phase."

The three of them were quiet, and then Apollo spoke. "So, it's true, Sughi is over Flint. Right?"

Pause... pause... bothersome pause. "Well... yes and no," said Brian. "Yes, in that Flint is an attempt to follow Sughi, but no, because I don't think B. Z. has ever come and talked to Gammon or anybody in his group. Gammon was gone to hear Sughi talk, but I don't think he's ever actually met him or been in a private meeting with him or anything like that."

"So, Gammon's just a wanna-be," said Dramos. "He's nothing more than a crazy fan of the Flash?"

"Well... no, it's more than that."

Dramos was getting frustrated. "Brian, give us the whole picture, not this piece-by-piece nonsense. Is Flint a legitimate Sughi group or not?"

Brian's head bobbed in nervous thinking. "Legitimate, I'd say."

Dramos leaned forward, wanting more.

"You see, Sughi doesn't formally start any of the groups."

"Groups?" asked Apollo. "You mean there are more than Flint?"

"Oh, yeah. Didn't you guys know that? There are B. Z. groups all over. There must be hundreds of them."

"Hundreds?"

"Yes. Maybe more. Each of them is independent of the other. They don't report to anybody except themselves. They are self-controlled. Nobody is in any chain of command above the local leader. Sughi probably has no idea who the individual leaders are, except those of the largest groups."

"You mean there's probably a Sughi group at the U—my school?" asked Dramos.

"Oh, for sure," said Brian. "Probably several of them. Nobody is controlling the thing. It doesn't matter if there's a group and somebody wants to start another one."

"Is Flint the only one at our school?" asked Apollo.

"Probably," said Brian. "Gammon is a freak. He'd go on the rampage against any competing group. He wants to be the only one."

At this, a thought occurred to Apollo. He looked over at Dramos, and it was clear that Dramos was getting something similar. "Maybe we can mess with Gammon," Apollo said. "What do you think, Dramos?"

"For sure, Apollo."

Brian looked confused as he scanned back and forth between the brothers. "What? What are you guys talking about?"

Apollo wanted to tell him, but Dramos spoke first. "We'll let you know... later. But first, my bro and I need to talk about it. Now, tell us more about Flint."

Brian stayed for another half hour. Extracting information from him was frustrating, but Apollo and Dramos finally had a better picture of Flint and groups like it. B. Z. Sughi was only a SunStar in the Puissance. He had no authority over anybody. He could not form sanctioned groups, nor could he officially tell people what to do or think. But he had a magnetic personality, and he had ideas that many ghosts found interesting. Sughi said he was not in opposition to Olam or any Quasar. Instead, his ideas were there to help everybody.

B. Z. encouraged ghosts to form their own groups, like clubs, saying that all ghosts were in this together.

"But what about the idea of forcing people?" Apollo asked.

"All Sughi says is that it's important for all of us to help each other. It's the most important thing we can do. Some ghosts think that means they should force ghosts to do the right thing."

"Like Gammon," Dramos said.

"Yes, like Gammon and Malta," Brian responded. "And because of that, I'm getting out."

Apollo asked, "I still don't understand why the Flash is spending so much time and effort on this. And the same with Gammon? Why do they even care? Why all this effort to form groups and attack people?"

"Apollo... think," said Dramos. "Look what this does for Gammon. Can't you see the power it gives him?"

Apollo understood, partially.

"This is perfect for Gammon to boss ghosts around. And that's exactly what he wants, power. He can take the high moral position that all he's trying to do is help people. And he can force ghosts to do things, supposedly for their own sakes."

"That's right," Brian said. "And you know, I wonder if B. Z. Sughi isn't doing it for the same reason? Maybe he doesn't want to advance in the Puissance like he should. Maybe he thinks he's too good to do it Olam's way."

"Yeah, Brian, maybe you're right," said Dramos. "The Flash can't come right out and say he thinks Olam is wrong. Instead, he says he wants to help everybody."

In listening to Dramos and Brian talk, Apollo could see that Brian was very smart. Maybe not brilliant like Tamir, but still a super brain. It was too bad that Brian was cursed with mush for a backbone. And his annoying habit of pausing right in the middle of a sentence... not good. He was in for some hard times over the next several weeks if he tried to break from Malta and Gammon.

"Who thought of that stupid name, Flint?" asked Apollo.

"Gammon," said Brian. "He says flint creates sparks, which can turn into a big fire. Gammon calls it Sughi fire!"

15

A Free Force

For the next several weeks, Apollo, Tamir, and Torith combined with other friends, including weird Brian and the red-aurora'd girl at school named Rachel. They worked to form a group to compete with Gammon and Malta's Flint. With the help of Dramos and Reemo, they came up with the name "AFF" for "A Free Force."

They banded together to protect themselves from Gammon, Malta, and others who had joined with Flint. Gammon continued to be mean and nasty, but he stopped the attacks. Still, he took every opportunity to ridicule Apollo for being a Momma's Boy. Malta, on the other hand, changed tactics completely. She continued attempts to recruit Torith, but she only used charm. Eventually, she and Torith came to a tenuous understanding. Torith was not joining, but there was a level of respect.

Malta also continued attempts to make contact with Apollo. This, for Apollo, was confusing. She was the enemy, but she was an intoxicating older girl. She no longer tried to fight. Instead, she went out of her way to see him at school—simply to talk with him—as if she had a personal interest in him. She frequently told Apollo she could see that he would be a great person one day. "You'll be a powerful ghost, Apollo," she would tell him. "I hope you don't forget me when you are."

Malta's contact with Apollo caused problems

between Apollo and Torith. Apollo would naturally give bandwidth to Malta. How could he not? And this made Torith jealous. For Apollo, it was all complicated.

"You're playing with forces you don't understand," Tamir would tell Apollo. "Malta might tell you she thinks you're a wonder boy. But you know she's trouble."

ᘐᐤᑳᘐᐤᑳᘐᐤᑳᘐᐤᑳ

Years passed. Apollo, Torith, and Tamir became older and stronger. Despite the Malta factor, their friendship remained committed and strong. Malta and Gammon went away to college, taking their nonsense with them. Apollo lost contact with Malta, and he hoped never to see Gammon again.

16

Twenty Years Later

Twenty years later...

Apollo watched the moisture-laden clouds rolling in off the ocean. Their bellies glowed orange, lit by the sun hanging low in the sky. Behind Apollo, to the east, coastal terrain rose slowly into gentle, rounded mountains wrapped in heavy clouds.

Apollo was resting on a small hill above a rocky coastline. The darkened ocean waters were white-capped from a blustery wind. Healthy-sized waves boomed onto the rocks below.

His thoughts wandered as he waited, and he drifted back in time. So much had happened since his school days. He remembered how he and his friends had innocently organized an opposition to Gammon. They had called it AFF. In the first year, it was only a moderate success. A few students joined, mostly trying to protect themselves from older kids who were Gammon's friends.

Things improved for AFF as Apollo and his friends moved into upper grades. AFF became dominant. Flint dwindled in strength. Gammon and Malta went on to the university, and without their strong personalities, Flint could not compete. Apollo, Torith, and Tamir's AFF—A Free Force—ruled.

Apollo remembered the night that weak but brave boy named Brian came over to the house to apologize. He remembered how surprised he and Dramos were to learn there were hundreds of groups following B. Z. Sughi, like Gammon's Flint. Soon after learning this, Dramos spent time looking for groups on his university's campus. His search was quickly rewarded with the names of three groups. One went by Critical Mass. Dramos decided to make contact.

He talked to a few of its members, and as soon as he showed interest, Critical Mass put on a well-organized campaign pressuring him to join. At first, they were gentle and polite, but when it became apparent that Dramos only wanted to know about the group, not join, they were more aggressive. Finally, they tried the force-feed approach, where six of them ganged up on him and attacked him, just like Gammon had attacked Torith and Apollo.

The attack did not go well, at least not for the attackers. Dramos was especially strong for his age. He withstood all of them and maneuvered the battle to a floor in the main campus library where he and his friends often studied. Unluckily for the attackers, Dramos' friends were there, and they quickly joined his defense. Soon, the attackers were overwhelmed. Dramos and his friends blew so many of their menapses that several of them were left unconscious. After that, Critical Mass stopped recruiting Dramos and considered him an enemy. Its members feared him and stayed away.

Apollo wished he could now fight alongside Dramos, but Reemo explained why that was a no. "Dramos is very strong," Reemo said. "He has special assignments." Apollo knew that was right. Then Reemo said, "You and Dramos together are too strong, Apollo. We need you elsewhere. Be patient and learn!"

Back when Apollo and Dramos were in school, they could not see where all the Sughi activity was going. They did not understand that B. Z. Sughi had a native fluency in the nuances of ghost relationships and behavior. He was setting up his followers for all-out war. He was training his followers to be soldiers in a battle against Olam. By extension, that war was against Diamond, the Puissance, Sapienti's guidance, Megantha, Tamir, Torith, and many others whom Apollo loved.

Apollo ached for the casualties of this war. His heart was broken over the loss of his older sister, Celti... Celestine. She had always been so good. But she defected to the Sughi side. Unlike Dramos, who had opted to attend a university close to home, Celti had attended one in the Light Source Mountains. That was two thousand miles away. There, she allowed herself to be recruited. The family had little contact with Celti while she was gone. That was by her choice. She rarely came home, and she seldom engaged via comm.

Apollo remembered, with a pang, the time Celti came home after having been away for months. He and the Pups, Jank and Natilia, had been counting the days until her return. She had always made time for them, weaving animals into almost every game they played. That suited Apollo and the Pups just fine. Any game was good, as long as it was with her.

But this time, when she arrived home, she was different. Her blue eyes and matching aura were less bright. She was not as happy, and she started to argue with Megantha. When Olam was there, she would argue with him, too. It was awful, and it was so different from her norm. In the past, as the older sister, she had always gone out of her way to be a peacemaker.

Celti could not accept all the pain that would exist in the next life as Bloods. She argued that Olam and Megantha's way meant unnecessary hurt for billions of people. "You can't let them do what they want without knowing why they are there," she would say. "You have to let them remember this life."

Olam, Megantha, and even Dramos would try to explain that the whole purpose of the Blood phase was to test people's internal character. They tried to tell her that you cannot know what people will do unless they are free to act on their own, sometimes without constraint.

But Celestine could not accept this. She said there would be too much unfairness and hurt. "People will torture each other. The strong will always take from the weak. There will be no justice. That's not a test! It's chaos!"

Celti was concerned about people, but she was more adamant about animals. "Animals will kill each other to eat! Why do they have to suffer? They aren't being tested! You say we have to suffer to test our internal character. But then you say animals must suffer, too, even though it isn't a test for them. It's like you want them to suffer for no reason. It's wrong, and it's senseless!"

Celti went over to Sughi's side. She had decided that force and control during the Blood phase were better than the free-for-all pain, misery, and chaos under Olam's plan. Celti—the peacemaker, the animal lover—sweet Celti. She said Sughi's plan for the Blood phase would limit freedom, but it would also limit pain. Celti bought into that plan. "I'm willing to give up my freedom to help others. That is the loving thing to do!" she told the family. "I did it because I love you!"

Apollo was young when Celti left the house. Like his parents, he had wept at her loss. If only there were a way to convince her to come back! He had stewed over this many times, wondering what he could say to convince her. Despite Celti's anger at Olam and Megantha, she remained friendly and loving towards Apollo. He visited her several times a year, and they talked frequently via comm. She was always happy for the contact, and she was not Apollo's enemy, despite his being a warrior for Olam.

17

Enemy Outpost

Apollo was pulled out of his reflective musing back into operational mode at the sight of Tamir and Torith. They were streaming towards him from over the ocean, coming in low and fast, barely above the whitecaps. Despite the waning sunlight, he could see that Tamir was flashing him hand signals. First, there was a three, followed by a four. Tamir repeated this, making the meaning clear. Apollo was disappointed. The number was only thirty-four. He'd hoped it would be closer to 334, or better yet, 1,034.

"It's only an outpost," said Tamir, now within speaking distance.

"Yeah," confirmed Torith. "It doesn't look permanent. I doubt Diamond Command will want us to attack. It's not worth the effort."

Tamir and Torith described the enemy outpost they had found two miles off the coast, under the water. Here, the ocean floor was seven hundred feet deep. Cutting through the otherwise flat terrain of the floor was a narrow canyon several hundred feet deeper than the floor itself. Torith and Tamir had worked their way down a steep face of one side of this canyon and found the entrance to a large sea cave. They were drawn to the cave entrance by a heavy flume of bubbles channeled out of the cave's entrance.

They carefully started exploring the cave. Torith explained how the cave sloped downward as air bubbles flowed along its top. The bubbles made a rushing sound and felt warm to the touch, far warmer than the ocean water.

"We kept going down," Tamir said. He told how it became pitch black in the cave, and they proceeded forward blindly, using the oncoming bubbles as a guide.

After following the bubbles for another forty or fifty yards, they were able to see some faint, red light. Soon, this light was quite bright, and they could tell there was now a surface to the water above them. The tunnel had widened considerably, and they moved to one side and mainly into the rock before coming above water level.

Tamir explained, "We found a huge, underwater cavern lit by volcanic lava. The gases put off by this lava had pumped the water out of the cavern down to the level where the gases could escape through the cave."

"Wow!" exclaimed Apollo, impressed with this geological wonder.

"You could put five hundred people in that cavern," said Torith. "It was amazing!"

"Well, if it's that big, why do you think it's only a transitory outpost?"

"Because two of them were using comms," said Tamir. "You'd never do that if you wanted to keep a location secret."

Tamir was right. The network supporting the comm system was completely open. Both sides of this war used it for communication. The comm users could encode their communications, making them secure, but the location and data volumes of comms were easily plotted, such as the links between comms or the login IDs communicating with each other.

Diamond Command had a whole group of techno-warriors dedicated to tracking the location of each comm in use on the planet at any given time. They ran programs against the usage patterns designed to locate enemy positions and strongholds.

Locating the outpost that Tamir and Torith had just visited was a perfect example. Using comms two miles out in the ocean at a depth of a thousand feet drew a hit on one of these programs, prompting Diamond Command to order an intelligence operation.

Apollo knew Sughi's people were doing the same thing as Diamond's. They, too, had programmers and analysts scouring the system for comm usage patterns that might tell them something about the army fighting for Olam—the army led by Diamond and guided by Sapienti. The army Sughi so badly wanted to defeat.

Apollo talked to Tamir and Torith for a few more minutes, and then Tamir left to go to Diamond Command. One of the facility's commanders needed his help with a defense analysis algorithm.

With Tamir gone, Apollo had time alone with Torith, and he switched out of operational mode. "So, how's your boyfriend, Jacob, doing?" he teased her.

Torith gave her head a dismissive flip, flashing the aquas in her brown eyes. "That guy is so annoying!"

"I thought you liked him?" Apollo's voice rang with jocular facetiousness.

She pulled a contorted face that showed disagreement. "He's like a lost puppy! Every time I'm at Command, he follows me around."

"I can't blame him, Tor. I would, too, but you always shoot me the get back signal."

Torith's face showed "not true." And she moved closer to Apollo, facing him straight on in mock confrontation.

"Besides," Apollo continued, "that's Jacob's job. He's an Intel. He's supposed to debrief you."

"Ya, right. One time, he even came in off-shift to debrief me. It was weird, Apollo."

Apollo knew Jacob was not actually a problem for Torith. Torith was Torith, which meant she could handle anything. The Jacobs of Planet Summa were nothing to her, and there had been many of them over the years. It used to make Apollo jealous, but then Celti pointed out to him how Torith always wanted him to know about these many Jacobs. "Don't you see, Apollo," Celti had explained. "Torith can swat those ghosties away like nothing, but before she does, she always makes a point of letting you know they are there. There's a reason for that."

Celti's insight was invaluable. "You'll know, Apollo," Celti once told him, "If Torith were ever actually interested in one of them. You'll sense it. It will be different. You're smart."

Apollo knew Torith had no obligation or commitment to him. He had talked to her about this multiple times. Some ghosts outed themselves as couples, but Torith never wanted that level of commitment, and Apollo himself had mixed feelings about it. As for friendship, that was different. There was no doubt that Apollo, Torith, and Tamir were the best of friends.

Today, with Torith, Apollo had no worries about Jacob, and hence the teasing. "He's a pretty smart guy," Apollo said. "And he has a nice aura. I think he's cute." Apollo winked.

Torith moved to within inches of Apollo's face and said, "Stop it!" She faked anger.

Apollo and Torith settled into a more normal conversation, communicating simply for the enjoyment of

communicating. This went on for a few minutes, and then
Apollo needed to go. They agreed to talk later.

Torith gave Apollo a short but lingering stare, then
she shot up to altitude and headed home.

Apollo's work for the day was far from over. First, he
needed to report the enemy outpost to Reemo, who, in turn,
would push the information up the line. To make this report,
good operational security required that he leave the area.
Calling up a comm here, so close to the outpost, might lead
Sughi's people to suspect their outpost was being watched.

Apollo headed straight south, following the coastline
for ten minutes, enjoying the day's last colors as the light
faded. He traveled twenty to thirty miles, passing over
alternating sections of ragged cliffs, rocky outcroppings,
wide, sandy beaches, lagoons, and coves. He chose this
shoreline route purely for its scenery and beauty. Then he
stopped and called for a comm.

Since the outbreak of war, the comm's opening menu
had always included the option of communicating in an
encoded mode. Apollo selected encoded and called Reemo,
who answered immediately. The network would see that
Apollo was talking to Reemo, and it would know the amount
and type of traffic, but the traffic itself was encrypted.

Apollo knew he was lucky that he could still report to
his Mentor. Tamir's, for example, had defected to Sughi. In
doing so, he tried hard to take his SunStar apprentices with
him. This had been tough on Tamir. Apollo knew he would
be bewildered if Reemo decided to follow Sughi.

Apollo remembered being worried because Tamir's
non-stop brain could generate hard questions much faster
than they could be answered. There had been hours on end
when Apollo would listen to his friend argue with himself

over the Olam-versus-Sughi position, and he'd do so on a level where Apollo could only spectate, not participate.

But Tamir managed to work it out. He finally came down on the side of Olam and agency, even though it would mean so much pain and sorrow during the Blood phase. "Olam's right," Tamir told Apollo. "As much as I wish it could be otherwise, there's no other way. You can't truly test character without making people forget about our Ghost phase here on Summa. And in the Blood phase, people must be free to do what they want, or you won't ever see their true character."

Tamir finally told his Mentor he would never join Sughi, which meant he no longer had a Mentor in the Puissance.

Apollo and Tamir were still on the Puissance's SunStar level. With some lobbying on Apollo's part, Tamir's new Mentor in the Puissance became Reemo. Now, as Apollo talked with Reemo through the comm, he was especially grateful for his many years of friendship with Reemo. It had been more than twenty years.

Reemo's huge smile was always there, as was his excellent advice. The smile would change depending on Reemo's mood and level of interest. Right now, as Apollo reported Tamir and Torith's finding of the enemy's underwater cavern, the smile was straighter and more serious than usual. Apollo knew this to be a sign that Reemo's interest was sky-high.

"We don't think it's a permanent outpost," explained Apollo. "They were using comms down there, which would immediately give it away. Wouldn't it?"

Reemo thought briefly. "Maybe... maybe not, A.P. They were only using two of them, right?"

"Yes."

Again, Reemo paused, looking down and thinking, but not revealing his thoughts to Apollo.

"What?" asked Apollo.

Reemo looked up and spoke more deliberately and slowly than usual. "Apollo, I want you to be very careful with your find. Don't treat it lightly. That outpost may be more important than you think." Reemo stopped and stared firmly into Apollo's eyes.

Apollo shifted uncomfortably. "Well... okay... yes... I mean... I'll be careful."

"And please tell Tamir and Torith the same thing. I don't want you three to let anyone know we found that place."

Apollo had a clear understanding of operational security, or "opsec." The concept was hammered into him and other fighters all the time. Apollo wondered why Reemo had been so definitive about keeping the outpost quiet. It was something Apollo would have done regardless, so why was Reemo so concerned?

Apollo and Reemo finished their business, and Apollo sent his comm away. He turned himself east and inland towards his next assignment. It, too, was intelligence gathering, and it would be in a city that, for a city, had an unusual name: Seven Valley.

18

Seven Valley

Megantha and Olam had guided several powerful Forzas in the construction of a series of coordinated buildings in a city known as Seven Valley. Many of these structures had no side walls. Their roofs were high and often supported by massive columns.

One of the Forzas working under Megantha had constructed a building that had one enormous column in the middle of a round structure about three hundred yards in diameter. This center column was two hundred feet wide. It alone supported the building's high ceiling, six floors off the ground.

The building was quickly and appropriately nicknamed "The Circle." Its gently domed roof was honeycombed with round, glass sky tubes, which channeled sunlight through the roof during the day. At night, these same tubes glowed brightly, mimicking natural sunlight. Night or day, the building was an impressive landmark, whether viewed on land or from the air.

Apollo's assignment tonight was to be in a building close to The Circle. This one was a more traditional rectangular shape. It had a few columns at its entrance, but otherwise, it was straight walls with large windows. There were no sky tubes for light, but there was plenty of internal lighting. This building had a second floor, and the middle section of this second floor was open, like the upper level of a stadium. This allowed people to see down to the first floor, which was set up as a large meeting hall.

At any one time, thousands of people were in Seven Valley. They came from all over the planet. Most of them were intellectual types or people who fancied themselves as such. They gathered here to discuss, argue, and theorize over endless topics. The split between Olam and B. Z. Sughi was a big hit on their debate parade. Most people in Seven Valley now supported Sughi. The city was a Sughi stronghold.

Tonight, Apollo's job was to watch a debate between four pro-Sughi advocates in the rectangular building. They would each present their positions on how much knowledge Bloods should be given versus how much they should be left to discover on their own. Apollo was to attend this debate and observe.

The arguments put forth by the debaters were of little interest. Instead, Diamond Command wanted Apollo to see what important people attended the debate. This would help Command better understand who was running things in Seven Valley. Like many Sughi-controlled cities on Planet Summa, Seven Valley's visible leadership was controlled by a hidden level of more powerful leadership. These hidden entities answered to Sughi himself.

Apollo was to mingle among the audience, in plain view, not trying to hide. Since all four debaters were on Sughi's side of the argument, Apollo and Command expected most attendees to be followers of Sughi. Some of these might be undecided fence-sitters, but none in attendance would be openly for Olam. The crowd would be too hostile for that.

Apollo traveled inland for half an hour before cresting the mountains west of Seven Valley. It was dark, and the high cloud cover made navigation by moonlight impossible. The lack of references had forced Apollo to stop twice en route and call for a comm to give him the proper headings. One of his course corrections was a full thirty degrees.

There were forty-nine buildings in Seven Valley. Seven times seven. One of these was The Circle. Apollo's altitude was about two thousand feet, and he immediately saw The Circle. It was a spectacular structure.

In the center of Seven Valley was an expansive, generously lit, stone-paved plaza. The plaza's shape was an even-sided heptagon. Long, narrow ribbon pools of shimmering water marked the borders of the heptagon's seven sides. Each pool was well-lit, and each showed a different color based on the rock from which it was built. The colors were red sandstone, jade, blue, aqua, purple, slate gray, and black.

Broad, well-lit, tree-lined walkways extended from each apex of the heptagon. These walkways divided the city's land into seven equal sections, expanding from the plaza.

Each of the seven sections of land had seven buildings, and the buildings of each section followed a theme. Those in the section with The Circle were all round or oval-shaped. Another section had pyramids, and one had squares. The section where Apollo was headed had rectangular buildings, the largest of which was a meeting hall—Apollo's assignment for tonight.

The magnificent buildings, built by loving Quasars and their apprentice Forzas, were now harboring children who openly defied and rebelled against their Quasar parents, the Forzas under the Quasars, and the Mentors who had nurtured them for years. They ignored the quiet, wise guidance of Sapienti, and they wanted nothing to do with Diamond's commanding presence.

Apollo approached the meeting hall, gliding low over the city, just high enough to clear the rooftops. Locals passed on either side. He made his final descent toward the two-story structure. Judging by the crowd streaming inside, the debate would begin soon. Two groups of about six people converged on the entrance. Apollo slipped in alongside them. He hoped each group would assume he was part of the other.

Once inside the building, it was clear that the first level was already full. Ushers directed them to the second level, accessed via a wide cascading waterfall made to look like stairs. The engineering was so perfect on this stairway that the moving water was smooth as glass. The liquid looked frozen as it slid down, one stair to the next, making almost no noise.

Apollo said little to those around him, keeping a low profile. At the top of the water stairs, Apollo stayed mixed with others as they filled the balcony level. Apollo tried to position himself where he could see as much as possible of both the main floor and the balcony level. The balcony was about half full, with maybe a thousand people so far. At the rate the Sughi ghosts were arriving, both levels would be packed in no time. *These Sughi-lovers sure love a debate*, Apollo thought to himself.

There were no seats on either level of the two-tiered, stadium-like building. Ghosts do not need to sit. On the main ground level, a raised platform stood at the front where the debaters would perform. The upper level's floor was angled to give everyone a clear view of this stage.

Proper etiquette called for attendees to stay close to the floor, aligning themselves so as not to block anyone's view. This system worked well—unless too many ghosts showed up. Then ushers would have to herd the overflow into a second, figurative level: a higher band of floating ghosts. These ghosts had to divert part of their attention from the debate just to hold their position and maintain a clean line. Marks on the walls indicated the ideal height and shape for that second layer, but once it filled up, the marks were hard to see, and order quickly unraveled. The ushers did their best, but it was always messy.

Apollo knew that if the debate became emotional, some people would break ranks and try to move closer to the debaters to voice their disagreement or displeasure. This meant they would leave their self-assigned area and crowd in tighter, try to fly above the debaters, or engage in other rude behavior. The ushers could control a little of that impolite nonsense. But too much would result in pandemonium and an end to the meeting.

Apollo also knew that if the crowd realized he was a soldier for Diamond Command, there might be chaos. At a minimum, he would be forced to leave. More likely, he would be attacked.

Hopefully, nobody would recognize him. Apollo might be a strong soldier, but he was no celebrity. Apollo tried to subdue his aura and ghost presence as much as possible.

The lights in the room dimmed except for those shining on the center platform area. Apollo liked the dimmed lights as they helped him blend with the crowd. The crowd quieted, and a man took the stage. His aura was very bright, and he was full of energy. He said his name was Pushkin. Apollo made a mental note of that.

Pushkin introduced the four debaters. Each would be allowed a three-minute opening statement to lay out their basic position, and then Pushkin would ask them questions and try to maintain control while they went at each other.

The first was a tall woman with black hair and an aura that surged so quickly it was more of a flicker. She immediately attacked Olam, saying it was ridiculous for him to completely delete a person's memory before sending the person on to be a Blood. She argued that Olam's plan to test a person's character was good, but you cannot separate the fiber of their being from their knowledge and memories. Doing so fundamentally changed their character. She concluded her opening statement by arguing that Bloods should have full memory of when they were ghosts on Planet Summa and should be as smart as they are now.

Apollo listened to her, but more importantly, he concentrated on the audience. Down on the main level, close to the front, he could see a man surrounded by at least four others who seemed to be protecting him. Despite the full crowd, people around the man and his contingent gave them extra room. The man was close enough to the stage that the stage's lights showed on his face, adding to the light of his aura and making it possible for Apollo to see him. His face was round and lacked firmness. He was shorter than the four men who watched around him. Despite the man's limited height and soft features, he projected power.

The second debater was now yee-yawing away. This one was a man. He was older than the female, and he had different ideas. He, too, started by declaring his opposition to Olam, but he thought the memory-erase thing was just fine. "It's one of the few things I like about his plan," he said. "And while they're Bloods, only give them enough brains to survive. Don't make them too smart, or they'll be too cocky. After all, look at us and how cocky we are!" The audience laughed.

Apollo noticed a dark-haired man working his way through the crowd towards the man with the four protectors. Dark Hair spoke to one of the four protectors surrounding Round Face, and that protector then addressed Round Face, who nodded in the affirmative. The protectors parted to let Dark Hair approach. Round Face and Dark Hair spoke briefly, then Dark Hair left, and Apollo soon lost sight of him in the throng.

Who is that round-faced guy? Wondered Apollo.

Pretty soon, it was the third debater's chance at an opening statement. He briefly announced opposition to Olam's plan, and then he made it clear he wanted only a dim memory of life as a ghost. He said Bloods should be given a lot of scientific knowledge so they could advance quickly. "We don't want them wasting time in caves," he said. "We want them civilized fast. Then they can get down to the business of choosing right from wrong." He explained that people are not tested if all they are doing is trying to survive. Only after they have the basics—food, water, and shelter— can their character be tested.

Apollo continued to scan the audience, checking frequently on the round-faced guy.

The fourth and last debater was a woman, and she started her opening statement. At the same time, Apollo caught sight of Pushkin, who was near the stage to announce the next part of the debate. Next to Pushkin was the dark-haired man who had recently spoken to the round-faced leader. That was significant, and it added importance to the stature of Mr. protected-round-face.

The woman on the stage quickly worked herself into a verbal frenzy as she denounced Olam. "His plan is completely and utterly ridiculous!" Her voice was edged with a shrill. "He's going to throw us down on some hostile planet, not tell us anything, and watch to see what we'll do? That's not a plan! What kind of parent would do that?"

Apollo started calmly working his way through the swarm to where he would have a better view of Round Face. Pushing through the crowd like that was rude, but Apollo hoped it would not be too suspicious. Apollo was not here to be polite.

The shrill-voiced debater continued. "The least he could do is send us to our earths already grown up. What's with this being born as naked, defenseless babies? All we'll know how to do is eat, poop, and cry!" That was funny, especially the way she said it.

Apollo noticed two women watching him with a disapproving look. He hoped it was because he was not conforming to social etiquette and holding his position. But other than these two, most other people were wrapped up in the Madame Shrill tirade.

After Apollo had moved far enough to have the women well behind him, he wanted to turn around to see if they were still watching. But he resisted. It would make him look guilty. They might be nothing more than two nosy gals more interested in people watching than the debate itself.

The audience relaxed a little after the fourth woman stopped. It was a natural breaking point, and people chit-chatted amongst themselves, allowing Apollo to make better headway through the crowd. Then, Pushkin took the stage and started to outline the next part of the debate. This quieted people, and Apollo slowed his progress. Even so, he was much closer to having a better view of the round-faced ghost.

Pushkin asked the first debater why she thought giving Bloods full memory of their lives as ghosts was so important. "I mean… we all agree that under B. Z. Sughi's plan, there will be controls to keep people from making too many mistakes. So why does it matter if we remember our lives as ghosts on Summa?"

Apollo did not hear the debater's answer because he saw that the two women who had been watching him took the unusual move of transitioning above the crowd to a place that was much closer to him. They were not being subtle. Apollo could only hope they were trying to figure out who he was. If they or security uploaded a good picture of him, recognition software would ID him as an enemy soldier. Things would then get interesting.

Apollo briefly weighed his options and decided to continue trying to get a better view of Mr. Round Face. Finally, Apollo was close to being directly above the man. He could see that Round Face was on a comm, and his protectors continued to keep the crowd clear of the area around him.

On the debate platform, Pushkin was having a hard time controlling The Shriller who, again and again, rudely demanded extra time to make her points. The debate focus had shifted to the question of awareness. One of the male debaters was saying that he actually agreed with Olam's plan to have Bloods living on planets that were thousands of light years from here and thousands of light years apart from each other. He liked the idea that there was no way Bloods from one world would ever be in contact with Bloods from another.

The Shriller could not contain herself. She raised her hand, bobbed up and down, and made obnoxious, child-like noises until Pushkin reluctantly gave her the floor. A man next to Apollo let out a frustrated sigh, as did others in the audience. Apollo seized on the cue and said out loud. "Where did they get that lady?"

"She's a freakin' idiot," grumbled the man.

Apollo nodded in agreement, trying to respond in a way that said they were on the same team.

The Shriller ranted on about how important it was for the Bloods to start out as grown-ups, having memories of ghost life here and already knowing right from wrong.

The man next to Apollo was shaking his head in disagreement. Apollo wondered what part of The Shriller's statements he did not like.

Pushkin managed to quiet the obnoxious lady and give the floor to the first debater. This was the one with black hair and a flickering aura. She, too, liked the idea of Bloods having a memory of ghost life, but she argued forcefully that they had to be born as babies to properly learn and grow. She said their memory of ghost life should return to them slowly as they became older and more responsible.

Apollo noticed the man next to him nodding, apparently liking the born as babies concept. Apollo also noticed that one of the two women who had been following him was missing. And finally, he noticed the dark-haired man coming back through the crowd towards the round-faced man, whom the four bodyguards still protected.

Apollo waited until Dark Hair spoke to one of the protectors, then he inched up to the man next to him and said, quiet and low, "What's with that guy?" Apollo nodded down below.

"I'm pretty sure he's a Magnate," the man whispered. "He's the guy who's really in charge. Not Pushkin."

Apollo nodded while quietly responding with an understanding "O-h-h..."

He had never been this close to a Magnate. Reemo had taught him that Magnates were like generals in Sughi's war against Olam. They had tremendous authority and commanded thousands of troops. Apollo was surprised that only four protectors guarded him. But then again, what did the Magnate have to be concerned about with this audience? This was Sughi-land, through and through. Besides, undercover personnel were probably spread throughout the audience to give him additional protection. Maybe the nosy women watching him were part of his U.C. contingent.

Apollo checked the two women. They were together and on a comm, which would normally be considered rude.

Apollo mentally recorded the face of the round-faced Magnate, doing his best to store it well. Now, it was time to leave, and Apollo weighed his options. He could work through the crowd towards the door and leave quietly. He could make a scene and leave rudely, blasting straight up through the ceiling. Or he could transition over the top of the crowd like the two women had done.

Apollo saw that one of the protectors was also using a comm. Maybe the women were talking to the protector? Apollo's guess was correct because, right then, the protector looked up and caught Apollo's eye. Their vision locked briefly and knowingly, where each understood the other had been spotted.

19

Myke, The Yellow Bull

Apollo knew he was out of time, and he started pushing through the crowd towards the water stairs. He was not here to fight. He wished he had time to learn the name of the Magnate, but he would have to use his memory to photo-ID him back at Diamond Command.

Pushkin announced to the audience that the debate was at halftime and that there would be a break for a few minutes. This would make Apollo's exit easier. He could mix with others who were leaving. But then The Shriller demanded to make one more point, and Apollo was disappointed to hear Pushkin reluctantly agree. The crowd moaned in protest, and the woman launched into a rapid-fire babble on a new topic of equality. She was furious that Olam's plan called for people to be born in vastly different circumstances, the bulk of them going to societies where they were likely to be poor and uneducated.

"She's right," Apollo heard somebody say near him. "Yeah, but what a witch," said another.

Apollo glanced back and could see the same two women following him. Their comm was gone. Apollo switched from normal, polite movement and began transitioning above the crowd towards the exit. He had avoided this until now, wanting to keep a low profile. As soon as he went airborne, the two women did the same.

How did they find me in the first place? Apollo wondered. There were thousands of ghosts here, so what made Apollo stand out? *Did somebody recognize me?*

Apollo looked back and saw that one of the Magnate's protectors had come to the upper level and was also following. That made things more serious. He would be a fighter.

Apollo was not afraid of the protector, but his assignment was to gather intel and not do battle. All he wanted to do was leave. Soon, he was at the top of the water stairs. He considered leaving the building by going straight through the second floor's wall, but the two women and the man behind him seemed to be following more than chasing, so he opted to go down the stairs, the more acceptable way. That turned out to be a mistake.

At the bottom of the stairs, there were ten soldiers. They were waiting for him and tactically divided into two groups of five. They were in attack mode. Apollo looked for a leader who might try to engage in dialogue. But instead, as soon as Apollo was at the bottom of the stairs, all ten attacked.

Apollo was no stranger to combat. Over the past ten years, he had been in many battles, and his skills were well-honed. His experience kicked in. He went right and slammed into the group of soldiers on that side. It was instant pain and mayhem. He plowed through them hard. He knew they would be surprised at how strong he was. Apollo's many years of fighting had made him formidable. He was confident in battle, experienced, and powerful.

Apollo demolished the first five soldiers, blasting their menapses. They would be stunned and out of the fight for several minutes. Apollo whipped around and plowed into the second five. *Boom! Boom! Boom! Boom!* In microseconds, Apollo hammered the first four soldiers. For each, he instantly mixed his ghost with theirs, read them, and violently manhandled them. His freight train of a ghost overwhelmed them, and each of the four crumpled immediately. He sensed their shock and surprise.

Then, Apollo hit the last soldier. *Wham!* It was like hitting a wall of steel. This soldier was a beast of a ghost. He was dark. His eyes and aura flamed yellow. He was a bull, and Apollo had never fought anyone like him. *Who is this guy? He's almost as strong as Dramos!*

Apollo's first microsecond with this dark yellow bull had been a brutal hit. Apollo rammed him again, harder this time. The bull rammed back equally as hard. Now Apollo knew the other soldiers did not matter. The real fight was with this one, and Apollo wished he had more time to fight this incredible specimen.

But Apollo was not there to fight. Apollo rammed the yellow bull again, but he also let the yellow push him back, which he did—hard—and Apollo used the momentum to make a run for it. Apollo blasted towards an outer wall of the building. Behind him, he could hear a woman gasping and a Sughi commander yelling orders. Then Apollo was through the wall and gone.

So much for being covert, Apollo thought. He set his ghost throttle to "max power" and began speeding out of Seven Valley. *Who was that?* Apollo wondered. *Diamond Command has to have intel on him. He's no ordinary soldier.*

Apollo thought he had stunned the attackers enough that he would be able to escape without any more fighting, but to his surprise, a ghost came out of nowhere and walloped him. The ghost was not strong, but he was extremely fast, and Apollo could not shake him. The ghost was all over Apollo like an attack hornet. Apollo swatted him away, and he came right back. He was more annoying than a true threat.

Then—bam! Apollo was body-slammed. The yellow bull was back. The hornet had slowed him just enough for Yellow to catch up.

Wow! That yellow ghost is as fast as he is strong!

Apollo knew he could not fight the yellow bull and swat the hornet at the same time. *I need a change in tactics.* Apollo dove straight for the ground. He had to lose these guys.

A thousand feet below Apollo was one of the pools that formed the borders of the heptagon plaza. This was the black pool. It was made from lava rock. Apollo zoomed down, aiming straight for it, and he slammed into the ground through the pool. Then he zigged and zagged, moving blindly through layers of rock, clay, and sand. Deeper and deeper he went.

To Apollo's surprise, he could not shake The Hornet or The Bull. They were amazing ghosts. Their ability to sense his next move and stay with him in the blindness was incredible. Taggers! Expert ones! The best Apollo had ever seen!

Apollo headed deeper. He fought off a hint of exhaustion. He was a strong person, but his strength had limits.

Apollo considered calling Olam for help, but he also wanted another crack at the yellow bull. Maybe it was pride, but beating him would be a score. *Who is this guy?* As for the annoying hornet ghost, Apollo knew he could be dispatched with a well-placed swat.

Apollo sensed the layers of the earth through which he traveled. He instinctively tried to stay in dense rock, hoping the density would help him escape two taggers. But it was no use. He could not escape. Running and running was going to burn him out. He had to make a stand. It was time to grab The Bull by the horns and have it out.

Apollo took some hard, underground turns. The Bull lost him temporarily, and Apollo used the seconds alone with the annoying hornet to smash him hard, working inside him and exploding through him. The hornet ghost went limp.

The yellow bull caught up. Here, in the dense underground, the blackness was violated by the intense blues of Apollo's fighting aura and the powerful yellows of The Bull. The fight was on. "I have the Puissance," Apollo yelled. "The Power of Olam! You cannot win!"

"Olam's wrong!" The Bull yelled back as they swarmed and tangled. "Olam has no compassion!"

Apollo always found it incredible how B. Z. had convinced his followers that Olam lacked compassion. All you had to do was talk with him face-to-face to be overwhelmed by his love and compassion. The ones who rejected him were the ones who stopped talking with him.

Apollo and The Beast were now one in physical space, with positive and negative charges, fracturing, imploding, blasting, and exploding. Matter was forced on matter. Will against conviction. Strength versus power. Each could read the other perfectly. The intensity of the battle revealed all.

"Sughi will never beat Olam. Come with me!" cried Apollo. "There's still time!"

"Time? Time for what? Time for a plan where so many of you will fail?"

The annoying hornet ghost had recovered somewhat and joined the fight. Apollo was surprised at his tenacity. The hornet was too weak to be effective, and he was ruining a wonderfully splendid fight. Apollo began using him to block The Bull.

"Move! Lucen," The Bull yelled at the hornet. "You're in the way!"

Hornet ghost Lucen tried to move out of the way, but he was still so discombobulated that Apollo easily continued to use him as a shield against the yellow bull, whose blows were all tempered by the hornet. Pounding by The Bull damaged Lucen more than it hurt Apollo. It became comical.

"Friendly fire, my friend," Apollo called out to Lucen. "You're collateral damage!" Apollo laughed.

The Bull swore, stopped fighting, and shook his head in frustration. However, to Apollo, it looked like this yellow bull of a ghost saw the humor, too. Then, The Bull blasted Lucen out of the way. "Move! I said! I can't fight him with you here!"

The interruption put a pause in the battle. Apollo and The Bull stared at each other. "Holy Summa, you're strong!" Apollo said.

The bull ghost continued to stare. The yellow in his eyes softened. Then he turned to Lucen. "Leave! You're in the way, and you're too weak. Leave!"

"But... but Myke... I..."

"Leave!" Myke, the bull ghost, said.

"So... it's Myke," Apollo said, pointing out the obvious. He now knew the bull's name.

Lucen was still there, hesitating.

"Brave," Apollo goaded, nodding at Lucen.

Myke continued, "Have you ever seen me lose, Lucen?"

"No... ah... Myke... never."

"Then leave. You're blocking me. Now leave!"

Apollo stayed put while the two enemies worked it out. Then, the annoying hornet of a fighter, Lucen, left.

Apollo thought Myke the bull might jump right back into battle. Apollo was ready. But Myke held his position.

Apollo asked, "Don't you ever talk to your mother?"

The question was out of place, but it also wasn't. They had fought. Maybe they now needed a verbal fight. Maybe.

"I love our mother," said Myke. "But she's wrong… like Olam is wrong."

"So," said Apollo, "the two most powerful people you know are wrong. And you're going to follow B. Z. instead? Tell me, does that make any sense?"

"They're wrong, Apollo. The Quasars' plan is mean-spirited and brutal."

"Don't you ever talk to Olam or Mom about it? How can you talk to them and think they're wrong?"

"I don't talk to them anymore. That's for sure. They won't answer my questions. They can't explain why everything has to be so unfair."

There was silence between the two of them.

"Do you want to fight?" Apollo asked. "Shall we finish it?"

"When I beat you down, are you going to call your mommy?" Myke asked.

"Nope. I'm calling yours," Apollo answered. "Gonna make you talk to her."

The verbal fighting had taken on a level of ridiculous. They were both talking about the same mother. And at that, the fighting was over. They both knew it had degenerated into banter.

"I'll tell you what," Myke said. "I'll stop fighting if you promise never to tell anybody. If that worm of a Lucen hears about it, he'll spread the word that I was afraid."

"Deal," Apollo answered. "I doubt you're afraid of anything." He was tempted to add, *except your mother*, but he held his tongue, not wanting to fight like a girl. "So... how did you get so strong? Normally, I clean house."

Myke hesitated, then answered, "Maybe another time."

"Okay, but your tagging ability. I've never seen anyone as good."

"I've always had that," Myke said. "It's a gift."

"From Olam?"

Myke was annoyed at that. "Yes, probably."

"Lucen was good, too," Apollo said.

"Unfortunately, that's true," Myke said. "It means I am often paired up with him. He's a good tagger, but he's weak and annoying. A weasel."

"Could I have turned him?" Apollo asked.

"You'd diffract your aura trying," Myke said. "I promise you, you don't want him."

"Don't tell Olam," Apollo said. "But I agree. He gives me the creeps."

"I thought you were supposed to love everyone," Myke asked, with some jest.

"I thought you were supposed to hate every Olam soldier," Apollo pushed back.

Myke shrugged.

Right there, Apollo knew he and Myke would be friends, as unusual as it might be.

Apollo had drawn energy from the small amount of electricity in the ground, and he knew Myke had, too. They were charged enough to fight. But no, they were done with the fighting.

"Do you want to go up top?" Apollo asked.

"No, no," Myke answered. "They'll be looking for us."

The two of them were silent, but the fog of a plan started to form in Apollo's mind. "Look, Myke," he asked. "Is there any way we can stay in contact?"

"So you can recruit me?" Myke asked.

"Of course, Myke," Apollo said, ribbing him. "That's always there. But you and I know this is different. Besides, you can try to recruit me. What I don't want is to lose contact. I've never met a Sughi fighter like you. You're not all about hate, and you're an animal!"

"My command would be spewing black light if they knew I was talking with you," Myke said.

"Mine might, too," said Apollo.

There was silence while both fighters were thinking. Finally, Myke spoke, "If we decide to communicate, we need to do it securely, and our commanders can't know what we're talking about. I don't imagine you would be willing to do that since you seem like a rule-boy."

"You mean we need a B-Channel, right?"

"Yes."

"They're hard to get," Apollo said. "I've never needed one, but my friend has wanted one for years."

"Tamir?" Myke asked.

"Y... Yes," said Apollo, surprised. "You know Ta—"

"I know a lot about you, Apollo," Myke interrupted.

Apollo was going to ask more, but then he realized Myke had played right into Apollo's foggy plan... a plan that was now becoming clearer. "Well... then... it sounds like we have a lot to talk about."

"Yes, but I don't want our conversations monitored."

"Okay, I can try to get one," Apollo said. "But I won't lie to my chain of command. You're right that I'm a rule boy or whatever you want to call it. But, will your Command allow you to have a B-Channel? We both need one for it to work."

"I'll tell them I think I can bring you over," Myke said. "I'll tell them we fought for a long time. We both were so exhausted that we nearly flatlined each other, and we lost track of each other underground. And I'll tell them I almost turned you in the fight."

Sounds reasonable, thought Apollo.

"I know that B-Channels require approval by a Forza. One of your Forzas will have to sign off and pass it to my side."

Apollo was again surprised by Myke. "I thought you were a fighter. How do you know the geek stuff?"

"More things we can talk about," Myke said.

Apollo thought there was a good chance he could obtain permission for a B-Channel. In addition to the Forza, whose network engineers would have to set it up, Reemo would need to approve it. Apollo thought he would. There was something formidable about this yellow bull of a soldier named Myke.

B-Channels allowed two or more B-Channel-authorized-comms to communicate without the network keeping a record of where the comms were located, who was using them, or the nature and contents of the comms' traffic. When a B-Channel was operational, all the network saw was that it was active. Everything else was obfuscated. B-Channel protocol required real-time wiping of logs, location addresses, and many other network housekeeping functions. The protocol also had built-in search features that scoured the network for rogue attempts to gather and store B-Channel data. Several engineers had lost their jobs, looking for ways to hack the B-Channel system.

"Let's meet in two days," said Myke. "I should know by then if Sughi Command will allow me a 'B.' If they do, we can share ID codes."

Apollo was a seasoned soldier and an experienced intelligence officer. He was well past the naïveté of trusting Myke. This could all be a trick and a setup. Hopefully, Diamond Command had intel on Myke to help them decide if Apollo should proceed.

But Apollo had just fought with Myke. They had slammed each other's menapses, overloaded the other's network, and blasted at each other's intrinsic cores. They had read each other's root programming. Apollo believed Myke was being straight up.

"Where should we meet?"

"Not here," said Myke.

"Where, then?"

"The cave."

"What? What cave?"

"You know," said Myke. "The one under the ocean… with the lava." Myke had a knowing tone in his voice, sprinkled with a hint of "gotcha."

Apollo was shocked. *The cave? How could he know about that? Did somebody tell him?*

"I followed you," said Myke, answering Apollo's question.

"Me? You followed? Since when?" Apollo's brain was spinning.

"I'm a tagger, Apollo. I'm excellent at following people. You've been my project for a couple of weeks now."

Apollo could not understand why Myke would tell him this. It had to be an operational secret. But he also did not doubt that it was true.

"So... that's why your side knew I was at the meeting tonight?"

"Yep." Then, Myke changed his tone into more of a hurry-up mode. "Look, two days from now in the cave, okay? We need to decide..."

"Yes, yes," said Apollo. "But you've been following me?"

"Yeah, yeah. We'll talk about it when we talk. Now go! Lucen will be back soon with others!"

Apollo set a meeting time with Myke, said goodbye, and left. He went sideways under the ground for several minutes, putting distance between himself and Myke. Then he transitioned straight up, finally emerging in the pyramid section of Seven Valley. He had come out of the ground between two pyramid-shaped buildings. He was far from the building where the debate had been held. Apollo wondered if it had continued after the commotion he had caused.

Apollo looked around. No soldiers were in sight. He rose to building height and again looked around. City residents were moving through the night air, but Apollo did not see any groups of soldiers. He shot up several thousand feet, where, in the night air, he would be invisible to any regular traveler. Then, Apollo headed for the coast. Hopefully, Myke, the yellow bull, was not following him. That guy was good.

20

Twisted Mountains

After his mission at Seven Valley, Apollo's original plan had been to meet Tamir and Torith and travel to Apollo's home for a family get-together. Although Tamir and Torith were not technically house brothers and sisters, everyone considered them adopted.

This was particularly true for Tamir. Many of his siblings had gone over to Sughi, and they wanted nothing to do with Mom, Dad, or Tamir's house brothers and sisters, who still supported Olam.

But Apollo had to delay going to the family bash because Reemo had ordered him to the command center for a debrief, which would take several hours. Tamir and Torith would go on without him.

After Seven Valley, Apollo had gone west to the coast to be sure he was clear. Then he turned northeast, slightly inland, and headed to command. It would take him an hour. Unlike his travel to the city named Seven Valley, now the clouds had mostly cleared, and there was a moon. Apollo knew where he was. The moonlit terrain was familiar enough to keep him oriented.

Apollo's line of travel to Diamond Command would take him over a spectacular section of terrain known as the Twisted Mountains. This range of low mountains looked like massive rock flows that had been twisted and turned before cooling, and then laid down intact on a flat plain. The geology's fascinating beauty was hidden in the low light, but Apollo had seen it during the day.

He remembered a time when he came to these mountains with his younger sister and brother, Natilia and Jank. Natilia had to do a report for school on these mountains, and Apollo brought her for her report. Jank wanted to come, too, and they set off from home one morning.

Getting to the mountains with the Pups was more of an effort than Apollo had expected. It should have been an hour and a half flight, but that was a long time for Jank and Natilia to concentrate on travel. They kept wanting to rest or look at things on the way. The ninety minutes turned into more than three hours. By the time they arrived, it was early afternoon.

Then Natilia wanted to play. Apollo could not get her to do anything on her report. She and Jank fiddled around. Their dawdling was so different from Apollo's Type A personality. He wanted her to jump in and get it done. In frustration, he called Megantha and complained.

Megantha told him to play with them while teaching them. That was the only advice she would offer. Apollo had to think about this, but then he told the Pups they would play hide and seek. His plan was to get them down in the rocks and canyons of the Twisted Mountains, and hopefully, by hiding in them, the Pups would absorb some of the mountains' secrets.

The plan was good. Apollo took them to a high, rust-colored section of twisted rock several hundred yards long. He told them they had to stay close to this rock for their game. "See that snake mountain over there?" he asked, pointing to a white, winding ridge line. "You can't go any farther than that." One part of the red, twisted rock line was humped, and he told them this was base. It was easy to find, and there was little chance of them getting lost. Then he told them he would be "it," and they had thirty seconds to hide. He added, "No fair going down into the ground to hide. If you do that, you're a cheater and you lose!"

The Twisted Mountains had little topsoil and sparse vegetation. There were a few places to hide, but it was nothing like a dense forest or a boulder-strewn hillside. Instead, the mountains were threaded with small, winding, rock-walled canyons. Centuries of wind had hollowed out shallow caves and niches in these walls, some of which were big enough to offer concealment. The Pups would need to use their imagination to hide well.

Each of them took a turn being "it," but Apollo took the most turns. The Pups wanted to hide more than they wanted to seek. Seeking was especially challenging for Apollo because the Pups were too young to be good at hiding. Apollo had to work hard to find ways to "seek" them while hiding from them so they did not know they had been spotted. Sometimes, Apollo would maneuver in ways that forced them to change their position to stay hidden from him. Apollo's objective was to herd them into different types of rocks and canyons to help them better absorb the nuances of this field of play.

After more than an hour of playing—and a little rest—Natilia was more agreeable to do her homework. Apollo helped while Jank stayed close by, exploring on his own. Apollo's trip home with the Pups was better. Their imaginations were worn out for the day, and they only cared about getting home.

As Apollo worked his way to the command post, high above the Twisted Mountains, his fond memories of that day with the Pups played through his mind. Natilia and

Jank were not kids anymore. They had grown up and were very much his equals. Thankfully, they had listened to Sapienti and stayed true to Olam and the Puissance.

21

Diamond Command

After forty-five minutes, Apollo could see the command center's lights. Judging distance at night was tricky, but Apollo estimated them to be twenty miles away. He headed straight for the center and stopped five miles out where he needed clearance. Apollo summoned a comm, which he used to contact Reemo. Once Reemo answered, they each put in memorized codes, allowing for more secure communication.

Reemo then told Apollo to proceed to the main gate, where he would be scanned and allowed into the complex. The sensors surrounding the complex constantly monitored everybody in the area. Without that clearance, a security team would be dispatched to force him outside the perimeter.

Early in the war, waves of Sughi warriors stormed the command center. It happened repeatedly. When they attacked, the computers in the center locked down. They did this automatically whenever an unacceptable number of unauthorized personnel were inside the center's boundaries. With the computers secure, everybody was available to fight the enemy.

Apollo had been present for several of these attacks. They were brutal. Overall, Olam or Diamond Command had more soldiers than Sughi. But this was only true for the entire Planet Summa. Sughi could plan and amass a large contingent of soldiers and attack any Diamond position with an overwhelming force. Apollo had seen attacks at Diamond Command where every defender was up against five to ten

Sughi warriors. Apollo's job was to be a fighter. He was good at it, and his personality embraced it. However, many of Olam's followers did not like to fight. They were not weak, but their expertise lay in network engineering, communications, analysis, and other valuable military fields. For them, fighting one hateful Sughi soldier was difficult, frightening, and sometimes overwhelming. The fighting left them with emotional scars that were a challenge. They were not like Apollo, who had a psychology that allowed him to take a severe beating and come back fighting the next day.

Apollo knew these other Diamond soldiers were, in many ways, braver than he was. For them, the battles were terrifying, and yet they stayed true to Olam. "I'm a knucklehead," he would say to those people. "I'm too simple-minded for it to bother me. If I were smart like you, I'd know better." Apollo admired people who were scared to death and still did their jobs. They were the real heroes.

The attacks on the command center were similar to the ones Sughi was doing all over Planet Summa. Apollo, Tamir, and Torith were often dispatched to fight in those battles. They had learned to be a powerful and effective team. At first, they fought near each other but separately. Then, in one of the attacks on Diamond Command, the three of them banded into a tight threesome, rolling over waves of Sughis who stood no chance. Usually, these large-scale Sughi attacks required Diamond Command to send out an alert for outside soldiers to come in and help. But the Apollo-Torith-Tamir threesome had been so effective that it turned the battle on its own. By the time reinforcements arrived, the Sughi attackers had fled.

The power of Apollo and his friends was a bright spot for many followers of Olam, especially those who needed protection. It was how it should be. Olam's soldiers should be the strongest.

The problem for many followers of Olam was that Mentors and Forzas were not allowed to fight in the battles. They could give advice and tactical suggestions to the regulars... the SunStars, but Olam forbade them from doing any actual fighting.

Two Mentors had the strength to defend any Diamond Command facility, such as the one where Apollo was headed. A Mentor would be unfazed by a hundred or five hundred Sughi soldiers. As for the Forzas, it would only take one to easily defend the facility.

When Apollo talked with Reemo about this issue, he answered Apollo's question with his own. "Apollo, how do you think we advanced to become Mentors?"

Apollo gave the pat answer. "By doing the right thing."

"True."

Apollo could see that his lack of effort was being reciprocated. He put more effort into it. "Okay... but... still... why not help us fight the hordes?"

"You're not always going to win, Apollo. Sometimes, you will lose... maybe badly."

Apollo learned that these battles were proving grounds. The SunStars had to show they were willing to stand up for Olam, even if it meant painful losses. Some ghosts fought bravely, even when outnumbered. Some fought to a state of unconsciousness, and then they fought more once they had recovered. Some refused to give up, no matter how bad it was. Apollo was one of these.

Apollo had been in battles where the enemy blew enough of his menapses to render him unconscious. Commonly, this was referred to as flatline. Being hammered into this catatonic state was a painful process. For many, it was terrifying to feel the enemy beat the life force out of you.

During these battles, a few Diamond Command soldiers would give up and go to Sughi's side. Others would leave after the battles. A big reason for leaving was resentment over the lack of help from the Mentors. Their Mentors, who claimed to love them, and who had spent years teaching them, would not fight to protect them. SunStars felt abandoned. "Sughi would not abandon us like that," they would hear the Sughi soldiers say. "And he won't abandon us when we are Bloods." This caused some Olam soldiers to switch sides.

Worse than the desertion of SunStars was the occasional Mentor who switched sides. This was a monumental loss. These were Mentors who could not stand to watch a hateful enemy destroy their SunStars.

Apollo had talked with Olam about all this, and his father's explanation was like Reemo's. "You have to prove yourself, son. I love you too much to always help you. You have to know you can be beaten in battle, and sometimes you will be. But we won't lose this war. I promise you. Learn to accept the pain. In the end, we will win."

In one of these discussions, Olam said something different to Apollo. He only said it once, despite Apollo asking him for more information. Olam started by reminding Apollo that he was one of Olam's strongest warriors and that his older brother, Dramos, was even more powerful. Apollo had heard that before and felt nothing but pride for his brother. But then Olam said, "I have a special gift I hope to give you, Apollo. The time will come when I will need you to have even more strength than you do now. A strength that will terrify every Sughi soldier. Stay true to me. Help me win this war. And that gift will be yours when the time is right."

At first, Apollo thought Olam was saying that Apollo would be a Mentor. But no, because Olam explained, "I hope you are a Mentor someday, Apollo. But the gift I have for you is very different. You'll know what it is when I give it."

Apollo looked forward to the gift, whatever it was, but he mainly concentrated on his current assignments.

Apollo arrived at the command center's main gates. The gates were symbolic because no physical gate could keep a ghost in or out of the complex. The gates and walls were delineations of who could go where. You needed clearance to enter, or there would be a fight.

Vanessa was the gatekeeper. Apollo had met her before, and she was well known. She was a favorite. She had a way of putting you at ease while also making it clear she was in charge, and you had better do what she said. She was perfect as a gatekeeper. Nobody was going to intimidate her, but every authorized visitor was going to feel welcomed by her.

Vanessa's aura was multicolored but primarily red. She was short, with a large head. Her eyes and smile were big. Her smile rivaled that of Reemo. With her oversized eyes and mouth, she could make endless, powerful facial expressions. Conversations with her were fascinating because she was so animated.

She greeted Apollo with a bright, "Hello," and she ushered him into a lobby large enough to hold a hundred people. As he stepped inside, Apollo knew his aura and the core patterns of his menapses were being scanned by sensors capable of reading down to his foundational lattice. His outer networks would have changed from constant battle damage, but his core structure remained intact—as did the emanation and pulse of his living aura.

Vanessa chatted with him, friendly as always. "Apollo, Reemo told me you had a little scuffle in Seven Valley?"

"Yes, ma'am," Apollo answered, looking down shyly.

"Oh, don't you 'ma'am' me, Apollo, my boy. You make me feel like a stranger."

"Yes, ma'—I mean... yes, Vanessa."

"So?" she asked, "tell me about it."

"Oh... somebody figured out I was for Olam, and a whole squad attacked me. I had to go underground, but two taggers stayed with me. Finally, I fought them. For a while, at least."

"Are you okay?" Vanessa showed genuine concern and came right up close to Apollo, looking him in the eyes and all over.

"Yeah, umm, I mean, yes."

She stared him down, wanting more.

"Really. It was okay. We fought, but then we called it off. It was a draw. I even think I ended up liking one of them."

"Liking?" Vanessa was surprised.

Apollo shook his head up and down, thinking about that bull of a ghost named "Myke," and scrolling through the events in his mind.

"Hey, buddy," said Vanessa, waving a hand in front of Apollo. "Are you still with me?"

Apollo came back to the present. "He was a good guy, Vanessa. He's the enemy... but a good guy. It was weird."

At this point, an image of Reemo appeared close to them. It was full-sized and could speak as if it were him. It was a mirror of Reemo, reflecting him and his speech without him being there. "Well, Vanessa, dear," said Reemo, "I see you've found my favorite SunStar."

"I have, Reemo, darling. I'm one of your favorites, too... right?" She batted her huge eyes at him in flirtatious mockery.

"Apollo," said Reemo, "watch out for that woman!"

Apollo did not respond, even though spoken to. He had enough sense to know the conversation was really between Reemo and Vanessa.

Vanessa turned towards Apollo. "I'm harmless, soldier boy."

Apollo was tired, but it was impossible not to be energized by Vanessa. "You know, Vanessa, ma'am, you should ask the higher-ups if Reemo could be your alternate Mentor. He's the best! Just ask Torith. We call Reemo her Uncle Mentor!"

"No, no, no!" Reemo's mirror answered. "I can't handle Vanessa. Apollo... no!"

"O-h-h, I thought Mentors are not afraid of anything!" she said, looking at Apollo. "Does he sound scared to you, Apollo?"

Reemo jumped in: "You know, Apollo. If I end up with a woman like Vanessa when I'm a Blood, I'll have it made. I won't have to make any decisions or figure anything out. Other than how to salute, of course!" Reemo was saluting with his hand upside down.

Vanessa gave Apollo a big wink and turned towards the Reemo image. "Why, thank you, Reemo. I'll remember your nice comment. Now, Apollo here is all cleared and set to come in. Should I send him your way?"

"Please."

"Okay, boss," she said. Then she waved her wrist in an upside-down go-away motion, signaling that she was done with Reemo. His mirrored image disappeared.

Now that it was just the two of them, Apollo wondered if he should joke or comment on the obvious chemistry between her and Reemo. But Vanessa surprised him by coming up close. Her demeanor changed one hundred percent. Her eyes were now sad and penetrating. "I know you had a hard day, Apollo. And I know you are out there fighting for us. I know you are hurt sometimes. I only joke to cheer you up. I'm so proud of you!"

Apollo could not respond. He had been steel for hours. Now she had melted him. Apollo did not want to show emotion going into the briefing, but he was afraid he would lose it.

"Nope... nope... no!" Vanessa shook her head. "Not yet, my strong boy. Come on. I need you to put your soldier face back on before I let you through those big doors. You can do this."

With that encouragement, Apollo was able to flush his emotions. There was still business to take care of.

Vanessa looked him over. Satisfied that he was back in his soldier mode, she gave him the thumbs up and pointed towards the access doors. "Be a rock!" she said.

Grateful for Vanessa's perception, Apollo went towards the far end of the lobby. The shiny black access doors opened for him. He walked through and heard a 'whoosh' as the doors closed behind him.

22

Lionah

After going through the large black doors, Apollo was on a small platform overlooking an enormous room. The room was constructed as if it were inside a vast sphere, shaped like the interior of an enormous globe. The inside diameter was over fifty yards across. Along the ever-sloping, single-round wall of the sphere, numerous workstations were outfitted with communication equipment. There were also small gathering areas, formal briefing setups, and places to relax with big-screen comms for viewing and entertainment. One part of the inner sphere was darker and less lit. Apollo had never inspected that area, but it appeared to be a bank of servers, electrical panels, and other equipment.

As far as Apollo knew, Megantha had not been involved in the design and building of this facility. Olam certainly had, and this one was similar to other command centers on Planet Summa. Sughi's army had taken over a few of those centers. Diamond's soldiers resisted some, but then they were ordered to retreat.

Apollo and everyone knew a few Mentors could have easily taken the centers back, but Olam and Diamond would not allow it. It seemed as if Olam and Diamond were purposefully giving Sughi and his army operations assets— almost as if Olam was trying to make the war fairer, whatever "fairer" meant.

Apollo knew Olam's reasoning had to do with agency, but that was a rough pill to swallow. Apollo had watched Sughi soldiers unleash their hell on people who had fought and protected these centers. Then, Olam told these same people to walk away and give them up. Why? Why give Sughi any advantage?

Free-floating in the middle of the vast command center room was an active and detailed globe replicating the entire Planet Summa. It was an excellent tool for tactical briefings and keeping track of opposition activity. The replica could be spun in any direction, and any part could be zoomed out for more detail.

A thousand people worked here regularly. But given that it was late in the day, only about a hundred were on duty, covering critical operations. Apollo looked around for Reemo, and he caught sight of his Mentor zooming towards him from across the sphere. Once they locked eyes, Reemo stopped and pointed to an area off to Apollo's right. Reemo headed that way, and Apollo took off to meet him.

Apollo had assumed Reemo would want to debrief in front of the globe so Apollo could do a detailed show-and-tell of what had happened today. But Reemo had gone to a secure room commonly referred to as a locker. This surprised Apollo. He did not think anything he had seen in Seven Valley warranted that level of security.

Lockers were rooms built with sensors geared to detect the proximity of any ghost. When a locker was in use, the room's door would shut and light up blue. This told everyone to stay away from the door and the room. If they approached too close, an alert would sound in the room, and any briefing or secure conversations could be stopped. Comms in the room would automatically go blank.

Apollo followed Reemo into the locker. Inside was a singular, circular table. A window with thick, double-paned glass was built into the wall facing the command room. It was one-way. They could see out, but nobody could see in.

Reemo told Apollo to wait because others were coming.

"Who are we waiting for, Reemo?"

"Another Mentor. Her name is Savana."

"Torith's Mentor?"

"Oh, yes," said Reemo. "You know her."

Apollo could tell there was at least one additional person, but Reemo had not offered that name. "And… someone else?" Apollo asked.

"Yes," said Reemo, who paused for effect, looking at Apollo. "A Forza."

"A Forza?" Apollo was surprised. First, a meeting that had to be in a locker. Then, Savana. And now a Forza was coming?

Apollo had seen Forzas in the Command Center. He had passed them in transit but did not know any of them personally. A Forza was a formidable ghost. This was a being who had progressed far. A Forza could move physical matter and had some ability to create physical things. A Forza was also learning how to make living creatures. They were nowhere near as capable as Quasars, but they operated on levels far above Apollo's capabilities and well above those of Mentors like Reemo and Savana.

Savana entered the secure room and greeted Apollo warmly. "Thank you for being such a wonderful friend to my Torith," she said. Savana then positioned herself next to Reemo, and they spoke briefly and quietly. Apollo could not hear what was said.

Savana concluded with Reemo and shut the door to the room, which would have activated the sensors to keep it secure. Apollo wondered if the plan had changed. Maybe the Forza was not coming.

But seconds after the door shut, the Forza appeared in the room, just inside the doorway. She nodded warmly to Savana and Reemo and went right over to Apollo. Unlike normal greetings between ghosts, Apollo was surprised when she embraced him. She was not physical. He could not feel her form. But he felt power and warmth from her spirit as it enveloped him. Then she stepped back. Her eyes were shiny, blue-green emeralds. She locked them onto his.

"Thank you for coming, Apollo." She said it as if he were doing her a favor. "I want to hear your story." She then moved towards the circular table, and they all gathered around. "My name is Lionah. I grew up in the Red River Desert."

Any middle school geography student knew where the Red River Desert was. It was an enormous, dry region, a thousand miles across. The name came from a part of the desert covered with red rock formations, many shaped like huge drops of dried, wet sand. The Red River wound its way through this same part. The river was deep blue in color, but the terrain was red sandstone, leading to the Red River name. Apollo knew the desert was near Summa's equator, a third of the way around the globe.

Apollo expected Lionah to tell more about herself, but instead, she asked him to describe everything that had happened, including the cave, the debate, and the fighting with Myke and Lucen. Apollo went through it all. They were interested in the Magnate, but it was clear that both Savana and Lionah were the most interested in Myke, the yellow bull.

"So… you want a B-Channel to talk with Myke?" Reemo asked.

"I think it would be good for Myke and me to talk on a B. When I say I 'want' one, I mean that I believe it's the right thing to do."

"Do you think Myke trusts you not to tell us everything?" asked Reemo. "He has to know your loyalty is to us, not him."

Apollo explained the immediate bond he had with Myke. He acknowledged that Myke could have been playing him, but when you fight with another person like that, you are part of them. You know what's inside them because you've been digging at them so hard.

"I want to be straight with Myke. I want an understanding that if I promise Myke I'll keep something confidential, then that also means I don't tell you or Diamond Command."

They talked about it some more. Lionah had not said much. Reemo and Savana seemed okay with the B-Channel if Apollo wanted to take on that responsibility.

Apollo was still curious why Savana and Lionah were there and what was so secret about this meeting. Why did it have to be in a locker? He wanted to be polite and wait until they told him, but they had not given any explanation. Finally, he asked, and the room went quiet.

Reemo and Savana looked at Lionah, deferring to her. But she said to Savana, "Go ahead. You first."

There was a distinct change in Savana's demeanor. A sadness came over her. "Apollo," she said, "Myke is my house brother. We're only a year apart. He was so good and strong. He was a Mentor. I love him so much." She choked up, and Reemo tried to comfort her.

A Mentor!... thought Apollo. *Wow!* He knew Mentors switched. Tamir's did. But he had never fought one. It was hard for Apollo to process. It also explained why Myke was such a beast and why he was so different from other Sughi soldiers.

"He's not a Mentor anymore," said Reemo. "Olam took it away. He has the Puissance, but not its power."

"No wonder he's so strong," Apollo said, shaking his head. "Now I understand why he's different."

Myke had been a Mentor!

Apollo turned towards Lionah, thinking he knew why she was there. "Were you his Mentor, Lionah?"

"No, Apollo," she said, sadly shaking her head. "No," she sighed. "He was mine."

Apollo was shocked and recoiled. He could only imagine Lionah's heartbreak. She was magnificent, and Apollo hated to think she had reason to be sad. Apollo absorbed and processed, and he hurt for her.

Lionah continued, "Apollo, we're talking in a locker because we think Myke has friends on our side. He was an excellent Mentor. His students loved him. I loved him. I still do."

Apollo understood.

"We don't want Myke to know about this meeting. When you talk to him, don't tell him that Savana and I are involved."

"Why?" asked Apollo, not seeing how it could hurt.

"Because we want Myke to think he's only dealing with you. We think he'll come back, eventually, Apollo. You might be the ticket to make that happen."

"But I want to be honest with him. I told him I would be."

Savana spoke up. "Apollo, we want you to be one hundred percent honest with Myke. He's smart. Tell him straight up you had a meeting at Diamond Command and that Reemo approved the B-Channel. Myke's very no-nonsense. He doesn't like politics. He'll understand there are parts of the meeting you can't divulge.

Apollo nodded his head in the affirmative.

"What Myke hates," Lionah added, "is when people dance around the truth. He does not want any sugar coating. Only straight talk. Tell him what you can, and then be upfront about what you can't. Direct is good. That is his style, which is why he likes you."

They talked some more, and then the meeting was over. Apollo wondered how it would look to people in the command room if Lionah came out, followed by him. People out in the center knew about the fight. It was their job to know. And they would now know Apollo and Reemo, and probably Savana, were briefing in the locker. If a Forza came out, too, it would be a big deal—and it might get back to Myke.

But Lionah and Savana were way ahead of Apollo. Before the door to the locker opened, Lionah and Savana stood arm in arm. "Ready?" asked Lionah. Savana said she was, and Lionah and Savana disappeared. Poof. Gone.

Apollo turned toward Reemo, astonished.

"They're still here, Apollo. Lionah can bend light. It's an optical illusion."

The door to their secure room opened. Apollo wanted to look more for Savana and Lionah, but people in the main room were looking their way.

"Come on, Apollo. We walk out normally like it's only you and me." Reemo started moving through the doorway, and Apollo followed.

"Can you do that?" Apollo said.

"Not like Lionah. She does it perfectly. When I do it, there is some distortion. I'll get better."

Apollo asked Reemo how it was that Myke was Lionah's Mentor. Usually, it would be a woman. "Was he like you are to Torith? An Uncle Mentor?"

Reemo said no and explained that there were a few exceptions where men were Mentors to women. Lionah was exceptionally capable. A wonderful, strong person from day one, even as a young child. She had a woman Mentor, but she was so strong they assigned Myke to her, too. Not because her Mentor wasn't good, but because they wanted Lionah to have double the exposure. She absorbed everything very quickly.

"What happened to Myke? He must have been a great Mentor to be assigned to Lionah."

"Well, Apollo, for one thing, I don't know what happened. From what I've heard, it sounds like Olam could see Myke struggling and hoped his interaction with Lionah would bring him back on track."

"Struggling? How?"

"I don't know, Apollo," said Reemo. "Hopefully, you'll get the chance to hear it from Myke himself."

23

Richard

Reemo took Apollo to the far side of the command center, near the darkened area housing servers and electrical panels. There, they would meet a network security officer named Richard. They needed Richard's help setting up Apollo's B-Channel.

Richard had five or six comms open, arrayed in a circle around him. He darted back and forth from one to another, checking their output and inputting data. Apollo had never met Richard, but Apollo knew he had a reputation for being intense and weird. Richard had no sense of personal space. He would come close, look you over like a detailed, inanimate object, then go back to his work, all without saying a thing.

"You know about this guy? Right, Apollo?" asked Reemo. "Don't be offended. He's brilliant, and we love him."

"Got it," said Apollo.

"Richard, my friend," said Reemo loudly, spreading his arms wide, open, and friendly. "How are you?"

Richard glanced over from his array of comms. Apollo could see Richard beginning to pause or hard stop the multiple mental processes he was juggling. The effort looked physically painful. Richard would now have to deal with illogical people. This mental reconfiguration was familiar to Apollo. He had seen Tamir do the same thing many times.

Pulling people like Richard and Tamir out of their deep mental forests was meant to be a careful process.

"Hello," was all Richard said. He looked back at one of the comms and then checked another. Apollo had no problem with this. He knew Richard was downshifting and applying the brakes. His mental momentum needed time to adjust.

Reemo and Apollo moved in closer and waited. Apollo could see the screens of two of the comms. One had at least six columns of scrolling data. The other had a dozen pie charts segmented into different colors. The charts were constantly changing. Apollo wanted to ask Richard about it, but instead, he waited patiently.

Richard finally stopped his scurrying around and came over to Apollo. He stopped close. "So, you are Apollo?" Richard looked him over from two feet away. "You're strong, aren't you? Fighting all those soldiers."

"He's a strong soldier," said Reemo. "With a special mission. That's why we need a—"

"B-Channel," interrupted Richard, glancing at Reemo. "I know all about that." Then, looking at Apollo, he asked, "What makes you so special? I know you are strong. Your brother… Dramos… he's stronger… and older. He doesn't have a B-Channel." Richard had a hint of challenge in his voice, but it was more admiration than challenge. "They won't even give me one."

Apollo did not expect tactfulness from Richard. Apollo responded by nodding affirmatively, knowing he did not have to explain himself.

"I received a message from a Forza," said Richard. "That's rare. Even more rare, the system blocked the name of the Forza. I don't know which one sent it."

Apollo wondered how Richard knew the message was legit if he did not know who it came from. But Richard was a network security guru, and Apollo stayed quiet, letting Richard work it out.

"The message told me to set you up right away."

Richard explained things about the B-Channel Apollo already knew, such as how the network would not record it was him using the channel. The network would encrypt where he was, who he was talking to, and the contents of the conversation. Now, whenever he called for a comm, the network would automatically encrypt his location until it knew whether or not he was invoking the B-Channel option. It would also scrub the logs of his B-Channel activity.

Richard had a portable scanner, which he used to map Apollo's core network for ghost authentication. Soon, Richard was finished, and he looked Apollo over one more time. Close. Very close. Apparently, Apollo passed scrutiny because Richard gave the faintest of nods and turned back to engage with his comm array.

"Done," was all Richard said.

Apollo and Reemo eyed each other. "Ahh… alright… thanks, Richard," Reemo said. "We'll see you later."

"Thank you, sir," Apollo added, and he and Reemo left.

Reemo caught Apollo's eye, and the two of them smiled at what they had experienced with Richard.

Apollo could not help but like Richard's strangeness, and he felt extremely protective of him. It would be terrible for Richard's brilliant, fragile brain to have to outright fight some hateful, numbskull of a Sughi soldier. *That's my job,* Apollo thought. *I'll trade punches with the ugly so Richard won't have to.*

Reemo said Apollo was done for the day at the Command Center, and he could go home. Apollo headed for the main door but was quickly stopped by several analysts who had heard what had happened. Their job was to gather intelligence on enemy movements and activity. They wanted specifics, including the names of any of the Sughi soldiers. Apollo realized he was facing his first dilemma. Normally, he would have given them the names of Myke and Lucen, but he only gave them Lucen's.

When Apollo told the analysts about the round-faced Magnate, one of the analysts said, "Oh, yes. We know him. He's very secretive, and he has others do everything for him. He claims it's for security purposes, but we think he's mostly a powermonger."

Apollo was tired. He needed to recharge for the flight home. He went through the big black doors into reception. Vanessa was still on duty. She was checking others in. She flashed him a big smile and mouthed, "Goodnight."

Apollo headed out the exterior doors into a courtyard area at the front of the building. It had big trees, a fountain, and sturdy stone benches. Apollo buried himself in the trunk of one of the trees. He relaxed and absorbed electrical energy from the massive, living organism.

Ten minutes later, he was topped off, and he started home. What a day!

24

Fight for the Good Guys

"Home" for Apollo still meant the same house where he had grown up with Dramos, Celti, Natilia, and Jank. Dramos, Natilia, and Jank still considered it home, too. Like Apollo, they were grown and often gone, but they kept their rooms at the house and stayed regularly. Megantha and Olam were often there as well.

Unfortunately, the house no longer meant home for Celti. Everyone hoped she would come back, but she was too unhappy with her parents' plan for life as Bloods. "Brutal, unfair, irrational, and just plain not right" were ways she described it. "At least save the animals," she would say.

Celti would sometimes come by the house, but it was rare. She might show up for an important family event, especially if it was related to Apollo or the Pups, but her visits did not last long.

Most of the time, Apollo was not home. Reemo kept him fully occupied in the war with Sughi, including operational missions, intelligence-gathering assignments, training younger fighters, and deployments for outright battles.

Tonight, when Apollo arrived home, the family party was over. Torith and Tamir had both left. Jank was there. He was grown now, but he was still as energetic as when he was a pup. Jank asked Apollo all kinds of questions. Normally, Apollo was okay with that, but this time, he cut Jank short.

"It's been a slammer of a day, Jank. Sorry, but we need to do this later."

Jank understood, and Apollo headed straight to his room. He'd make it up to Jank tomorrow.

In his room, Apollo called for a comm and tried to contact Tamir. Tamir answered, but was busy, so Apollo called Torith. She was anxious to talk. "Apollo... I heard your op went bad! Are you okay? What happened?"

Apollo summarized much of it but was intentionally vague about Myke and said nothing about the B-Channel. Then he asked, "I need your help, Tor."

She was happy to help.

"The problem is, I can't tell you why I need your help. I can't tell you what we're doing."

Torith said okay, but she sounded concerned.

"Can you be at my house in two days?"

"Not the Command Center?" asked Torith.

"Better here. Or at the Pacos Mountains Server Complex, if you prefer, since that's where we'll probably meet Tamir. I need his help, too."

Apollo knew Torith was still confused. He also knew she trusted him completely, as he did her. For him to withhold information was not the norm. Apollo, Tamir, and Torith were regularly positioned as a three-person special team. Usually, they briefed together, so they all knew everything. And if something was passed only to Apollo, he always tried to forward it to the other two.

Apollo knew Torith could read him well. Sometimes, she knew more about what was happening in his head than he did. Torith was an incredible person, and it often made Apollo uncomfortable to be assigned as her team leader. Apollo had asked Reemo to have her lead the team, and he said no. Apollo countered that her instincts were better than his, and that he and Tamir would always fight to the "ghost death"—flatline—to protect her. They would do anything for her, even if they disagreed with her orders.

That was when Reemo explained something new to Apollo. He said Torith was being prepared for bigger things. Reemo knew Torith could lead the team, but the Forzas had other things in mind for her. They wanted to protect her from some of the ugliness that came with leadership in battle.

"You are forced to make hard choices, Apollo. You have to live with those choices, and they are painful when you make mistakes."

Apollo knew that to be true.

Reemo continued, "Torith is more than capable of making those same hard decisions. But do you want her to bear those burdens? The ones you have to bear?"

Apollo did not.

"She loves you, Apollo. And she wants to support you. So let her. Now is not the time for her to lead. Her time is coming. She is a superstar."

What Reemo told him about Torith was not surprising. Apollo was happy she was being prepared for more important assignments. He would expect no less. So, rather than worry about giving her the chance to lead, Apollo was glad to have her total support. He would miss her when they took her from him.

Torith looked nothing like a warrior, and Apollo often used that to the team's advantage. She was a striking ghost, poised and composed—more like the head of an art academy than a fighter. Her black hair shimmered with aquas and browns, contrasting sharply with her fair complexion. The browns of her eyes sparkled aqua, as did her predominantly brown aura. Her essence was magnificent.

Ghosts were naturally drawn to her, and they trusted her immediately.

Apollo, of course, trusted her, too. He had been talking with her on the comm without video, using audio only, not wanting to invade her privacy. But Torith switched them to video.

"Apollo... please look at me," she said.

Apollo lined up with the comm. *Oh, boy*, he thought. *Here it comes.*

"I'm worried, Apollo. First, your op goes bad today. It sounds like you had a nasty fight. Now you're telling me we're going on some secret mission? One you can't describe?"

Apollo looked at her, but he offered no explanation. Her instincts, as he had told Reemo, were superb.

"I know you, Apollo. I'm worried about you."

Apollo was worried, too. "Talk to Savana," he told her.

"My Mentor... Savana? What does she have to do with it?"

"Tell her the same things you've told me. Tell her I won't give you more explanation. She can decide if you should know more. She knows what's going on."

Torith's face showed surprise and then even more concern. "You're scaring me, Apollo. What have you gotten yourself into?"

Torith's concern set off more warning bells inside Apollo. Her worry heightened his. But Apollo also knew he needed to go forward for Myke, the yellow bull, for Myke's sister, Savanna, and for Myke's former student, the Forza named Lionah.

Later that night, Apollo had a similar conversation with Tamir. Tamir was more amused by the secrecy than bothered by it.

"Okay, boss," said Tamir. "I'll meet you at the Pacos Mountains RSC. Sounds like fun, whatever it is. Torith and I will save your ghostness when things get ugly. And I won't talk to anybody but Torith about it."

Apollo was tired and rested in his room for hours, replaying the day. First, there was the underwater cavern, then the gathering of Sughi followers in Seven Valley, then the fight with Myke and his soldiers, then Vanessa and the command center meeting with a Forza. Finally, there was Richard and the B-Channel. It was all a lot to digest.

Apollo knew all the fighting had to be changing him. He thought he was handling it well, but he was not big on self-analysis. Somebody had to fight, and he was good at it. So many others on Olam's side hated the grinding horror of one-on-one physical battle. These were "love thy neighbor" people, not "pound your local Sughi soldier people." They had a hard time coping with the fighting that Apollo, Torith, Tamir, and many others did on their behalf.

Apollo wondered how it would be for him when the fighting was over. *Olam will win—of that, I'm sure*, he thought. *So, then, what do I do?* Apollo hoped he'd be sent on as a Blood before the fighting on Summa ended. For sure, there will be fighting on my earth, wherever that is. *I can fight for the good guys there.* He could not see himself sitting around teaching Sunday School for a living. "Please send me on before we win," he verbalized to Olam.

Later that night, Apollo spent time with Megantha, talking to her about the assignment with Myke. He told her everything, knowing she already knew. Apollo was an adult, but he still let her hug him. There was nothing like it. Such power and love. It made Apollo look forward to when he would be a Blood. He would be able to touch and feel everything.

Then he switched subjects with Megantha. "What about Celti?" Apollo asked. "Is there any way to get her back?"

"There's a plan," Megantha told him. "Your sister loves you, and you are part of that plan."

Apollo wanted to know more, but he did not ask. That plan would have to unfold on its own. "Okay, Mom. But please promise to hit me over the head if I don't see my part in the plan."

The next day, Apollo made a point of spending time with Jank. They went to a training seminar together, where Jank and several hundred others were learning about light, its speed, and its composition. More importantly, they were learning about the concept that light is truth. Both Sughi and Olam's followers were there. Other than Apollo, there were no soldiers. These were science nerds, and for the most part, the two factions stayed on different sides of the room. These types of meetings were considered no-fight zones so all could learn. This did not mean there were not occasional insults or arguments, but, for the most part, people kept an uneasy truce. When Apollo entered the room with Jank, they positioned themselves in the back, wanting to stay low-key. That did not work because some of Jank's friends knew Apollo was an experienced Diamond soldier, and they came back to greet him with awe. Apollo tried to downplay it, not wanting to rile up the Sughis at the meeting.

Apollo knew Jank was more intelligent than he was. Maybe not like Tamir, but close. Jank understood the lecturers; Apollo followed only on the surface. He could grasp that the speed of light was a constant, but concepts like mass increasing exponentially near light speed—those he could only repeat, not truly comprehend. The proofs linking light and truth were far beyond him. He could recite some of the formulas, maybe even sketch the logic, but his actual understanding hovered just above zero.

Jank was not like Tamir. Jank was meant to be an analyst or scientist helping Diamond and Olam in the world war. Apollo did not want to see this brother on the battlefield, although some fighting might be inevitable.

Tamir was an anomaly and different from Jank. He could do the ugly, down-in-the-mud fighting. He was a hardened soldier, but he still managed to keep his intellect keen and cooking.

Of course, there was Apollo's older brother, Dramos. Not a Jank or Tamir intellectually, but a lot smarter than Apollo and ten times the soldier. Apollo would always wish he could fight alongside Dramos. Reemo always said they were too strong together. This made Apollo sad. He missed Dramos.

25

Torith's Intuition

The next morning, Torith arrived early and came in to see Natilia and Jank, who were both home. Torith doted on them both. With Celti gone, Torith had partially filled the vacuum left by the departure of their older sister. The Pups adored her as she did them. Apollo appreciated her kindness towards them. Apollo could see that Torith was distracted, but it would not show to the Pups. Apollo knew she was worried about today.

After an hour, Apollo and Torith left and headed for the Regional Server Complex, or RSC, in the Pacos Mountains. Apollo was not surprised when Tamir asked if they could meet there. Tamir had managed to gain clearance to use a tiny fraction of the complex's nearly endless computing power. That small percentage was still immense. He was using it to study how sound waves traveled through water under tremendous pressure, such as at the bottom of a deep ocean. Tamir was fascinated not just by pressure but by how changes in temperature and water composition could bend and shift sound waves in surprising ways. Leave it to Tamir to be blissfully immersed in such complexity.

The Pacos Mountains were southeast of Megantha's and well inland from the ocean. They were old and rounded, with no jagged peaks, arranged in a partial circle, with a wide, high valley in the middle. The floor of that valley was covered with scattered pine trees. There were a few shallow lakes. At times, the valley and mountains were covered in snow. The RSC was on relatively high ground in the middle of the valley.

Apollo knew the Pacos Mountains RSC was impervious to attack. RSCs were different from command centers like Diamond Command. Nobody could take down an RSC because each was guarded by a Forza. Unlike command centers and other military targets, Forzas had full authority from Olam to use their considerable powers to protect their respective RSCs. It was important to Olam that everyone on Planet Summa, regardless of persuasion, have full access to the network, and the RSCs were the central nodes of Planet Summa's comm network.

B. Z. Sughi and his followers were heavily critical of this approach. They said it made no sense for Olam to ensure full access to information here on Summa but then provide so little information when his children were physical Bloods on their earth planets. They would argue points like, "When my kids are dying from starvation, it sure would be nice to have access to a comm to find out which plants are edible, or where to hunt for food, or how to make a better bow and arrow."

Apollo knew, however, that Olam did not see it that way. The test here on Summa was totally different than the one they would be subjected to as Bloods. On Summa, people were indestructible ghosts, coddled by their parents, blessed with troves of knowledge, and under no obligation to work to feed and clothe themselves. What choices would they make under those circumstances? That was one kind of test. Then, if they passed Summa, they would go on to be clueless, vulnerable physical beings on some earth. That was a completely different type of test. To Apollo, the process was brutal and brilliant.

As Apollo and Torith approached the RSC, a group of five flyers formed up on their left. Normally, that was not unusual, but the five seemed to be carefully staying about two hundred yards away, moving in a parallel track. The fliers were too far away to be recognized by face, so Apollo could not tell if they were friends or foes. He asked Torith what she thought, and she said it was not good.

Apollo and Torith dove for the RSC. The five stayed with them. If they were Sughi soldiers, Apollo knew their efforts were pointless because the Forza at the RSC would protect him and Torith. Still, it was concerning.

Apollo and Torith arrested their descent, stopping in a courtyard outside the main RSC entrance. Apollo could feel the power of the Forza who controlled this place. The five flyers broke off, low and fast, and disappeared over a nearby tree line.

The Forza would know Apollo and Torith had arrived. The main doors opened, giving them access. Once inside, Apollo called for a comm and told Tamir they were there. Tamir did not keep them waiting. He was out of his computer lab within a minute, anxious to get on with whatever it was Apollo had pulled them into. Soon, they were off again. They had a good hour of flying ahead of them. Apollo told them where they were headed but not why. Apollo could tell they were not happy.

Apollo beelined for the ocean shoreline near the sea cave that Tamir and Torith had found two days ago. During the flight, he scanned for the flyers who had tracked him and Torith. They were not in sight.

Once at the shoreline, Apollo told Tamir and Torith more about the fight he'd had with Myke. He explained how Myke was a beast of a ghost and how he and Myke had come to a sort of understanding. Apollo explained he was going into the cave alone to meet Myke. "I don't know what will happen," Apollo told his friends. "I need you here as backup."

Neither Tamir nor Torith liked it. "It's probably a trap, Apollo," Torith said. "Myke could have an army in there waiting for you. You're not invincible!" Torith was angry. Her aura flashed, as did her eyes. "They could blow all your menapses!"

Tamir was not afraid of a fight, and he knew Apollo was not either, but he, too, had huge reservations. "You can't trust this Myke guy... whoever he is."

Apollo knew his friends might be right. Apollo also knew that if Tamir and Torith knew Myke had once been a Mentor, they would be doubly concerned.

"You want us to wait here while you go down there alone?" Tamir asked.

Apollo nodded in the affirmative.

"That's crazy! How long do we wait?"

"Till I come back," said Apollo, knowing that sounded ridiculous when he said it.

"Oh... good plan, Apollo," Tamir mocked.

"I can't give you more, Tamir. I know you want it, but this is the plan. Reemo knows what I'm doing."

Tamir seemed skeptical.

The three friends were in the cover of a clump of coastal pines near a cliff that dropped down to the beach. The surf was pounding hard, thumping against the rocks. Tamir and Torith both looked around for threats as they argued with Apollo. There could be hundreds of Sughi soldiers in the area right now.

Apollo knew his friends were not convinced of the plan, nor had he expected them to be. It was time to play his ace, and he held up his hands and looked at his friends, pausing the conversation.

Tamir and Torith stopped talking, their focus riveted on him.

"Let me show you something that will convince you," said Apollo. Apollo called for a comm. Apollo authenticated himself, then said, "Look," pointing to the screen.

Torith looked, hunting on the screen, and then she gasped.

Tamir did not have to hunt. He noticed it immediately. "Holy Summa!" said Tamir. "You have a B-Channel!"

Torith moved right to Apollo. Her anger had melted to concern. She looked at him from inches away. "What, Apollo?" she asked, definite fear in her voice. "What did they task you to do?" She continued to stare him down, her eyes wide and glowing.

Apollo could hear Tamir saying something, but it was Torith, right in his face, who had his attention. "I haven't told you everything," Apollo said. "I can't."

"You don't always have to say yes, Apollo," said Torith, still locked on. "They should not have sent you to Seven Valley alone, and whatever they have you doing now sounds even more dangerous. Tell them no! Or I will for you!"

Apollo knew Torith would do whatever Diamond Command asked her to do. Her words were out of concern for him.

Torith took a step back and brought her hands up to her head. Clearly, she was upset.

"Apollo, how did you get a B?" asked Tamir. "I've wanted one for years. What in the world are you into, boy?"

Tamir shook his head. "Holy Menapses! You're one in a million." Tamir was impressed. "I've never actually seen one of these... but... Apollo... why?"

"To talk with Myke," Apollo explained.

Torith had stopped saying anything. She looked sad and worried.

Apollo told them he did not know what would happen. He explained that there was supposed to be a level of trust and a truce between Myke and Apollo, which was why Sughi Command had not sent an army.

"But I'm not naïve," Apollo said.

"Yes, you are," Torith countered.

Apollo sighed, pausing slightly, then continued. "That's why I want my two best friends here in case it goes bad."

Soon, it was time for Apollo to go. Tamir and Torith finally convinced Apollo to agree that if he had not checked in with them within an hour, the two of them would call Diamond Command for help. It was too dangerous for them to attempt a rescue on their own.

Torith gave Apollo a ghost hug before he left. Unlike the normal friendship he felt through her hugs, this one transmitted tremendous worry and concern. Apollo knew her intuition was saying no to this op. He also knew it would be foolish to ignore her concerns, but he had to go forward.

26

Underwater Cavern

Apollo called for a comm a mile offshore and brought up a beacon channel. This caused the comm to broadcast both an audible noise and a pulsing signal, making it easy for anybody to know that Apollo was coming. Apollo also used the comm to pull up a map of the seafloor to help him navigate to the entrance of the underwater sea cave. He then started transitioning above the water in that direction. Myke might have already known Apollo was in the area, but Apollo wanted to make it obvious he was not trying to hide his approach.

Apollo could not call Myke on the B-Channel because they needed to be together in person to complete the setup. He considered calling Myke on an open channel but decided he did not know enough about Myke's status to chance that.

He thought back to the fighting he had done with Myke a few days ago. The fact that Myke had been a Mentor explained why he was still such a powerful ghost, even if he had lost access to Olam's Puissance. Apollo wondered if Myke had been faking it and was actually much stronger. If that were the case, Apollo was in trouble. But Apollo doubted Myke was anything more than he appeared to be. Myke was formidable, but he was no longer a Mentor. He was nothing like Reemo or Torith's Mentor, Savana.

Apollo normally loved flying over the water, especially near the shore in seas where the water was shallow and clear, and where he could see marine life and the bottom. Today, the water was rough and silt-laden. A stiff wind blew, and the sea was cold, blue, white-capped, and foreboding.

The comm was still with Apollo, and it said it was time to dive. He slowed so the comm could stay with him, and he broke the water's surface and started down. The noise of the wind cutting over the waves was replaced with a muffled chorus of sea sounds. The water's cold was much more intense than it had been in the air above. Apollo's ghost could feel the pressure and temperature changes as he descended. By the time he passed through two hundred feet, Apollo knew that if he were a physical Blood, he would be dead or nearly so. He would be out of air, incredibly cold, and crushed from the tremendous water pressure. Apollo's ghost essence registered these forces, but they were no challenge. *Being a ghost is awesome*, he thought.

On the surface, it was a sunny day, but less and less sunlight was finding its way to the depths. At four hundred feet, things were very murky. Apollo could tell he was starting into a canyon and going deeper, heading into total blackness. Tamir and Torith had to feel their way to the cave, not having the luxury of a comm to guide them, and it would have been difficult for them to find it had they not been able to follow the bubble stream down to the cave entrance. Apollo's navigation was much easier. The comm was drawing the terrain for him, marking depth, and allowing him to see the canyon walls virtually. At seven hundred feet, darkness prevailed. The comm was showing little signal strength, coming close to its network connection limits. There was no longer any visible sunlight.

The comm had enough network connection to draw the cave entrance, showing it to be at the base of a steep rock wall. Apollo could hear the escaping gas bubbles.

The comm was still in beacon mode, and its light would have been easy to see by anyone hidden in the dark. Apollo knew he could be attacked at any time. A few fighters as strong as Myke could flatline him. Apollo had some fear, which he embraced. The right amount of fear kept his edge sharp.

Apollo moved towards the cave and found the stream of bubbles rolling off its ceiling and racing to the surface. Apollo was looking forward to seeing the cavern and the lava at the end of the cave. Apollo felt the bubbles. Torith and Tamir were right. They were warm. *Hot lava gases*. This was a phenomenon.

There was a disturbance in the darkness. Apollo tensed and turned the comm so its screen projected light. It was Lucen, the tagger who had been with Myke in Seven Valley.

"He's waiting for you," Lucen said. "You're late." There was disdain in his voice, and he muttered something else that was unintelligible.

Apollo knew he had not been more than a few minutes late. Lucen was picking at him, probably insulted that he had been assigned to wait for his enemy. Somehow, Apollo knew Myke had given that order, probably to mess with Lucen, who would think his superior tagging skills put him above escort duty. Apollo remembered that Myke had said Lucen was a worm and a weasel.

"Follow me!" Lucen snapped. "And turn off that bantet comm." Lucen started into the cave.

Apollo released the comm to the network and followed Lucen, trying to figure out what "bantet" meant.

Clever swearing was an art form, one well-practiced by some Sughi soldiers. "Bantet" certainly would be an insult. Was it artful? Apollo did not know. Tamir would. As he did frequently, Apollo wished Tamir were with him now.

The heavy cold of the deep ocean water suppressed Lucen's aura. In the cave, it was intensely dark. Apollo hoped to see some bioluminescent sea life, but he saw none.

To navigate the cave, Tamir and Torith had told Apollo to follow the bubble stream, which Apollo did, rather than trying to follow Lucen's aura. Lucen was moving faster than Apollo wanted, and Apollo felt no obligation to keep up with the worm of a ghost.

After some travel, the cave's pitch black released the beginnings of a faint, orange glow. *The lava... and the cavern! Myke will be there.* Apollo did not know if that was good or bad, and he tensed and readied himself for possible pandemonium.

Apollo and Lucen broke through the water's surface and were now inside a vast rock room partially lit by pools of molten lava. The gases coming off that lava had forced the water level down to the cave opening, where they could escape. Visibility in the trapped air was good but distorted by waves of tremendous heat. Tamir and Torith had said five hundred ghosts could easily fit in this room, and they were right.

Lucen did not stop and took Apollo towards the middle of the cavern, where lava had cooled and formed a wide rock island twenty feet above the water level. Apollo had never seen anything like this. He stopped, wanting a few seconds to set his bearings and absorb the magnificence of this geological wonder.

Lucen reversed back to Apollo. "Keep moving!"
There was a sneer in his voice, and Lucen jerked his head
towards the island, where Apollo could see Myke waiting.

"I see him," Apollo said with pushback. He was tired
of the worm, and now that Myke was there, Lucen was
irrelevant. "Time for you to bounce." Apollo moved right
into Lucen's face and held firm.

"He's mine, now, Lucen!" Myke called from the rock
island. "You're done!"

Lucen huffed and attempted to project strength. This
close, however, both Lucen and Apollo knew Lucen's
voltage was nothing compared to Apollo's. Lucen shot
sideways out of Apollo's view.

Apollo headed towards Myke, stopping four feet in
front of him. "Here we go!' he said to himself.

Myke's eyes and aura blazed yellow, contrasting with
his black hair and dark complexion. Apollo was powered up,
too, his blue eyes and aura gleaming. The two warriors
looked each other over, judging, reading, and evaluating.

Apollo could not help but be drawn to this man.
There was instant chemistry between him and Myke. It was
something Apollo had never experienced before. Myke was
the enemy, but it was as if Myke and Apollo had been
friends for a long time.

"Sorry about Lucen," Myke said. "Like I said before.
You can have him, but I recommend you don't take him.
Leave him to the Sughis."

Apollo smiled. Two squads of soldiers were behind
Myke, twenty to thirty yards back. "Why the
reinforcements?" Apollo asked.

"I didn't want them," said Myke, sounding miffed.
"They're not here for you. It's for me. Command doesn't
trust what we're doing, and Sughi demanded they be here."

"Sughi?" asked Apollo, surprised and not sure he believed Myke. "Sughi himself?"

"Oh, come on, Apollo," said Myke. "Your Puissance is strong. You're almost a Mentor. Sughi is worried you'll change my mind and beat up a bunch of us in the process."

Apollo was surprised that Myke thought he might soon be a Mentor. "I don't want to be a Mentor," Apollo said. "I'm too much of a fighter."

Myke nodded. "That, I get."

"If I were a Mentor, I couldn't be here." Apollo expanded his arms and looked around in an exaggerated manner.

Again, Myke seemed to agree. Then, businesslike, Myke said, "Let's get this B-Channel thing done." Myke pointed over his shoulder to the squads behind him. "Before they lose it."

"Are they going to attack?" Apollo asked.

"All I know is that they hate you, Apollo."

From the looks Apollo could see on some of their faces, Myke was right.

"If they attack, you take the squad on your right," Myke strategized. "I'll pummel the other one."

Apollo and Myke's eyes met. Each understood the other. What was important in this cavern was what was going on between them. Everybody else's concern was the noise of minions.

Apollo called for a comm. One appeared immediately. It showed a steady, albeit weak, connection. Myke called for one, too. They both navigated to their secure B-Channels. Their comms then asked for the electrical DNA of the person they'd be talking to. Apollo stepped back, and Myke touched his comm. Then Myke let Apollo touch his. Each was now authenticated. That was the final step. Now, when they went to their B-Channel, they could call each other in secure mode, unreadable to anybody other than a Quasar and a few designated Forzas. The system would mask their locations, traffic, and who they were talking to.

Myke continued in his business mode. "Good. Now... about your friends, Torith and Tamir. Can you tell them to leave?"

Apollo was not surprised at Myke's comment, but he asked anyway. "How did ..."

"The five soldiers following you back and the server complex," interrupted Myke. "Two of them were taggers. They tracked you."

"Okay," said Apollo, embarrassed that he had not picked up on the tail. "But aren't we done for today, Myke? We can talk later on the B's."

Myke shook his head. "Actually, no, we're not. Unless, of course, you want to be. But we have another idea."

"We?" Apollo did not know who Myke meant by "we."

"Well, me," Myke clarified. "I had an idea, but my command had to approve it, which they did. Yours has, too."

Now, Apollo was perplexed. The commands were at war with each other, and they did not co-approve anything. "What are you talking about, Myke?"

Myke hesitated, making an obvious point to do so for effect.

This is going to be big, Apollo thought, readying himself.

Then, Myke spoke. "Apollo, I want to take you to Sughi City. Just the two of us. You and I. To Sughi City,"

27

Travel Plans

Apollo was shocked. He did not know how to respond. "What?"

"To Sughi City, Apollo. I want to take you."

Sughi City was on the other side of Summa. That was far away, maybe fifty days of travel. It was Sughi's stronghold and the center of all Sughi activity. It housed Sughi Command. There were thousands of Sughi soldiers there. Most of the people in the city opposed Olam, and anybody openly supporting Olam was persecuted mercilessly.

"Why?" Apollo asked, struggling with the concept of going alone to the heart of enemy territory. "It will be war if I show my face there." Apollo could not conceive of going to Sughi City. "It will be me against thousands."

"Not true, Apollo. I got you a pass. They say they won't fight you if you don't fight them."

The infinite connections in Apollo's subatomic ghost brain fired rapidly. "My command agreed to this?" Apollo asked. "How?"

"I don't know," Myke said. "I think they called your Mentor and talked to him about it. Weird, I know, but your Reemo agreed, as did some Forza."

To Apollo, it felt like he was being thrown to the wolves. "Why would I want to go to Sughi City? Isn't that the last place I would want to go?"

"Look, Apollo. I know it's a lot to ask. But think about it. Wouldn't you want to go if your protection was guaranteed?"

As Apollo thought about it, he knew entering the heart of enemy territory would be wild and exciting. What true warrior would not want to go? If protected, of course.

Apollo debated whether to ask the obvious question of whether he could trust Myke. He decided there was no need. He knew he trusted Myke.

The two squads of Sughi soldiers behind Myke were far enough back that they could not hear Myke and Apollo's discussion. Apollo noticed they were starting to grumble, probably unhappy at the attention and courtesy being given to an enemy. Apollo was still churning on the Sughi City thing, but he had not forgotten where he was—deep under the ocean in a lava-laced cavern with enemy soldiers. Not at all a friendly environment.

"Don't worry about them," Myke said. Then he turned and looked them over. All grumbles and slouches immediately ceased. They straightened back at attention.

Apollo was impressed. Not only was Myke strong, but he apparently had powerful command authority as well.

"I have juice in Sughi City, Apollo. And I'll ghost slam anybody who tries to hurt you, not that you need my help."

"For how long?" Apollo asked. "How long in Sughi City?"

"Maybe a couple of weeks."

"But, Sughi City is fifty days' travel from here. How are …?"

"You'll take care of that."

"Me?" asked Apollo, surprised.

"Yes. You need to find a Forza to spring us there. Only you and I, not the minions," said Myke, thumbing backward at the squads behind him.

"Lucen, too?" Apollo asked.

"Oh, summa shake, no!" Myke snapped. "Not him."

Apollo was beginning to accept the possibility of going to Sughi City. "Are you sure you want to do this, Myke? They'll detest me in Sughi City. I can deal with that. But they are your team, and many of them will be angry with you for bringing me. Look at the ones behind you!"

Myke smiled. "Apollo, most of the people in Sughi City are hate-filled fools. They don't know what they believe. All they know is they can't stand Olam or the flavor of his people. They pick Sughi's side without working through the logic. Their choice of Sughi is emotional, and they try to cloak it in logic. I have no respect for them. I have my reasons for fighting against Olam's plan, but I'd much rather spend the day with you than any of those numbskulls."

"So... I'd be doing you a favor?" Apollo asked, with a hint of flair.

"Yep. Absolutely. And we'll watch each other's backs. They're afraid of you, Apollo. And they're afraid of me. So, we'll be good."

Apollo was looking for more guidance. He decided to try a quick mental check with Sapienti. *I believe I can trust him,* Apollo projected. *Right?* To Apollo, it seemed like it could be right. And he did not feel any pushback from Sapienti, although, admittedly, his checking was quick and cursory. But Apollo knew he would be receiving a hard confirmation from Reemo, and as he worked it over in his mind, a trip to Sughi City was looking like a reality.

Apollo and Myke worked out some quick logistics, and then Myke turned to the cavalry behind him and said the meeting was over, instructing them not to interfere with Apollo's departure.

Apollo then took off straight up, through the lava rock that became the seabed, then the ocean itself, and finally, he exited into regular air. The wind was still blowing, but less so, and the sea was calmer. Apollo headed for the beach and what he knew would be an ugly session with Tamir and Torith. But first, he stopped and called Reemo on a comm.

Reemo confirmed that Diamond Command had signed off on Apollo going with Myke to Sughi City. Reemo said he disagreed with the plan, but Lionah had overruled him. "Please be careful, Apollo," Reemo said. "There is more going on here than you or I understand. I trust Myke's intentions, but I don't trust Sughi Command to keep its word."

Apollo agreed. Sughi Command might go back on its word. Apollo doubted the Sughis would have any qualms about backstabbing their own soldier, Myke.

Reemo's last advice to Apollo was about Torith. "She's going to be furious with you, Apollo. She won't hold back. Tamir will, but you'll get a volcano's worth out of Torith. Please don't be angry with her. Understand the real reason for her reaction, and don't reciprocate her anger. Who knows when you will see her again…?"

Apollo ended with Reemo and headed towards the beach hiding place of Torith and Tamir. *Who knows when you will see her again?* That sounded ominous.

Minutes later, Apollo was standing in front of Torith and Tamir, explaining that he was going to Sughi City with Myke and would be gone for several weeks. The conversation did not go well.

Torith took it badly, as expected. She planted herself firmly and resolutely in front of him. Eyes, hair, aura—all at full power—flashing and pulsing. She attacked him for being foolish. "You don't know Myke. You just met him. How can you trust him? Are you crazy? How do you expect Tamir and me to protect you when you are on the other side of the world? The whole plan is ridiculous!"

"A Forza approved it …" Apollo tried to say.

"Yes. Because you have your agency, Apollo! Do you think it will be some kind of boys' camp? Maybe a little surfing... a few campfire stories... telling jokes?" She was yelling and almost crying. "You're crazy, Apollo! They're going to break you down! You're going to end up like Celti!"

At that, Apollo recoiled. He was willing to let her rant—she needed to—but bringing up Celti was too painful, and it started to make Apollo mad.

Luckily, Tamir jumped in. "You're not invulnerable, A.P. They'll pound you. I know you'll whomp 'em back... hard... but you can't fight them all."

"I'll call for help," said Apollo. "I'm a Momma's Boy and proud of it."

"Beuf-f-f-f," scoffed Tamir. "Just like you were a Momma's Boy at the Dunes?"

Apollo gave Tamir a hard stare. Torith didn't know about the Dunes, and Tamir and Apollo had a prior agreement that she wouldn't. "Tais-toi, Tamir."

"No, Apollo. I'm not going to shut up. I don't care about our agreement. They pummeled you at the Dunes because you were too hard-headed to ask for help. You flatlined, and they almost took you. You were too stubborn. So, what makes us think you'll do it in Sughi City?"

"You flatlined!" exclaimed Torith, back in Apollo's face again. "They were going to take you?"

"Ah, well, it wasn't that bad."

"Yes, it was!" growled Tamir. "You were stupid that day, A.P.! A danger to yourself."

Torith had stopped yelling. Instead, she showed resigned sadness. She moved close to Apollo, her head down, crying. "I don't want to lose you, Apollo." She moved into his space.

Apollo knew how to fight with Torith, but he had no defense against this. Apollo eyeballed Tamir, wanting his help. Tamir looked too mad to try, instead giving Apollo the *it's-your-problem* look.

The Dunes had been a tough mission, where secrecy had been paramount. This prevented Apollo from telling Tamir the whole story. It was true that he had been flatlined, and Apollo remembered how helpless he'd become. He knew they were going to take him, and they would have, except a rescue team from the Command Center found him at the last minute. There was an essential part of the mission that Apollo could never tell Tamir. Apollo had fought as hard as he could, but he could not take on all twenty fighters. He had to stand his ground while the asset he was protecting escaped undetected. The fighters needed to think Apollo was the prize, and the attackers could know nothing about the critical source Apollo had been debriefing. All in all, Apollo thought it best not to call for help from Olam, Reemo, or anyone. He wanted the attackers to believe they had won a routine fight and write the mission off as a success.

Apollo wished he could tell Tamir what actually happened at the Dunes. He needed Tamir's support for this Sughi City mission.

After additional hard discussion and some difficult goodbyes, Apollo left Tamir and Torith. Torith was still crying, and Tamir was awkwardly trying to comfort her. The last thing Tamir said to Apollo was that, although he disagreed, he would always support Apollo. That was a huge boost. Apollo hoped he would have the same support from Torith once she accepted that he was gone.

Apollo headed away from the rocky shoreline out over the water. Then he went sub-surface and turned right. Staying below the water line, he traveled for a long time in a direction that he guessed paralleled the beach. He surfaced briefly to get his bearings. He was quite a ways offshore. He went back to his submarine mode and turned inland. When he hit dry land, he would be many miles north of where he had left Torith and Tamir. At the beach, he mainly stayed hidden beneath the sand and worked his way up into a clump of scrawny pines. These wind-shaped trees offered limited cover. There, he called for a comm and brought up a B-Channel. He hailed Myke and waited.

Ten minutes later, Myke responded. "Are you alone?"

"Yes. My guess is I'm twenty to thirty miles north of the cave. I'm right at the coast, hidden in some trees. I stayed hidden the whole way."

Apollo knew Myke's comm could find Apollo's while in B mode, and without the network recording their location.

An hour later, Myke showed up.

28

Ask Me, Myke

Apollo and Myke traveled inland for about ten minutes, wanting to disassociate themselves from the coast. Then, Apollo called for a comm and reached out to Reemo, who responded almost immediately. Apollo explained his need for a spring to Sughi City. Reemo was colder than usual. He did not respond in his normal jovial style. Reemo said he doubted any Forza would spring them to Sughi City. Apollo knew that Lionah might, but given that Myke had once been Lionah's Mentor, Apollo could understand why Reemo might want to leave her out of it.

Apollo's comm session with Reemo became awkward, especially because Myke was right there listening in. "Can you at least try a Forza?" Apollo asked. "You already told me the op is approved. We need a spring. Won't a Forza do it?"

Reemo shook his head no. "A Forza won't do it," he emphasized. Reemo would typically provide the reason, but this time, he said nothing. Apollo knew it was because Myke could hear the conversation, but Apollo could not figure out why that mattered, nor could Apollo figure out why Reemo was so reserved.

The conversation between Apollo and Reemo came to a weird impasse. *What am I missing here?* Apollo asked himself. *Why this administrative blockade?*

Seconds ticked by. Reemo did not provide any answers or explanations. Apollo looked at Myke, then back at Reemo. "I... I don't understand."

More seconds. Reemo just looked at Apollo. Finally, Reemo said, "Ask Myke, Apollo. He knows."

Apollo checked with Myke, who moved to the comm and said, "Alright, Sir. I know. We'll do it. I didn't want to, but I will."

Apparently, that was what Reemo wanted to hear, and he said, "Be strong, Apollo. You're going to need everything you have on this mission."

Apollo acknowledged, "Yes." He could only imagine what Reemo was referring to.

"And, Myke ..." Reemo said, "... remember what you promised. Olam will hold you accountable if you don't."

"I know," Myke said.

At that, the comm screen went blank.

Apollo looked at Myke for an explanation. "Promised?"

"I promised to protect you, Apollo. No matter what happens. That is the only way your Command would agree to let you go."

"And Olam holding you accountable? That sounds like a threat."

"It is," Myke said. "It definitely is, one I take seriously."

"But what about the spring?" Apollo asked. "Why wouldn't Reemo help us?"

"Because... Apollo... because they want a Quasar to do it."

"Okay?"

"And... they insist I be the one to ask. Another part of the deal. They're forcing me to interact with a Quasar."

"Who... Mom?" Apollo asked. "Or maybe Diamond?"

Myke hesitated.

Apollo could see how hard this would be for Myke, and Apollo had no interest in making it any harder. Apollo waited, giving Myke the time he needed. Then he asked, "Myke, if this is so hard, why are you doing this? What do you get out of taking me to Sughi City?"

Myke gave Apollo a frustrated look and shook his head. At first, Apollo thought Myke was unhappy with him, but Myke explained, "It's the management. Sughi Command. They are so jacked."

Apollo absorbed, nodding his head up and down, slowly. "So, showing up with me is maybe an in-your-face move... or something?"

"Yes, something like that," Myke answered. "They're insane, Apollo. Just come with me."

Myke's explanation only gave Apollo a taste of why Myke wanted this to happen, not a concrete explanation. Apollo decided to let it rest at that for now.

It was quiet between them for several moments. Finally, Apollo asked. "Who, Myke? Who do I call?"

"Megantha," Myke muttered, head down.

"Okay... ready?"

Myke indicated he was, and it looked like he was bracing himself.

Apollo called for their mother, Megantha. All he had to do was reach out to her mentally, hoping she would respond in person. She came immediately.

Apollo and Myke were on a relatively flat section of a forty-five-degree slope on the side of a small mountain, many parts of which were covered with scrubby bushes and sagebrush. The face of the slope was oriented southwest.

They were too far from the coast to see the ocean. There was a rounded coastal range between them and the water. The sun had nearly set, and it was getting dark. When Megantha came, her natural light lit up the surroundings.

Megantha hugged Apollo, and he hugged her back, feeling charged and warm. There was a tinge of unease at hugging her in front of Myke, but he loved his mother so much he could not resist, and he wanted to feel her power.

After their long embrace, she turned towards Myke, who was ten yards away. He faced them but looked down, not wanting to meet her flashing eyes. Apollo could see that Myke was visibly struggling with her presence. He might have melted if he were made of ice or soft metal.

"Myke, we have missed you. And we love you, son."

Myke was shaking and looked like he might cry.

"Come back to us."

Myke met her gaze for half a second, then looked down, crossing his arms and hunching in, trying to protect himself. "Please... Apollo," Myke muttered, his face contorted. "Just ask her."

"I will spring you," said Megantha. "Both of you. But Myke, you have to ask me... and come to me." Megantha held out her arms, ready to embrace him.

Apollo knew Myke had no choice and watched as Myke forced himself to move forward to where she could take him in her arms and embrace him. When she did so, Myke crumpled and began to cry. He said no words and sobbed like a child. Apollo knew Myke could feel the love and power of Megantha. How he must have wanted to give in to that. Apollo did not understand why anyone could remain loyal to Sughi after being in Megantha's presence.

"Look at me, Myke," she ordered, pushing him back but holding him by the shoulders. Myke looked.

"You've chosen your path. Now, what do you need?"

"Please spring us to Sughi City," Myke said.

"And your promise?"

"I promise I will protect Apollo." Then Myke added, "You know I would do it anyway—protect him—without the promise. I think Apollo, my enemy, is my best friend. It makes no sense, but Apollo and I are like one... on different sides of this war... but still like one."

"He does that to people," said Megantha. "You can feel his strength. But he's not invincible. He needs you, too."

Myke moved forward and put his head on Megantha's chest, a move of submission and commitment. "I promise I will, Mom. I promise."

Megantha released Myke and moved back, transitioning into more of a business mode. "Okay, boys. You're getting your trip to Sughi City. But before I send you there, you'll be taking a little side trip to visit some physical Bloods."

Apollo and Myke looked at each other in surprise. "Bloods?" they mouthed to each other. What was this?

"You'll be with them for about twelve hours. Then you'll move on to Sughi City."

Apollo thought, *But Bloods don't exist, at least not from this world. How ...?*

"Time travel," said Megantha, interrupting Apollo's thought struggle.

Apollo was trying to absorb, and he could see Myke was equally confused. Apollo had never heard of anybody going on a Blood visit. He knew Megantha could do anything, but ...

"You're going to another world and another time," she said.

Apollo knew time and place were no obstacles to her.

"Ready, boys?" she asked with a knowing smile.

No! thought Apollo. *We're not!* But Apollo could tell it was happening—now.

Megantha made a sweeping motion with her right hand, and everything changed.

29

Pirates

Apollo and Myke were together, transitioning five hundred feet above an ocean different from the one with the lava cave. This ocean was more turquoise, and Apollo could tell the waters were much warmer. The sun was up, but it was early in the day, still well before noon. The air was warm and muggy. Apollo's ghost sensed these changes, even if they did not have the quantitative effect on him that they would on physical Bloods.

Apollo could tell the air was thinner than it was on Summa. There was less gravity. He could travel faster here compared to home. He knew he was not on Summa, and this planet had less mass. It was probably a lot smaller.

Apollo heard a swooshing noise, and the "boys" saw a wooden ship on the waters below. Its sails were full from a medium breeze. Apollo did not know much about sailing, but it looked to him like the ship was sailing directly away from the wind, and Apollo thought how fortunate it was that it needed to go in that same direction.

Apollo and Myke transitioned toward the ship, whose speed was not a challenge. The boys, as ghosts, were much faster. They could see the bow cutting through the waves, sea spray rising, and a wake trailing behind the vessel.

There were people on the ship. "Bloods," Apollo said to Myke. "Real Bloods!"

Myke's eyes were wide with excitement, and he pointed behind them. Apollo followed Myke's view and saw another ship behind the first. It, too, was full-sailed and coming in the same direction. It was about five hundred yards behind. Nothing else, other than the sea, was visible. Wherever Megantha had sent them, they were way out in an ocean with no land in sight.

Closing in on the lead ship, Apollo could see people on the top deck scrambling around in panic, sometimes taking worried glances at the trailing boat. Soon, it was apparent to both Apollo and Myke that this first ship was trying to flee from the other. Men, boys, and a few women were visible. They looked sweaty, tired, and terrified.

Myke wondered why there was so much fear on the lead ship. It was significantly bigger than the one giving chase. It had more masts, and its main deck was much higher off the water. It seemed well protected from the attacker.

As Apollo and Myke watched, they could see people throwing things overboard. *Why?* Wondered Apollo, but only briefly. He and Myke realized the passengers were trying to lighten their ship, wanting it to go faster and escape. The fact that they were willing to throw their possessions into the sea to avoid being caught must mean that being caught was a very bad alternative. Given the size of the ship, Apollo doubted the cargo being thrown overboard would make much difference.

The boys were fascinated at how the Blood people could pick up physical objects, carry them to the railing, and launch them into the sea. All their lives, they had been taught Bloods could do this, and they had seen Olam and Megantha move things. But to see regular Bloods do it was amazing.

One man was struggling with a heavy chest, dragging it across the deck and then trying to leverage it up onto the railing. After considerable effort, he managed to get most of the chest's weight onto the bulwark, but then the ship lurched sideways from a cross wave, and the chest crashed onto the man's shin. It raked downwards and crushed his foot. The man was wearing knee-length knickers, and the sharp edge of the chest scraped the skin off his bone. Blood poured from the gash. The man screamed and then cursed in pain. Myke and Apollo could not understand what he said, but his pain was obvious, as was the blood. Seeing it was intense. They watched as a woman rushed to the man. She helped him clear of the chest and then down onto the deck, forcefully giving him instructions and rushing away. Later, they saw this same woman return and quickly bandage up his leg. Nobody else gave him any help, apparently too focused on efforts they hoped would save them all.

Apollo and Myke moved alongside the running ship, transitioning through the air at an equal speed. They were only about thirty yards off the starboard side, at a height close to the top of the main mast. Nobody on the ship was paying any attention to them. In the ghost world, they would be obvious, but not to Bloods. "It looks like they can't see us," said Myke.

Apollo nodded in agreement, then said, "Let's go check out the other ship." He started towards it, and Myke followed in agreement. It took them about ten seconds to get there.

As they approached, Apollo pointed out that they could move quicker here than on Summa. "Yep," said Myke. This must be a smaller planet." Myke had also paid attention in science class.

The activity on the chasing ship was busy but much more focused. It was not frantic. Only men were visible, as were many weapons—swords mostly, but also spears and grappling hooks tied to long ropes. Apollo watched two men unpack a series of pistols and muskets. Each was wrapped in oily rags. *To protect them from the salty sea air,* Apollo thought.

"Look at that guy," said Myke, pointing to a man on deck who was missing the bottom part of one of his legs. He had an artificial, wooden leg from the knee down. Apollo and Myke could see the wood, but they could also see the ghost leg, the whole thing.

"I wonder if they can see his ghost leg," said Apollo, knowing the answer as soon as he asked the question.

"No way," answered Myke. "Or they could see us, too."

Myke and Apollo went back and forth between the ships for about two hours. It was clear that the attacking ship was going to catch the runner. What was unclear was what the attackers would do with the much larger ship. To board, they'd have to rope climb twenty or thirty feet up its side, all while being shot at from above. The fleeing ship had weapons, too.

Apollo could see that both ships had cannons. The attackers had mounted two of them facing forward on the top deck at the bow of their ship. There were also six cannons on each side, but none in the back. *I guess they're just an attack ship,* thought Apollo. *No need to defend their tail end.*

The fleeing ship had five cannons on each side but none in the back. To Apollo, that seemed like an obvious and crucial weakness, but he also knew that he knew nothing about maritime warfare. The captain of the big ship surely had some tricks up his sleeve.

Despite the cannon advantage of the attackers, Apollo thought the big ship would be challenging prey.

At one point, Apollo and Myke went below the deck of the big ship. As they transitioned through the decks, it was soon obvious why the attackers were so motivated. Down in the ship's hull was a large amount of merchant cargo, including dried foods, tools, clothing, spices, glassware, and many other trade items. Also, there were over a hundred passengers, each with their own belongings.

The "boys" were disturbed to see some children on the fleeing ship. One was a young, grade-school-aged girl who was old enough to know what was happening but too young to do anything about it. An adult woman was trying to hide this child behind some discarded barrels deep in the stern of the ship. That area was dark and wet, with no fresh air and months of filth. Apollo thought most of the below-deck living quarters looked uninhabitable, but the dark corner this terrified girl was being told to endure was worse. She had been wearing a long dress, colored green and blue, but her mother changed her into a dirty pair of men's black pants and a dark top. The girl had long, dark brown hair, and the mother cut it all off into a ragged Tomboy cut. Unfortunately, the girl was still a girl, and a pretty one. She was young enough that she was mostly flat-chested, but Apollo worried about what the attackers might do to her. He could tell Myke was worried, too.

By noon, the attacking ship had caught the runner, staying tight on its back end and out of the line of fire of its side cannons. The men on each ship were taking musket rifle shots at each other. Those on the back of the larger ship had the advantage of high ground, shooting down onto the lower ship with a better angle on the ship's forward decking. They had a dozen long-barreled muzzleloader rifles. The men on the attacking ship had to stay behind cover, especially those at the front operating the two cannons.

The men on the big ship had organized themselves so that there were six shooters, with others doing the musket reloads. Some of the reloaders were boys, not men.

"Pirates," said Apollo loudly to Myke, who was nearby.

"What?" Myke responded with a surprised look. Apollo blurting out that word was out of context.

"Yes," said Apollo. "That's what they call them," said Apollo, pointing at the attacking ship. "Those are pirates! I've been trying to remember the word."

"Whatever," mumbled Myke, much too interested in what was happening to worry about terminology.

Apollo thought of his friend Tamir, who would be proud of Apollo for coming up with the word "pirate" from some language class they'd had together.

The pirate ship was quicker and more maneuverable, and it stayed close to the back of its intended victim. It was close enough that the musket fire from the men on each ship was becoming effective. Some were firing pistols, too, but from what Apollo could tell, hitting anyone from that far with a pistol was pure luck.

Apollo and Myke could see how each side had set up a system with people reloading weapons behind cover and passing ready weapons to shooters who had to briefly expose themselves when firing. Apollo was fascinated with this kind of warfare. It was so different from what he was used to, where you had to personally mix with an enemy to fight them.

One of the men on the big ship was especially impressive. He was no taller than the others, but he was barrel-chested with broad shoulders, and he was strong. Rather than using a muzzleloader, he had a beautiful crossbow. It was ornate with engravings and brass trim. Apollo thought it must be his personal weapon and not from the ship's armory. The man could load it much faster than the rifles. The tip of the front of the pirate ship was only fifty yards away. It was not that far, but it was still difficult to hit a man-sized target while both ships bounced on the seas. Even so, the bowman hit one of the pirates up front, loading the cannons. His arrow hit the attacker in the eye.

Myke and Apollo moved right over to the injured man, horrified and fascinated at the same time. The man was screaming and rolling on the deck, clutching his eye. Two men dragged him behind some protective bulwark. A third man approached—this one seemed to have authority—and he barked orders at a teenage boy, who hurried off and soon returned with a bucket of seawater and some rags. Mr. In-Charge barked again, and they all climbed on top of the injured man, holding him down.

In-Charge forced the wounded man's head firmly against the deck planking. The injured man screamed in protest, but there was no hesitation. In-Charge pulled out the arrow, and the eye came out with it—like a shish kebab. Discarding the arrow and its bloody cargo, he poured seawater into the gaping socket, then soaked a rag and forced it in. The man screamed in agony.

Finally, In-Charge spoke to him in a deep, threatening voice. Apollo and Myke could not understand the words, but the meaning was clear—the ordeal was over. "It's done," he might have been saying. In-Charge then left, leaving the others to wrap the victim's head while the rest of the ship continued its attack.

The attackers working the two cannons at the front of the pirate ship appeared shaken by what had just happened. But soon, they were back at loading and firing. It would take them several minutes to load a cannon, and as they loaded, several pirates held up thick planks of wood to protect the crew from shooters on the big ship. The defense was not perfect, and another pirate was hit in the thigh, this time from a musket ball. He, too, was dragged to cover and treated.

So far, nobody on the big ship had been hit. They were a much more difficult target, being higher and behind better cover. The rear bulwark and railing of the ship were thick enough to stop any musket balls fired by the pirates. It also gave them a more stable firing position.

The forward cannons on the pirate ship were not part of the original ship's layout. The top forward decking at the bow had been widened considerably to accommodate two cannons. The carpentry looked makeshift, but it was doing the job, much to the detriment of the targeted ship.

Each forward cannon on the pirate ship was angled slightly so that, rather than shooting straight forward and damaging the bowsprit and its rigging, they aimed about twenty degrees off-center. Firing the cannons with any accuracy required precise crew coordination. Once a cannon was ready, Myke could see the gun crew signal their status, and the helmsman would steer the ship so the cannon was lined up for a shot. The gun crew would light the cannon, which had a short delay before firing. Despite the difficulties, the pirate crew did well at slamming cannonballs into the back of its prey. Everyone on the back of the big ship knew when one of the cannons was going to go off, and they would duck for cover before the boom.

At first, Apollo thought the pirates were bad shots because they were hitting in the middle of the back of the ship and not high up where they might kill some of the defenders, nor were they hitting low at the water line where they might sink the ship. But after about ten shots, it was clear they wanted to hit in the middle of the stern or back end. Apollo wondered why, and he went inside the big ship to look at the target area. Nobody was back there, not

wanting to be slammed by a fifty-pound metal ball. Some
crew quarters were in the stern, including the captain's. His
dwarfed the others in size and luxury. One ball had ripped
through it, shattering a large mirror and dresser. The room
was covered in wood splinters and dust. Shards of glass were
embedded in the ceiling and walls.

Apollo instinctively knew the target of the cannon
fire could not be the captain or crew quarters. He kept
looking. One level had a food gallery, and a deck near the
waterline had storage for ship repair materials.

Then, Apollo figured it out. Running through each
deck at the ship's rear was a main beam, linkage, and rigging
for the ship's rudder. "Of course," Apollo said to himself.
They're after the rudder! And... given the damage the cannon
shot was having, Apollo could see that unless the big ship
could shake the pirates, it was only a matter of time before
the rudder would be damaged or destroyed. As Apollo
observed, a metal ball slammed into a cross beam supporting
the rudder assembly. It was not enough to render it
inoperable, but a few more lucky shots like that would cause
the captain to lose control of the ship.

30

Save Marika

Apollo could see a man on the upper aft deck of the defending ship, who was probably the captain. He was giving orders, and the crew was taking them seriously. The captain had to know his ship's rudder was on its last legs, and he had to do something different. His boat could not outmaneuver or outrun the pirates. Apollo sensed a change in tactics was coming, and the men on the back of the defending ship suddenly moved to the port side railing, and the captain had his ship make a hard left turn. At the same time, the big ship dropped its main sails. The defender was hoping for a chance to use its five cannons on the smaller ship. Apollo understood that had the captain not dropped the mains, the change in the wind would have pushed the big ship over to starboard to the point that its port-side cannons would be shooting too high to hit the pirate ship.

The pirate ship also made a hard-to-port turn, and now the ships were close and parallel to each other. The big ship's port-side cannons went off. They had been loaded with shot, not ball. The purpose was to kill enemy personnel rather than damage the attacking ship itself. Apollo watched as parts of the pirate ship were shredded. One man in the middle of a shot group disappeared in a splattering of flesh and bone.

The pirate ship did not fire its cannons and kept all its sails up. Now it reversed its turn, hard to starboard, putting it on a collision course with the big ship. As the vessels converged, riflemen on each ship successfully killed and wounded enemies.

Apollo saw that each pirate who was preparing to board had several pistols strapped to his waist. Other pirates were preparing grappling hooks attached to ropes.

The big ship did not have time to reload its cannons before the pirate ship had moved alongside, dropping half its sails as it did so. Now, the pirate ship was so close that the big ship's cannons would only be able to blast at the rigging and masts of the pirate ship and not at the body of the vessel itself.

The pirate ship let go with all its starboard cannons, shooting at point-blank range. The cannons had been preset to aim high at the big ship's gun deck, and they tore it apart.

Smart, thought Apollo.

The attackers began throwing grappling hooks onto the big ship's railing. At least ten of them were thrown, and men started across. The defenders threw some of them back. But it was not easy. With the weight of a man on the rope of the hook, it was hard to pull it away from the railing. The pirates were also pulling on the ropes to keep the hooks in place. One man on the big ship was shot while trying to remove a hook. Another ran and brought back a sword and started hacking at the rope. He ended up being shot in the neck, the first of the defenders on the upper deck to die. Several pirates were shot as they tried to cross over. But there were many more pirates shooting rifles to protect them than riflemen on the big ship defending. It was obvious to Apollo that the pirates were going to board.

The first pirate to cross had great upper-body strength. He pulled himself up so his left arm was on the railing, and he palmed one of his pistols with his right.

Several defenders were in his line of fire, and it did not take much of a shot to hit one of them. The pirate dropped the smoking pistol on deck and grabbed a second one. Ducking for cover as a rifleman shot at him, he then heaved himself up enough to shoot over the railing and hit another defender, sending all the defenders for cover. The pirate climbed over the railing, pulled a saber, and ran around and away from the defenders, maneuvering behind them and taking cover behind a wooden bulwark.

The defenders were starting to panic. There was a threat behind them and the horde in front of them. They knew they had already lost control. But the crossbowman did not panic. He knew that the rear pirate had to be eliminated. He had a pistol and his bow, and Apollo saw him go hunting. There was no time to waste. The bowman clearly was tactically trained, as he efficiently used cover to protect himself each time he cleared a section of the upper deck. Apollo saw another pirate come over the deck. He was shot. But then two more came over, and the four pistols between them took out two defenders. Only two defenders were left, plus the bowman on his hunt, who successfully located the pirate sneaking behind some water barrels, attempting to gain an advantage over the remaining defenders. The crossbowman quickly shot the pirate in the lower back, slowing him down enough that he could then use a saber to take the pirate out, stabbing him repeatedly. To Apollo, it was awful. Finally, the pirate was dead, and Apollo saw his ghost separate from his Blood body. Apollo moved close, and it was apparent the pirate's ghost could see Apollo now that it was separated. The pirate ghost looked evil and seemed angry at Apollo's presence.

"What do you want, you piss-pitner?" scoffed the pirate's ghost to Apollo with menace. Until now, Apollo had not understood anything the Bloods said, but now that the pirate was a ghost, his language was perfectly understandable.

"Why?" is all Apollo could ask. "Why?"

But there was no time for the dead pirate's ghost to respond. He was being pulled away. His time on this planet was done, and he was off to another realm. The ghost moved towards the sky. Slow at first, then faster and faster until it disappeared. Apollo saw the same thing happening to the ghosts of other Bloods dying today. Their dead bodies were strewn all over the decks of the two ships, bleeding and mangled, and their ghosts would rise and be channeled upwards, disappearing into the sky.

Three more pirates had come over the big ship's railing, and the crossbowman shot one of them with a pistol. He reloaded his bow and managed to shoot another one.

The other two defending riflemen were soon killed, as were the boys who had been doing the reloading. The crossbowman fought sword to sword and then hand to hand, but a pirate stabbed him in the back, and another knocked him out with a wooden mallet. The bowman fell with a crumpled thump at the base of the ship's rearmost mast. A pirate daggered him in the heart.

Brutal, ruthless, and so wasteful, thought Apollo.

The crossbowman's ghost rose from the deck, and Apollo rushed over, hoping to feel the power of the man's ghost.

"Are you okay?" asked Apollo, instantly knowing his question was ridiculous. The bowman's ghost did not respond. He seemed dazed and confused but not in pain. It was clear that he immediately understood he was no longer a physical Blood.

Then, a terrified look came over the bowman's face. "My daughter! My daughter, Marika," he said anxiously. "Is she safe?"

The bowman's ghost was talking directly to Apollo, obviously seeing him.

"I don't know who your daughter is," Apollo said. "Let's go down and find her."

The man hesitated, still shaking off the physical and reacquiring his former ghost bearings.

Apollo said with insistence. "Come on, sir! You're not going to have long before you are taken. You need to go now!" Apollo moved towards midship, motioning to the man to follow, ignoring the chaos that continued on deck.

The bowman followed Apollo, and Apollo then pointed down and started to descend through the deck towards the inner midship. The man followed.

"Find her!" ordered Apollo.

The bowman's ghost quickly took over the hunt.

The woman and children below deck were terrified. They could tell there was a lull in the fighting above, and they correctly feared their protectors were dead. So far, the attackers had not come below deck. The bowman transitioned through this terrified misery and eventually found a woman Apollo presumed was his wife. This was the same woman who had hidden the young girl. The bowman tried to speak with his wife and comfort her, but she did not sense his presence. He repeatedly asked her where Marika was, but she could not hear him. "She's back there," said Apollo, pointing to where the woman had hidden the girl earlier.

With Apollo's help, the bowman found Marika. He was overjoyed to see she was still safe. Weeping, he told her how much he loved her and tried to embrace her. Unlike her mother, Marika sensed the presence of her father.

"Papa!" she said through tears. She hugged herself. "Papa!" She lay and curled herself into a fetal position, crying and terrified. "Papa," she said repeatedly, rocking herself and remaining as small as possible in this dark, nasty corner of the ship.

Apollo could see a portal tunnel opening for the bowman. His time had come. He knew it, too. His session in the Blood phase was done. "I love you, Marika," he said, trying to hold her face. Then, as he was pulled into the portal, he turned towards Apollo and pleaded, "Please... please... protect her! My beautiful Marika. Protect her from those awful men. Please." Then the portal closed, and he was gone.

Until now, Apollo had no investment in this fight. But the bowman's request changed everything. Could he save Marika?

"Well?" asked Myke, surprising Apollo, who had no idea Myke was there.

"You heard all that?" asked Apollo.

"Yes. I've been right behind you."

Apollo had been so engrossed in the bowman and Marika that he had no idea Myke had joined them.

"I think we can fight them," said Myke.

"Maybe." Apollo was thinking. "Okay, okay, yes, let's try!"

Apollo was shifting from observational to operational. *Can we fight a physical person who does not know we're there?* He wondered about this. *We have to try!*

No attackers had come down into the lower decks yet. They had been in control up on top for several minutes. Apollo and Myke went up to see why they were delaying.

Apollo also noticed for the first time that as many men who had defended on the upper deck were also waiting below deck, ready to attack anyone who came down the main staircase into the ship's bowels. This was a deadly choke point and a logical strategy for the defenders.

The captain must have known he'd lose to the boarding parties, Apollo surmised. Otherwise, he would have allocated more resources up top. Apollo wondered if the men and boys assigned to fight off the boarders knew they were pawns to be sacrificed. Some probably did. Such bravery. Incredible! Apollo hoped Olam would reward their selflessness.

Apollo saw that the attackers were too experienced to launch headfirst down the main stairway. Instead, they resorted to terror and torture. First, they opened the doorway to the stairs and brought over one of the defenders who was still alive. They tied his hands behind his back and tied his ankles together. Then they tied a long rope around his waist, beat him with a club, and pushed him down the stairs. With the rope, they stopped him halfway down and kept him there while he screamed in agony, which terrorized his loved ones and shipmates below. The attackers kept him out of reach of the defenders and potential rescuers below, and this went on for several minutes. Eventually, the defenders got smart. They broke the legs off a thick table and used it as a protective shield, allowing two of them to work their way up the stairs far enough to cut the man free. But the rescue was a wasted effort. Once it was apparent he would be freed, the attackers shot him several times, and the tortured man died. His screaming stopped, and Apollo watched his ghost leave his body. It was quickly pulled into a portal and vanished. Compared to the bowman's ghost, who had been given time to see his wife and daughter, this man was taken almost immediately. Apollo did not know why. Maybe he did not deserve that small mercy.

The attackers switched tactics to gain access to the lower decks. They shut one of the two doors to the stairwell and started throwing burning, oily rags down the open one. Then they shut that one, too. Apollo wondered how smart that was because it seemed like they risked burning the whole ship down. But it was quickly apparent that the panic of the people below dwarfed any such concerns. They had to put the rags out quickly or be smoked out.

The attackers went to one of the ship's smaller sails, lathered it up with some greasy oil, lit it on fire, and then stuffed it down the stairs. Apollo went below and could see that this was working. There was too much fire to put out without a bucket fire line, and the smoke was becoming intense. Apollo went back to where Marika was hiding. She'd covered her face with something her mother gave her. She was safe for now.

The defenders below had no choice but to rush up the stairs. Some of them severely injured the attackers, even killing a few of them. Two of them managed to fight through the pirates and scramble overboard, putting their fates in the hands of the warm seas. But it was not long before the pirates had control of the stairs and the main deck.

Following the defenders, some of the older women came up. The attackers herded them to one side of the deck. Children followed them, and then younger adult women. There were about ten of them, and these were stripped naked and lined up against a central bulwark. They were humiliated and terrified, forced to stay there at sword point.

"We need to do something now," said Apollo.

"Let's see who's in charge and attack him," said Myke.

"Pretty sure it's that guy," said Apollo, pointing at a big man to whom all attackers seemed to look for guidance. He looked better fed than the others, with a respectable belly, big belt buckle, sturdy shoes, and loads of unkempt facial hair. His second-in-command was Mr. In-Charge, who had pulled the arrow and the shish kebab eye out of the injured pirate.

The boss pirate broke from the others and walked to the naked women. He had the first pick. He made his choice, grabbed her by the back of the neck, and put a knife to her throat. She whimpered but complied as he walked her off to another part of the ship. There was no doubt that he would slice her up if she resisted, and maybe he'd do it anyway when done. Her pale skin flushed with horror at what was coming.

"Now!" yelled Myke, and he and Apollo rushed the boss, unsure what would happen. They were both experienced fighters, but that was with ghosts. Can you fight a ghost that's locked into a Blood? Could they take control of this evil man's physical being by attacking his inner ghost? Neither knew, but they had to try.

Once inside the man, Apollo could feel the boss's ghost, but the boss's Blood was overwhelmingly powerful. It seemed there was no way to make it do anything it didn't want to. But even as Apollo thought this, the boss stopped in his tracks and shook his head, still keeping a firm grip on the girl and the knife. Somehow, Apollo thought he, too, could feel the knife and the girl. Physically feel them. It was faint... but there. "I can feel what he's doing!" yelled Apollo.

"Me too," said Myke. "A little. But I can't begin to control him."

The boss shook off the weirdness inside him and continued forward with his human spoils. Apollo could sense that the man had no regard for the woman beyond his own physical satisfaction.

"We need a better plan, Myke. We're not going to stop him."

Myke and Apollo dug at the man's essence, looking for a weakness. The man's subatomic ghost was insulated by the mass and power of his physical Blood. Myke and Apollo's efforts seemed puny.

But despite their frustrations, they were having some effect. The boss stopped again, shook his head, and pulled his knife hand back from the girl's throat long enough to wipe his eyes on his forearm.

"You try to attack his brain, Myke!" said Apollo. "I'm going for his heart."

Help me, Sapienti! Apollo implored. *Help me know what to do!*

Apollo tried to explode with power inside the boss pirate's chest. Screaming at the man's ghost, Apollo exerted as much outward force as possible, trying to completely overwhelm its essence. But the man's ghost/Blood combination was powerful. How could he fight this?

Boss Pirate had pulled the woman to a secluded part of the top deck. He threw her hard to the ground, and Apollo heard her heels, buttocks, and head all slam to the wooden planking. The impact to her head left her dizzy, and Apollo sensed satisfaction on the part of the pirate. He was enjoying hurting her.

Now that Apollo was part of the pirate, he also felt satisfaction, which amazed him. It was like the power of the pirate's physical Blood was overpowering Apollo more than he was trying to overpower it. He liked it in the wrong kind of way. Apollo could sense the evil intoxication. How incredible the physical Blood experience must be.

The boss pirate did not bother taking off his shirt or boots. He looked filthy. He undid his giant belt buckle.

"Come on, Myke!" yelled Apollo.

"Let's both attack his brain, A.P.," Myke yelled.

Apollo agreed and moved into Myke's space. It was like he was fighting Myke, but it also wasn't. They were inside each other, but also inside the evil man. They churned and yelled and tried their best to confuse.

It worked. The boss pirate stopped what he was doing. He dropped the knife and started to wobble around. He stumbled towards the ship's railing, leaning against it, holding his head.

Apollo had a flash of inspiration. "Keep fighting, Myke! I have an idea."

Apollo rushed into the young woman's brain." He tried to get inside her and into her ghost. "Now is your chance, he yelled to her... now, now, now! Push him over the railing. Do it now!"

All Apollo needed was to implant a faint impression of the idea in the woman's conscience. She had a small window to execute. But would she? Was she a fighter like Torith? Could she step through her fear?

Apollo could feel her terror. He could feel the physical pain in her head from smacking the deck. A lot would depend on her personality. "Come on!" he yelled at her ghost. "Now, now, now! Push him over the rail."

Apollo felt the woman reset. A rage rose from her core. Then, she surprised Apollo. Rather than slam the boss pirate, she swooped up his knife, rushed him, and stabbed him repeatedly in the stomach and chest. The pirate was too confused by Myke's continued onslaught to resist. The woman stopped and looked at him, amazed that he did not fight back. She then looked around to see if anybody had seen what she did, but she and the filthy pirate were still hidden.

"Push him over... now!" Apollo tried to yell at her ghost. "Hurry, before he falls to the deck!"

The message got through. She backed up a few steps, lowered her shoulder, and charged. She hit him like a fullback, and the boss pirate went over the railing, tumbling to the sea. This was on the opposite side of the ship from where the pirate ship was attached. Nobody saw him go over, and with his stomach stabs, he could not cry for help.

Apollo went down to the water and followed the man's body as it floated away, face down. Apollo wanted to see the ghost of the man he had helped kill.

The knife wounds inflicted by the girl would be fatal. So would floating face down in the ocean. Either way, he would die. Five minutes later, death's job was complete, and Apollo saw the boss pirate's ghost separate and come out. Apollo was right there, angry with this horrible person. Apollo moved directly into the pirate's face and yelled at him. "I did that to you! You scum! You are dead because of me, and you deserve it. You child of hell. May you burn forever!"

Apollo thought his yelling at the dead boss would be powerful. But it only made him feel small. *I killed a man! This was not a temporary flatline. It was permanent death. I took away his agency!* Apollo watched as the pirate's ghost rose towards the sky and disappeared.

The sea, the ship, and the horror of the last hour all blurred away as Apollo looked inside himself. What would Megantha say about the killing? Why did she send us here?

Apollo was shaken back to action by Myke. "Come on, Apollo. We need to check on Marika! Forget about that dead man! We have to go. Come on!"

Apollo shoved the killing into a mental corner. He would deal with it later, and he followed Myke into the ship's body to find the girl. Protecting Marika, the bowman's daughter, was imperative. Apollo was sick of death and wanted to leave, but he had to act.

Inside the ship, it was pure confusion. There were frequent skirmishes between pirates and any males over the age of ten. Some would give up, only to be killed. Others were spared. There was no order or reason to it. Parts of the inside of the ship had been damaged by the point-blank broadside from the pirates' cannons. There were body parts and the mangled dead everywhere.

Hunting parties of pirates were going through the ship, deck by deck, assessing the spoils and looking for stragglers. Women and children who were not assaulted were herded into various sections of the ship, huddling on the floors, terrified of what would happen next. They needed little controlling. There wasn't anywhere for them to go unless they wanted to fight and be killed.

Myke and Apollo found Marika. She was still safely hidden. They wished they could comfort her.

"What did you do to the pirate boss, Myke?" Apollo asked. "You totally had him confused. How did you do that? I didn't think I was affecting him at all."

"I don't know. Maybe we can't tell what we are doing because their Bloods are so strong. He could have ignored us if he'd wanted to... or at least sloughed us off as an annoyance."

"Maybe it depends on the Blood," Apollo said.

"Could be," Myke responded.

A pirate hunting party was working towards Marika's hiding area, and the boys switched back to tactical. They surveyed the men. The one in front was their leader, and there were three others with him. Both Myke and Apollo rushed the leader to churn at his inner ghost. The pirate stopped and shook himself. He grimaced, and Apollo could feel him forcing himself to concentrate. He also looked around and brought up his pistol, threatening whatever was attacking him. He fought against the enemy inside him. The leader pirate then did with his Blood what Myke and Apollo were doing to his ghost. He growled and projected himself outward, attacking Myke and Apollo and trying to eject them. Somehow, this man knew he was being possessed and wanted nothing to do with it. His reaction was much different and stronger than the boss pirate's had been. His Blood was too powerful. Myke and Apollo had to extricate themselves.

"Holy smokes," said Myke, who looked beat up. "That guy manhandled our menapses!"

"No kidding," Apollo responded, shaking his head. "Let's try somebody else. We need to shake them."

They picked the pirate in the back. He appeared weak and unkempt. He was skinny and had a facial wound that appeared to be recent. And he had no pistol, only a sword. It looked like he was at the bottom of the pirate food chain, and Myke and Apollo hit his ghost hard.

They had immediate success. The wounded face pirate stopped in his tracks and recoiled in terror. Then he screamed and looked around for the evil spirits attacking him.

"This guy is vermin!" yelled Myke as he frantically churned and hammered at the weakling.

Sensing victory, Apollo projected harder and harder onto the pirate's ghost, trying to put confusion and fear into him. It worked. Between the two of them, Apollo and Myke totally destroyed the man, who crumpled into a heap, yelling, wide-eyed, and terrorized.

The strong leader pirate stopped the search and came back to Wounded Face, looking down on him in disgust. He yelled at the man and pointed down the dark hull cavity they had been searching. He then pointed to himself. He made a symbol of strength and fighting back. Apollo and Myke could not understand his words, but it was clear the pirate was saying he'd been attacked too and fought it off. Wounded Face needed to suck it up and fight, too.

Wounded Face was now scared of the evil spirits and the leader pirate, who kicked Wounded Face in the buttocks and gestured for him to get up. Wounded Face did, cowering. Then the strong pirate took another look down the dark hull cavern where Marika was hiding. Something bad was down there, and there were plenty of other gold mines on the ship. He pulled his crew out, and they set off another way. Myke and Apollo knew they had won, at least for now.

After a few hours, pirates and prisoners settled into unwritten routines. Women who were old enough to be mothers of the pirates were mostly given their freedom. They started to care for the wounded, both pirates and passengers. The pirates allowed a few of the big ship's mess crew their freedom, with the idea that they would use the mothers to do most of the work and distribution of food. Despite the pirates' ruthlessness, they and everybody had to eat. Pirates ate well. Passengers and prisoners, much less so. Water had to be distributed, and people needed to be escorted to potty holes.

This obviously was not the first ship the pirates had raided. Captors and prisoners all fell into their roles. Small children were allowed to roam but were swatted if they got in the way. Apollo was surprised that, as ruthless as the pirates had been, there had been no deliberate killing of small children. Even filthy pirates had some sense of restraint.

Able-bodied teenagers and men who were still alive were formed into portage chains. The pirates began systematically looting the ship, transferring anything of value to their ship. The pirates also organized a crew to dump dead bodies overboard. Sometimes, this included the seriously wounded. Women would wail as the bodies of their loved ones were taken away. They would wail harder for the near-dead who, moaning in pain, were dumped, too. There were no funerals.

As night fell on the ocean, lanterns were lit, and the alcohol came out. The day's work was done, and the pirates began to drink. Some of the ship's cargo was expensive wine, and it was distributed freely to all pirates. Apollo saw that even Wounded Face was given multiple bottles, which meant every pirate was drinking as much as he wanted. By nightfall, with the ship firmly under control, most pirates were basking in an alcoholic stupor.

And that's when it happened. From deep within the ship, thirty men emerged, armed to the teeth and ready to take back their vessel. The big ship's captain had been killed—Apollo had seen the boss pirate execute him—but evidently, the captain had laid down a plan to save the ship, and now the plan was going into effect. These thirty men looked strong and well-fed. Each had pistols and swords. They started to work their way through the drunken pirates. Death was swift and ugly as they exacted revenge.

Myke and Apollo watched them clear some of the lower decks, mainly using swords to keep things quiet. There would be more resistance as they went to the upper decks.

Apollo was looking forward to seeing Marika's area secured. But that was not to be.

A portal opened. This one was not for the dead. It was for Apollo and Myke. They were drawn into it and soon found themselves floating in the night air above the ships. The vessels were still tied together, and Myke and Apollo could see movement on both top decks.

Two moons were aloft in the night sky. One was full, and the other showed three-quarters. Their light bounced off the ocean and lit the ships in shades of gray. Apollo wished he could stay here long enough to see if the counterattack would succeed. Would Marika be saved? Apollo looked at Myke, who was sure to be wondering the same thing. Then, the boys were taken, and the ships were gone.

31

Sughi City

Apollo and Myke were sprung from the sea battle to Mount Merritt, twenty miles east of Sughi City. Mount Merritt's summit consisted of three rocky peaks, all at about the same height of eight thousand feet. This was seven thousand feet higher than Sughi City at one thousand feet. The elevation difference was impressive.

Only two of Mount Merritt's peaks were "peaks" in the traditional sense. These rose to definite, pointed summits. The middle peak was very much the opposite. It was a geological wonder in that it was a flat surface, made of solid rock, hundreds of yards in diameter. From Sughi City, its one-dimensional flatness looked surreal.

Everybody referred to Mount Merritt as "Flat Top" because of the unusual middle peak. Flat Top was a primary reference point for ghosts giving directions or orienting themselves in Sughi City. It was a perfect place for Megantha to have sprung Apollo and Myke, giving them a place to breathe and recover after what they had been through with the pirates on another planet's faraway ocean.

The boys processed as they looked down towards Sughi City. "Do you think Marika made it?" Apollo asked Myke.

"Probably. It looked like the attack team was taking it to the pirates. I hope they killed every one of them."

Apollo almost answered in agreement, but then checked his response. *Was it right for him to wish for the death of the pirates? Even if the pirates were killers themselves?* Then Apollo asked, "Did you see if Marika's mom was still alive?"

"Yep," said Myke. "She survived. I even saw her sneak food to Marika."

Apollo was relieved. He wanted Marika to live—for her sake—and for the sake of her brave father, who died to protect her. Apollo hoped he could be as courageous as the crossbowman.

Neither of the "boys" was in a hurry to move on to Sughi City. It was going to be an intense time for both of them. "I'll take care of you down there," said Myke.

"I know," said Apollo. "You promised Megantha, but you'd do it regardless." Apollo knew he and Myke were now tightly bonded, even if they were on opposite sides of the Sughi/Olam conflict.

They stayed on Flat Top for another thirty minutes, recharging physically and emotionally. They talked about how smart Megantha had been to send them where she did. Her choice of putting them into a life-and-death conflict, far out at sea, gave them intense exposure to a critical Blood environment without showing anything about broader Blood society or its living conditions. Apollo and Myke had no idea of the types of cities the ship goers had come from or their societal structures and politics. It had put both of them in a very narrow operational theater, intense with a life-and-death conflict.

"That Megantha," said Myke. "She's crafty."

Apollo agreed, then commented, "In the physical world, there are so many ways to die. You can be shot, drowned, stabbed, starved, crushed, frozen... and it goes on and on!"

Myke nodded.

"And there's no escape. You can't fly away like we can. If pirates attack, you have to fight. If you're thrown into the sea, you swim till you drown. If you're on a cliff and pushed, you're done. There are so many ways it can go bad."

Apollo was stating the obvious, and Myke did not need to respond.

They were silent for another ten minutes. They could have checked the time on a comm, but they could tell from the sun it was probably early afternoon. "Let's go," said Myke. "Time to start the show." At that, Myke began to move—slowly at first, to make sure Apollo was coming—and then at regular speed toward Sughi City.

Apollo followed close behind, tense and apprehensive. *Into the belly of the beast I go*, he thought as he shifted into warrior mode, gearing up for anything.

Much of Sughi City's buildings had been built by a Forza named Pacifica, under the direction and assistance of Megantha. Pacifica had been a house sister to B. Z. Sughi. She was quite a bit older, but they still lived together for years while Sughi was a young child. Given that Pacifica was a Forza, Apollo was sure she would have been a wonderful older sister to Sughi, but he had no idea how their relationship was now. He doubted it could be as good as his and Celti's. Sughi was aggressively fighting Olam, which would break Pacifica's heart. Celti, on the other hand, was not actively fighting against Olam, even if she strongly disagreed with Olam and Megantha's plan for Blood life.

Pacifica had designed the city as a coordinated community environment, featuring many multi-unit dwellings separated by generous open spaces that included gardens, parks, small forests, and lakes. The bulk of each building was underground, like icebergs. This allowed for much open space at ground level while keeping the living and working spaces close to each other. Many of these buildings extended hundreds of feet underground. They each had extensive, well-lit open spaces inside, such as expansive common rooms, tall and wide hallways, and large, majestic fountains. There was nothing claustrophobic about the city's design, above or below ground. It was magnificent.

Sughi City looked more like a rural community than a political and military power center. To say the city had an understated look would be exactly that: an understatement.

As Apollo and Myke approached and transitioned over the city, the city looked calm and appealing, very much in contrast to how Apollo felt.

Apollo knew most people living in Sughi City strongly favored B. Z. Sughi's views. The rest either kept quiet or made it clear they did not care. Few, if any, would openly favor Olam or Diamond's plan. To do so would invite disdain or attack. Apollo would never want to live here, but here he was. Despite Myke's promise to protect Apollo, Apollo was under no illusion about the next several weeks. There would be skirmishes or all-out battles. Apollo and Myke might be lions, but enough hyenas can eat a lion. Even with Myke's protection, he was not safe.

Apollo and Myke were running at about five hundred feet above the ground. Myke slowed and then pointed downwards to a sky-blue building ringed by a grassy park with a few trees. That park was, in turn, ringed by a blue lake. "There," said Myke. "I'm sure that's our building," and Myke headed for it.

If Myke was correct, Apollo was happy because the building would be easy for him to find as he worked out his bearings in this unusual city. The sky-blue color and the ring-upon-ring configuration were distinctive and should be easy to locate from altitude.

They stopped at the entrance to the building, and
Myke touched a comm embedded in the wall. Apollo noticed
signage saying the building was named "Azure," probably
due to its color. "Welcome, Myke and Apollo," wrote the
comm. It also told them what rooms they were in. Myke was
assigned the Dolphin Room, and Apollo was in Stingray.
Great, thought Apollo. He had always liked stingrays. The
word was as compelling as the animal itself. Both rooms
were five floors down. The building's main doors opened,
and they headed in.

The entryway consisted of a landing and then fifty
stairs down to a lower level. There, the building expanded
underground into a large foyer. In the center of the foyer was
a majestic glass fountain that looked like water frozen in
time. The foyer had benches and tables, making for natural
places to relax or congregate in small groups. At one end was
a lit hallway that went straight down—no stairs this time—
which was the usual way to get to the lower floors. It would
be rude not to take the hallway and run the risk of
transitioning through personal space assigned to others.

They found Myke's room first. Apollo looked inside,
and on one of the walls, there was a large screen playing
footage of dolphins swimming, surfing, jumping, and
hunting. The screen could be turned off or dimmed as
desired. It could also be controlled to show endless other
scenes, such as mountains, jungle animals, polar bears,
extreme weather, waterfalls, or even real-time views of
certain public places in Sughi City and many other locations
on Planet Summa. The room had no washroom, as there was
no need. But for aesthetics, it had a nice table and chairs, a
couch, a bed, and some other furniture. The room was lit via
a ceiling with a default mode of projecting the same sky that
was outside the building. If it were bright and clear outside,

so was the ceiling. If it were dark and stormy, the ceiling looked the same, even projecting raindrops, snow, or any other precipitation. Dark, clear nights showed the same on the ceiling, including the stars in the same patterns and movements as outside. Like the wall projecting the dolphins, the ceiling could be turned off, dimmed, or adjusted to show other things, such as solid colors, at any desired level of brightness. Some ghosts preferred total darkness when rejuvenating, and the room could easily be set to one hundred percent lights out.

Apollo's room was three rooms down the hall from Myke's, and it was the same setup but with an ocean stingray theme. Myke took a look and nodded his approval, and then he headed back to his room. While leaving, he told Apollo they had a meeting in two hours, suggesting that Apollo get some rest. "It's a routine discussion group type meeting. There will probably be several hundred to a thousand people there, with more attending via comm, so you should not stand out. But if somebody starts to bother you, I'll get in their face until they back off. And we can leave anytime you want."

In his room alone, Apollo wanted to check in with Tamir and Torith to let them know he was okay. But first, he used his B-Channel to talk with Megantha. She could have come in person, but there was no need. It was quick, and Apollo told her he loved her and thanked her for the time he and Myke had spent with the Bloods. Megantha asked Apollo not to say much to Tamir and Torith about his Blood experience. "That was for you and Myke," she explained.

Apollo understood. "It's a lot to absorb, Mom."

"As it was meant to be," she said.

"But Mom... I killed a man... or helped kill him. Did I do the right thing?" Apollo doubted she would answer the question directly, but she surprised him.

"The man you killed is not some man. He's your brother, Apollo, and I love him as much as I love you."

Apollo now felt terrible.

"His ghost name is Jacob. He fought hard against Sughi here on Summa. But when he was sent to his earth, he lost his way and fought hard for Sughi. He has broken my heart."

Apollo could feel the pain in his mother's voice. "I'm sorry, Mom, for what he became. But I had no choice. I had to kill him... didn't I?"

"Yes, son. You did the right thing. Your sister, Sarah—the one you saved—will have the chance to thank you someday."

Apollo was relieved, then asked, "What about the little girl, Marika? Did we save her?"

Megantha did not answer that question, telling Apollo the day would come when Marika would tell him herself.

Apollo's conversation with Megantha was sobering. Thankfully, it also left him at peace. Apollo then used his B-Channel to send one-way messages to Tamir and Torith, telling them he had arrived safely. Sometime in the future, he would tell them he'd been in battle on an ocean with Bloods. But for now, he needed to rest and prepare for whatever was coming when he went out with Myke.

For an hour, Apollo put the room in dark mode, and he tried to use the time to shut himself down. He and most ghosts could put themselves into a quasi-sleep mode, where they were aware of their surroundings but not engaging. Some ghosts could detach into a total meditative trance. Not Apollo. He had too much trouble shutting off his brain, and this afternoon, he randomly drifted back to a time he had been with his sister, Celti.

32

Celti and the Beetle

Apollo's sleepy mind took him back to years ago when he and Celti were out on one of her excursions to hunt for animals. They were miles from home in a relatively arid area, working their way through a sandy wash. The wash was in the bottom of a shallow canyon, and the surrounding soil was nutrition-starved, supporting only scrub, sagebrush, and small, hardy plants. The wash itself had no vegetation other than scattered wisps of dry, juvenile grass.

In the middle of the wash sat a triangular-shaped boulder, its pointed end facing upstream. When water rushed through, the boulder split the flow smoothly—until the current rejoined at its downstream edge in a turbulent collision. The resulting eddies churned and carved into the sand, forming a steep-sided hole behind the boulder. And in that hole, trapped and unable to climb out, Apollo and Celti found a large black beetle.

The shiny bug was a Blood. Its mass was hundreds of thousands of times more than Apollo's subatomic ghost. Neither he nor Celti could do anything to help the creature escape its predicament. They watched as the beetle's long, spindly legs worked and worked at the sand, moving the fine, granular rock but doing little to promote a climb to safety.

Apollo felt bad for the beetle, but Celti became frantic. She insisted they call Mom, but Mom would not come. She called Dad, and he said no as well. She tried Diamond and Sapienti, but neither would help her.

Apollo did not understand why all four said no. It would have only taken a flash for one of them to pick up the bug and send it on its way. Why not do that? More importantly, why not do it for Celti? She was crying and extremely distraught. The beetle would die. Water flow in the wash might save it, but no rain was predicted for days. Celti checked.

Celti and Apollo went home, and Apollo heard Celti pleading with Mom for hours to save the beetle. Mom gave little explanation for why it was still no, except to say that Bloods died. It was part of the process. Apollo was surprised Mom would not offer more.

The next day, Celti was finally able to convince her Mentor to help her. Mentors do not have the ability to touch, hold, and move physical things like Quasars, but compared to SunStar ghosts like Apollo and Celti, they were much more powerful. Celti clung to the hope that her Mentor could figure something out.

Apollo loved Celti, but he deliberately chose to be needed elsewhere and not go back with her. Dramos had warned Apollo it was not going to end well. "Things die," Dramos said. "Celti needs to learn that."

Dramos was right because when Celti and the Mentor found the beetle, it was at the bottom of the sandy hole, on its back, legs sticking up, dried out and dead.

Celti came home and went straight to her room. She was quiet and withdrawn for the next several days. Apollo felt bad for the beetle, but he had moved past it. Celti, however, did not.

33

Outdoor Debate

Apollo and Myke left the Azure building and headed west. Myke took them up to one thousand feet, giving them a good perspective on where they were going. Behind them was Flat Top, and it was late afternoon. Myke had a comm that was giving him directions. Like Apollo, Myke had never been to Sughi City, so neither of them knew their way around. After about five minutes, Myke released the comm and pointed down to a horseshoe-shaped lake that partially surrounded an outdoor amphitheater. The seating levels of the amphitheater were made of gray and pink marble, layered into the ground, and spacious enough to accommodate several thousand people.

Myke and Apollo arrived only a few minutes before the meeting started. Apollo guessed about five hundred people were in attendance, and more were coming.

Apollo and Myke settled into the crowd, positioning themselves in an open area on one of the marble step levels toward the bottom of the amphitheater. Nobody paid any attention to them beyond courtesy greetings. Soon, a man stood up in front and announced he was the moderator and there to encourage discussion. He asked that people feel free to express themselves. "We are here to share ideas, and we'll not always agree. Be polite," he said with authority. He also explained that the discussion topic was Sughi's plan versus Olam's.

Of course, thought Apollo. *What else would it be?*

A middle-aged woman with long, dark hair and a bushy aura stood up and began to speak. The acoustics of the amphitheater were excellent. As long as people were quiet, she could be heard well. She expressed concern about the Sughi side versus Olam's. She said that even if most people wanted Blood life the Sughi way, Olam would never allow it. "We're wasting our time," she said. "We can blah-blah-blah all we want. We can delude ourselves by living here in Sughi City. But if Olam wants horror and mayhem when we are physical beings, there's nothing we can do about it. B. Z. Sughi is strong, but his power is nothing like Olam's."

Apollo thought the woman had a good point. Not because he agreed with her Sughi views but because he knew Olam would never, in the end, allow for Sughi's plan to go forward. Olam was not going to have Diamond head up a plan that was wrong. This concept was frustrating for Apollo, and he often spoke with Reemo about it. He had tried to talk to both Megantha and Olam about it, but both were purposefully vague with him, telling Apollo that agency applied here as ghosts just as it would later as Bloods... and that because of that agency, people could follow Olam, Sughi, or whomever they wanted. "Right," Apollo would say, "but how can it be agency here? We all know that your plan is going to win. How can it be agency if we already know the outcome?" And that is where both Olam and Megantha would tell Apollo they loved him, but they were not going to explain it further. So, Apollo would talk with Reemo about it because at least there could be a discussion, even if it were partially speculative. Reemo admitted the concept was unclear to him, too, and he did not have a good answer. Like Apollo, Reemo could not understand why people chose to follow Sughi when they knew they would lose in the end.

"Of course," Reemo had said to Apollo. "When you and I say they will 'lose,' what does that mean to them?"

This question by Reemo was a good one. Reemo continued, "A lot of the Sughis say they prefer to stay as ghosts rather than go to be Bloods in a world with Olam's conditions. B. Z. Sughi seems to be promoting that himself. He says that if the only way to be a physical Blood is Olam's way, then it would be better to remain in our Ghost phase."

"I've heard that too," Apollo had told Reemo. "And it sounds like B. Z. is more than happy to be the boss of all the ghosts who stay that way."

"Right," said Reemo. "The B. Z. Man is not stupid. He has to know it's Olam's way or no way. So maybe he's really after control of ghosts who refuse to move to the Blood phase."

The woman with the black hair continued to speak. Myke moved close to Apollo's ear and urgently said, "Heads up, A.P. Check out those two guys over on the far left, upper row."

The "guys" Myke was referring to had just arrived, and they were not acting as if they were part of the regular crowd. Both were looking at a comm and then over the audience. Apollo wondered if they had a photo of him and were trying to find him. Apollo kept an eye on the two without being obvious. Soon, he could see that they had started to focus on someone off to one side, away from Apollo and Myke. *They must be after somebody else,* Apollo thought.

The men moved to a woman and positioned themselves on each side of her, invading the space of those next to her who moved out of the way. This woman had short, somewhat spiked red hair. Her aura glowed bright with nervousness as she was now their target. Apollo could not tell if she was confident or scared. But as Apollo watched, it became apparent they were asking the woman questions, as if trying to obtain information, but not confronting or interrogating her.

"Who are those guys?" Apollo asked Myke.

"I think they're Intels," said Myke. "I wonder what they want?"

Apollo knew there were "Intels" in Sughi City. They were not enforcers or police, but they were information gatherers. Diamond Command had Intels, too, although their roles were more in the background. Not cooperating with an Intel in Sughi City could lead to more aggressive action on the part of the Sughi establishment. It was a smart move on the part of the Sughis to have Intels gather information. They were not threatening like a Sughi soldier or enforcer. You could be next to an Intel in line somewhere and think little of it, whereas being next to a Sughi enforcer made people nervous.

The woman and the two Intels moved from the crowd to an upper and more isolated part of the amphitheater. The woman's aura had dimmed, and whatever was going on between them looked routine and likely had nothing to do with Apollo.

Down on the amphitheater floor, the woman with long, dark hair sat down, and a male and female couple started talking about the amount of pain and suffering Bloods would need to be tested properly. The man and woman were both in favor of pain, but there had to be restrictions. Take young children, for example. Their suffering from extreme pain taught them nothing. Why was Olam going to allow it? The couple said children would have to die and suffer some, but there was no place or need for a two-year-old to be burned alive, crushed, starved to death, raped, or seriously abused. Such terrors served nothing. "But Olam doesn't care about that!" they said. "He's happy to sit by and let it happen! Sughi wouldn't. He says his plan would not stand for it!"

"What about the adults who commit such atrocities?" asked a man from the audience. "Aren't they being tested?"

The couple agreed they were, but said those adults could be tested in other ways. Sughi's plan would prevent these depraved adults from any such action. Besides, they argued, most adults who willingly torture or abuse children are mentally ill. Olam would let these degenerate people run around with their agency and torture babies, and then Olam would let them off totally free because they did not know what they were doing. That's insanity on all levels! Sughi would never allow it!

Apollo had heard many versions of this same argument. Its conclusion always was that full, unrestricted agency should never be allowed. There had to be controls. Protecting the little children seemed obvious, but where to place controls after that was all over the map. Another area was severely handicapped children. Why have them suffer any pain? It seemed unnecessary. The couple down on the floor tried to make the point that severely mentally handicapped Bloods, even if adults, were really just children and should not have to suffer pain. There was a healthy amount of back-and-forth discussion about this.

Apollo was surprised that the conversation had remained reasonably civil. *Not bad for Sughis,* he thought.

The next person to take the floor was a mature man with bright blue eyes. There was a gentle, disarming look to him. "Look," he said, "we may disagree with Olam and Diamond's free-for-all terror and mayhem, but it's still supposed to be a test, and it needs to be a hard test. To be fair, everyone should live the same number of years. Fifty years, for example."

Mr. Blue Eyes' idea was not new, but it was controversial. "We can't control everything," someone yelled out.

"Right," responded Blue Eyes. "But if we're going to control, let's do the best job possible. I don't see anything wrong with a lot of control, as long as the test is hard and a good test of character. People have to live to a certain age. A boy who dies at the age of two never gets tested."

"Yes, but everybody is different," said someone. "Maybe living to thirty is plenty of time for one person. Say they are terribly sick, and given their character, they've been fully tested. And say they have a terrible, painful disease. In your world, they would have to suffer for another twenty years until they are fifty and can finally die. That's not right!"

Apollo was interested in how contentious the audience became with Blue Eyes and his age-of-death topic. *It's all irrelevant,* Apollo thought. *Olam is never going to agree to restrictions on age of death, or to any of the other limitations they are talking about.*

The next Sughis to stand up were two women who addressed Apollo's thoughts directly. They argued that even though they agreed with some of the limits discussed today, Olam would never allow them.

Someone responded that if Olam loved us, he would, and many in the audience loudly agreed. "It's what we want, and it's not unreasonable," said another. We have our agency!"

By the end of the two-hour meeting, nothing had been resolved. As the crowd started to disperse, Myke and

Apollo stayed put for a few minutes to see if anyone was waiting and watching them. Nobody seemed interested.

Apollo knew Myke probably agreed with some of what the Sughis had said in the meeting. But more than anything, he seemed to have disdain for them, and Apollo asked him about that while they waited for the crowd to clear.

"A lot of them are making excuses," Myke said. "They are weak. They think they can't handle Olam's plan, so they are looking for an easier way. They talk about wanting to protect innocent children. They mostly want to protect themselves."

Apollo understood why Myke would feel that way. He had been a Mentor. That was no small accomplishment. Whatever Myke's problems were with Olam, they were not because he was afraid.

Apollo doubted it would take long for Sughi's intelligence personnel to pick up on the fact that Apollo was in town. "Don't you have to tell them we're here?" Apollo asked. "Or... maybe you already did?"

"I'm going to let them figure it out," said Myke.

"Yes, but won't they chew you out for not reporting?"

"Probably," Myke said, looking far off and smiling slightly. "I don't care if they have a conniption. They'll do their yelling, and then it'll be over."

Apollo sensed that Myke had little respect for Sughi's Command structure. "Won't they suspect I've turned you?"

"I'll tell them I think I am turning you, Apollo. That's the reason they let me bring you to Sughi City in the first place. They won't know what to think, which is good because they won't know what to do."

After the meeting, Apollo and Myke headed back to the Azure building. They made no plans for the rest of the day. Apollo went out briefly several times. He stayed local. Mostly, he stayed in his room to process the last twenty-four hours. There was a lot. He also used a comm and his B-Channel to write down some of his thoughts about the time he and Myke spent on the ocean with the pirate attack, and he documented his first impressions of Sughi City.

Apollo was grateful for Megantha's clarity that his role in killing Jacob, the pirate, was not wrong. *I killed my brother,* thought Apollo. There was nothing sweet about it, even if it had been the right thing to do.

Apollo wrote about watching ghosts rise out of the bodies of Bloods who had died. He was fascinated by how, as Bloods, they could not see Apollo, and they spoke another language. However, as soon as a person returned to being a ghost, they could see and speak perfectly.

Apollo also wrote about how different Bloods responded to his and Myke's attempts to control their actions. They could partially control the boss pirate—enough for Sarah to kill him. They could do nothing with the squad leader hunting Marika. He threw them out like rotten trash. And then there was the weak pirate with the wounded face who crumpled in terror. Each resisted differently.

Finally, Apollo pondered in his writing about the fear Bloods had of the endless things that could hurt or kill them. The fear was justified and so different from being a ghost, where death did not exist. For the physical Blood body, staying alive would be the most basic of driving forces. Apollo could see why some Sughi followers had no interest in moving beyond the Ghost phase.

34

Day Two in Sughi City

It was day two in Sughi city, and Apollo doubted it would be as calm as the first one. Apollo and Myke went to a large stone plaza to meet one of Myke's cousins. She had lived in Sughi City for over twenty years, and she was an early and ardent supporter of the B. Z. Man.

"You'll like her, Apollo. She's smart, and she's nice. She'll take time to listen to you and then patiently explain her position, if you let her. If not, she doesn't push it. You can have a calm and intelligent discussion with her, even if the two of you totally disagree. She has a gift."

The stone plaza was round and divided into four equal quarters. In the middle of the plaza was a large water fountain, and in the middle of each quarter circle was an oak tree. Each of these four trees was magnificent and enormous, providing a tremendous amount of shade. The entire plaza was surrounded by a line of tall, thin trees. The plaza was another example of Pacifica's supreme architectural skills combined with Megantha's power of execution. Apollo hoped to meet Pacifica one day.

Myke's cousin was named Darcie. Myke and Apollo had not been waiting long under one of the oak trees when Darcie showed up. Apollo liked her immediately. She had shoulder-length curly brown hair, green eyes, and she was about as tall as Apollo. She greeted Apollo and Myke warmly and seemed happy to be with Myke, whom she had not seen in person for more than ten years.

Prior to Darcie's arrival, Myke had told Apollo that all he had said to Darcie about Apollo was that he was a friend being shown Sughi City. Darcie did not know Apollo was a powerful enemy soldier. Darcie had agreed to be a tour guide, but she needed to know who Apollo was before they spent much time together. Apollo readily agreed.

Darcie asked how long it took them to get to the city, knowing it could take two months from Myke and Apollo's side of the planet. Myke said they had a good trip, but told her he could not say how they got there. That confused her, and then Myke explained that Apollo was an enemy soldier. This confused her more. Myke told her that Apollo was one of his best friends and someone he trusted. "There are many things I can't tell you, Darcie."

Darcie looked Apollo over, keeping a respectful distance.

"Check him," Myke told her. "You'll see. He's the real deal."

Darcie moved right up to Apollo... close to where she could read his aura. Then she moved closer. Apollo did not resist. Now, her ghost was partially mixed with his. For Apollo, this close often meant he was fighting. But not this time. He could read Darcie just like she could read him. Apollo could tell she was a keeper.

Darcie moved back. "Okay, Myke," she said, looking at Apollo. "He's good."

"Just good?" Myke asked.

"More than good," Darcie responded, staying locked on Apollo. "And I don't think he needs your or anybody's protection. He's a strong one."

Myke explained that, at some point, Sughi Command would figure out Apollo was here and would come for both of them. "They say they won't attack him, but we don't trust them. And they wanted me to check him in, which I never did. So, we might be swarmed at any minute. I don't want you to be blindsided. Maybe you don't want to hang out with us."

Darcie took a few seconds to absorb, and she looked back and forth at Myke and Apollo. "Alright," she said. "I'm good with it. And I assume you want to keep this quiet—about him being who he is."

"For as long as possible," said Myke.

"What do you want me to do when they come after him?" she asked.

"Well, you don't need to protect him."

"Obviously," she said.

"Just stay back and out of the way, Darcie. And if somebody with authority asks you why you're hanging out with him, tell them the truth. I'm your cousin, and I asked you to show us around."

Darcie turned to Apollo. "You're a pretty tough guy to come here alone, aren't you, Trouble-Boy?"

Apollo liked that she would tease him with a nickname. "I'm with the Yellow Bull—Myke. What's to fear?"

Darcie gave Apollo another good look, and then she turned to Myke. "Okay, now, let me show you around."

The first place Darcie took them was the regional command center. This was a server complex combined with Sughi Command, Sughi's main military operational center. She kept them several miles away and stopped on some low hills where they could see it plainly. "We'd better not get any closer," she said. "The security over there is tight. Besides...

Apollo... chances are that's where they'll want to take you for questioning. You'll probably be getting your own, up-close, in-person tour." Turning to face Apollo, she added, "Go easy on them. They're paranoid... cockroaches."

"It sounds like you're not a fan," Apollo said.

"Not of Sughi Command. I don't believe we should force our beliefs on anybody. But, Apollo," she said, winking at him, "it also doesn't mean I won't try to reason with you. I think you're smart enough to see things right."

Apollo smiled. He liked her, but he knew she could not change his mind. "I look forward to it," he said, and he meant it. He wanted to understand why someone as impressive as Darcie could be so wrong.

After showing them the operational center from a distance, Darcie took them to Pacifica University. Darcie had degrees in mathematics and social sciences from Pacifica. She explained that she loved the balance and logic of math and the humanistic aspects of social sciences.

So lovely... and so smart, thought Apollo. *I wish she were ours.*

The university's main campus library was particularly impressive. Here, virtual shelves of books were organized into logical topics and areas of interest. As one approached each section, it would expand into thousands of pictures representing the titles and contents of the books. These images surrounded the library patron, providing a visual scan of what was available. Specific searches could be done on comms, but the visual cues were tremendously mind-opening. They allowed the researcher to see ideas not thought of. If one entered the dog section, they would be surrounded by images representing books on dog nutrition, medical care, dog stories, and dog psychology. Touch an image, and the book would open for contents perusal. Step back, and the sections would generalize. Moving towards a more specific area, such as dog training, the images would change to books focusing only on that topic. The whole experience could be duplicated on a lesser scale on a comm, but walking through the books and seeing them was deeply immersive. It made Apollo hungry to learn. He could spend all day working his way through the evolving book tunnels in this library.

More excellent design of Pacifica, Apollo thought. *She's amazing, and what a shame that it's now all controlled by the Sughis.*

After visiting the university library, Darcie took them to an island in the middle of a small lake, where they spent about thirty minutes doing nothing specific. She was a perceptive tour guide who understood the importance of time to reflect and rest—another thing Apollo liked about her.

Darcie asked if they wanted to see the Anti-Blood building. "Those people will get in your face, Apollo," she said. "Even you, Myke. You might be in Sughi Command, but you're all for becoming a Blood. These people don't want anything to do with the Blood phase. They think we're good right where we are, and they'll argue with anyone who disagrees. They are nuts."

"You don't agree with them?" Apollo asked.

"Nope," she answered. "Sure, we have it great here as ghosts. No physical pain, nobody chopping off our heads with swords or any of the other crazy nonsense we'll have to endure as Bloods. But we have to go and be Bloods. We need to be kicked around to see what we're made of."

Apollo wanted to hear more, but decided to leave it alone.

"I want to go," Myke answered. "I won't mess with them if they don't mess with me."

35

Anti-Bloods

Apollo, Myke, and Darcie took off towards the Anti-Blood center, which was about ten minutes away. Darcie explained that it had previously been a large Olam conference center used for worship services and religious administrative matters. But so many of Olam's followers had left Sughi City, the center had been abandoned, and the Anti-Bloods took it over.

"Is it going to bother you, Apollo, that one of your churches is now an enemy building?" Darcie asked.

Apollo looked off and then back at her. "I've seen it before. Sughi Command, which we saw earlier today, used to be Olam's, too."

Soon, the three were in the building's large foyer, and several Anti-Bloods approached them. "Are you here for the protest meeting?" one of them asked.

"No, just lookin' around," said Darcie. "My friends are from out of town and want to see your center."

The Anti-Bloods' mood changed and darkened. "Are you here to make trouble?" one asked aggressively.

Darcie kept her voice level and calm. "No. Can you show us around?"

"We'll get one of the new guys to help you," they said, clearly believing it was beneath any of them to babysit the tourists. "Wait here." The Anti-Bloods left, saying something between them that could not be heard but sounded derogatory.

"Friendly bunch," quipped Myke.

They waited about ten minutes, clearly not a priority for anyone at the center. People were coming and going to and from the building, but no "new guy" showed up to help them. They were about to start wandering around on their own when a young, college-aged man walked over.

"Are you the people wanting a tour?" he asked. "I was told to come help you." The young man showed neither disdain nor warmth.

"Yes," said Darcie. "Can you show us your facility? My friends are from out of town?"

"Are you here to argue with me?" the boy asked.

"We're not Anti-Bloods," said Darcie, "but we're not here to argue. Just to learn."

The boy seemed comfortable with Darcie, but Apollo and Myke made him nervous. The boy was no dummy. Apollo and Myke looked strong.

"Don't worry about those two," Darcie told the boy. "I have them under control."

Darcie winked at the boy, and Apollo thought the boy might melt on the spot. Apollo wondered if he would, too.

The young man started them on a tour. The building itself was nothing impressive. As expected, it had offices, classrooms, and large rooms for seminars and conferences. It wasn't the building itself that interested Apollo and Myke; it was what they were doing here.

After being shown around for a while, they passed a large meeting room where several hundred people had gathered. "Is that the protest meeting?" Apollo asked.

"Yes," said the young man.

"Can we sit in and listen for a few minutes?" asked Apollo.

The boy was unsure, but any objections he might have had were overruled by Myke and Apollo, who went in anyway. Darcie and the young man followed.

The four of them stayed in the back of the room. Up front was a meeting leader talking about a protest rally planned for a nearby city. It would take place in two days. Given that city's proximity to Sughi City, most of its population would be pro-Sughi, but not necessarily pro-Anti-Blood. The leader was trying to fire up the group and remind them that they wanted to help people see that moving on to the Blood phase was a bad idea. "We have it good here." The crowd agreed. "Why do we want to become Bloods? What if you are born into a country where people are starving or into a tribe that is at war? Do you want to see your family suffer or be killed?"

"No !" shouted the meeting attendees in unison.

"If you are born into war, do you want to have to hurt, maim, or kill people you don't know? You'll have to, because they'll be trying to kill you!"

"We don't want that," yelled a man up in the front.

"Do you want to live in a place where you watch your mother or father slowly die a horrible death from cancer?"

"No!" the crowd responded.

"Is Olam right to force us to be Bloods?"

"No!"

"Is Sughi right to say we need to be Bloods?"

"No!"

The meeting continued as the attendees self-motivated and discussed logistics and tactics for their upcoming protest. The young man who had been with

Apollo, Darcie, and Myke left, evidently seeing no need to continue his escort role.

The meeting was winding down, and Apollo thought they should leave before it ended. But that's when everything changed. Six Anti-Bloods entered the room and set up behind Apollo, Myke, and Darcie. These were not regular attendees. They projected aggressively and looked like a security team. One of them called out over the crowd to the meeting leader. "Hey, everybody, look what we have here!"

The meeting leader stopped, and the crowd turned around.

Here goes, thought Apollo.

"Looks like we have some spies with us today," said the aggressor. There was a rumbling response in the crowd.

"We're not spies," said Darcie loudly. "We're here to observe."

"Are you from Sughi or Olam?" the meeting leader asked.

The correct answer would be "both," but Darcie was savvy enough to avoid the question. Instead, she said that they meant no harm, and that all they were doing was visiting to understand the Anti-Bloods better.

"Are you joining?" somebody asked.

"No, sir," Darcie responded.

A woman in the crowd then came to Darcie's defense. "Hi, Darcie," she called out.

Darcie recognized her and waved to her in a knowing, friendly way.

The woman told the crowd that Darcie was friendly and open-minded and that they should leave her alone.

The group leader then asked, "What about you? You with the black hair and yellow eyes?" He meant Myke. "And your friend, Mr. Blue Eyes?" meaning Apollo.

Myke responded with a dismissive head nod but said nothing.

The leader was too taken with himself to understand he was poking the bear. "Why don't you come up here?" the leader suggested.

Foolish man, Apollo thought.

Myke turned to Apollo and quietly said, "I'm gonna hurt this guy." Then, Myke started moving to the front of the room.

Apollo stayed put.

One of the six aggressors behind him said, "Hey, spark-pusser? You scared? Why don't you go up front, too?"

Apollo said nothing and did not acknowledge the remark. They would soon learn they were making a mistake.

Darcie was watching Myke work his way to the front. "Don't, Myke," she said, shaking her head. Then, turning to Apollo, she asked, "Can you stop him?"

"It will be quick, Darcie. I know you don't like fighting, but this is what Myke does, and he's good at it."

The tough guys behind Apollo and Darcie heard what Apollo said, and Apollo could sense they were pulling back. They would be able to feel his confidence.

Myke was now up front, facing the leader, who asked, "Where are you from, pretty boy? And what's wrong with your friend? I won't hurt him. Tell him to come up, too."

"You don't want him up here," said Myke with confidence, and Myke started to project himself onto the leader, who was immediately taken aback and unable to speak. "You shouldn't mess with people you don't know. The real puss bags in this room are you. You are all afraid of being Bloods."

The leader had crumpled, and the crowd in the front row was petrified.

"The Blood phase is coming!" Myke boomed. "Whether you like it or not!"

At that, Myke rammed himself through all the Anti-Bloods in the front row. They all collapsed. The crowd gasped.

Apollo sensed the panic of the security team behind him. Clearly, they could not stop the yellow-eyed devil. What about the blue-eyed one?

Apollo answered the question for them, ramming all six and knocking them unconscious.

The crowd was now in a state of full panic, but Myke positioned himself above them and yelled at them. "You people are fools! You have no idea what you are doing. You can't stop the Blood phase!"

Myke then moved deliberately and slowly over the top of the people toward Apollo and Darcie. "We're leaving," he shouted to the frightened ghosts below him. "Your menapses are wack-a-doodle!"

Myke headed towards the door and said to Apollo and Darcie, "Come on. Let's go."

36

Darcie's Reprimand

Apollo, Myke, and Darcie left the Anti-Blood building, and Darcie took them to a nearby forest. There, they regrouped under the trees to assess what had happened. She was not happy with Myke's behavior, but she was impressed with his power.

"We should have left, Myke, before you attacked them. We were guests!"

Myke and Apollo looked at each other while she scolded. They both knew the Anti-Bloods were pathetic. It had felt good to pound them, especially the arrogant ones.

"I'm sorry your friend will be mad at you, Darcie," Myke said. "But the rest of them are clueless."

"I know they are nano-brains, Myke. That's why I took you—so you could see how ridiculous they are. But I don't like fighting. That's why I hate Sughi Command."

Her tone and demeanor had shifted from that of a finger-pointing schoolmarm to one where she felt bad for what had happened. Then her projected mindset shifted further, and a sly look came over her face. "But... I agree... that pompous leader of theirs needed a ghost whipping."

The three of them chuckled. The tension between them was evaporating, and she said, "I saw Trouble-Boy take out that security team behind us. They were jerks, and they also deserved it."

They were silent, and then Darcie asked, "Myke, is Apollo as strong as you? Maybe with a little more self-control?"

"*Trouble-Boy* and I have fought hard, and I don't want to ever fight him again."

Darcie turned to Apollo. "Maybe you can teach my cousin some patience."

"He's pretty hard-headed, Darcie. His melon is a rock."

The three talked some more and agreed that today's beatdown at the Anti-Blood building was sure to put Myke and Apollo on Sughi City's radar. The Intels would report it to Command. Sughi's people would not care about some Anti-Bloods having been beaten up, but they would be unhappy that Myke had not reported his arrival, and they would be nervous about Apollo, the Blue-Eyed Devil.

"Remember, Darcie," Myke said, "If Command or some Intels approach you, tell them the truth. I'm your cousin. I showed up and asked for a tour, and you helped out. Yes, you saw us pound on some Anti-Bloods, but they were hassling us. You're innocent in all this."

Apollo was impressed that Darcie did not seem worried or bothered about the possibility of dealing with Intels or Command. She did not like fighting, but that did not mean she was a pushover. "I'll be fine, cousin."

After splitting from Darcie, Apollo and Myke went back to the Azure building. Apollo B-Channeled one-way messages to Tamir and Torith describing some of what happened today, including Myke's pummeling of the Anti-Bloods.

Myke and Apollo discussed possibly attending the Anti-Blood protest planned for several days from now. Not to fight with them again, but to see how regular Sughis reacted to the Anti-Blood protests. Would Sughi soldiers be there trying to interfere? Would regular Sughis give them an aggressive pushback?

"If we do it," Apollo told Myke, "we'll need to reassure the protesters we're not there to fight with them again."

"Yep, especially their leader," Myke said. "Stupid man."

In the end, Myke and Apollo kept attendance at the Anti-Blood rally open as an optional field trip. It was two days away, and a lot could happen before then.

Several hours after they had returned to Azure, Myke messaged Apollo on their B-Channel, saying that two Intels were waiting for him outside the building. He told Apollo that, right now, they were only asking to speak with him, Myke. "I'll try to keep you out of it, Apollo. I suspect they don't know who we actually are. Amazing, I know, but otherwise, they would have asked for you, too."

"Somebody's not doing their job," Apollo said. "The Azure Building knows who we are. How can Sughi Command not know?"

"That's why we're going to lose," Myke said. "I already know Olam will win. Our people can't get it together."

Apollo was surprised at what Myke said. *If he knew Sughi was going to lose, why did he switch to Sughi's side? And... come to think of it... it seemed like Myke did not like any of the Sughis. So... again... why did he switch?* For a moment, Apollo wondered if Myke was actually an undercover agent for Diamond Command. But Apollo dismissed that idea after quick consideration. The fight he'd had with Myke was real. There was nothing covert about it. Myke was who he said he was.

Myke and Apollo went up to meet the Intels but split before topping out. Apollo went another way and set up a surveillance position from which he could watch the interaction. Myke kept his talk with the Intels in the open in front of the building so it would be easy for Apollo to observe. The conversation lasted about fifteen minutes. From what Apollo could tell, the Intels seemed deferential and polite as they should be to someone on Myke's level.

After the Intels left, Myke explained that all they wanted was to understand why he pummeled the people at the Anti-Blood meeting. The Intels did not scold or admonish. They only gathered information. Myke told Apollo that if a junior-grade fighter had done what Myke did, Sughi Command might have disciplined him for overreach. However, since Command did not like the Anti-Bloods, any punishment would have been cursory. "They won't do anything to me," said Myke. "Case closed. Done."

"But what about the whole thing of you being on two sides of the planet so fast?" asked Apollo. "Did that come up at all?"

"It didn't. It probably would have, but they wanted to wrap it up quickly once they knew who I was. They were wise enough not to stray from their assigned task. They would have no idea that I'm really from the other side of the planet or that we were supposed to report."

"Still," Apollo reflected, "how is it possible Sughi Command doesn't know we're here? Wouldn't they have an alert in the system for us?"

"For you, yes. But not for me. I'm on their team, and I'm no first-level recruit." Myke took his index finger, put it to the side of his head, and then plunged it repeatedly into his brain. "I have zero confidence in Sughi Command," he said.

Regardless, Apollo knew it was only a matter of time—a short amount of time—before Sughi Command would be at Apollo's throat.

Apollo continued to find it fascinating how defiant Myke was of Sughi Command. He seemed to have no respect for his superiors. *It's like he wants to be on their side, but he also wants nothing to do with them.*

37

Shumaker

It was the morning of day three in Sughi City. The night before, Apollo had managed to sleep soundly for several hours. Normally, that would not be the case. Nights after busy, stressful days often left Apollo's brain gnawing noisily on the day's highlights, resulting in fitful, low-grade sleep. Torith had tried to teach Apollo meditation techniques to counter his overly active brain, but Apollo had not been the most patient of students.

Last night was different. Apollo had felt cooped up in his Azure Building room, five floors below ground level, so he went up on top, where he found a quiet place to rest peacefully on his back and look up into Summa's night sky. The air was clear, and the view was as grand and spectacular as always. The unimaginable distances between celestial bodies rendered his present dimension insignificant. Apollo's concerns melted away as he pondered immensity. The astronomical canvas was a marvel. Pacified, Apollo returned to his room and slept well.

Apollo was awake and ready for day three. While waiting for Myke's call, he thought back to the pirates and wondered what had happened to the body of the dead pirate boss—the one the woman had knifed and pushed over the railing. The body would have been in the water for several days now. Had it been eaten piece by piece by many small fish? Or maybe gobbled whole by a whale? If not, what would the warm waters of that planet do to whatever was left of the body? Had it sunk to the bottom? If so, how far down? Thousands of feet? Or was it bloated and bobbing on the surface, rotting in the sun? Apollo's theoretical knowledge of what happens to dead, floating pirate bodies was, of course, limited. He had an image of a school of tiny fish eating the man's eyes. Apollo did not feel bad for him. He was a vile creature. Hopefully, the woman who knifed him survived to tell the tale. It would comfort those who had lost loved ones, especially the bowman's daughter, Marika. Mortality in the Blood phase was endlessly fascinating.

Apollo's thoughts were interrupted by Myke, who hit him up on the B-Channel. They would be leaving in half an hour. "What about Darcie?" Apollo asked. "Is she coming?" Apollo hoped she was.

"Naw," Myke responded. "She is still mad at me for what I did. We talked it out last night, and I think we are okay, but she says we're on our own."

Apollo's ego was slightly wounded. He had hoped she would want to come to see him, even if she were mad at her cousin. But that was not to be. Apollo knew it was better, anyway. She might be attractive, but she was firmly entrenched on the Sughi side, and that was trouble.

Despite not coming, Darcie had been gracious enough to continue helping as a tour guide. She had suggested to Myke that he take Apollo to see a man she knew who was pro-Sughi, but who also was very smart about it and not one to fight with Apollo. She told Myke that this man frequently spoke to large groups of pro-Olams. These groups wanted to learn more about Sughi's side, even if they had no intention of joining. Many wanted to understand why their loved ones had left Olam for Sughi.

"His name is Shumaker," Myke said to Apollo. "A lot of people call him 'the Pulse.'"

"Why?"

"Darcie says he has an uncanny ability to read the room. He can sense the mood of the person or audience and tailor his arguments accordingly. Darcie says people love him, even when they disagree with him."

Darcie had made an appointment with the Pulse for Myke and Apollo, and the boys headed out to meet him. Myke had a comm whose directions he followed for about fifteen minutes. At first, they traveled east towards Flat Top, but then they veered left and over a large forest of deciduous trees and small, winding rivers. They were now outside the boundaries of Sughi City. Myke let the comm go, and they descended to the top of a prominent hill that was clear of trees. The cleared area was mostly covered with short, field grass, and it also featured several structures, including a modest, single-level, ranch-style home. This was Shumaker's home, and he was waiting outside for them.

As Myke and Apollo were on short approach, four men and two women emerged from a nearby bunkhouse and set up near the Pulse.

"Are the guards here because of me?" Apollo asked Myke. But Myke did not know.

The guards held their position at a respectful distance from Shumaker but remained close enough to assist immediately, if needed. Soon, Myke and Apollo were standing before Shumaker, who seemed pleased to see them and said they should not worry about the guards. "Sughi wants me to have protection. Supposedly, my opinion is important." Shumaker said this with self-deprecation that was laced with sarcasm. It was disarming, and Apollo could see why people liked him.

In the front yard of Shumaker's home was a round stone table with stone benches. The table was big enough to seat a dozen people. An open, airy gazebo covered it, making it the perfect place to talk. They all moved there. Shumaker released the security detail. Had he known who Apollo was, he might not have.

Despite the release, one guard from the detail came over with a comm and asked for DNA signatures from both Myke and Apollo.

Myke intervened. "Do mine," he said.

"I need both of you," the guard said.

"Do mine first," said Myke, "and then we can discuss it."

The guard was not happy but took Myke's imprint, which brought back a summary of who Myke was, including his rank and fighter stance. The guard's demeanor changed immediately. Myke was a powerhouse in the military structure, and Myke substantially outranked the guard.

"Like I said," Myke reiterated. "Just my signature... not his," meaning Apollo.

"Y... yes, sir," said the guard with stiffened respect. "Please have a good day, sir." The guard moved away quickly.

Shumaker watched the interaction with interest. "Wow," he said. "It looks like the two of you have some juice. Can you tell me who you are? All your friend Darcie said was I'd be interested in meeting you two. She gave me no details."

Myke was about to respond, but Shumaker cut in, "That Darcie... she's a special one. I'd do anything for her."

"I know," said Myke. "She's my cousin. One of my good cousins. You know how relatives can be."

"Oh, yes," answered Shumaker. "Oooh, yeess."

There was a pause while all three chuckled, and then Shumaker looked at Apollo. "You're an Olam fighter, aren't you? A strong one at that." Shumaker did not seem intimidated at all, nor was he being aggressive.

"I can see why they call you the Pulse," Apollo said.

Shumaker smiled but did not respond. Instead, he asked, "What house did you grow up in?"

"One on the other side of Summa, near Lake Minnick."

Shumaker lit up. "Not the one with the glass dome?"

"Yes. The dome over the entryway. High up."

"Yes, yes!" Shumaker exclaimed. "I know that house well, Apollo." Shumaker paused, purposefully so. "We are house cousins!"

38

House Cousins

"Where did you grow up? Apollo asked Shumaker.

"Not far from the Pecos Mountains. And I used to play at Lake Minnick all the time. Do you surf the canyon, Apollo?"

"Yes, of course."

"There were years when I went to the canyon almost every day to surf. To keep my head clear," Shumaker said.

"Hence your wisdom today," Apollo half-joked with Shumaker.

"Yes. And your home. The one with the skylight dome. My best friend lived there. I was at that house all the time. I liked it better than mine. So, we're house cousins."

"I think so," Apollo responded. "And your best friend... that's one of my house brothers?"

"House sister," Shumaker corrected. "Astella."

Apollo remembered Megantha telling him about an older house sister named Astella. She had been out of the home for a long time, and she never came to visit. Apollo thought she had gone over to Sughi's side. "I've heard of her. She's a Sughi, now. Correct?"

"Yes, we're still good friends. She's a reasonable Sughi like me." Shumaker winked. "You should talk with her sometime, Apollo."

Shumaker reminisced more about the geographic area surrounding Apollo's house. As he did so, Apollo's memory chose to settle backwards in time on the fight he'd had years ago to protect Torith on the island in the middle of Lake Minnick. The fight with Gammon, Malta and that dweeb of a ghost named Escue.

Apollo and Shumaker stopped talking for a few seconds. Both were awash in old memories. The lapse in conversation was punctuated by a myna bird that landed on the table and flitted around, looking at the three pre-human ghosts. The bird had nothing to fear, but it was unusual to be so uninhibited. The bird was a ghost, too. Otherwise, it could not have seen them.

"Well, hello, Bucky," Shumaker said to the bird. Then to Myke and Apollo, "This is my friend, Bucky. He comes by almost every day. I wish I could tell you why. All I know is that he has decided we are friends, and I'm great with that."

"Maybe he senses your gift," said Apollo. "I suspect he can tell you're different."

"Could be," said Shumaker. "My gift, if that's what it is, has never seemed to apply to animals."

"So, your gift, the Pulse," said Apollo, "is that how you could tell who I am?"

Shumaker explained that he had been partially lucky, but he could feel Apollo's power, and it was also clear to him that Apollo was still with Olam. Shumaker said his gift allowed him to read more from a person's aura than most. "I can tell you're a good man, Apollo." Then he had a quizzical look on his face, and he looked back and forth from Myke to Apollo. "I can also tell that the two of you are strong friends. And that interests me. You should be enemies."

"We were," said Myke. "We met fighting each other a few days ago."

"No better way to get to know a person fast than to go all in," said Shumaker. "I take it neither of you won the fight?"

"Correct," said Apollo. "But we won each other's respect."

"Pure gold," Shumaker said.

There was another pause in the conversation as Shumaker absorbed and analyzed. "So," he said, "I can sense things, but I'm not a mind reader. What are the two of you doing here? Especially you, Apollo. Why come to talk with me?"

"There's a lot we can't tell you," said Myke. "For example, how we got here."

"Oh, that's easy," said Shumaker. "You were sprung here. Did Megantha do it?"

It was apparent to Myke and Apollo that Shumaker was more intelligent and intuitive than either of them had thought.

"We are going to have to be careful with you, sir," said Apollo.

The myna bird had decided to take a nap in the middle of the table. *A good sign,* thought Apollo.

Myke and Apollo never acknowledged Shumaker's conclusion about being sprung to Sughi City. But they explained that Sughi Command had agreed that Apollo could come, and there would not be an all-out war when he did. "They don't know we're here yet," said Myke. "But they'll figure it out soon. We were hoping for a few calm days before it starts."

They also admitted that each hoped to bring the other to their side. "I might get him," Apollo said with some jest. "He won't get me."

Myke shook his head "no," but said nothing.

"Okay, but what's so special about you guys? Especially you, Apollo? Why does Sughi Command want you here, and why are they treating you differently?" Shumaker paused. "And Megantha? She's on board, too? How is it that both sides are good on this?"

Apollo said, with some jest, "How about if we ask Mom that question?"

"Oohh, Nooo," said Shumaker, backing up with his hands forward in a defensive move. "I know Mom loves me and will talk with me anytime. But I can't deal with her."

"Normally, I would get that," said Apollo. "But I would have suspected it might be different for you."

"Nope, guys. I might be the tolerant and understanding Sughi representative, but I'm still firmly on Sughi's side. Which means I've split from Megantha and Olam. I can't take their presence, at least not for long."

Myke changed the topic. "And that brings us to why we wanted to see you, sir. Can you tell Apollo why you follow Sughi?"

"I will, but you have not told me why Sughi Command treats Apollo so specially."

"We only know part of it," said Myke. "Once Apollo and I figured out we were friends, I thought it would be good for Apollo to come to Sughi City. I said so in my debriefs, and somebody pushed it up the chain. One of my higher-ups reached out to Apollo's Mentor, who strongly disagreed but said he would go up the chain. Surprisingly, they agreed, and here we are. But, to tell you the truth, neither Apollo nor I know more than that."

Apollo was a little too quiet, and Myke looked at him. "Well? Apollo? Do you know something more?"

Apollo shrugged and looked around in an exaggerated manner, as if he did but was not telling.

"A.P.?" Asked Myke, leaning towards Apollo, wanting more. "What is it?"

Apollo hesitated, purposefully squirmed a little, and said, "Look, Myke. There's something I haven't told you."

"What?"

"Well... look... ummm... I'm not supposed to tell you this... but remember how I said I had a debrief at our command center after my fight with you?

"Yes, and... ?"

"Well... there were some people at that debrief I didn't tell you about."

"Okay."

"My Mentor, Reemo, wasn't the only Mentor there." Apollo paused for effect. "There was another Mentor. It was your sister, Savana."

"Oh, boy," said Shumaker, rolling his eyes. "We're back to family."

Shumaker and Apollo looked at Myke, who had now looked down and was not saying much. Then, he shook his head in obvious discomfort. "Savana... my sis... I'd heard she was a Mentor."

"Were the two of you close growing up?" Shumaker asked.

"Yes... very."

The three of them were silent for a few seconds. Then Apollo added, "But that's not the only person, Myke."

"What... more?" Myke showed frustration with Apollo's piecemeal tactics. "Who else, Apollo?"

"There was a Forza there, too."

"I don't have any Forzas in my family." Myke's tone was dismissive.

"No, not a relative," Apollo said. "One of your students."

"Holy Summa!" Shumaker exclaimed. "Your student? You had students? That means... were?... Myke, were you a Mentor?"

"Yes, yes," answered Myke, with some tenseness. "Who was it, Apollo?"

"Her name is Lionah. She said she was from the Red River Desert."

Myke sighed. "My best student." There was a hint of sadness in his voice. "That is a wonderful person. I wish she and I could have seen eye-to-eye."

"The student becomes the master," said Shumaker. "That means you were a good teacher, Myke."

"I was... at first."

"But at some point, you knew you no longer believed it," Apollo said. "How could you still teach it?"

"By then, I wasn't teaching much. My Forza could tell I was struggling, and they pulled all my students before I could do any damage. It was for the best. I was miserable and conflicted—and I had no desire to pass that confusion to them."

"And what about this Lionah?" asked Shumaker. "Did you try telling her what was happening or why you were out?"

"There were a few students I went to—not to change their minds—but to be straight up with them. I wanted them to understand for their peace of mind, and I only went to the mature students whom I knew would not be swayed. Lionah was one of them. She was shocked but told me she didn't feel betrayed. She'd had plenty of loved ones in her family who had already gone to the Sughi side—people she cared for dearly. She cried, told me she loved me, and offered to help in any way she could. I expected nothing less of her."

Myke hung his head, and Apollo understood why. Apollo had been given a taste of how incredible Lionah was when he met her during the debrief. Any normal person would feel terrible letting down such a magnificent friend, especially Myke.

Apollo and Myke spent several more hours with Shumaker. He explained why he could never support Olam and Diamond's plans for life in the Blood phase. His arguments were not versions of anything Apollo had not heard before, but Apollo thought his reasoning was better thought out. Many Sughi supporters chose sides based on emotion, and then they hunted for logical justifications. Shumaker, on the other hand, stayed with logic regardless of the emotions.

For example, the pain and suffering of animals. Shumaker said animals had to have pain. However, he saw no need for animals to experience the same level of physical pain as humans. "The character of animals is not being tested like ours needs to be." Shumaker wanted the pain levels in animals' brains to be limited. There was no need for an animal to suffer painfully for many hours or days. He wanted pain programming that would lead to death if overloaded. He wanted animals to die from pain to prevent them from suffering too much.

Apollo liked Shumaker's idea. It didn't mean he agreed with it, but it was appealing. Myke seemed to like it as well.

Shumaker added, "No need for my friend here, Bucky the myna bird, to suffer too much. Bucky is not on trial."

Bucky stirred, then returned to sleep, content and secure on the table.

Shumaker had logical arguments related to death, pain, and abuse of children. He also had sound logic for how long people should live in pain. Most of all, he had the ability to explain why people thought the way they did, on both sides of the argument. None of what Shumaker said did anything to convince Apollo to switch teams, but it was tremendously helpful in understanding why a loved one might have chosen the other side.

Apollo asked, "But what about Sughi's statements that he can make it so everyone passes the Blood phase? That seems like a dream to me. People will have to be forced to do the right thing. How can that be a test of character?"

"You're looking at it the wrong way, Apollo. However, before I say anything more, please understand that I disagree with Sughi on this matter. I'm all in favor of us being tested. And I'm in favor of failure."

More logical thinking, thought Apollo.

Shumaker continued, "But assuming things could end up the way Sughi says they could—with every Blood passing the test—somehow Sughi has to make it so the law of equals is satisfied. Right? I mean, for every action, there must be an equal and opposite reaction. It applies to physics, and it applies to behavior. If a Blood steals a hungry person's food, there needs to be payment for that action."

"Of course," said Apollo. "Maybe not immediately, but sometime... yes."

"Okay. Who has to make the payment? The person who stole?"

"Not necessarily," Myke piped in. "Somebody else could pay."

Apollo agreed.

Shumaker continued, "That's right. And Sughi says he'll pay."

"What?" asked Myke. "Sughi pay? That's ridiculous. There's no way. He doesn't have that kind of power. It's a promise he can't keep!"

"Maybe, but he says he will recruit many followers to help pay. Thousands, millions of them, each taking on part of the payment for all the bad things people have done. He says they will make the payment, all of them, together. He says that's the loving way. Everyone will help out."

"So, a bunch of people have to pay for all the bad guys, and then the bad guys get a pass."

"Partial pass," said Shumaker. "They still have to pay, but others will help them."

Apollo did not like the logic. It seemed wrong. But he was reacting emotionally, and he did not have a logical argument against it.

Shumaker continued, "Everybody is going to have to pay. Everyone is going to be thrown into the burning forest or the acid tub or over the cliff or whatever the punishment of the day is. Everyone has to pay for at least part of what they did. But some people will pay extra to help those who really messed up."

"So," said Apollo, "in the end, maybe ten or a hundred or a thousand years down the road, the law of equals is satisfied, and everybody ends up with a pass."

"Right. Sughi says it might take a long time, but in the end, the law is satisfied, and everyone wins."

"I hate that," said Myke. "Some people should not get a pass, even if good people are willing to help them make payment."

Mercy, thought Apollo. *Putting it this way, Sughi's plan sounds more loving than Olam's.*

Just then, one of the guards came out. He had an open comm with him. "I'm sorry to interrupt, sir... sirs," he said.

"My command wants to know if you are okay, Mr. Shumaker?"

"Yes. You can see that I'm fine," answered Shumaker. "What are they worried about?"

"They know Myke is here." The guard turned towards Myke and gave him a respectful nod. "But they are worried about somebody who might be with Myke. An enemy. A dangerous one." The guard then took a brief look at Apollo, likely wondering if Apollo might be that enemy.

Shumaker started to say something, but Myke stopped him. "Is your commanding officer on the comm?"

"It's my LT, sir. Not the CO."

"Give us a few minutes of privacy. Then I'll come over and talk with whomever we need to." Myke indicated with his hand that the guard should move off, which he did.

"I didn't want you to say something that would upset Sughi Command," Myke told Shumaker. "You are doing us a favor." Then Myke turned to Apollo and asked, "What do you think I should tell them, Apollo?"

"I'd tell them where we're staying, although they probably already know, and see if you can negotiate a time for us to meet with them tomorrow. Tell them we'll meet with anyone they want."

Myke seemed fine with that.

Apollo added, "Oh, and tell them they can assign me an escort if that makes them feel better."

"I'm not going to do that," said Myke. I'm your escort, not some random security troll."

"I know you're high up, Myke, but do they trust you?"

"No, but they have to pretend like they do. Otherwise, they would be forced to demote me. They're scared of that." Myke jokingly put both arms up into a strongman flex position. "I have serious guns. Nobody wants to mess with these babies!"

Apollo gave Myke a thumbs-up. Shumaker chuckled. *Good logic,* thought Apollo.

The myna bird must have sensed a rise in tension. It woke up, gave Shumaker a quizzical, sideways look, and then darted away.

Myke left the table, too, and he went over to the guard. They conversed, and Apollo saw Myke speaking into the guard's comm.

"It looks like he's having to explain," said Shumaker. "Probably some pin-headed admin."

Myke returned, and Shumaker asked, "How'd it go?"

"Some of them are in a tizzy because I did not bring Apollo directly to the command center when we arrived in town. My bosses are okay with it, but one of the uptight commanders is having a fit."

"You must have had a good reason you didn't," Shumaker asked.

Myke and Apollo looked at each other, then back at Shumaker. "Like I said before, there are things I can't tell you. But I'll say this…" Myke paused. "Megantha didn't exactly send us straight here when she sprang us. She took us on a detour. An intense detour."

"Intense is an understatement," Apollo added. "And because of the detour, we needed time to regroup when we arrived here."

Myke nodded in agreement.

Apollo continued, "Plus, I think Myke wanted to show me a little of Sughi City before it all became formal and tense."

"A detour?" asked Shumaker. "Can you tell me more? Maybe a hint?"

Myke and Apollo eyed each other. In doing so, they came to an agreement to tell Shumaker more.

"If we tell you," Myke said, "we need your promise not to say anything about it to anyone. Megantha asked us to keep it quiet."

"Mom says 'Mum' on this one," Apollo added, proud of his cheesy play on words.

Apollo's feeble humor generated a half smile from Shumaker, who said, "It's double encrypted, locked in my core."

"Okay, we trust you," said Myke. "Right, Apollo?"

"Yes," Apollo responded.

Myke hesitated for effect, then said, "Megantha sent us to another planet—to some Bloods—and they were killing each other."

"A war?" Shumaker asked, showing intense surprise.

"Pirates," said Apollo.

"Ships on an ocean, fighting," Myke clarified.

"Where?"

"We don't know," said Apollo.

"It had to be a different planet," said Myke. "The gravity was different. And there were two moons."

"Holy Summa!" muttered Shumaker.

"The Bloods were fighting. There were good guys and bad guys."

Shumaker shook his head in amazement.

"And... and Apollo and I helped save some good people."

Shumaker was thinking, then asked, "You mean you helped save some of them from being killed?"

"Yes," said Myke, with tremendous satisfaction. "But that's not all. We helped kill one of the worst of the bad guys."

"Kill?" asked Shumaker. "But... you're a ghost. How can you kill a Blood?"

"Oh, we didn't actually do the killing. There was a woman who one of the pirates was trying to rape. She killed him. We confused his ghost, and then Apollo told her to attack him, which she did."

The explanation was confusing, and Shumaker had to process it. He asked a few more questions and finally understood. "Incredible," he said. "Simply incredible."

Myke and Apollo left Shumaker about an hour later. He again promised not to say anything about their visit to another planet, the Bloods, the pirates, or the pirate they had killed. Sughi Command would certainly debrief Shumaker on his impressions of Apollo, most of which he could freely discuss. "I'll tell them I tried to bring you to our side," Shumaker said. "That's true. As for your pirate adventures, well, I'll tell Bucky, but no one else."

39

Sughi Command

It was day four in Sughi City. Myke and Apollo were about a mile from the entrance to Sughi Command. It was a few minutes before ten in the morning. They had stopped to look over the area and gather their wits. Per instructions Myke had received the night before, they were ordered to be at the command entrance at ten.

Apollo was tense, and he could tell Myke was, too. Rightfully so. Myke had the tricky job of protecting Apollo while also showing loyalty to Sughi and his soldiers. If things became too overwhelming, Apollo could fight or take a dive into the ground and escape. He could even take the extreme step of calling for Olam or Megantha. Myke, on the other hand, did not have those options. Whatever Myke did had to be justifiable to Sughi Command. However, Myke had made it clear that Apollo was his first priority. "If Command asks me to do something I think is a threat to you, I will refuse. If they come after you, I will push back full force. They can cry about it all they want."

Apollo knew Myke was a powerhouse, and Apollo was sure Sughi Command's leadership was cautious about upsetting him, especially the line leadership. But these were Sughis. They were not loving social workers. Power and status were important to them. Defiance of power was, too, and if upper management thought Myke was out of control, there would be war.

Sughi Command was located in the middle of Sughi City, in the same building complex as the local Regional Server Complex. Like all of Summa's RSCs, this one provided networking and comm services for hundreds of surrounding miles. Although Sughi Command and the RSC were in different parts of the complex, they shared a common entrance and some common walls.

A Forza, named Gerard, oversaw the RSC and protected it from any Sughi incursions. Olam had insisted that planet-wide communications remain uninterrupted. Followers of both Sughi and Olam were to have full network access. Gerard made sure that was the case for this RSC. However, his protection was limited to the RSC's space and any adjoining infrastructure, such as power sources and data lines. The Forza did not interfere with the Sughi parts of the complex.

Despite Olam's order to protect this and all of Summa's RSCs, it did not mean the RSC in Sughi City had not been attacked. Several times, whole battalions of Sughi soldiers had tried to take it over. The attempts failed miserably. Gerard was too strong. Other times, the Sughis came at the RSC via intelligence operations designed to covertly turn one or more RSC staff away from Olam. These had resulted in a few successful conversions but never any substantive damage to the RSC's network operations. Gerard could read his employees well. Anyone thinking of turning for the enemy was told to leave, and their clearance was pulled.

Cyber-attacks were another thing. Sometimes, they had limited success. The Forzas and their staff were not perfect. They were hackable. But they were highly skilled, and Apollo had not heard of any recent attack that had taken a significant portion of the network offline for more than a few minutes. Even massive brute force and denial of service attacks were unsuccessful. The network filters were good enough that they generally could siphon off the billions of bogus network requests generated by these malicious methods. The harmful traffic was relegated to nodes that went nowhere. The network engineers called those nodes "dead heads." They often insulted each other with the same term. Apollo had heard Tamir use that term when talking about someone he thought processed information uselessly. "Dead heads... all of them!" was a Tamir expression. Too bad Tamir was not here today.

Those working in the RSCs could easily obstruct or corrupt Sughi traffic. But they were ordered to protect those data streams as if they were Olam's. Apollo used to think this was not fair. Why not interrupt the communications of Sughi Command? But then Apollo sat in on a training session led by Diamond, where it was explained that every ghost on Summa was given full access to vast amounts of information to help them choose. It would be easy, for example, to set up a system where only Olam followers had keys to the library, figuratively speaking. Every ghost's DNA could be registered to all kinds of access controls. But that was not the point. Instead, all ghosts were given vast access to help them decide. Were they going to follow Sughi or Olam? Were they going to sit on the fence? This was the core struggle of all of Olam's children.

Somebody in the training responded that when ghosts were Bloods on earths somewhere, it would not be like that at all. Most Bloods would have very little information.

"Correct," Diamond had told him. "The Blood phase is a different kind of test. It's a test of internal character—the character you are refining and building here on Summa. The whole point of being a Blood is to see what we will do when we have little or no information."

Apollo had gone over this in his mind many times. *The Blood phase is going to be brutal,* he thought. *We are going to be clueless.*

Apollo was pulled back to the present by Myke. "Time to go, buddy. Are you ready for this?"

"Y... Yes," said Apollo, surprised at himself for having gone so deep in thought. Now was a time for action, not reflection. Apollo quickly shifted to the present. "Let's fly."

Myke and Apollo took off and quickly closed the last mile to the RSC/Sughi Command Center complex.

Apollo could tell that Pacifica had designed this RSC and command center. She and Megantha had built it like much of the rest of Sughi City. Most of it was underground. The real estate above the structure had many shallow ponds whose water constantly flowed to keep them clear. The bottoms of these ponds consisted of clear crystal, ten to twenty feet thick, which became the ceiling for many of the large rooms below. The crystal conducted light to the rooms, and at night, it channeled light from the rooms up to the night sky. During the day, it was spectacular down below, and at night, it was equally magnificent on top.

As soon as Apollo and Myke arrived near the RSC's entrance, ten Sughi fighters appeared and surrounded them in a tight formation. Myke told them to back off, and when they did not, he attacked one of them and repeated his demand. They backed off another ten feet. Apollo could feel their mixed emotions. They respected and feared Myke. They hated Apollo.

The above-ground level of the RSC/command complex was a large, round structure, one hundred yards wide, consisting of a domed roof supported by forty-nine columns. The dome was solid rock, as were each of the massive columns. Inside the columns, the base of the dome roof was fifty feet off the floor, giving the covered space an outdoor, airy feeling. The gaps between the columns were unobstructed, allowing for access to the complex from any direction. The floor under the roof was smooth stone and completely flat. In the middle of this floor, equidistant from the columns, was a circular security access counter. It, too, was stone, and employees from both the RSC and Sughi Command worked there to control facility access. This was one of the few places on Planet Summa where Olam and Sughi followers worked side-by-side with common security goals.

The ten soldiers who had surrounded Myke and Apollo stayed close as they all approached the round RSC building. Their formation entered between two of the columns and transitioned over the stone floor to the big, round control desk. Every ghost under the domed roof stopped to watch this unusual procession.

At the desk, the soldiers tightened their formation. Myke snarled at them, but the group captain said, "Sorry, Myke. I have my orders."

"Really?" answered Myke. Then, pointing at Apollo, but looking at the captain. "Don't you get it? That guy could take you and your whole squad out like that." Myke popped his hand open in the captain's face for emphasis.

Although far less powerful than Myke or Apollo, the captain stood his ground. "It needs to be this way for now, sir."

Apollo intervened in the mini-standoff. "It's fine, Myke. They need to do their job." Apollo respected this captain and wished he could talk to him alone.

Myke grumbled and then checked them in at the desk. Both he and Apollo had to touch a comm for their digital DNA. When the woman at the desk saw who Apollo was, she immediately beamed. She was obviously under Gerard's command, which meant she was an Olam follower, and having a powerful Olam fighter here was exciting for her. Apollo could tell she wanted to engage with him, but there was no time. Instead, he asked her for her name and gave her a firm, warm look.

"Flora," she answered. "Nice to meet you." She glowed.

"It's very nice to meet you, too, Flora. I wish we had more time. You have an important job here."

The ten soldiers also checked in. Then, the floor behind the desk opened, and all twelve proceeded into a vertical hallway down to the main foyer a hundred feet below. At the bottom, there was a door on one side for the RSC. They would not be allowed into that side. The other side was the Sughi command center, where they headed. Soon, they were in a large, high-ceilinged room, lit by the sunlight passing through the light ponds up top. The room reminded Apollo of the command center room he'd gone to for debriefing after his fight with Myke in Seven Valley. Like that room, in the middle of this one was a large floating globe depicting the entire planet. Sughi tactical personnel were gathered around parts of the globe, and sections were expanded outwards, probably as they monitored or planned operations. Apollo was surprised nobody was stopping him from looking that way.

"Quit your spying," said one of the soldiers, coming close behind him. "We're going over there." He pointed to another hallway. "Keep moving."

The "keep moving" comment was annoying because Apollo was right with the group and never stopped. But he expected no less from a small-minded regular.

Once in the next hallway, Apollo could see that it was lined with classrooms and conference rooms on each side. Some were occupied, sometimes with a teacher at the head of the class and students in rows facing the teacher. In other rooms, people were arranged equally, more or less in a circle, like teams. The classroom doorways were mainly open, and those that were not had hallway windows. Apollo assumed he would be led into one of these rooms, but surprisingly, they arrived at the end of the hall, where there was a mandatory left turn and then entry into another large room, similar in size to the first one that had the interactive globe.

This room also had a high ceiling, with space to accommodate several thousand people. There was a large screen on one wall and an area in the back of the room that would be an audio-visual station for controlling sound, the room's lighting, and whatever was being projected on the large screen. The room's walls were primarily black, and the floor was finished with squares of beautiful black tile embedded with crystal specks. This tile was laid in various flowing patterns. It was spectacular. *Pacifica,* thought Apollo.

The room had no natural lighting, and the electrical lighting was off except for the middle part of the room, where the floor was raised five feet into a circular stage, big enough to hold dozens of people. The stage was well-lit.

When Apollo, Myke, and the escorting soldiers entered the room, twenty to thirty ghosts were already there. Apollo scanned them for threats. He could see none, and they looked like random Sughis going about their own business. Several were looking at a comm and talking to each other as if trying to work something out. Another small group appeared to be casually conversing as friends. Others in the room were spread around, sometimes alone and sometimes in twos or threes. The ghosts in the room looked over at them, naturally curious, but none appeared hostile or overly interested.

Then, Apollo saw a woman up on the stage. She was the only person up there, and she turned to face them as soon as they entered. It looked like she had been waiting for them. The overhead lights showed her well. Apollo could see that her hair, eyes, and aura all showed purple. In an instant, he knew who she was. *Malta!*

40

Malta

Apollo re-scanned the entire room. Still no threats. Only the always intoxicating, purple Malta. Apollo had heard that she had moved up high in the Sughi ranks. She would be trouble.

The soldiers ushered Myke and Apollo towards the waiting woman. She stared at them as they approached, and as Myke and Apollo neared her, the escort backed off. Apollo noticed their actions and realized they were afraid of her. Not surprising.

Malta was unforgettable. Apollo had not seen her since middle school. That was over twenty years ago. Yet, he had recognized her immediately.

Apollo quickly decided he would not give her the satisfaction of thinking he remembered her. She was the enemy. *Time for some acting!*

"Do you know who this is?" Apollo asked Myke.

"She's an area commander," said Myke. "But not over soldiers. She's part of the Intelligence Bureau."

"Okay. A spook. I get it." *I'm not surprised,* thought Apollo.

Then, Myke shot Apollo a mischievous look. "We call her the Purple Mamba. She's a poisonous snake." He grinned.

Apollo barely had time to process what Myke said.

The "boys" were close to the woman now, and she spoke.

"Hello, Apollo." Her voice was confident. "Do you remember me?"

Apollo was trying to see the Mamba in her. That he could not pick out, but the danger he knew well. "I only know that we've met," faked Apollo.

"Yes," she said. "It's been years since we met. We know each other, Apollo. I, for one, could never forget you."

Apollo moved off the main floor and up onto the stage, close to Malta. Apollo feigned mental searching, as if still trying to place her. At the same time, Apollo could sense the tension of the security detail as he approached one of their commanders.

Malta moved towards him with a hint of a slither.

There's the mamba, Apollo thought. She was beautiful, mesmerizing, and lethal, as he had always remembered her.

"You don't remember me, Apollo?" She sounded disappointed and hurt.

"From a long time ago? Right?" Apollo acted.

"We have a mutual friend," Malta said.

Apollo forced a blank look to his face.

"Torith. Your friend, Torith."

Apollo delayed his response. Then he lit up as if finally remembering. "Gammon's friend, Malta!" Apollo exclaimed. "Yes... Malta from school. I remember you now."

Malta gave him a look of: *How could you forget?*

"But," Apollo continued, "you said Torith is a mutual friend. That threw me." Apollo had injected sparring into his acting. "I don't think Torith would agree."

"I wanted her to be," said Malta. "But Torith always rejected me!" Malta paused. "Is she mean to everybody like that?"

This was the Malta that had tried so hard to recruit Torith over to the Sughi side.

"Torith's only mean to mean people," said Apollo. "Oh... and to me, all the time."

Apollo was missing Torith, and he was using her now as a weapon against the Mamba. Switching tactics, Apollo complimented her. "You look fantastic, Malta! As you always have. You have a power glow."

What Apollo said was true, and he knew she would know it.

"The Sughi world is treating me well," she responded. "When you do the right thing, Apollo, you radiate power."

Not the kind of power I want, thought Apollo.

"I'm surprised you're still with Sughi," said Apollo. "I thought you would eventually smarten up." Apollo had always wanted to like Malta. "Are you still picking on people younger than you?"

"Children need to be taught right from wrong," she shot back. "We try hard to undo the brainwashing. But I never could get into Torith's stubborn head."

"You know," said Apollo sarcastically, "I never could either. She's a strong one."

"Yes, but she listens to you."

"And then does what she wants," said Apollo. "Is that why I'm here... to give you another chance at Torith?" There was a challenging tone in Apollo's voice.

"Not exactly. But... yes... that, too."

Apollo found Malta's answer confusing, and he showed it on his face.

"Maybe we can't bring you or Torith over, but Myke thinks you are a reasonable person. We hope to show you our side... to help you understand it... so you'll stop fighting against us."

"Maybe a little of... keep my enemies close... or... a dose of... frenemies?" Apollo offered.

"Sure," said Malta. "Look, Apollo, you already think one of your best friends is Myke, correct?"

"Yes," said Apollo.

"Well, then, my command, and I think you'll stop fighting us if you better understand us. You're already at peace with Myke, and he's one of our battle tanks."

Apollo looked at Myke, who seemed uncomfortable being discussed this way. Apollo wanted to point out to Myke that a purple mamba thought he was a tank, but Apollo held his tongue and fought to keep his face locked in business mode.

Apollo turned back to Malta to re-engage. He'd so much rather fight her. She was so attractive. He would love to slam her hard.

"You don't understand, Malta," Apollo said. "I don't care what you and your Sughi ghosts think. That's not why I fight you."

Malta did not respond, but she seemed annoyed.

"Where are you in the command structure, Malta?" Apollo asked. "Are you higher or lower than Myke?"

"Higher," said Myke, appropriately answering that question for her.

"Technically, Myke is right. On an org chart, I'd be higher. But everybody in this room would rather have Myke around when things are bad. Myke gets it done."

Apollo agreed. "So, you're not an operational fighter like Myke? It sounds like I won't have the pleasure of fighting you on the field someday?"

"Probably not," she said. "At least, not the way you fight."

"Are we fighting now?" Apollo asked. "Maybe we should cut the yak-yak and fight for real. We might come to like each other—like Myke and I do."

Apollo had not been in a good fight since his quick flatlining of the security team in the Anti-Blood building. He missed it.

"How about it, Malta?" Apollo asked. "Shall we put on a show?" Apollo shuffled in a hint of a boxer's dance like he was preparing to spar.

"I already like you, Apollo. I always have. I'm not going to fight you—not your way."

"Like girls, then?" Apollo countered. "Shall we fight that way?"

"You mean like civilized grown-ups? Smart fighting? Not like little boys in the sandlot?"

"Yes."

"Aren't we already doing that?"

Apollo knew she was right.

She continued and switched subjects. "I know you and Myke went to the Anti-Blood building. What did you think?"

"Myke worked them over pretty hard." Apollo looked at Myke, and they both smiled. "Those fraidy cats had no idea what hit them."

"*Fraidy cats?*"

"Yes," said Apollo. "They are afraid, and they feed their fear to each other. They are afraid to go on to the Blood phase."

"Do you agree with them?" she asked.

"Of course not." Apollo could tell Malta was probing—playing mind games.

"What about Shumaker?" she asked. "Tell me what you thought of him?"

"I will. But first, tell me what you think about the Anti-Bloods. There is no way you agree with them either... correct?"

"As long as they don't agree with Olam or Diamond, we'll take them."

"Yes, but it can't mean you agree with them?"

"They are an enemy of my enemy," she said.

"To be used and abused at your convenience," Apollo countered. "There is no way Sughi will ever agree with them. He wants the Blood phase—his way, of course. The Anti-Bloods are his enemy. And yours. Why don't you attack them like you attack Olam?"

"They are harmless and no threat," Malta said. "You and I both know the Blood phase is coming. There is no stopping it. The day will come when they will have to choose Olam or Sughi. We're confident most of the Anti-Bloods will choose Sughi. They are too weak to choose Olam."

Apollo knew she was right. "The fence sitters, also," Apollo added. "You're going to get most of them, too."

"Yes, and we'll take'em!" Malta's purple eyes flashed victory. "No need to fight them or the Anti-Bloods. We already have them."

Right again, Apollo thought. It was discouraging. He tried not to show it.

"They're all too afraid of Olam's plan. Sughi says he'll save everybody. They'll come our way."

Apollo wondered if Malta truly believed Sughi could help everyone pass the Blood phase. He doubted it. In response to Malta, Apollo shook his head negatively and said, "Sughi's plan is nothing more than a power grab. He knows he can't save them. All he wants to do is control them... and you."

Malta's purple aura brightened, and her eyes went dark. Apollo could tell he was making her mad.

"I thought Shumaker talked with you about that," said Malta. "We'll all help each other—together."

"There is no way people will want to pay for all the bad things others did. Sughi certainly can't pay up to make it all equal. The fence-sitters aren't going to pay—that's for sure."

"But Apollo..." Malta said, showing irritation, her voice laced with sarcasm. "What about the love you are supposed to have for others? Huh...? Isn't that what Olam preaches? Love your neighbor? Help your neighbor? Don't judge your neighbor and help them regardless. What is so different about Sughi's plan? We may not have powerful people like Megantha, Diamond, or Sapienti, but we'll have millions who can pay for their own failings and then pay some extra to help others. In the end, the law will be satisfied. It will take longer, but we'll get everybody. It's worth it!"

Malta's demeanor had become more intense and emotional, and she moved close to Apollo's face. Apollo held his ground. He could feel her power, and he could not help but be attracted to her despite their enormous differences. He badly wanted to fight her, her purpleness, the mamba, everything. *Come on! Let's fight like soldiers fight! You slam me, and I'll slam back!* But, despite what his mind told him, he held his position and remained outwardly cool.

Malta continued. She talked about Sughi's plan... everyone paying... everyone making it... and on and on. Apollo heard little of it.

Finally, Malta backed off, much to Apollo's relief. He was done with her words. Then, Apollo sensed that Malta would let him have the floor—at least temporarily—now that she'd done her thing. "May I?" asked Apollo, making a sweeping motion with his arm toward the big screen on the wall.

Malta agreed, and Apollo switched places with her so that now, in addition to facing her, he was also facing Myke, the soldiers, and others who had gathered to watch the scene. Some of the gatherers were being told who Apollo was, and Apollo could sense their surprise that he was there. He could see that some of them were hostile to his enemy status. Others seemed frightened of him, as they should be. The room now had close to a hundred people.

"I have nothing to tell you that you haven't heard before." Apollo used a comm to bring up an image of their planet on the screen. "As you know," he continued, "every physical thing here on Planet Summa was made by Quasars like Olam and Megantha or by powerful ghosts like Pacifica under a Quasar's direction."

This was old stuff to everyone in the room. People were quickly showing distaste at being lectured by the opposition.

"There was a time when we all loved our parents. We all remember how powerful, warm, and loving they felt to us, and how we can physically touch them and feel their warmth and power. They can physically hold us or move us, just like they can a mountain, a lake, or an entire planet."

As Apollo talked, he called up a video of a Quasar creating a whole part of the planet, with mountains, rivers, and forests, and then building parks and homes for the ghost children who would live there.

"Why do they do all that?" Apollo asked. He doubted anyone would answer, and no one did. "Because they love us and want us to progress," he said. "They are doing all of this for us."

"Not true," said one of the Sughi soldiers. "It's all for them. They want to control us, and they want power over us."

"Partly true," countered Apollo. "Power over us for a while... as we learn... but they are trying to help us grow so that they can eventually share power with us, not control us."

"Sughi wants to share too—all of us will share," said someone in the audience.

"What power does Sughi have?" Apollo asked. "He's nothing like Olam or Pacifica. Sure, he's a convincing guy... and I know you think he loves you... but he's nothing compared to the Quasars."

"He's honest with us," said Malta. "When he says he loves us, he really does!"

To Apollo, that was nonsense. But he knew they did not see it that way, so he tried more reasoning. "Okay, let's say you are right... about everything you claim to believe. Do you think Olam is going to let things happen your way? Is he going to say, 'Alright, my children, I had a plan, but you want another plan, so... I love you... and let's do it your dumb way?'"

"He gives us agency now. Why won't he let us decide the plan?" The question had come from Myke's direction. At first, Apollo thought Myke had asked it. But Myke pointed at a guy next to him, and he did so with a condescending look that read, "The idiot next to me asked that."

"He will let you decide the plan," said Apollo. "Of course, he'll let you decide..."

"So, we've decided," interrupted the same guy near Myke.

"Yes, you have," said Apollo. "But just because you decided doesn't mean it's going to happen the way you want it to."

Apollo knew this was another concept that was not new to the Sughi followers. The audience grumbled and moaned.

"The Quasars are not going to follow Sughi's plan. How can that not be obvious?"

There was more grumbling. Apollo was surprised Malta let him continue. "Even if you think the Quasars are wrong, isn't it crazy to fight them? They're so powerful. Fighting them is nuts!"

"Exactly!" shouted Malta, loud and with authority. She swooped over next to Apollo but faced the group. "Some loving parents they are. They tell us how much they love us. They smother us with their love. We've all felt it. They tell us we have agency. It's amazing. But it's a drug—and look what it produces." At that, she stepped back from Apollo, holding out her hands, indicating him. "This is what you get. A dim-witted boy who loves his mommy and can't think for himself. He'll do anything she says, and he'll believe her to the end, because he thinks she loves him!"

Apollo let the "dim-witted" comment slide. He knew Malta did not believe that. More challenging to ignore was what she said about their parents' love. It was no drug. It was amazing, and it was real. It cut hard at his soul to hear Malta reframe something so wonderful as bad.

"Ask Olam," Apollo said back, his voice steady and firm. "Or ask your mother. Talk to them! They'll tell you!"

"Oh, yes," retorted Malta. "Of course they will. They'll tell us all day how much they love us, and make us feel it, too. It's all part of their control."

Apollo now understood why Malta had given Apollo time to talk to the group. She had set him up, and he should not have taken the bait. They were never going to listen, and all he had done was ramp them up.

Malta paused, and Apollo jumped in, "You can delude yourself all day that somehow you know better. Are you saying you know more than Pacifica, who worked with Megantha to make this whole city?"

Sughi ghosts had been streaming into the room ever since Apollo's arrival. Now, there were several hundred, and the number was growing fast. Nobody looked friendly.

Apollo caught Myke's eye, who signaled for Apollo to cool it. It was going to erupt into a war. The ten Sughi soldiers who had stayed back had now moved to the front of the crowd, looking ready to pounce. Like before, Apollo was not worried about them, but he had no idea of the capabilities of others in the crowd. Most of all, he did not want to put Myke in the position of having to fight his own people.

Apollo knew he was wasting his time, but he wanted a final word, so he moved to the edge of the stage, held his hands up, palms forward, fingers spread, and projected as much of his blue aura as possible. "Ask Olam! Ask him! He'll tell you. All you have to do is ask him!"

41

No More Olam!

Malta rushed next to him. "We're done talking with Olam!" she cried. Then she started into a loud chant. "No more Olam! No more Olam!" Then louder. "No more Olam! No more Olam!"

Apollo stepped away from her and back. He wanted nothing to do with these disgusting antics. How could she rail against somebody who loved her so much?

The crowd started chanting in unison with Malta's chant. They were motivated, loud, and aggressive. To Apollo's sadness, he realized he was the one who had fired them up. He had let Malta take advantage of him badly.

Suddenly, the big screen displayed the words "No More Olam" in a pulsing, rhythmic manner. Every time the words flashed, the crowd yelled them, everyone in unison, growing louder and more intense by the second.

As the chanting continued, people from all over Sughi Command rushed into the room. Many came through the walls as they filled the room. The hundreds turned into several thousand. The room's floor capacity was maxing out, and ghosts were forming levels in the air above the ground. Others crowded on stage to spur on the mania. The stage became filled to the maximum, and Apollo was soon buried in a massive show of hatred for Olam.

The words on the screen now changed to "We Love Sughi!" The pulsing words were accompanied by the sounds of thunder, and the house lights flashed like matching lightning. The energy in the room exploded.

Apollo was horrified to be part of this frenzy. He was on stage, mixed with those leading the mobs, as if he were leading them himself. The guilt by association was overwhelming. Malta's plan had been brilliant.

Apollo debated calling Megantha or Olam. If either came, they would shut down this rebellion immediately. But Apollo knew better. The Sughis had made their choice. Mom and Dad would not intervene. Not today.

Apollo also debated leaving. But, no, he wasn't going to run. Mostly, he wanted to smash a few of them. But that was not an option unless they attacked him. And even then, he could not fight all of them. His options were not good.

Apollo started working through the crowded stage, looking for especially obnoxious Sughis. Finding one, Apollo moved right into the man's space, projecting strength but not battling him. The man was not a fighter. Apollo interrupted his whole séance, and the man slinked away. Apollo found another and did the same. On his third, it was a woman. She started to fight back. Apollo did not want to fight her, so he backed off a touch and became a mental wall. He was much stronger than she was, and he let her attempt to beat on him. He merely stood his ground and projected strength. She could flail all she wanted, but she did not have the power to hurt Apollo. Finally, distraught but unhurt, she moved away.

Apollo picked another victim. He knew his actions would change nothing, but he had to do something.

After five long minutes, Apollo saw Malta signal to the back of the room, where several audiovisual Sughis controlled the lights and sound. Suddenly, everything shut off—lights, sound, the big screen, thunder—everything. The people shut off, too. The room went totally dark and silent. Obviously, the Sughi people had done this before. They did not seem surprised. The sudden silence was a powerful end to the pandemonium.

In the dark, Apollo did not know what would happen. He thought he might be attacked, and he was ready for it. Somebody moved close to Apollo. Apollo tensed. But it was Myke. "I'm here with you, buddy. I'll kick the Summa out of anyone who comes at you."

But no attack came. Finally, only one light came on. It was a spotlight in the ceiling, and it was on Malta, who was still on the stage, about twenty feet away from Apollo. The light on her was an intense, soothing bluish-green light that oozed warmth and comfort, like a deep pine forest mixed with a warm tropical ocean. This was called RR4 light. Apollo knew about RR4, although he only vaguely understood its technicalities. The light was produced via refraction, reflection, and various filters. Tamir would have to explain the rest.

Malta moved towards Apollo, the RR4 tracking her perfectly. Contrary to the intense chanting of a minute ago, she was now calm and composed, and Apollo sensed zero aggression in her. Instead, he was surprised to feel love and warmth emanating from her, like the RR4 bathing her. Malta was a beautiful person, mamba and all. The power of her aura showed strongly, and she was now two feet from Apollo, looking at him with affection and smiling.

Myke had moved off the stage, leaving Apollo alone with Malta. Apollo debated what to do with her. It was all mind games with this woman. He wanted to punch her, and he wanted to embrace her. But Apollo did neither.

Malta broke concentration with Apollo long enough to shoo people away who were on stage. They scattered. Then she locked back onto Apollo.

Apollo stared at the purple light emanating from Malta's eyes. She said nothing, staring back. She continued to project affection and warmth, in total contrast to the "I hate Olam" session she had barely finished. Apollo did not have the patience to understand it and was tired of the manipulation. He decided to go on the offensive. He moved into her, mixing himself with her. Usually, this was a battle move, but he was not fighting her, and she did not resist. He wanted her to feel the power he had. She was not the only one with juice. What he did was not socially acceptable, but this was not a time to worry about norms.

Apollo projected love of Olam. This was not his style, but he did his best. He projected loyalty to Diamond Command, and he made it clear he was not switching. He could feel her affection for him. He accepted her affection, but he returned only friendship. As attractive as she was, she was not the person for him.

She pulled back, separating herself from him. "I get it," she said. "I'm not surprised. We are too different."

"You knew we would be. So why? And why all this?" Apollo asked her, sweeping his arms across the room. "Why the Olam hate session, Malta? You express affection towards me, but you also deeply offend me at the same time."

Malta made a pouty face.

Apollo backed off another few feet. "Look, Malta," Apollo said, holding his hands up, "You are incredible." He gave her a slight nod and a knowing look. "And you have loads of sway over people here at Sughi Command." Apollo cocked his head toward the room.

"Yes."

"Yes, but," Apollo said, "I can never join you. What you are doing is wrong. And you are responsible for all the Sughi followers you've influenced."

Malta said nothing, and Apollo continued.

"You are a powerful person, Malta. People look up to you and follow you. You're respon—"

Malta interrupted Apollo by moving back towards him, then partly into him, half-mixed with him, and half not. She kept her head out so she could look into his eyes from inches away. "Stop, Apollo," she said with gentle firmness. "I know I'm strong. You are, too." Despite the scolding, her tone and demeanor were not threatening.

Apollo knew he should move back, but he did not want to.

"Stop fighting us, Apollo. We are good people. We're simply trying to do the right thing."

Apollo looked over and saw Myke about twenty feet away. Myke showed a "that's gross" face. Apollo understood.

Apollo looked back at Malta. "How about you come over to my side?" Apollo maintained steady eye contact with her, inches away. "I know you're dedicated, but you have to feel conflicted. You're too smart not to see how untenable your position is."

Malta's eyes and aura glowed bright. Waves of purple light coursed through her, projecting outward. Her aura and projection were more potent than most. Apollo was always taught that people like Malta would have an unseen power when they were Bloods. Other Bloods would not be able to see this projection, but they would feel it, and Bloods would be drawn to people like her for reasons they could not explain. She had a gift that was obvious here on Summa. But her gift would be a powerful, invisible weapon in the physical Blood phase.

"You have a special power, Malta," Apollo told her. "Why not use it for Olam? Why not use it to help all of us while we're traipsing around in the dark as Bloods?"

"I am using it, Apollo, for Sughi. He needs me more than Olam does."

"Malta... please," Apollo pleaded, trying hard not to let anger build inside him—anger she would surely feel. "Sughi is a sham. He's nothing. Everything he is doing is exactly what you say Olam does. He's all talk. He doesn't love you, Malta. He's the one who wants to control you."

"Are you done, Apollo?" she asked, still maintaining her position right with him. "I could be here with you all day, Apollo. I want to be with you when we are Bloods. Please come to my side, or at least please stop fighting me. We can work together, like you and Myke. We can be friends, even if you stay with Olam."

Apollo needed to resist Malta's intoxication. It was time to sober up. "Malta, let's be realistic," Apollo reasoned. "Most likely, we'll never meet as Bloods. We probably won't even be on the same planet."

"Oh, I disagree," she said. "Come over to Sughi, and we'll make sure we live close to each other, on the same earth. I will find you, Apollo."

Apollo knew Olam could work that out, but Sughi would never have that level of power. This wonderful woman was delusional, as much as he wished it were not so.

Apollo was done with the love fighting, and he backed away from her. He wanted a change. He looked around in an exaggerated fashion, then asked, "How about if you let Myke show me more of your command? I'd like to see your academy where you train new soldiers. Would that be okay? Could I sit in on one of your training classes?"

Apollo could see the disappointment on Malta's face.

"We could be a team, Apollo."

"We can be. Like I am with Myke. But I'm not coming to your side. And no more of these love fights."

"I can't promise that," she said. "I quite liked it. I know you did."

Apollo looked at her and said nothing. She was right, but he was not going to admit it.

42

Brutus Beatdown

For the rest of Apollo's day at Sughi Command, Malta sent the ten escort soldiers away and spent time showing Apollo around. Despite her affection towards Apollo, he was still the enemy, and she was not going to take him into sensitive command areas. For example, Apollo asked if he could go into their world room, but Malta said no. Myke also wanted to see it, so she sent him off on his own, and she took Apollo to one of the classrooms where there were thirty inexperienced soldiers. They were made up of young male and female ghosts, and they were talking about force multiplication versus individual fighting.

Malta pulled the instructor aside and asked if the soldiers could talk to Apollo directly. The instructor was far outranked by Malta, but he rightfully had concerns. She assured him Apollo would be helpful. The instructor relented. Apollo could tell the instructor knew he had no choice. Apollo introduced himself to the class.

At first, the students did not want to talk. Some said they thought it might be a trick by the instructor to have Apollo there. Others seemed intimidated, and most of them were hostile. One asked Apollo how many Sughi followers he had fought.

"Hundreds, maybe thousands," Apollo said.

Another asked Apollo if he had ever lost a fight, and Apollo said he had many times. But he added that, even when he lost, it never made him want to switch to the Sughi side.

"Who would win in a fight? You or Malta?" asked a woman.

Malta was still in the room, and she quickly said, "He would!"

Apollo laughed and said that even though he and Malta were enemies, they were also friends and respected each other.

"He likes to say we're frenemies," Malta said. She spoke in the tone of a commanding officer.

The classroom discussion became more serious when one of them asked why Apollo was fighting against Sughi. "Why not let us do what we want?"

"Good question," Apollo responded. "And I ask the same of you."

Apollo could see that his reasoning needed expansion. "Please understand that most of the fighting I do is defensive. We rarely attack you guys—unless it's a preemptive attack where we're stopping you from attacking us. We want you all to follow Olam, but we don't fight or force you to. We fight because you fight us."

Apollo could see the class was not buying it, nor was he naïve enough to think they would. They had been indoctrinated for years. His little speech would change nothing.

"Look," he said. "Here's another way to think about it: We have Mentors and Forzas, including Gerard, the Forza in the RSC right next door. If we wanted to force you, don't you think we'd use a few of them to clean up? A couple of Mentors could wipe out Sughi Command—all of you. A Forza could do it in his or her sleep. But that's not what Olam wants. He has people like me do the fighting, so you have a choice. You have fighters as strong as I am, if not stronger."

"Like Malta!" one of the toadying female cadets shouted out.

"Correct... like Malta!" Apollo echoed, looking at Malta, one eyebrow raised and flashing a slightly crooked smile.

The class asked him a few more questions, and then Malta had a suggestion. "How about if we do a little test?" She paused.

The class members looked at each other, uncomfortable. It was never good when a high-ranking officer wanted a test.

She continued, "Apollo says he's allowed to fight because he's not powerful like a Mentor or Forza. Do any of you want to fight him?"

The class instructor objected. "Please, ma'am. Not here. In the gym, maybe, but ..."

Apollo knew the instructor was wasting his time. Malta would shoot down his objections. But she did not have to because one of the male soldiers stood while raising his hand.

"I'll fight him!" the young man announced. He looked strong for his age, and he was overflowing with confidence.

This soldier had said nothing in class up until now. Apollo had noticed him immediately upon entering the classroom. This cadet was in the front and off to one side. He seemed alert, but there was much more to him. Apollo sensed aggressive contempt. He was probably a hardline Sughi follower. Unlike Malta, who had an aura that projected outward, this young man showed the opposite. His persona absorbed light, black hole style.

"What's your name?" Malta asked him.

"My friends call me Brutus, ma'am," he responded.

Apollo thought it interesting that Brutus chose to show respect for his superior officer by using "ma'am" but also showed disrespect by not telling her his real name. This Brutus creature looked like trouble.

Malta looked him over, sizing him up, and then she looked at the teacher, whose face showed no happiness. Turning back to Brutus, she asked, "Are you sure?"

"Yes!"

"I can promise you he's much stronger than you or anyone in this room. By far."

"Don't care," snapped Brutus.

Apollo saw Malta's eyes flare at his flippant style. He thought she might take him out in the hall and whip him herself. But, instead, she came over to Apollo and said crisply under her breath, "Eat him up, Apollo. That pitza needs a reboot."

"Pitza" was short for "pitner" and less offensive. Her word choice made it clear she was asking him to kick the snotty insolence out of Brutus.

Perfect timing, Apollo thought. *I need a good fight.*

"I don't think this is a good idea," said the class instructor, nervously moving into the middle of everyone. Then, looking at Malta, he pleaded, "Ma'am, please... I don't want a fight in my classroom."

"You are a good instructor, Mason," she answered him. "But when have we ever had the enemy right here for practice?"

Brutus had moved into the open area at the front of the class, and several classmates cheered him on. "I'm ready," he said.

"No, you're not," Malta answered. Then, turning to Apollo, she looked him in the eyes while angling her lips at Brutus. "Just him. Nobody else unless they interfere."

"Of course," Apollo answered, and then he launched himself at Brutus.

Apollo had no doubt he would flatten Brutus within seconds. He could have toyed with the inexperienced student, but Apollo had no interest in prolonging the fight. Brutus was dark and disgusting. Had it been Malta, it would be different. Apollo could love-fight with her—take his time and enjoy it, maybe even let her win. However, with Brutus, the goal was to eliminate as fast as possible.

Apollo slammed his billions of infinitely fine ghost particles into Brutus, mixing with his and Brutus' menapses micro-spec by micro-spec. Then, Apollo exploded the power in each of his particles and blasted those of Brutus, frying them like overloaded fuses. Brutus immediately lost consciousness and went limp.

Apollo withdrew, unscathed, and faced the classroom. Brutus was in a heap on the floor, and the students were stunned.

Apollo backed off and moved over near Malta. He tried not to show it, but he immediately felt bad about how he had manhandled the boy. Reemo would not be happy. Apollo's combat abilities were not for show.

Instructor Mason went to Brutus and asked several of the students to help him infuse Brutus with enough power to bring him back to consciousness. Brutus would eventually recover without assistance, but pushing power into him was faster.

Malta intervened and went over to Brutus. Taking him by both hands, she powered him up with her incredible presence. He immediately started to come to, and he looked around, dazed.

"You'll live," Malta said dismissively. Then, turning to the class, she said, "We have fighters as strong as this one," meaning Apollo, as she pointed towards him. "There is one in the building right now." She meant Myke.

Brutus was conscious enough now to know what had happened. He had a beaten-down look on his face.

Malta continued, still addressing the whole class, "Let this be a lesson to you on how far you can go if you train well... and how strong Olam's soldiers can be. Work hard!" she commanded.

Apollo wondered which of these cadets he would meet on the battlefield someday. He had a premonition that Brutus would be one of them.

Malta walked out of the classroom, and Apollo followed. They headed towards the world room to meet Myke. Apollo's tour of Sughi Command was over, and Malta escorted them out.

Malta stayed with Myke until they were clear of the dome and columns that marked the RSC and Sughi Command. She said goodbye and made it clear to Apollo that she would like to see him again while he was here in Sughi City. Outwardly, Apollo was noncommittal. Inwardly, he knew he wanted to see her, too, despite their differences.

Malta told Myke and Apollo that her intelligence people had heard rumors of rogue pro-Sughi groups who were unhappy with Apollo's presence and might attack him. "They'll go after both of you," she told Myke. "You are protecting him, so you are their enemy, too."

She explained that, although Sughi Command was the official pro-Sughi entity, other anti-Olam groups operated on their own. "The Brutus kid you beat up will probably end up in one of those groups. They are extremists, and he seems like the type."

"You beat up a Brutus?" Myke asked, confused. "What happened?"

Apollo said he would explain later.

Malta continued, "We have a protective order out on you, Apollo. You are here as an official visitor, and as long as you cooperate with Myke, nobody is supposed to touch you."

Apollo had noticed two guys waiting close by but out of earshot, and Malta then called them over. She explained they were Intels assigned to watch Myke and Apollo. "Their job is to ensure you two are not harassed," Malta explained.

Myke did not seem pleased. "I can handle it. We don't need babysitters."

"They'll monitor and report," Malta went on, ignoring Myke's objections. "They're not going to fight to protect you, but they'll report any problems."

43

Rogue Attack

It was getting late in the afternoon. The sun was still up, but the light was heavier. Some clouds had formed east of them, and the sun would drop behind the mountains to the west in an hour. A slight breeze moved a cluster of dry leaves on the ground nearby. Their crackly carcasses rustled, skipping in circles. Apollo knew this was their final dance. Automatic sweepers would pick them up in the middle of the night.

Apollo and Myke took off and rose to an altitude of one thousand feet. The Intels followed, not far behind. The weather continued to deteriorate. The clouds to the east were expanding upward. They seemed to grow out of nothing. Apollo remembered a college meteorology class and the concepts of rising air, lapse rates, dew point, and visible moisture. Apollo could feel the cooler air at altitude. Clouds were also starting to form in the west. Below him, the sunlight streamed in at a hard, low angle, leaving long shadows off the trees, buildings, and anything rising from the surface. The lighting was eerie.

They had only been traveling for a few minutes when Myke pointed to the left and said, "Over there!"

Apollo could see eight flyers, about two hundred yards off, at their same altitude and speed, tracking parallel to them. This was not good. "There, too," said Apollo, pointing right this time. "Another group." Apollo could see six more off to the right, also on the same flight path.

Myke stopped, and so did Apollo. Myke signaled to the Intels and pointed out the threats. One of them brought up a comm. He would be communicating with Command.

"What do you want to do, Apollo?" Myke asked. "This looks like a fight to me. We can run or fight. Whatever you want. I think we can easily take these guys."

Apollo was less confident. He was sure there were strong fighters here in Sughi City, even if he and Myke had not come up against any yet. "I thought we were off limits," said Apollo.

"We are to Sughi Command. But who knows who these guys are? Rogues, probably," said Myke. "The Intels should be checking on it now. If these guys are regular Sughi soldiers, we're good."

The Intels rushed over. One of them said, "Command does not know who they are."

"Get us reinforcements," ordered Myke. The Intel immediately complied.

"And leave," Apollo ordered. "Unless you know combat, go!"

The two Intels looked at each other. They were scared. "Yes... Go!" ordered Myke. "Now!"

The Intels shot away towards Command, and one was still reporting via comm as they went.

"We only need to hold them off until Command sends backup, Apollo. Let's do this."

"Okay, let's work together and hammer on the six first," said Apollo, and he turned towards them.

Myke agreed, and within an instant, they were both speeding toward the sextet. There would only be a few seconds to fight them without the other eight joining. Apollo hoped to take several of them out before the others got there.

Apollo had often faced groups of attackers. Typically, they spread out and came at him from all sides, allowing him to fight them one by one. It was a standard tactic—logical and requiring minimal coordination because each fighter could act independently. But that independence came at a cost: they fought as individuals, not as a unified force.

As he and Myke approached the group of six, Apollo expected them to break apart—maybe split into two teams of three. Instead, they did the opposite. They closed ranks, tightening into a single unit, moving as one. At first, Apollo was relieved, knowing that coordinated fighting like this was great in theory but difficult in reality. He should be able to break their coordination by hammering hard on one or two of them.

But the moment he engaged, he realized his mistake. Not only were the six disciplined, they were elite. Each fighter was strong, skilled, and moved in synchrony with the team. Their capo was calling the plays, and the others followed with precision. They had training, structure, and roles. Apollo was in trouble.

The other eight were on them almost immediately. They also fought as a whole, and they concentrated on Apollo. The sextet took Myke, separating the "boys" so they could not help each other. Apollo felt like he was fighting eight Mykes. He knew he could not win.

"I'm going to ground," he yelled to Myke, not knowing if Myke heard. Apollo shot for the safety of Summa's earth. In the seconds it took him to get there, the densely-packed team pulled chunks of power out of Apollo, blowing his menapses. Apollo fought back panic.

Apollo picked what looked like a dense rock formation and plowed into it, then zig-zagged furiously through the rock, deeper and deeper into the ground, expecting to lose the attacking team. But to Apollo's surprise, they stayed right on him, painfully breaking him down. Apollo had to do something soon, or he would go inert. *Who are these guys?*

Apollo was slowing, and the eight were becoming stronger, partially powering off Apollo, a skill few fighters had mastered. There was no getting away from them. Apollo knew he was going to lose. He was hundreds of feet under the ground. He wanted to return to the surface, but the power team was pummeling him so hard he could not tell which way was up.

Then things got worse. The attack team pushed him deeper and deeper and seemed to be forcing him in a specific direction. Not that they could actually "force" him, but they could vary the intensity of their attack depending on which way he was going. Suddenly, Apollo ended up in a deep, underground aquifer. The problem was that this water was totally pure, with no salt or minerals, which meant it conducted almost no electricity. There was nothing to recharge Apollo. It was an energy desert.

The power team held Apollo here, and he was now too weak to resist. He called for a comm to ping his location, but no comm came. He was too deep, sub-network, out of range. His only choice, then, was to call for Megantha or Olam. They could hear his call anywhere.

Apollo called for Olam, who came immediately, and the power team scattered. But to Apollo's surprise, Olam told him he would not help him. "I love you, son," he said. "But you're on your own. Don't forget that we love you." That was all Olam said, and then he was gone. Apollo did not understand. He had never been abandoned like that.

With Olam gone, the power team returned with a vengeance. It tore at Apollo until he passed out. The aquifer's dark, cold, extremely pure, and lifeless water offered no recovery. He was lost underground, beyond the search capabilities of the comm network and deep in the bowels of Summa. How would anybody ever find him?

44

Darkness

Torith:

Dear Apollo:

Where did they take you? You've been gone for two weeks, and we can't find you. I'm so worried. I've pleaded with Olam and Megantha for help finding you. They say we have to work it out on our own.

I've begged the Forzas, and none of them will help. Reemo doesn't know where you are. He wants to help, and says he might be able to figure it out, but he's forbidden from helping. He'll only give us general advice. Nothing specific. Please be strong, Apollo, wherever you are... please ...
It hurts.

I want to save you... Like you saved me so long ago at Lake Minnick.

...Apollo had a vague sensation of movement and being in the wet cold. It was dark, and he was so tired. Powerless. There were other presences. They were zealous and vile, and they were taking everything from him. Now, there was a tunnel down into nothing. And then nothing...

Torith:

You stupid, stupid man. Why did you ever agree to go to Sughi City? What did you think was going to happen?

It's been twenty days since you disappeared. They found Myke a week ago. He says the rogues took him and finally let him go. He was very damaged, but he's recovering, and he's becoming strong again. He's been looking for you since. So has that horrible Malta person. She's helping with the search. She claims to care about you and says it's not her people's fault. I don't believe her.

Where are you ...?

… Apollo felt the charge surge through him. It was too much, too fast, especially after being so cold and dark for so long. It ached deeply. Then he was awake. He was down in the dark earth, still in the water. Many dark souls surrounded him. Twenty of them. More. He could feel their hatred. They had charged him to torture him. They wailed at him. He tried to fight them, but it was too much. They sucked the power out of him, and he went dark, this time relishing the darkness, away from their misery…

Torith:

Tamir is trying so hard. I've never seen him use his brain more than now. He won't rest, and neither will I. He has some ideas. He and his geek squad are burning their brain circuits.

We'll find you, Apollo. We will. We have to.

> *This is hell, and I'm afraid you are also in hell. You are so strong. How could they capture you? Why don't you escape?*

… Again, they charged him, forcing him out of deep oblivion and back to a harsh consciousness. And then, before him, was that young soldier… Brutus… the one he had so flippantly beaten at Sughi Command. The others pulled life out of him, keeping him awake just enough so Brutus could exact his revenge, savagely burning inside Apollo. In and through him, pounding his brain. Stripping his soul. Apollo could no longer judge time. The beating went on and on. Apollo knew he deserved it. He never should have flatlined this boy. It was not Olam's way and not what he had been taught. He tried to let Brutus know he was sorry. But Apollo only felt Brutus' intense desire to hurt. Finally, Brutus was exhausted, and Apollo's menapses were shot. His captors sent him back to the darkness. Apollo began to relish the darkness, away from it all…

Torith:

> *Thirty days, Apollo. Thirty days! We've looked everywhere. Endless comm sweeps. Endless in-person searches. Malta has given us twenty-five of her soldiers to help. They are not nice people, but they are soldiers doing their duty, which means they are helping.*
>
> *Mom won't tell us where you are, but she agreed to spring Tamir and me to Sughi City so we can be on scene. I feel closer to you now. It helps, but it also makes it harder.*

Reemo talks to us every day on the comm, and he helps us with search ideas. That Shumaker guy is helping, and so is Myke's cousin, Darcie. Your older brother, Dramos, is here, too. He's had a couple of good fights with groups of Sughi followers. I know you are strong, but Dramos churns them into cream puffs. Dramos really should be a Mentor, as I'm sure you know. The Sughis have learned to stay out of his way.

I'm a wreck, Apollo. Please come back to me... to us!

… Apollo no longer had any sense of reality. They were constantly waking him up and then draining him, pulling him in and out of nothingness. All he wanted now was his friend, the darkness. Oh, how he loved the darkness. He craved the darkness. It had become an addiction. His will to fight was gone. So was his will for light—only darkness. Dark and empty was what he craved. If only he were in the Blood phase. Then, he could die and be away from his captors. He envied the people he had seen die in the pirate attack. Death would be such a relief. He remembered his conversations with Myke about Bloods and death. Now, he saw beauty in death. If only he could die and be released from this misery…

Torith:

Last night, Megantha came to see Dramos, Tamir, and me. She continued to insist she wouldn't tell us where you were, but she also powered us up. She cleared our minds and supercharged us... I love Megantha.

Megantha also told me I needed to go to Malta and work it out with her. I'm having a hard time with that, Apollo. I detest Malta. I'm jealous of her affection for you. I don't want Malta's ghost to come back to Olam because I don't want her ever to be a Blood, and that's because I don't want her to have a chance of being with you. I know that's terrible, and I know you are not mine. But you have talked about us being together as Bloods. You bring that up, not me. I've always pushed back when you do... but come back, Apollo. This time I'll talk to you about it. Please... come back...

...Now, when Apollo felt the pain of light charging into his being, he did everything he could to expel it. Darkness and nothingness. That's all he wanted. Go away, everything. Go away! Leave me in the void...

Tamir:

Hi, Apollo. Torith insisted that I write to you. Okay... you are my best friend, and we miss you. Yes, we are working like mad ghosts trying to find you. I've caught Torith crying a few times. I think she loves you more than she says. You are lucky.

There are many things I want to tell you about what we're doing to find you. But they are extremely close hold. So, I'm writing them in the attached encrypted file. When we find you, I'll give you the password. Hang in there, buddy. We're coming for you.

Parts of the Attached Encrypted File:

...Torith detests Malta, but Malta thinks that Brutus' kid, whom you beat up, might know where you are ...

...Brutus is more radical than most. He'll probably be expelled from Sughi Command... He'll be a rogue someday ...

... Malta has a lot of ears to the ground in the Sughi Command Center, and one of her sources overheard Butt-Faced-Brutus bragging about having kicked the photons out of you ...

... Myke says the guys who attacked are rogue extremists who support Sughi... He also thinks that Sughi might be behind them... even if that's not public... so maybe Sughi himself ordered the hit on you, Apollo... we don't know ...

... One of the network engineers has put a trace on Brutus' comm activity, focusing on locations. We are building his patterns and those of his friends. We know they know we can do this, so we're sure they are being careful ...

... we've been mapping location patterns for more than twenty days. There are answers in the data, but we don't have them yet. We will. ...

... We're also running some undercover agents against Brutus and his friends. The UC's are mostly females. These are Malta's people. She has many resources.

For all we know, sir-Brutus-Buttockness will lead one of these agents right to you ...

...We're gonna get you back, Apollo. It's only a matter of time...

...I hope you are still "Apollo" when we find you. I'm sure they have been tearing you apart...

...No matter what they are doing to you... and how much they are breaking you... you can count on me to help you recover. Reemo says you will be damaged when we finally find you. Don't worry; I'm there for you as long as it takes to fix you...

...We're also doing everything possible to learn more about the rogues. Malta assures us they are way off the reservation and not affiliated with the normal Sughi Command. Torith believes nothing Malta says, but I think Malta is right. Malta's people are sharing some data with me. They want to find the rogues as much as we do. Once we do, I wish we could sic Dramos on them, with me, Myke, and Torith as backups. But that would be revenge, and Reemo won't approve. Hopefully, we can figure out their next attack and then attack them first. Reemo would be OK with something like that. Dramos is so strong. You'll be like that someday...

...There's a lot of debate about whether or not the rogues take their orders from Sughi vs. Sughi Command, which is supposed to be the official conduit. Reemo

says the rogues might be a precursor to how this war is going. Right now, the war seems to have rules—at least on some levels—and that's why Sughi Command let you come here. However, it seems the rogues are only bent on destruction and hate. There is no civilized talking with them. If they become stronger, it will force everyone to choose sides—much more so than now. In a way, it might bring back some of the Sughi soldiers like Myke and Malta ...

... Anyway... the rogues were strong enough to take you down, and nobody expected that. We have to get a handle on them. Funny story: The same pack of rogues who took you down tried to take Dramos. He wiped them clean. Your brother is scary awesome! ...

... This is close-hold, very sensitive. Have you heard of the Mordax? Do you know what that is? Supposedly, Olam gave one to Dramos. Apparently, it's a game changer... Don't ask anyone about the Mordax, except Dramos directly. Nobody is supposed to know he has one.

... Hang in there, buddy. I'm with you all the way... regardless...

… Apollo's motivation was zero. He weakly tried to remember his life before this void. He did not care about that life. All he wanted was darkness and nothingness…

Torith:

It's been two months, Apollo. I don't cry anymore. I'm done with that. The search urgency has changed to routine. It makes me feel guilty, but it's impossible to stay in crisis mode forever.

Malta continues to offer to help, and she will give us soldiers, but we don't know what to do with them. There is nowhere else to search. We can't find you.

Tamir is working on some secret stuff. That gives me hope, although I know few details. He would tell me more about it, but there is plenty for me to do on the overt side.

Your friend, Myke, remains incredibly dedicated to finding you. But he's a Sughi person. His morals are different. He's super strong. Maybe as strong as you. But he hurts people, Apollo. He'll flatten anyone who he thinks might know where you are. Even Malta's people have had to tell him to back off. There are things I can't tell him because he'll take that information and go on a rampage. Did you know he used to be a Mentor? No wonder he's so strong... but he's dangerous!

I finally had it out with Malta. One-on-one. It was long. At first, it did not go well. She tried to recruit me as if nothing else was happening. I was furious and almost left, but then she told me to follow her, and we left the Sughi Command Center together. Once we were away, she totally changed her demeanor. She said she had to recruit me while we were at Command. It was part of her orders from her superiors. But once we were away, she apologized, and we spent the next three hours talking. She told me why she's with Sughi, and I told her why I'm with Olam. We didn't argue. She told me how she feels about you. For her, it is complicated. She knows she stands no chance of ever being with you as long as she is a Sughi. I told her I had no realistic expectation of being with you either. I mean, even if you and I were a couple here on Summa, there is no guarantee we'd ever know each other as Bloods. Then I asked her if she would come back to Olam if Olam promised her she would know you as a Blood. Maybe the two of you would be neighbors, classmates, or warriors together. Would that be enough to bring her back? She told me the offer was tempting if it ever came, but she probably would not take it. "I have to come back to Olam because I believe Olam, which I don't," she said. I respect her for that. In the end, Apollo, I still don't like Malta, but I think we at least understand each other. I trust her now, and she and I will keep working hard to find you...

...Apollo felt himself waking and consciousness returning. Unlike the many times before, this time, it was coming slowly, and he was no longer in the cold. It was not the brutal, painful awakening of too much power being forced into him too fast. This was a gentle transition from nothing to something, and he awoke without the usual pain. He no longer knew who he was or why he was here. His past memories were still there, but they were faint, surreal, and unimportant. Only the present mattered, and it was no longer filtered. His ghost had been stripped clean...

There was no attack or hate this time. There was no swirling mass of rogues poised to hold him down and tear him apart. Instead, there was one man in front of Apollo. And Apollo was no longer in the water. He and the man were in a cavern, deep underground. The cavern had some lava, providing light and warmth.

Apollo could have fled, but he had no reason to. Apollo had no fear of him, and there was nowhere Apollo wanted to go. Apollo was a "nothing." You cannot hurt, offend, or manipulate a "nothing." All that mattered was here and now. He did not care why the man was here or what he wanted.

At first, the man said nothing. He was simply there. In the lava light, Apollo could see his face. It was handsome, beautiful, and compelling.

I am nothing. I have nothing for him.

Contrasting the man's visible appeal, darkness emanated from him. It was a powerful darkness, very different from Summa's comforting blanket of sanctuary, rejuvenating darkness.

The man may have been with Apollo for a few minutes or an hour. Apollo did not know and did not care. Here and now was all that mattered.

The man extended a hand towards Apollo, contacting Apollo's cheek, as if offering comfort. Power flooded from him to Apollo. A dark power. A weapon. A controlling force. It differed from Apollo's friend, the darkness of Summa, where Apollo had found solace.

Apollo sensed the man expected Apollo to fear and respect him. Apollo was defenseless and weak, now up against a powerful ghost. Maybe Apollo would have feared him if Apollo had been someone. But he was nothing, with nothing to lose. No amount of power can hurt nothing.

The darkness from the man wanted to enter Apollo. It wanted to become part of him. Apollo was not alarmed. His ghost said no to the man's darkness. "You cannot be part of me." But Apollo did nothing to tell the man to leave. He merely said no. It was simple. It took no effort. He did not have the strength for effort. Apollo did not care what the man did or what he wanted. The answer was no.

The man was angry. Apollo did not care. The man cursed. The expletives were hollow. He threatened. Apollo was an inanimate object, unaffected. The man tried love. Apollo felt nothing.

The man tried again and again to infect Apollo. It should have worked. Apollo had been stripped of all defense, strength, and ability to reason. He was operating at a fundamental root level. He was at his core. He had no antivirus, no protection, and he was totally open to attack. He had no ability to parry, dodge, thrust, or thwart.

But Apollo's very core said no. This darkness was not Apollo. It did not compute. It was one plus one equals three. It was a wave of negatives. It was a full-stop… No.

The man brought his handsome, powerful face within inches of Apollo. Yes, he was truly beautiful, but his aura was cold and dark.

Apollo did not flinch, pull back, or resist. He was too weak to struggle. His core simply rejected what the man forcefully offered. No.

Apollo saw defeat in the man's strong face. The man pulled his power out of Apollo, gathering it back to himself like a valuable and limited quantity. Then he was gone. His darkness was, too.

Now, Apollo was alone. He did not know where he was, and he had no desire to know. He was nothing, and he wanted to stay that way. Dust, vapor, sand, or clay. It did not matter. He did not care. Inanimate. Nothing. The angry people were gone. So was the pain.

Apollo's ghost took power from the minerals, rocks, and dirt surrounding him. He melted into them, wanting to be one with them—part of Summa herself.

Soon, Apollo's ghost was fully recharged. But he was still nothing and wanted nothing—except to stay here, somewhere deep inside Mother Summa, in her arms and shielded from all.

45

Summa's Embrace

Apollo's ghost felt the heat of molten rock interspersed with solid minerals. It was powerful. He had never been this deep into Summa because there had never been a need. The pressures at this depth must be massive, and Apollo's ghost sensed their enormity. He could see nothing. Everything was pitch black and dense, and it wrapped him tightly. He wandered slowly and aimlessly in the bowels of Summa, relishing the supremacy of her spirit, letting it surround and flow through him. He might be a "nothing," but Summa was an "everything," and he was part of her. To wander freely and unmolested in her depths was paradise. She offered comfort, protection, and relief.

After he started his wander, he did not see the dark man again, nor did he see any of the hate-filled tormentors. Apollo doubted they could find him. He was too deep. Only a Quasar could find him now. Apollo's empty mind knew he could reach out to Olam or Megantha if needed. Maybe he would—eventually—but there was no need in his current present. His protector was Summa. Her spirit asked nothing of him, and she gave him everything he wanted.

Apollo's ghost was strong, fully powered, and healed. But his mind was far from healthy. It was empty, wanted little input, and absorbed sparingly.

Once, the sweet darkness of his wandering was interrupted by a spectacular vein of bright light caused by a concentration of minerals full of magnesium. They were igniting spontaneously from the heat and depth. Another time, a group of four or five ghosts passed by him within inches. They stopped and tried to engage, but he did not know who they were and did not care. He moved on and lost them immediately. He should wonder what they were doing so deep. But he had no interest in wondering.

Time had changed from meaningless to inert. Hours, days, weeks, and months were irrelevant. There was only the now. Summa was home. He moved forward, concerned little about direction—except to stay deep below the surface, always seeking tremendous heat and pressure. Summa's cooler crust extended thirty to fifty miles below the surface. Apollo wanted nothing to do with that. *Deeper,* he thought. *Deeper.*

Most of the huge veins of rock and magma that Apollo pushed through were hundreds or thousands of feet thick. There were different consistencies: solid layers, gritty or crumbled layers, magma, highly pressurized mud, or changes in the substance itself, such as from magma to silicates to igneous rock. Traveling through these changes allowed for a sense of forward motion.

Apollo's mind was healing slowly. He started to think about the beautiful, handsome man of darkness at the end of his torment. Apollo knew the man was significant, as was the man's forced effort to infest Apollo's soul with his heavy darkness. It was a darkness that would have consumed him. It was completely different from Mother Summa's darkness. It was a powerful, active darkness—alive and life-changing. A darkness Apollo wanted no part of. A darkness that was Apollo's polar opposite. Its rejection had been effortless.

More travel through the depths. More recovery. More self-awareness. Apollo was deep. So very deep. A hundred miles? Maybe. Thousands? More likely.

Apollo had felt no guidance, no plan, except to stay deep. Slowly, that changed. He became aware of subtle guidance. The kind Sapienti gives, not the bold, throw-open-the-door, give-you-a-hug guidance from Olam. Sapienti's guidance was quiet; nothing more than faint thoughts in Apollo's foggy brain. Had it been Olam driving, he would have taken Apollo by the shoulders, turned him right, left, up and down, moved him in the correct direction, patted him on the back, and told him, "You're doing great, son!"

The remote, misty, hard-to-decipher guidance continued. Apollo listened, sometimes. Mostly, he did not care. Deeper and deeper he traveled. A rough semblance of time returned. Days more of descent. *Where are we going, Sapienti?*

Then Summa changed. Apollo found rock inside her that was like none before. This rock was perfectly consistent, cooler, harder, and much denser than anything Apollo had ever encountered. He could only traverse it slowly, maybe a tenth of his normal speed through granite. Apollo knew he had found something unusual.

"*Found?*" The word came to Apollo. *What do you mean by "found?"*

Apollo corrected himself. *Led to, by Sapienti. Led to. I know Sapienti brought me here. Thank you, Olam, for letting Sapienti quietly lead me.*

Darkness prevented Apollo from seeing the color of this unusual rock. He doubted he'd ever seen rock like this. Its electrical qualities were superb. It was much more alive, as if it were generating its own power. The rock surged with smooth, clear, rejuvenating energy. Apollo's ghost fed from it, charging and healing. Apollo considered stopping and basking in the rock's purity. But Sapienti told him to keep going. Apollo's link with Sapienti was especially clear in this rock. *What is this substance?* Apollo wondered.

Don't stop. Keep going. His mental misfiring could not obfuscate the message's clarity.

Apollo continued down, damaged brain and all, clear on the need to continue forward. Also clear was that his long, peaceful, rejuvenating wander in the darkness of Summa's bowels was coming to an end. He would forever love the nighttime because of it.

Apollo tried to maintain a constant course, picking a direction he thought to be straight down. Tracking any course in this environment was difficult. The only sensory queues were gravity and friction. Apollo, however, was not helpless. He had been deep in the ground for a long time. Despite his overt brain's lack of motivation to engage on any level, his subconscious had learned a few things. Whether he realized it or not, he was now far better than most ghosts at deep underground travel.

After pushing through thousands of feet of this incredibly dense, vibrant rock, Apollo suddenly broke into another realm. It was a world deep within Summa. A planet within a planet. This world extended as far as Apollo could see. One hundred miles... two hundred? Maybe much more. Apollo was in the ceiling or sky of this world. There was plenty of light, although he could not see a sun. He estimated his breakthrough point to be five or six thousand feet off the ground. He held his position and stared. Below him were forests, lakes, low mountains, and an entire wilderness ecosystem. Apollo could see no buildings. If there were ghosts like him, he could see none.

Apollo understood that the incredibly dense rock he had passed through protected this world from the rest of Summa. He had to be hundreds or thousands of miles below Summa's crust, beyond the abilities of any surface-based sensors, protected in a world within the womb of Mother Summa herself. Unlike the hot temperatures outside this subworld's rock layer, Apollo found the temperatures normal here.

"*Go to the meadow,*" Apollo heard in his brain, more forceful and straightforward than usual.

OK, Sapienti. Got it.

Below Apollo, there was a large, colorful meadow surrounded by a healthy forest of aspen and pine. Some of the aspen trees were changing colors, showing off their yellows and oranges, contrasting nicely with the evergreens. With clouded admiration, Apollo realized this inner world had seasons.

Soon, Apollo was on the ground in the meadow. He looked around and absorbed. The light, colors, and natural beauty chipped away at his defenses. It was impossible to ignore the beauty of this place, even if he, himself, remained a nothing.

46

Wolves

Apollo had only been in the meadow for a few minutes when his eye caught movement off to his left. Two ghost wolves had come out of the tree line, now eyeing him from a distance. Apollo keyed on them while he continued to sort through his bearings.

The wolves moved forward, towards him, quickly working the terrain in his direction. Apollo knew he should worry that they might be hostile. But in his detached mental state, he cared little for his personal safety.

The wolves clearly were ghosts, which meant they were not restricted by objects on the ground or by the ground itself. And yet, as Apollo watched them approach, he saw that they were determined to maneuver as if they were physical Bloods. Sometimes, they acted like proper ghosts and transitioned through obstacles, such as through a large fallen log, but mostly, they followed the type of path they would have to track when they became physical. *Their programming is strong,* thought Apollo.

Apollo was no wolf expert. He thought they both looked like mature adults, probably males. The leader was big, with bright blue eyes and an equally bright blue aura. He was primarily gray, highlighted with streaks of black. His nose was jet black, as were his lips, whiskers, and the soft flesh surrounding his eyes. The other wolf was gray and brown, with some brown in the coloring of his nose and other features. His eyes and aura shifted between brown and

green, the same way Torith's shifted between brown and
aqua blue.

The blue of the wolf leader's eyes and aura matched
that of Apollo in depth, warmth, and tint. Apollo wondered if
that was meant to be, and he sensed an immediate, powerful
bond with this animal. Blue eyes came right up to Apollo, as
if he had been coached. There was no hesitation. He seemed
to already know and trust Apollo. The blue touched his nose
to Apollo's outstretched hand. Apollo went down on all fours
and looked the beast in the eyes. The wolf immediately
looked away, only re-engaging eye contact when Apollo
stood and moved back. Apollo understood this was not a sign
of weakness. It was deference.

Both wolves then came to alert and turned towards
the forest from which they had come. At the same time, they
craned their necks to keep Apollo in sight. Apollo could tell
they wanted him to follow them. Apollo motioned them
forward and stepped with them. The wolves headed out,
constantly checking on Apollo. Soon, they were all on the
move, a coordinated threesome.

Thank you for guiding me here, Sapienti, Apollo
projected, confident his message of gratitude would be
received. *And please thank Olam that it's wolves. I'm not
ready for my friends and family.*

The wolves entered the tree line, glanced at Apollo,
then continued deeper into the aspen and pine. They
followed a logical path, although there was no sign of any
wear on the ground or the vegetation. This told Apollo there
were no Blood animals in the area. These wolves, like
Apollo, would eventually become Bloods on an earth
somewhere. Apollo wondered if they had any sense of their
future.

During most of Apollo's wandering in Summa's blackness, he had felt no direction. But now it was obvious his travels had not been random. Olam and Megantha had not abandoned him. It was no coincidence he was here following these four-legged beasts.

The wolves' route took them to rising terrain where the aspen thinned, giving way to more pine. Eventually, the aspens were gone, and the pines were so thick that they blocked any direct sunlight. There was little growth on the forest floor, which was covered with inches of pine needles. Sounds in this temple were muffled, and the chirping of birds in the tops of the evergreens was distant.

The wolves halted in a small clearing, a break in the trees about twenty yards wide. Towering trunks encircled the space, and a weave of branches blocked most of the sky. On two sides of the clearing lay the skeletal remains of massive fallen trees, their trunks forming half-round benches. It was a natural place for resting or gathering.

The wolves took a rest in the middle of the clearing. Blue eyes went to the ground with his legs directly under him, his chin on one front paw, and his eyes steady on Apollo. Although resting, he remained alert. The gray and brown wolf lay on his side, much more relaxed and only partially facing Apollo. Any guard duties were apparently the responsibility of blue eyes.

From the wolves' demeanor, Apollo could see it was now time to wait, and Apollo was fine with that. All of this was magic, and he had no agenda beyond simply being here.

Night came, and they were still waiting. The birds were quiet now, and the wolves had hardly moved. Blue eyes dozed lightly but frequently tracked Apollo. Apollo had no idea what they were waiting for, but he could feel this world within a world changing him, bringing him back.

The darkness of the night was friendly, like the darkness inside Summa. For the first time in weeks, he thought about Torith, Tamir, Myke, and others who were important in his life. *What did they think happened to me? Did they try to find me? Did Dramos help?* Instinctively, Apollo knew they all had looked for him.

Through the tree canopy, Apollo could see sprinklings of moonlight. Wanting to see more, Apollo assured the blue-eyed wolf he would be back, and then he went up to the top of the pine trees for a better view. A three-quarters moon was hanging at about forty-five degrees. There were no stars, nor could he see any clouds. *Does it rain here? It must.*

Apollo knew the moon could not be real. Otherwise, it would have to be hundreds of thousands of miles away. He wondered how the creator of this sub-world had simulated the real thing. *Who was the creator of this world? Olam? Megantha? Some Forza with help from a Quasar?*

Apollo left the treetops and went back down to the comfort of the wolves. He positioned himself close to blue-eyes and lay down on the ground as much as a ghost could lie on anything. Eventually, the moon set, and the forest became multiple layers of darkness. The soft auras of the wolves provided some light.

Two more wolves joined them. They first headed towards the blue, seeking his approval, and then they came to Apollo for his. It was surprising to Apollo that the wolves were so deferential towards him. These were pack animals. Why would they consider him anything other than a tolerated outsider? The two newcomers were a mix of young and old. The old one went off to one side of the clearing, but the young one took up an alert position, down on its folded fours, about five feet from Apollo, watching him closely.

Apollo's sense of time was returning. If the nights in this world lasted the same as those on Summa's surface, Apollo thought they were probably well past midnight and closer to dawn.

Blue eyes suddenly shot to his feet and turned to face the direction they had come from hours ago. All four wolves were now on their feet, their ears forward, straining to hear. They looked excited, not threatened. Apollo could neither see nor hear anything in the forest, and he stared hard into the black, trying to understand what had brought them to alert.

Blue eyes began shaking with anticipation, and the youngest wolf started an excited barking howl, prancing in place.

"Hello, my babies," said a woman's voice from the darkness. Now, all four wolves bark-howled, their bodies shivering with delirium.

Apollo still could not see the woman, but her voice was clear, and it was familiar. He knew she was close, and he was surprised he could not find her aura in the dark. *Surely, she has one... right?* Although Apollo could not see her, Apollo felt power and goodness radiate from her.

"I'm playing with my babies," she said to Apollo. He could tell she was only twenty or thirty yards away. "I'll show myself soon." She continued to keep her distance. "It's fun to watch their excitement."

She was still invisible to Apollo, but the wolves were able to track her. She had apparently moved sideways, and he saw all four beasts shift their intensity to the left. "I'm hiding my aura, Apollo. It's so much fun to watch how perceptive they are."

Apollo noticed that the blue, in addition to his intensive focus, was also taking in large, sensory nosefuls, searching for the woman.

Suddenly, the woman illuminated her aura, and she entered the clearing. All four wolves were overcome with happiness. She was a ghost, so they could not physically hug, but she wrapped her spirit around and through them, showing and telling them how much she loved them. Apollo was not a direct participant in this, but her majestic presence projected on him, too.

Now Apollo knew who she was. She was the Forza from the command center named Lionah. This was Lionah from the Red River Desert. The Lionah, who had been in favor of Apollo going to Sughi City with Myke. Yes, Lionah, who had once been one of Myke's apprentices, back when he had been a Mentor.

Lionah finished greeting her wolf pack. They had calmed enough that she could now have a conversation with Apollo. Her presence was a vivid contrast to the man of darkness—and all those before him—who had beaten Apollo down for months.

Lionah looked at Apollo for a long time. Then she started to tear up. "I'm sorry, Apollo, for all the pain you've been through." She continued to look at him closely. "I never thought it would be so bad. Olam and Megantha would not allow me to rescue you. I still don't know why. I'm sure they are right, but I never understood their reasoning. I was not allowed to help you."

Apollo could feel her emotions. It was unusual to hear a Forza openly disagree with Olam or Megantha. But Apollo was still in the cocoon where he had retreated to protect himself. He could hear what she was saying, and her power was undeniable, but he was largely unmoved.

"You are going to need time, Apollo," she was saying. "Time to heal and time to come back to us. That's why you are here, in this sanctuary."

"Did you even look for me?" he asked, detached.

"Yes, yes!" Apollo! Not me... I could have found you quickly. But your brother and your friends searched for you, frantically and endlessly, for months."

Apollo absorbed that. He knew he should feel more grateful for what they went through, but he struggled to generate empathy for himself or anyone. "I am broken," he said to Lionah. "I'm not the same. I don't care about anything. And nobody can hurt me."

"I know," she said with compassion.

"And who was the man trying to give me darkness?" Apollo asked. "He was at the end like he was important, but he was nothing to me."

"Yes!" she said with excitement. "Someday, you will understand how singular your reaction to him was. That was B. Z. Sughi himself. He thought he had you, Apollo. You were beaten down. You loved the darkness. He was sure he could give you the darkness you so craved. But you rejected it. Just like that. With zero hesitation. I've never seen that before. You did it without thought or effort. You knew what he offered was different, and you turned him away. And you did it while in the lowest of lows. Your reaction truly was one in a million, and Sughi was floored—totally taken aback—surprised and confused."

Apollo only partially understood. Mostly, he did not care.

"We had a deal with Sughi," said Lionah. "He had one chance at you. He wanted to make you one of his commanders. He thought that if he could break you, you would readily agree. But you threw it right back at him.

Right in his face. Outright rejection and proof positive that no matter what he tries to do to you, you are inherently on Olam's side and reject what Sughi has to offer."

Apollo heard the words. He tried to be interested. He knew this must be important.

"Why did it end?" Apollo asked. "The breaking and torturing?"

"Two reasons, Apollo," she explained. "One was the deal with Sughi. We were only going to give him one chance. And, secondly, your friends had found you. Sughi's time was limited. He had to take his shot when he did because Dramos, Myke, Tamir, and Torith were all bearing down on your location. They were within minutes of being there to free you. Dramos alone, as you know, could have taken out the rogues guarding you."

"They found me?" Apollo asked, struggling to understand. "I did not see them."

"Because you needed to heal, Apollo." Lionah was close to Apollo, looking him in the eyes. Apollo could feel her power surge through him. "I told them they had to let you go. You needed time to wander and heal in Summa, and now you need time here in this Sub-Summa."

"Sub-Summa?"

"Yes. Had I let you go with them, they would have needed too much from you. Instead, you need to build yourself back in layers, and the first layer was your wandering time inside Summa."

Apollo barely understood what she said, and instead, he asked, "But where were they? Were they close?"

"Yes, they were close, Apollo. They could see you. Torith begged, cried, pleaded to come to you."

Apollo processed slowly and incompletely. "I'm broken," he said again.

"You are," said Lionah, ghostly embracing Apollo. "But we're fixing that."

"Okay," said Apollo.

"This Sub-Summa is a sanctuary, Apollo." Sughi and his followers cannot come here. Nobody can come unless they are brought here, like you have been."

"The wolves?" asked Apollo.

"The wolves are for you. That way, you are not alone."

"Thank you," said Apollo, starting to understand why he was here. "I like the blue-eyed one."

"His name is Glacier," Lionah told him. "He knows he's supposed to take care of you. Treat him right, Apollo. He wants to be with you."

Apollo and Lionah talked some more. Then she told him she would come back in a few weeks. "You'll have more questions then," she explained. "Your brain will be working better."

Lionah spent time with the wolves before leaving. She pulled Glacier aside, and Apollo watched as she spoke to him directly. It looked like she was giving him instructions about Apollo, and they both repeatedly glanced at Apollo as they spoke.

Lionah then left. The last thing she said to Apollo was, "You've done more than you can know, Apollo. Now, heal yourself in this special place. Your friends need you, and we need you back in the fight."

47

Sub-Summa

Soon after Lionah left, the second set of wolves left, too. Before doing so, they did nose taps with Glacier and hand-to-nose goodbyes with Apollo. Not long after that, Sub-Summa lit up as if a sun had risen. It was daytime. Apollo wondered how that was happening, but he was in no rush to figure it out. He did, however, want to look around this fantastic world. "Come on, Glacier," he said to blue eyes.

Glacier jumped to his feet, as did Glacier's companion, the gray and brown wolf. If that wolf had a name, Lionah had not shared it with Apollo. "I'll call you Wolf Two," Apollo said to the gray/brown. *Not very original,* Apollo thought to himself. But he did not want to give it a real name if it already had one.

During yesterday's hike to this meeting spot, they had passed the entrance to a valley that gently climbed over the span of several miles. The valley was flat and carved out, with a stream running through it, making for interesting terrain that might be home to other wildlife. Apollo hoped for a closer look. He wished the wolves could talk with him like they could with Lionah. They could tell him where all the interesting places were. On the other hand, it would not hurt for Apollo to search it all out on his own. *Part of the healing process,* he surmised. *Probably something I need.*

Apollo started back the way they had come yesterday, and the wolves came, too. As the trio progressed, the wolves were often in front, crisscrossing and scouting ahead, but always looking back and keeping track of Apollo. To make things easier for them, Apollo soon learned that all he had to do was quickly yelp when he was changing direction. They'd key on his new path and immediately adjust. It was interesting how they were following Apollo from the front. Apollo thought it was probably possible to teach them voice commands for "turn right" and "turn left," but the system of simple yelps and their constant attention to his movements worked well enough.

Like yesterday, the ghost wolves followed paths on the ground that were similar to what they would have to do when they were physical Bloods. At one point, the threesome reached the top of a hundred-foot cliff. There was a long way around, but Apollo transitioned straight down the sheer face. Had he been a Blood, the "fall" would have killed him. Once at the bottom, Apollo turned and called for the wolves. They hesitated, prancing and whining, but refusing to come down the cliff. Apollo knew it would not hurt them. He watched as the wolves took off in a hard run to take the long, roundabout way.

Once Glacier and Wolf Two had circled and joined Apollo at the bottom, Apollo chose to praise them rather than express disappointment. Apollo also told himself he would not do that to the wolves again. These were his friends, and they were programmed the way they were programmed. No need to try to change them, and he had no interest in causing them anxiety.

Apollo continued towards the valley, with the last part of the journey along the spine of a low ridge, then down a long slope to the mouth of the valley itself. The stream exiting this valley could almost be called a river, and it had plenty of water and catch basins for mountain fish such as rainbow trout or whitefish. Apollo transitioned over various parts of the river, looking for fish. He could not see any. "Where are the fish?" he called to Glacier.

Glacier looked at Apollo with attention, but he also had a look on his face of, "What are you yammering about, human?"

"The fish?" Apollo asked. "How come there are no fish?"

Glacier came into the river and began sniffing and looking around, copying Apollo's search, most likely wondering what they were looking for. One part of the river was deep and much deeper than Apollo's height, so he went under to explore. Descending about twelve feet, Apollo looked up and saw Glacier swimming on the surface, looking distraught and sticking his head into the water to check on Apollo. Apollo returned to the surface to assure Glacier that everything was all right, and then he went back under to explore the bottom. There wasn't much down there other than mud. Apollo resurfaced, a little disappointed, hoping to have at least found some kind of bottom feeder, but he had seen nothing.

Apollo headed towards the left riverbank, and then he started up the valley, the wolves "following" him from up in front.

The dominant trees continued to be aspen and pine. The terrain was beautiful but not particularly unusual for a mountain valley. They saw some deer. There were also marmots in a long rock fall area below a nearby cliff. Apollo spotted two mountain goats up on steep terrain bordering the valley. They seemed out of place, but he did not pretend to have expertise in where they should be. He was surprised he had not seen more things out of place in this remote world. He wondered if that was the whole point. If this were a sanctuary, it was meant for calm and healing. Maybe it was meant to be beautiful, but also predictably boring. Glacier and Wolf 2 were, by far, the most interesting things he had seen so far.

Apollo spent the next two weeks exploring with the wolves. They covered new terrain every day, resting in different places each night. Their overland progress was much slower than he could have made had he flown or transitioned. The wolves' ground maneuvers forced him to be one with the land, and he loved it. Sometimes, he quickly transitioned above the trees or higher to improve his bearings, but then he would return to the wolves, not wanting them to feel abandoned. They soon became accustomed to this and would wait patiently for him to return.

Once, they traveled to one of the border walls of this inner world. The terrain came to a halt at the wall, with the wall of the world rising thousands of feet above them. Apollo shot up, tracking the wall itself. After a thousand feet, he could tell the wall was slowly curving inward. Four thousand feet up, the amount of the curve was fairly pronounced, and by the time he was an estimated five or six thousand feet, there had been enough curve that, as he tracked the wall, he was traveling much more parallel to the ground than in an upwards direction.

He did not want to be away from the dogs too long, so he returned to his starting point. From there, he looked side to side along the wall. If there was a curvature along the horizontal line, he could not detect it. This inner world was much wider than it was tall. It might be shaped like an enormous arena, or maybe it was more square-shaped with actual corners, where the walls took ninety-degree turns. Apollo transitioned into the wall. Here, its substance was the same as he remembered it when he had first come through it.

Like before, it was much denser than anything else he had previously transitioned, and it was energy-rich. He thought of the tremendous heat and pressures inside Summa on the other side of this wall. He assumed the wall here was thousands of feet thick. How wonderful this place was. Apollo knew he was lucky to be here. What a tremendous gift, and he hoped it would not end soon.

When Apollo considered how he felt about being here in Sub-Summa, he realized he was becoming less broken.

It had been weeks since Lionah's last visit, and she came again to see Apollo and her wolves. She said Wolf Two's name was Fjord. She also asked Apollo how he felt about Glacier. There was no question that Apollo had become tightly bonded to the animal, as had Glacier to Apollo. "Do you want him, Apollo?" she asked.

"What do you mean?"

"You can take him with you, Apollo, if you want."

Apollo thought about this. Of course, he wanted Glacier with him, but... "I think he'd be happier here with Fjord," he said.

"You're right that it's probably best for him to be here. But he's going to miss you, Apollo."

"Can I come back to visit him?"

"Probably not. But there is another option if you want it."

Apollo looked at her. She had paused.

"Yes?" he asked.

"You can have him when you are both Bloods."

"You can promise that?" Apollo asked with surprise. "Really?" Apollo was thrilled. "But how... I mean—"

"Megantha told me I could promise him to you... if you want him."

Apollo was taken aback, and he felt something burst inside him. Large segments of the protective shield he had put up during the torture and abuse by the rogues were shattered by Lionah's offer. The love building inside him for Glacier overwhelmed that shield. Apollo was thrilled. His journey back to completeness required shedding his internal, protective barriers.

"Yes… yes… of course," mumbled Apollo, barely able to speak. "I can have him as a Blood? Yes... Yes."

Apollo tried to compose himself. "Can you tell him he's mine?" But then Apollo had a worry. "But... but isn't he yours? Doesn't he want to be with you, Lionah?"

"Yes... but we can both have him, right? I'll have him here, and you'll have him for the short time you are both Bloods."

"Short time?" asked Apollo.

"Relatively short time. Even if your Blood life is one hundred years, that's still short."

"Yes."

"And Glacier's will be shorter. If he lives a full life, it won't be more than ten or twenty years."

Apollo's joy at the prospect of having Glacier as a Blood was saddened by knowing he would not be with Glacier for more time. He fell silent, thinking about that.

"When I'm a Blood, I won't know he's a gift," Apollo said. "I won't remember you gave him to me."

"True, but you'll know he's special. And you might have enough insight to understand he's a gift. Hopefully, you'll be able to hear Sapienti when you're a Blood."

"Either way, I want him. Of course, I want him, Lionah. Thank you!"

Apollo and Lionah talked for a while longer, and then she left. One nagging—maybe silly—question he had was why there were no fish in the rivers and streams. She explained that this sanctuary was never designed to be a complete world. "It's a place for healing, Apollo. Fish are a less important part of that, unlike wolves, which can be so loyal and loving.

She was right on that. It's hard to feel warm and fuzzy about a fish. But a wolf. That was totally different.

Apollo was surprised she had said nothing to him about the need for him to move forward. There was no pressure to rush his recovery or to hurry up with his healing. He expected her to tell him he was needed on the surface and that it was time for him to reassume his responsibilities in the real world. But there was none of that from Lionah.

Despite Lionah's lack of pushing, Apollo knew he was making progress. His sense of obligation and responsibility was returning. Glacier and Fjord were a big part of that. Apollo's defenses against empathy and caring were breaking down. He was building himself back into a complete person.

During Apollo's first weeks in Sub-Summa, his detached mental state dictated a certain type of exploring. Every day, he and the wolves would move to a new place, always miles from where they had stayed the night before. There was no sense of attachment or permanence. But Apollo was changing, and not long after Lionah's visit, when they found a place they liked, they made it their home base for days or even an entire week. They still did their daily exploring, but it was always from that base. Then, they would move to another location.

Once, during their travels, they found a family of beavers. Apollo located their den inside a good-sized beaver dam. The dam was old, and Apollo could see that it had been constructed years before by actual, physical Blood beavers.

There was much evidence of old beaver activity, including fallen trees. The beavers living in the dam now were ghosts.

Apollo wanted to look inside the beaver den. He left Glacier and Fjord on the bank of the beaver pond, transitioned under the water, and came up through the entrance into the ghost beavers' den.

There were three beavers in there, and Apollo's sudden appearance freaked them out. From nowhere, this human ghost head had invaded their space. All three chittered aggressively and dove for the water, shooting out of the den.

Apollo felt bad about his abrupt invasion. Rather than follow them, he went straight up through the roof of the den and then across the pond, back to the dogs. Apollo chuckled and said to Glacier, "That was mean of me."

Glacier cocked his head sideways, trying to understand.

"I'll need to work on my beaver etiquette."

Glacier nodded as if he agreed.

"Come on, boys," Apollo said. "Now that I've ruined the neighborhood, let's be on our way." At that, Apollo headed downstream from the beaver dam, and the wolves followed.

Occasionally, the other two wolves from the pack would join them. Evidently, they were following and keeping track of Glacier and Fjords' movements. Apollo could never figure out what made them join or go back out on their own. That was wolf business to which he was not privy. When they joined, it was never for more than a night, although several times they joined in the morning and participated in the day's explorations, leaving the next morning.

When there were four wolves, the usual traveling formation was Glacier and Fjord out in front, then Apollo, followed by the other two wolves in back. It was always clear that Glacier was in charge of the pack. In turn, Glacier deferred to Apollo.

Apollo's bond with Glacier was becoming strong. It was different from times in the past when Apollo had formed bonds with other animals. For example, his sister, Celti, often had pets in the house while they were growing up. She had a horse she especially loved. She would sneak it into her room. Megantha constantly had to tell her it should be outside. Since the horse was always around, Apollo was friendly with it and would try to talk to it. When Celti left the family and moved away in protest, she took the horse with her, and Apollo missed it.

There was also a time when Tamir had a pet dolphin. This was while he was in college. Somehow, he had convinced the dolphin to live with him, rather than in the water where it belonged. Unlike the wolves who refused to transition or fly, Tamir taught the dolphin to fly, and they would go to school together. Some of his professors didn't mind. Others asked him to keep it out of the classroom. Apollo liked that dolphin, and he went with Tamir when Tamir took the dolphin back to the ocean. It took some coaxing, but they convinced the dolphin to stay.

Apollo thought about Celti's horse and Tamir's dolphin. His relationship with them was nothing like what he was experiencing with Glacier. His bond with Glacier was as strong as his with Tamir, Torith, or Myke. It occupied a different place in his heart than his feelings for his friends, but it was of equal weight.

One night, they stopped for the day on a flat area on the side of a steep hillside. The flatness was formed by a prominent outcropping. All four wolves were with him this evening. From their position, they had a good view of a lake below that had turned dark and colorless now that the day was ending. Apollo knew the Sub-Summa moon would be up soon. It varied in phase, but it never was a no-moon, and most of the phases were half to full. Unlike a real moon, it came up at about the same time each night.

Once the moon rose enough to illuminate the lake and the landscape, Apollo decided to have some fun with the wolves. All four were lying on their sides, including Glacier, who was intermittently tracking Apollo with one eye. Apollo moved into the middle of the wolves and suddenly fell onto all fours and barked twice, facing towards the lake below. All four wolves were instantly on their feet, focused intently in the same direction as Apollo, their auras glowing bright in the moon-laced night.

Now that Apollo had their attention, he shot down into the ground and came up right next to Glacier. Apollo meowed at him loudly, like a deranged cat. Then, Apollo laughed loudly, hoping Glacier would understand it was a game. Apollo then went underground and shot up next to Fjord, meowing loudly at him, too. The wolves were pumped, although they were still unsure what was happening. Back underground and up next to the other two wolves, then barking loudly—not at them, but between them at something imaginary. Back underground and up by Glacier. Staring him in the eyes, meowing and spinning on all fours, then racing around on all fours between the wolves.

They got it now. It was a game, and they all jumped in. Yelping, spinning, jumping, and generally making a racket, waking up the night in the quiet forest.

Now that they were riled up, Apollo scampered on his fours over to the edge of the rock outcropping and started howling at the night's moon. The whole pack joined in. It was wonderful. They howled and yelped, and when the wolves seemed to stop, Apollo would howl even more, and they joined in again with enthusiasm.

After that night, Apollo regularly played with the wolves, sometimes teasing them. There were times when they did not seem to realize it was a game, maybe classifying it in their minds as the incomprehensible acts of crazy humans. But there were also plenty of times when they knew he was playing a game, and they tried to join in. Glacier might have been in charge of the pack, but Apollo was definitely the camp clown.

Life with the wolves was good, and this splendid life continued for months. But things were about to change.

48

Glacier's Warning

One day, Apollo, Glacier, and Fjord were on the move, working their way through a relatively flat terrain covered with heavy timber. Given the density of the trees, forward visibility on the ground was minimal. Apollo had been up above the trees several times to see where he wanted to go, and he knew that up ahead, the timber gave way to a large, circular, flat clearing that looked like it was covered with wild grass. There was dense forest all around the clearing, except for the far side, where the clearing was up against a vertical cliff several hundred feet high. Apollo wondered why the clearing was there when it logically should have been more forest. It seemed to have a purpose rather than being a random break in the trees.

Approaching the clearing, and before they broke into the open, Glacier's demeanor started to change. His pace slowed, and his head began to hang low. He was no longer scouting aggressively. Something was wrong, and he seemed unhappy. Apollo noticed this immediately. Glacier started looking back at Apollo as if wanting assurance or support or something that Apollo could not read. Finally, Glacier turned around and came to Apollo and put his head into Apollo's knees, not wanting to move.

Apollo reassured the ghost wolf and encouraged him to move forward. Glacier looked up towards Apollo. The look in his eyes was different. Apollo wondered if this was

Glacier's form of pleading. "Come on, Glacier. It's okay. Let's go."

Glacier held his ground briefly, then nuzzled up to Apollo briefly, then turned and moved forward with a demeanor of resignation.

After another hundred yards, Glacier veered hard right, clearly trying to change Apollo's mind about where they were going. This was still well before the clearing, and Apollo thought it was before Glacier could have known the clearing was there. Apollo called him back on track, which the wolf did, reluctantly. After more forward progress, Glacier again veered right. Apollo called him back, with some firmness this time. Glacier complied. His ears sagged, as did his head and tail. Then, rather than follow from the front, Glacier moved behind Apollo. This was not at all Glacier's M.O.

Unlike Glacier, Fjord did not react in the same way. He seemed to have little sadness or foreboding about heading towards the clearing. But Fjord knew his place in the hierarchy, and he stayed back with Glacier. Unlike the past months of exploring with the ghost wolves, Apollo was now in the lead. "It's okay, guys," said Apollo. "There isn't anything up there that will hurt us."

Up ahead, Apollo could see more light through the trees, and he knew the clearing was close. Behind him, Glacier sat down on his hind legs and refused to go further. Wolves normally do not bark, but Glacier did, clearly wanting Apollo to stop. His ears were still down, and the wolf started whining.

This created a dilemma for Apollo. Ever since trying to coax Glacier off the cliff during the first days of their exploring, he had vowed never to put the ghost wolf in that position again: one where Apollo knew the wolf would not be hurt but where he was forcing the beast to go against its deeply ingrained programming.

Apollo had no idea what was bothering Glacier, who showed that he wanted nothing to do with the clearing. Apollo was sure that whatever it was, it would not hurt them. After all, Lionah promised this mini-world would be a sanctuary.

As Apollo processed this, he realized how much he had returned to himself during these months of wandering with Glacier and Fjord. The warrior in him was rejuvenated. When he first arrived in Sub-Summa, he was not afraid of a fight because he did not care what happened to him. Now, he was not afraid because he was strong. He could fight back—hard.

Apollo returned to Glacier, got down on all fours, and looked Glacier in the eyes.

Glacier moved his gaze sideways, programmed to never do a close-up eye-to-eye with his leader.

"What's wrong, boy?" Apollo asked, knowing there would not be an answer. Like before, he wished he could talk with Glacier like Lionah could.

Apollo conversed with Glacier for a few minutes. It was a calm, one-way discussion. Apollo knew his words meant much less than his tone and demeanor.

Glacier was paying attention, sometimes flicking his eyes for an instant to meet Apollo's.

"I'm going to go on and into the clearing," Apollo explained. "You can follow or not. It's up to you."

Glacier moved into Apollo as if wanting comfort. This was not the strong, powerful ghost wolf Apollo was used to.

Apollo stood up. He started walking towards the clearing while calmly talking with Glacier.

Glacier stood on all fours, but he would not advance.

Apollo decided not to push it. "It's fine. You can stay." Then, turning to Fjord, Apollo said, "Come on, Fjord. Come."

Apollo started forward. He watched as Fjord hesitated. Apollo called Fjord again, and after some hesitation, Fjord followed.

Apollo knew it was killing Glacier to be left behind, and Glacier let out one whimper. As Apollo and Fjord progressed and put distance between them and Glacier, Apollo looked back to see Glacier prancing in place and sometimes spinning, clearly distraught. Apollo felt bad for the wolf, but now Apollo was determined to find out why the clearing was such a scary place for a strong ghost wolf—a wolf that had been savvy, loyal, and fearless.

Apollo and Fjord passed the tree line and now stood in the open at the edge of the clearing.

Fjord seemed willing to go forward, although he constantly checked behind him for Glacier, of whom they had lost sight.

At first, Apollo could see nothing unusual about the clearing. It was about one hundred yards wide. Then he had a better look at the cliff at the far end. He had seen the cliff from his previous far-off checks at altitude. But now he saw that, at the bottom of the cliff, there was a perfectly shaped, rectangular doorway. The door was cut directly into the mountain. It was obvious that the entryway into the cliff was the reason for the clearing. Apollo was determined to learn the doorway's significance.

Apollo started across the clearing. Fjord stayed at his side. Halfway across, Apollo looked back for Glacier, but the wolf was too far back in the trees to be seen. Apollo continued.

Now Apollo was at the rectangular cave door. The cut continued into the rock. It extended as far as Apollo could see, disappearing into the darkness. It was a long, perfectly cut rectangular cave.

"Shall we go in there, Fjord?"

Fjord looked at Apollo and sat down. He moaned a little, and when Apollo motioned him to go forward, he refused. Fjord was not as worried about the cave as Glacier, but Apollo could see that Fjord had no intention of going inside.

Apollo sensed nothing about the tunnel. There were no markings, signs, or anything to tell him if entering would be good or bad. On the other hand, he had been given clear indications from the wolves not to go in. *Should I go in anyway?* He asked himself. *Of course I will. I'm strong again. I can handle it.*

Suddenly, Apollo heard a long, mournful howl from across the clearing. It was Glacier who had appeared at the tree line. He was no longer whining, prancing, or sulking. Instead, he was standing firmly, head and ears up, howling to Apollo and the world.

Seeing his Glacier so distraught was heartbreaking. *I'll make it up to him,* Apollo thought. Apollo was confident in his ability to handle the cave, whatever was there. He looked Glacier's way and tried to tell him it would be all okay.

Glacier held his position and continued his howling, louder and more mournful, as if the world itself were about to end.

"See you soon, Fjord," said Apollo as he stepped into the cave. One step, two steps, ten steps. There was nothing in this cave. It was getting darker. The sound of Glacier's mourning was fading.

Maybe I should turn around, thought Apollo. *There is nothing in here, and I'm scaring my wolf friends for no reason.*

Apollo took three more steps forward.

Suddenly, everything changed.

49

Return

In a split second, Apollo found himself back on the surface of Summa, no longer in the Sub-Summa sanctuary. One instant, he had been in the long, rectangular cave, thinking he should turn around, and the next he was here, somewhere on Summa, far from the safe place he had grown to love.

Apollo immediately ached for Glacier. Clearly, Glacier knew what was going to happen and that he was losing Apollo. How terrible that must have been for him. And now, for Apollo, it was equally as terrible. He would see Glacier again—he was sure of Lionah's promise—but it would not be for a long time. Oh, how he wished he could say goodbye to his wonderful ghost wolf friend.

Apollo fell to the ground and cried. He wanted to call Lionah, Megantha, or Olam and plead with them for a chance to see Glacier again. *I want to tell him goodbye!* But Apollo knew that was not going to happen. Somehow, he understood that this last, awful event was his final cleansing from all the abuse and negativity he had endured with the rogues. Now, all he thought of was the wonderful times with Glacier and Fjord, and the times they would have together in the future when they were physical Bloods.

It took hours for Apollo to pull himself together. Not only was he back in the real world, but he had lost something he loved as much as anything or anyone. It hurt.

After several hours, Apollo called for Olam, who came immediately. Megantha came, too. They both told him how much they loved and were proud of him.

"Myke is back with us," Olam said. "It's because of you, Apollo. What you went through brought Myke back."

Apollo did not ask how. He knew he would hear it from Myke later. "Is that why I went through all that?" asked Apollo. "Was it all a plan?"

"Yes," said Megantha. "And we were hoping it would bring others back too, she said."

"You mean... Malta?" asked Apollo.

"Yes, for one," she said. "Malta is still trying to figure it out. She worked very hard to find you... and she has a tremendous dislike for the rogues. We may still get her back. If we do... a lot of it will be because of you, Apollo."

Apollo could not get Glacier out of his mind. "Can you tell Glacier goodbye for me? And tell him I love him and will see him again?"

"Lionah will do that," said Olam. "Glacier will understand you did not abandon him."

Apollo was comforted knowing that Glacier would understand, as much as a wolf could. Apollo talked with his parents for another half hour. Then they hugged and kissed him. "Now it's time to get back to work, my boy," said Olam.

"I know," answered Apollo.

At that, both his parents were gone, and Apollo was left totally charged and loved. Things were not perfect, and he was still very damaged. But he now had a clear understanding of where he would be going. He might be forever scarred, but he was going to be a force to be reckoned with by Sughi, who had failed to recruit him. The breaking and repairing gave him a better understanding of what Sughi and his people could do. Apollo was now battle-hardened and better able to take the ugly that would be unleashed on him in the future. His innocence was gone. He was ready to fight.

50

Special Ops Squad

Five years later…

Apollo, Tamir, and Torith were waiting in a briefing room for Reemo's arrival. They were in a protected command center a thousand miles east of Lake Minnick, far from where they had gone to school and played together as children. Their mood was tense, knowing that whatever assignment Reemo was bringing to them would be difficult. But "difficult" was not what bothered them. These magnificent ghosts thrived on difficult. No, it was the nature of the difficulty that had them concerned, and that concern centered around protecting Torith from being hurt.

The three of them were part of a small, four-person special ops squad, all hand-picked by Apollo. Their fourth member was Myke, who was also in the room. Myke stayed a little off to the side, wanting to give space to the tight threesome who had been a lock since first grade.

Apollo and Myke had a different kind of relationship. It was incredibly bonded and as strong as Apollo's with Torith and Tamir. But with Myke, Apollo's relationship was more hardcore. It was based on the harsh reality of battle and conflict. It was not tempered by the soft innocence of childhood, or surfing at the canyon, or sitting together in grade school writing reports about fish. No, Myke and Apollo first met fighting each other, and that first battle led to immediate respect. There was a unique chemistry between Myke and Apollo. It was more blunt and real. Myke could say anything to Apollo, and there was no offense. Apollo's style with Myke was more reserved, but still harsher and more direct than with Torith and Tamir. Apollo expected directness from Myke and welcomed it.

Apollo knew Myke was an anomaly among Olam's ghost warriors. Many knew Myke had been a Mentor, like Reemo, then left and fought for Sughi, and now was back with Olam, stripped of any authority. He was a powerful fighter, but he had no leadership duties. He took orders and did his job, especially when those orders came from Apollo.

Torith had often expressed her dislike of Myke to Apollo. "I know he's a good friend of yours," she would say, "but he really messed up. Think of all the people he hurt."

Apollo would tell her she should be happy he was back.

"I am," she would acknowledge, but then she would launch into an anti-Myke rant, and that was where Torith could be intense.

Apollo thought of these as Torith's "Myke-a-tribes." The problem for Apollo was that Torith would get right into Apollo's face, monologuing hard about Myke. When this happened, for Apollo, it was no longer a conversation. This was fighting, not talking. He knew in his brain it was only Torith expressing strong feelings, but to the rest of his sensory feedback, it was a personal attack, and it was almost impossible not to treat it as such.

This left Apollo the options of fighting back, evading, or retreating—none of which were the type of honest communication Torith wanted. Those conversations, if they could be called that, always went bad.

Apollo liked Torith, and he had spoken with Megantha about this communication problem. "She gets so intense, Mom. I can hardly talk to her when she's like that."

"Myke is intense, too," Megantha would tell him.

"Yes, but that's different. With Myke, it's not directed at me. With Torith, it feels like she's yelling at me as if I'm the reason Myke is the way he is."

"Wait until you're no longer a ghost," she said. "Then it's going to be even harder.

Apollo knew where this was going.

"When you're a Blood, the attraction you feel for her will be physical, too. It's going to be very strong."

Apollo had heard this many times.

"Torith will still be Torith when she's a Blood. Many of her characteristics will be the same."

"I know," said Apollo. This was a repetition of lessons already taught.

"Do you think Torith will be physically attractive, Mom?"

"That depends partly on what she decides is best for her," Megantha said. "Just like you, Apollo, Torith will have to decide if she wants to be physically attractive."

Apollo thought.

"You'll have to decide what you want when you are a Blood. As you know, it's a big decision. You're my beautiful boy. And you always will be. But do you want to be a beautiful human? I mean, beautiful on the outside? The way you look will affect how people treat you. A lot more will be handed to you if other Bloods want to be with you because of how you look. It's a tough decision."

"Yes, so you make the choice for me," Apollo said, joking.

"Not a chance, son. That one is all yours... the consequences too."

Apollo remembered how she had reached out and tousled his full ghost hair when saying that. Only she and Olam could touch him like that.

Apollo's perspective on what he wanted to look like as a Blood had become very clear since coming back from his days in the Sub-Summa world... the days of healing... the days of coming out of an internal darkness into the light. He hoped that as a Blood, he could somehow be friends with Tamir, Torith, and Myke, but his heart ached the most for Glacier. That's what he wanted the most: to live in the forest with Glacier. And to do that, he doubted Glacier would have any opinion on what he looked like. So, he didn't care. Now... what he smelled like... might be a different matter. If he were going to be given a choice in what he would look like, could he also choose what he smelled like? After all, stinky feet might be a turn-off to humans, but maybe they would be just the thing to seal his relationship with Glacier, and hopefully other wolves. *Yes,* he thought to himself. *The only thing I'm asking for is smelly feet. Whoo-hoo!*

Apollo was lost in thought, but Tamir snapped him back to reality. "Hey," said Tamir. "Hey, boss?" he pressed.

Apollo did not like being called "boss," but he was the squad captain, so he did not argue. "What, 'T'? What?" Apollo faked annoyance with his friend.

"Did you get any intel from..." Tamir paused for effect, "Secret Sauce?" Tamir paused again. "You know... for this op?" There was a hint of feigned reverence in Tamir's voice at the term *Secret Sauce*. "Did you have a chance to use that fancy B-Channel?"

The squad knew Apollo had developed a well-placed source in Sughi's command who sometimes fed Apollo operational and tactical information. Apollo also knew that everybody in the room suspected it was Malta, but they understood the importance of keeping that close hold, and they never spoke of her name or hinted at who she might be. The quality of too many ghost lives was at stake, including the source's. The team definitely had strong personalities that liked to go at each other, but they also had enough operational savvy to keep quiet about this issue.

"Not this time... at least not yet," said Apollo. "I reached out but heard nothing." Apollo knew that Tamir wanted to hear more about the B-Channel. "The fancy B-Channel has been quiet." In saying that, Apollo angled the comm he was using toward Tamir so Tamir could have a look. Tamir glanced but did not look hard. He and Apollo both knew the comm activity could be buried, and Apollo's move was more symbolic than substantive.

A minute later, they all received a message from Reemo saying he'd be there in five minutes, followed by another message that said, "Gear up. This one might be rough. You'll dispatch in an hour. Clear your to-dos."

51

Deer Canyon

Sixteen hours later, Apollo and Torith were concealed as best they could in a thicket of scrub oak, looking down at a target area hundreds of feet below. They were in a canyon named Deer Canyon, just below the upper ridgeline on the canyon's south side. Myke and Tamir were on the other side of the canyon, also concealed. They, too, were in scrub oak, well hunkered down because Apollo—despite knowing where they were—could not pick them out.

The mouth of Deer Canyon was at about five thousand feet of elevation, and the canyon ran five miles east to west. Its east end was closed off in a large, wide bowl. To the west, the canyon opened onto many miles of flat, sparsely inhabited terrain.

It was winter, and many parts of the canyon were covered in one or two feet of snow. It was old snow, more gray than white, probably from a week ago. The snow had melted off much of the rock surfaces that faced the sun. The scrub oak, which dominated this canyon, was deciduous and without leaves. The color of this tough tree's spindly branches was a bland gray. Overhead were gray, cold, stagnant clouds that had no texture. The lighting in most of the canyon was a diffused gray upon gray.

Apollo was happy about the lack of direct sunlight. The boring gray offered nothing to the eye, and chances were that any Sughis in the canyon would have no interest in a detailed look at the lackluster scenery, reducing the risk of Apollo's team being spotted.

Deer Canyon was about seven hundred miles northeast of the command center where they had briefed with Reemo. To arrive in their current positions without detection, about twenty-five miles out, they had split into two groups and then "went to ground" to avoid detection. "Going to ground" meant traveling much slower and mostly underground or in thick brush, or via some other cover, such as under the water of a lake, all to avoid detection.

For the past hour, Apollo had been checking with Myke via their B-Channel. Most units did not have two members with B-Channels, and this was one advantage Apollo's squad had over Olam's other special operations groups.

Both teams had their eyes on a school that had been built in the bottom of the canyon. This school contained the canyon's only structures. The rest of the canyon was untouched, and the whole canyon was considered school property. Like the canyon, the school was named Deer Canyon, or Deer Canyon School.

The school had a reputation as one of the region's best primary or elementary institutions. It was built of bricks that were a deep maroon in color. The rectangular shape of the bricks contrasted with the school's classroom buildings, which were all round or oval-shaped. Most were single-story, high-ceilinged structures.

Apollo and his team had been briefed that these classroom buildings also had full basements, which would be important to today's operation. In addition to the classroom buildings, the campus had one large administrative building. It, too, was made of the deep-maroon-colored bricks, but it was not round. Instead, it was more traditional, rectangular in shape, and had three floors.

The school no longer had students. This was because of the war between Olam's Diamond Command and Sughi. Five years ago, the war still had some boundaries. People on both sides often got along, or at least tolerated each other. It was far from peaceful, and there were many skirmishes, but there was some civility.

Then the rogues became more prevalent and emboldened. The conflict turned into all-out war, and it was not easy to sit on the fence. Either you fought for Olam, fought for Sughi, or you went and lived somewhere out of the way, even off the grid.

Apollo's sister, Celti, the animal lover, had been forced to relocate. She had problems with Olam's side because of Olam's plan for animals as Bloods, but she detested the Sughi side, too. She had found a small village where people were neutral and mostly cared about animals. So far, the rogues had left her alone. Of course, people knew she was Apollo's sister. Apollo had a reputation, and those who might harm her knew there would be hell to pay with Apollo, or worse yet, Dramos, if she were bothered.

Deer Canyon School had been mostly filled with students who favored Olam. As the Sughis became more extreme, the school had to close and send its children to institutions located in better-protected areas.

After the children left, a group of pacifists took over the school. These were fence-sitters to the max. They preached love of all, both Olam and Sughi. They were anti-war, including any war by Olam's ghosts to protect their side. Apollo had never met or spoken with any of these Deer Canyon pacifists, but he could not understand their delusion. Like it or not, all of Summa was at war, and that war was not going to end until one side won. Peace was coming, but it would be peace through victory, not through delusional love chants.

During the briefing with Reemo about this operation, Tamir had immediately started calling the Deer Canyon pacifists "peace-turds." Apollo thought that was too childish and unbecoming of the powerful status of his team. He asked that it be "peace-nerds." Tamir saluted, meaning he wasn't thrilled but would comply. Myke rolled his eyes and said something under his breath. Apollo was not threatened by Myke's reaction. That was Myke, and his bond with Myke was ironclad. Apollo did not blame Tamir for the use of "peace-turds." It was because of the stupidity of the "peace-nerds" that he was now being asked to put his team in danger.

Apollo suspected that many of the pacifists at Deer Canyon were weak and actually looking for reasons not to take a stand. Only a few of them would be genuine. Those few could be people like Shumaker, the man Apollo and Myke had spent a day with in Sughi City. The one with the pet myna bird.

Wow! Apollo thought. *That seems so long ago!* Things had changed so much! As he thought about Shumaker, he knew there was little chance Shumaker was still being allowed to openly share his quiet, well-thought-out, tolerant views—even if those views supported Sughi. Gone was the patience for that level of intellect, analysis, and tolerance. Now, it was much more black and white, hardcore.

Apollo had tried to reach Shumaker via an open comm several years ago. But there had been no response, and Apollo wondered if his reaching out had been a mistake. Apollo suspected Shumaker was afraid to respond because

Apollo was definitely a number one enemy on Sughi Command's list of deplorables. Unless Shumaker decided to come back over to Olam's side, he would be better off avoiding all communication with Apollo. Even so, Apollo hoped to see him again someday.

"No sign of any peace-nerds," messaged Myke from across the canyon. Then... "No sign of anybody. Tamir says there aren't any Sughi-turds either."

Apollo knew that "Sughi-turds" was pushback on his request about the term "peace-turds." *Good one,* thought Apollo.

Torith was also looking at Apollo's comm. "Those two are children," she whispered, close and personal into Apollo's ear. Then she added, "I haven't seen any movement either."

"Weird that nobody is around," responded Apollo. Intelligence said there were at least a hundred Sughis still at the school.

"They're probably all down in the basements, cheering on the psyops teams.

"'Psyops' ..." huffed Apollo. "That almost makes it sound legitimate."

Reemo had told Apollo's team that a large group of Sughi soldiers—probably at least two hundred—had swarmed the school four days ago and captured some of the peace-nerds. "Capture" meant flatlining them and setting them up for "behavior modification," which was probably going on in the basements of the school's classrooms.

It was thought that at least a hundred Sughis were still here. "Maybe it's Sughi-siesta time," Torith said. "Could be laziness."

"Yes, but you'd think we'd see a guard contingent or some sign of life," Apollo responded. "They have to know we're going to attack at some point."

"Maybe that's the whole point," Torith responded. Maybe they're ready and waiting, hiding and hoping to draw us in."

Apollo agreed that it was a possibility. Then he said to her, "I'm worried about you, Torith. This is a dangerous mission for you. You don't have to do this. We can do it the regular way. I can call in the battalion, and we'll slam them with a thousand ghosts."

"We already briefed it this way, Apollo. The decision-making is done. Give me my thirty minutes, then come save me."

Apollo had the authority to call the mission off. The on-scene leader always had that authority; at least, Olam's leaders did. And with that authority, Apollo was looking for a reason to cancel. He knew killing the op was not logical. They had seen nothing so far to warrant calling it off. But he could not help wanting Torith out of it. Looking at her again, he said, "You high-tail it out of there if it gets too crazy. Remember, they brought this on themselves. We don't have to save them."

"I know," she said, returning his stare. For a few long moments, neither said anything.

"You have to let me go, Apollo. I need to get down there. We have a mission to do. C'mon, A.P.! Give me the green light!"

With an anxiety Apollo tried not to show, he said, "Go get'em, Torith!"

"Fantastic," she responded, and she was gone.

Apollo then went to his comm. "She's on the move," he messaged.

"Got it," was the response.

Apollo started the timer on the comm. He knew Myke had done the same. It was going to be a long thirty minutes.

52

Sasha

A few minutes later, Apollo saw Torith appear near the entrance of the school. She chose an approach path that made it seem as if she had come up the canyon, the way a normal person would approach. It was time for her to put her acting skills to work. If the Sughis had not spotted her, they would soon. Torith was no nameless soldier, and it was only a matter of time before they figured out who she was.

The school had a camera system, and it was probably still operational. The system was air-gapped from the net, so there had been no way for Tamir or his brain trust to hack into it, at least not with the prep time they had. If the system was working, the Sughis would use the camera system to take pictures of Torith's face and use a comm to upload them to Sughi Command for facial recognition. If the camera system was physically broken, the Sughi ghosts had no way to repair it. Instead, they would have to approach Torith with a comm and demand that she submit to facial or DNA recognition.

Once the Sughis figured out it was Torith, they would be concerned that she was with her team. Apollo's team was well-known to Sughi Command. Torith alone was a threat, but the addition of Apollo, Myke, and Tamir was a whole new level of threat. Plus, Sughi himself had been humiliated by Apollo, and everyone knew it. Many on Sughi's side hated Apollo.

If they attacked Torith, Apollo, Myke, and Tamir would race to her rescue. She could hold off twenty or thirty regular soldiers for a few minutes, which was plenty of time for her to be extracted.

The other possibility—and the one they hoped would happen—was that Torith could convince the local Sughi commander not to fight and hear what Torith had to say. Five years ago, that would have been the norm. But now, there was so much hatred and intolerance that attacks often happened without any attempt at dialogue or negotiation. "No more talk!" was a common theme of the Sughi ghosts. Unfortunately, ghosts on Olam's side were also adopting this policy, making things more volatile.

But Torith had an ace up her sleeve, and that was why she was today's tip of the spear. Operational Intel had managed to determine that the local Sughi commander here at Deer Canyon was Torith's younger house sister, Sasha. Torith and Sasha grew up at the same time in the same household. They had been tight. Torith was only a few years older, and there were years when they were at the same school and knew the same people. Apollo and Tamir both knew Sasha.

It was not until late in high school that Sasha decided Sughi was a better fit and soon left the house. Sasha and Torith had stayed in touch for a few years, but finally Sasha stopped answering Torith's calls.

Sasha was like most who left Olam for the Sughi banner. They almost always cut off communication. Hopefully, despite that, Sasha would talk things through with Torith and agree to have her people clear out without a fight.

Apollo continued to watch Torith as she cautiously but openly approached an outside plaza area beyond which were the round, single-story classroom buildings and the rectangular admin building. Three Sughi soldiers came out of one of the classrooms, and three more came from the admin building. They rapidly headed for Torith.

In the middle of the plaza was a large fountain raised three or four feet off the ground. The base of the fountain was rectangular, and it was made of smooth, dark stone that was almost black. Torith was walking toward that fountain.

The top of the fountain was a shallow pool of water, out of which shot ninety-eight water jets. The jets were organized into two rows of forty-nine, seven times seven, one row on each side of the fountain. The rows were parallel to each other, and the jets were angled to shoot water up into a high arc that came down on the other side of the fountain. The effect of these jet streams was the creation of a high-arched water tunnel.

Inside that tunnel was a magnificent stone deer. The deer was a large buck with a powerful rack of antlers. The stone of the deer itself was marbled with intricate browns and blacks. The deer faced the entrance to the plaza, which meant it was facing west, in the direction from which Torith was approaching. On sunny days, when the sun was low to the west, the light rays would shine into the front of the tunnel and illuminate the face of the deer as well as the inside of the tunnel. The effect was spectacular.

Today, with the high clouds and diffused light, the deer inside the water tunnel looked dark and menacing. From Apollo's perspective, off to the side and above the fountain, the deer was mostly obscured by the refracted light coming off the arcs of jetting water.

"She's on the plaza and headed towards the fountain," said Myke, calling out the play-by-play.

Apollo saw no snow or moisture on the stone plaza. *The stone must be heated,* he thought. He watched as Torith approached the fountain and then stopped. He also watched the six Sughi soldiers streaming towards her. Again, Apollo wanted to call off the op. But he couldn't. Torith was going to have to take whatever came, and Apollo knew she was ready for it. He hoped it would not be bad.

"She stopped short of the fountain," said Myke. "Six soldiers are there, too."

Apollo could see everything Myke saw, at least for now.

"And now I see some Sughis moving near one of the classroom buildings. It's like Torith woke the whole place up."

So far, only six Sughis confronted Torith, and no more were on the way. Apollo, Myke, and Tamir were too far away to hear any conversation or see any facial detail that might help them understand what was going on. Only full-body movements could be seen.

Suddenly, a group of about twenty Sughis came flying up the canyon. "Red alert," said Myke. "Two squadrons coming in from the west."

To Apollo's relief, the group of flyers went right over the top of the fountain and continued to the classroom buildings, landing in front of one of them. They seemed unconcerned with Torith at this moment.

Seeing the two squadrons partially confirmed what intelligence had said about the Sughi takeover at Deer Canyon. It had been a significant play by Sughi, and many peace lovers were believed to be missing. Some were thought to still be here at the school, held as captives.

Captive peace-nerds would be undergoing mind manipulation. Likely, this meant they were being repeatedly torn down into a comatose-like state and then brought out under the control of a trained Sughi psychologist. It was a brutal process. Depending on the person, it made the brain malleable, like soft clay. It had already been four days since the takeover, and Apollo had to assume many of the peace-nerds had already succumbed to the Sughi mentality.

Diamond Command had a battalion standing by to back up Apollo's team. It was three hundred miles away, engaged in a mock training exercise. Sughi's people would be tracking the battalion, but hopefully, they would not associate it with the Deer Canyon operation until it was too late. Once Apollo's team called for the battalion, it would take at least two hours for it to arrive. This meant that Apollo's team might have to fight a hundred Sughis for two to three hours.

Apollo and his team were well-trained and experienced in fighting large groups. They were much more powerful than the average soldier, and if overwhelmed, they could dive into the ground and lose their attackers. This would give them the short time they needed to fully recharge and get back into the fight.

The big variable was the experience and skill of the taggers Sasha had at her disposal. If she had a capable group, it would be more difficult for Apollo and his team to disengage, lose the attackers, and recharge. Myke was a superior tagger, and he could use those same skills to shake a tail. Apollo's time wandering inside Summa had made him better, too, but he did not have the gift Myke had. Tamir and Torith were exceptional fighters, but not exceptional at losing a good tagger.

Tamir had started research on an underground decoy system, like chaff, where a ghost could drop energy one way and go the other. In theory, it could work, but he had not yet figured out a real-world implementation.

Apollo's biggest concern today was Torith. Some of the ugliest Sughis took great satisfaction in violating anyone they had flatlined—especially women—and especially someone like Torith because she was a notorious enemy soldier. It was a warped power thing. It had happened to Torith before, and it clearly had changed her. Because of it, she was more hardened and aloof. Apollo, Tamir, and Myke always tried to protect her over themselves, and it bothered all of them that she was so exposed on this mission.

This all weighed on Apollo as he watched. Torith and the six Sughis surrounding her had been standing near the deer fountain for about five minutes. It looked like the conversation between them had mostly stopped, and to Apollo, they appeared to be waiting for something. Apollo wasn't sure, but it seemed that the six were less threatening than they had been at first. The tight, aggressive circle they had formed on her was wider now. They might not yet have figured out who she was, but they would be able to feel her power. They would be afraid of her, but they also would be afraid to show fear to their commanders. Apollo knew Torith could take care of the six soldiers, but if they were joined by ten more, it would become too much for her to handle on her own.

"Looks like something is happening behind the admin building," Myke messaged on the B-Channel. Apollo could not see that area from his viewpoint. "Somebody is out—maybe a female. She's all in black, and now others are coming out, too. They are setting up a protective formation around her."

Apollo suspected it was Sasha.

"Probably Sasha," Myke confirmed. "Now they are moving. You'll see them soon."

The formation came around the admin building and into Apollo's view. It headed towards the deer fountain and Torith. The formation remained tight and protective around its leader, but when arriving at Torith, it maneuvered to keep the leader protected while also allowing Torith to approach. These would be stronger soldiers with the leader, and Apollo knew Torith could not fight them all.

Now Torith was face-to-face with the Sughi leader. Torith put both hands on the sides of her head in what may have appeared to the locals as a sign of amazement or awe, but which Apollo's team knew to be a confirmation that the leader was Sasha. This was good. Torith had said she doubted Sasha would order that Torith be attacked, unless Sasha thought there was no other choice. Sasha was no pushover, but she was reasonable—or at least she had been when Torith knew her years ago.

Apollo could see that Torith offered to greet Sasha with an embrace, as much as two ghosts can embrace, but Sasha clearly refused.

Apollo hoped Sasha's refusal to embrace was no more than part of the image she needed to show to her troops as their commanding officer. Hopefully, Sasha still felt something for her sister, despite having cut Torith off years ago.

"Two more squadrons coming up the canyon," said Myke. Apollo knew it had probably been Tamir who noticed them. His job was to watch Apollo and Myke's backs as they focused on Torith.

These two squadrons did not go to the classroom building like the first set had. Instead, they landed and set up in a wider U-shaped formation around Torith and the others. Part of their U included the fountain itself. Torith was now outgunned, especially if the taggers assigned to the squadrons were any good.

"Looks like things are getting heated," messaged Myke. Apollo could see that both Sasha and Torith were moving their arms and bodies as if having an argument. Sasha's movements indicated resistance, whereas Torith's indicated pleading.

Then, Torith pointed towards the canyon rim, up in the direction where Apollo was hiding. Sasha pointed, too, and their communication seemed to intensify. A comm appeared in front of Apollo—not the one Apollo and Myke were using as a B-Channel, but an open one. If Apollo answered, the network would plot his location for everyone to see, including all the hostile Sughis in the canyon below. The comm showed that it was Torith calling.

"Hey, guys, she sent me a comm," Apollo messaged over to Myke. "I'm going to answer."

This would not be a surprise to Myke or Tamir. The team had gone over this possibility in the pre-op briefing. "Kick'em hard, Apollo," responded Myke. "We have your back."

Apollo took a breath and opened the channel with Torith. "She wants to see you, Apollo. Sasha wants you to come down."

"Okay. Coming." At that, Apollo shooed both comms away. He then took off down the steep side of the canyon, towards the fountain.

53

Negotiations

As Apollo traveled down, he came across two female deer in between clumps of scrub oak about one hundred yards below his tactical position. They were well hidden, nestled on a small flat that was covered with trampled, muddy snow. *Appropriate for Deer Canyon,* he thought. *In the summer, when the scrub is green, this place must look a lot better than it does now. Today, it's so drab.*

Apollo landed inside the protective U formed by the two Sughi squadrons, but outside the tighter wall of Sughis immediately surrounding Torith and Sasha. Apollo did not advance, not wanting to appear threatening, and he gave the next move to Sasha. Apollo could see fear in the eyes of many of the closer Sughi soldiers. Apollo understood that they all knew about him. He was the one who survived months of intense Sughi torture only to reject the in-person and direct attack of Sughi himself. They had felt Sughi's power and did not understand how Apollo could have done that, especially in such a weakened state. Apollo knew it had not so much been his strength as his core DNA.

Sasha's protective guard moved to let her walk to Apollo. They then started to closely follow, but she held up her hand and stopped them. "You can't protect me from him," she said to her guard. "Stay back." The guard held its position, and Sasha continued forward, followed by Torith.

Sasha stopped in front of Apollo, close enough to appear as if she had no fear. She launched into a series of questions. "Why aren't you a Mentor, Apollo? What gives you the right to be here? You're too strong. How does that help anybody? There's no freedom of choice with you around."

Sasha's questions were surprising. Apollo started to answer, but Sasha cut him off.

"You need to leave," Sasha said. "And take your people with you."

"No, Sasha," answered Apollo, shaking his head and keeping all emotion out of his voice. Then, with a pause, he added, "Why don't you call your sister anymore? She loves you."

"I love my sister too," Sasha answered. "But it's too painful to talk with her. I can't do that anymore."

Normally, the feisty Torith would have injected herself here, but Apollo caught her eye, and she held her tongue.

"We're not leaving, Sasha. And you know why we're here. At least seventeen people are still missing." Apollo said this, knowing that Diamond Command had not been able to locate seventeen of the peace-nerds.

"I have some good soldiers, Apollo. You can't force us to leave."

"Look, Sasha," I have a battalion standing by. And I have two more on my team here in the canyon. You—"

"Is Myke the traitor one of them?" Sasha cut in with bitterness.

"Myke, my friend, is here... yes," said Apollo.

Sasha showed disgust. "You brainwashed him, Apollo. There's no way he'll ever be happy with Olam. Send him back!"

Apollo saw that Sasha could be just as intense as her older sister, and he looked at Torith. "I see it runs in the family, Tory." Then, facing Sasha, he said with some finality, "Sasha, we're here now. We're going to find the people you've taken. Myke will blow through your troops like water, and the battalion will mop up the rest. Show us where the seventeen are or get out of our way."

Sasha took a step back so she could face both Torith and Apollo. "You're all so self-righteous. You talk about love and good and other nonsense. But look at you now, forcing us. It's disgusting!"

Apollo was not here for a debate. "Fair or not, I'm giving you one minute to order your people out." Apollo then called up a comm and linked with battalion command, which responded immediately. "If I don't call you in two minutes," Apollo said, "Send in the troops."

"Affirm," said the voice on the other end.

At the same time, Myke appeared off to the left side of the school grounds, about fifty yards above ground, and one hundred yards away. Apollo pointed him out to Sasha.

She was not happy. "There's the traitor," she said loudly to her troops. "Myke the traitor!" There was a rumbling in her ranks.

"The clock is ticking," said Apollo.

Apollo could see that Sasha was starting to lose her composure. He had been ordering her around in front of her own people.

"Who else is here?" Sasha asked. "Do you have any more scum with you?"

Apollo was not going to tell her about Tamir, whose first assignment was to try to sneak in and hack into their local network.

Apollo knew he had backed Sasha into a corner, and even though that was satisfying, his main goal was a resolution to the matter. He tried to think of a way to help her save face while also getting them past the impasse.

As Apollo thought, Torith jumped in, "Look, Sasha," Torith said, "We know there were about a hundred people here when you attacked a few days ago. We also know that most of them escaped, and that you let others go. But there are seventeen we can't account for. And if you're holding them, we're not going to let you torture them."

"We're not torturing anyone," said Sasha.

"Okay," continued Torith, "show us. That's all. Let us talk to them. Each of them. Alone."

"They're not here," Sasha said.

Apollo knew that was not true, but he let Torith continue.

"Yes, they are, Sasha. We know they are."

Apollo knew Torith had to be careful here. Olam's people had a well-placed source who was a soldier under Sasha's command. The information from that source was key to the decision to commit a large amount of resources to today's op. Torith could not say anything that would alert her sister to that.

Torith continued, "Our Intels have interviewed some of the people who escaped. We even talked with a few you let go. We know, Sasha!"

It had been more than two minutes since Apollo had spoken with his command. This meant the "go" order had been given to the battalion. Apollo said to Sasha, "The battalion is on the move. ETA, two hours and fifteen minutes."

Sasha swore and cursed at Apollo, "I thought we were negotiating!" She was angry, and Apollo could hear a hint of desperation in her voice. No matter what she did now, she would lose when the reinforcements arrived.

"Maybe I'll call my own battalion—maybe two of them!"

Apollo knew those were idle threats. There were no Sughi battalions close by. He was surprised that Sasha would throw out such a threat. It made her look childish. But he said nothing, hoping Torith could make better progress. Apollo was the hammer. Torith was the mediator, albeit a mediator with a big hammer of her own.

Sasha forcefully said, "You can't simply come in here and take over. You say you are the good guys. Act like it!"

This was an illogical argument, and Torith was too smart to engage. "Please, Sasha. Let me talk with you alone. Come over here." Torith pointed towards the side, where they could talk in private.

Just then, the comm in front of Apollo beeped. This time, it was Tamir, who evidently no longer cared if his position was discovered. Apollo could see that Myke was being copied. Tamir wrote, "I got what we need."

Apollo replied, "Good," and then he blanked the screen. Tamir's message was excellent news. He then looked at Torith, who had moved away with Sasha, and he hand-signaled to her a letter "T" and then two thumbs up. Torith would know it meant Tamir had scored.

Apollo, feeling more relaxed, turned towards the closest Sughi soldier and asked him his name. The soldier did not respond. "Who is your squad leader?" Apollo asked the group.

"I am," responded a soldier standing four places to the left. Apollo felt no ill will towards any of them, including the squad leader. "I'm like you," Apollo said to the man. "I have a squad. Sometimes one of them screws up. How do you handle that?"

The leader was rightfully uncomfortable talking with Apollo. He began stammering a broken answer.

"Apollo!" Sasha yelled. "Don't talk to my soldiers!"

"Sorry, guys," Apollo said to the nearby Sughis, and he backed off. No need to aggravate them.

Tamir's message meant Tamir had been able to sneak in and gain access to their local network. It also meant he had seen what was stored about the location of the missing seventeen people.

The thought flashed through Apollo's mind that Tamir sure had been fast. There was no question that Tamir was a good hacker, but... still... it seemed like he had gotten in quickly. *Maybe they had left the main comm open and unattended,* thought Apollo. That would be careless from an operational standpoint, but possible.

Apollo could see that Sasha and Torith were still negotiating. Both seemed frustrated. Apollo was surprised it had been going on this long. Sasha was on the clock. The battalion was coming. She needed to fight now or get her people out. *What was she waiting for?*

Apollo moved over towards Torith and Sasha. "I'm running out of patience, Sasha."

"I'm not stopping you," she responded. "Go look around all you want."

"W... what?" Apollo asked, surprised. "I can look around?"

"Yes, go. But you only. I don't want Myke looking. He disgusts me."

Apollo was churning all of this over, trying to make sense of why Sasha would let him have free rein.

"Can I take that squad captain with me? The one I was talking to?"

"Not him," Sasha replied. "This one." Sasha then called to one of the elite who had been part of her personal guard. "Bronson, come over here, please."

The soldier named Bronson came over. "Bronson," she explained to him, "you go with Apollo. Go with him wherever he wants. Don't tell him where anything is. But don't stop him, either. And make sure the others let him go where he wants."

Bronson said hello to Apollo in greeting.

Apollo nodded, then to Sasha he said, "It'll go a lot faster if you let Bronson tell me where to go."

"Tamir can tell you," she responded. "He already knows."

So, she knows about Tamir's hack, thought Apollo. Alarms were starting to go off in Apollo's head. Clearly, Sasha was several steps ahead of them. *What's happening here?*

Apollo hesitated, and Sasha said, with some in-your-face-ness, "We're not stupid, Apollo."

He looked at her.

"And we're done with those seventeen idiots you're calling victims. They are worthless nubs. We don't want them. Peace lovers... not! They are spineless, and they can't take a stand. They are no good to us, and they'll be no good to you. Take them!"

Apollo considered what she said, then asked Torith, "Do you want to come with me or stay with your sister?"

Sasha answered for Torith, "Let me have her, Apollo, for another hour. Then my soldiers and I are leaving this place. Your battalion won't have anybody to fight."

"Go ahead, Apollo," said Torith. "I want more time with my sister."

"On one condition, Torith," Apollo said. "Stay here, near the fountain and up top. I'm going to tell Myke to watch over you. If you disappear or get attacked, Myke will be told to unleash at full power."

"Relax, Apollo," Sasha said. "I'll keep her safe."

Apollo did not trust Sasha, but he told Bronson to come with him. The two of them took off and transitioned over to Myke. Apollo explained what was going on.

Myke was skeptical. "I think you should wait until the battalion arrives before searching for victims. Let's not split up now."

Apollo knew Myke's suggestion was logical, but the situation seemed under control, and he wanted to rescue the victims as fast as possible. Also, he thought there was something different about Bronson. Apollo wanted time to talk with him alone, and that had to be done before the battalion arrived.

Apollo called Tamir and told him to set up on the other side of the fountain, above and back a little on the canyon hillside. That would give Tamir a good view of Torith, and it would allow him a fast response time to protect her if things went bad.

Tamir gave Apollo the coordinates of the seventeen peace-lover victims. Most of them were in the basements of the round classroom buildings, which was where pre-ops intelligence thought they would be. Six of them, however, were somewhere deep in the ground. They might be tricky to find without help.

Before Apollo and Bronson left, Myke pulled Bronson aside and asked him, "Do you know who I am?"

"Yes, sir."

"That's my best friend you're going with. You take care of him... or I will take care of you."

Bronson seemed tough, although he would be no match for Myke. Bronson did not flinch at Myke's threat. Instead, he responded, "I would expect as much, sir." His eye-to-eye lock with Myke was steady and firm, but also neutral and not threatening. It was hard not to like this Sughi soldier.

54

A Setup

Apollo gave Myke a nod of appreciation, and then he and Bronson took off toward the classroom section of the school grounds. Looking over at Torith, he could see she was still talking with Sasha, or maybe sister fighting, who knew? For Apollo, female talk was hard to comprehend. The same general configuration was in place. Sasha and Torith were alone, with her guard nearby and a wider U-shaped guard formation around them. Myke and Tamir should be able to back her up if anything happened. Still, a distant alarm continued to go off back in Apollo's brain. He heard it, but he decided it was normal battlefield jitters.

Arriving at the first classroom building, there were a few Sughi soldiers milling around who looked hard at Apollo. Bronson obviously had some juice because they turned away once he told them to stand down. Apollo went downstairs into the basement of the building, and there he found a series of well-lit underground classrooms, five of which contained "rehabilitation" setups. One peace-lover was being worked over in each of the five setups. Two or three Sughis were in each setup, too. Apollo knew the drill. Two of them were assigned to be flatliners, and they were strong fighters who could permeate and blow the menapses of a ghost to the point of no energy. The other person was a psychologist. Tamir referred to them as "psychos." That person's job was to work on the victims in their weakened state and convince them to change over to Sughi's side.

Apollo drove all the Sughis out of these setup rooms. He pounded on the ones who argued or did not go immediately. He had no tolerance for their form of torture. The Sughis could not understand why Bronson was standing around and letting it happen, but Bronson told them he would fight them too if they did not leave immediately.

The five peace-lovers were in various states of consciousness, but none were alert enough to understand they had been freed. It would take some time for them to recharge and come out of their days in the darkness. By the time they understood things had changed, the battalion would be here with its medical personnel.

After clearing the first basement, Apollo wondered if the teams would go back in after he left, but Bronson handled it. "Sasha says no more," he told the soldiers. "A Diamond battalion will be here soon. Get ready to move out."

Apollo and Bronson then cleared two more basements. In total, they had found eleven of the seventeen peace victims. Tamir had said the other six were being held way underground. "Why?" Apollo asked Bronson.

Bronson said he did not know. He speculated that maybe those victims were different. All he knew was that somebody had found an underground cavern, about twelve hundred feet down, beyond the comm-link limit. "The cavern is pretty big," explained Bronson. "And it's extremely secure. We keep it lit with some comms we took down there."

Apollo was surprised that Bronson was giving him this information. Sasha had told him not to tell Apollo where to find victims.

"But how do you find it each time?" Apollo asked Bronson. Since it was subnetwork, they could not use a comm to find it.

"You have to feel your way down. There is a long break in the rock. It's a thousand feet or more. And there is some water trickling through it. There is enough change in the density that you can follow it. You'll see," said Bronson.

Wow! He's going to show me! Apollo knew there was a risk of a trap if he went down into the ground with Bronson. But Apollo's time in the ground before had changed him. He liked the dark, and he liked the sense of maneuvering through layers of Summa. He was good at it, and he was much stronger now than he had been when he had been taken five years ago. It was worth the risk to save the peace-nerds. He doubted the Sughis could hurt him.

"Where do we start?" Apollo asked.

Bronson pointed at a nearby side of the canyon that was a steep rock face. The rock showed horizontal geological layers. The pattern of the layers suddenly stopped, only to continue in the same pattern a thousand feet lower. The remnants of an enormous crack showed between the shift in the layers, and it was obvious that the rock on the lower side of the canyon had broken away and fallen as a whole, down many hundreds of feet. If the fall had happened at once, it would have been a spectacular geological event. More likely, thought Apollo, the shift happened over millions of years.

"We follow that break in the rock," said Bronson. "It'll take us right to the cavern."

Apollo took Bronson back to the fountain, where he checked in with Torith. She said everything was fine, and he told her he was going to free the last six. Then he suggested to Sasha that she gather her troops and leave before the battalion arrived.

"I still have an hour, Apollo. My guys are tracking it."

Apollo debated telling her goodbye or thanking her for her cooperation, but he checked himself. The Sughis never should have been here in the first place, and what they did was wrong. She should be thanking him for not crushing them with a battalion from the get-go. He opted to say nothing.

Apollo brought up a comm and told Myke and Tamir how to find the cavern, per Bronson's explanation. "I should be back before the battalion gets here. But if not, have the commander send some people down there."

"I don't like it," said Myke.

"Me neither," said Tamir.

Myke reiterated his concern. "Why can't you wait one hour? One hour and the battalion will be here?" Myke sounded frustrated.

"Just protect Torith," said Apollo. "I'll be fine."

Apollo then took Bronson and headed for the fault line crack through the earth. Before going in, he stopped Bronson. "I want to talk with you before we go in."

"What?" asked Bronson, matter-of-factly.

Apollo liked talking with soldiers because you could be direct and not sugar-coat. "I want you to come with me after we're done here today."

"I'm not a traitor," said Bronson.

Apollo liked that answer because it was not a no.

Apollo had spent enough time with Bronson that he could sense this ghost's inner makeup. "I could say that the traitors are those who left the family and went to Sughi, correct? I mean, if we want to frame it in terms of being a traitor, aren't Sughi followers the real traitors?"

Bronson did not respond, but Apollo could tell he was thinking about it.

"I want you working with me," said Apollo. "I would be proud to have you on my team."

"I'm not a good person," said Bronson.

"I don't care," said Apollo. "You can work that out with Olam. Are you a good soldier?"

"Yes."

"Then be a good one for me. And, over time, you can get yourself back on track with Olam."

Apollo knew there was an Olam spy in this Sughi camp. It could be Bronson, but Apollo's read on Bronson was that he was a straightforward personality and not someone who would be playing two sides.

Bronson looked at Apollo and said nothing. However, Apollo could feel the soldier's respect.

Apollo knew they had to get going. "Think about it, Bronson. Today would be a good day to come with me. But I'll take you tomorrow or a year from now. Okay?"

Bronson nodded in the affirmative, and then he started into the crack in the ground. Apollo followed.

They found the cavern with ease. It was exactly as Bronson had described, and following the enormous break in the rock was not difficult. Once in the cavern, they found a dozen comms whose brightness had been set to max. Their combined light was enough to illuminate the cavern. To Apollo, it looked as though this vast space had formed when a massive section of rock sheared away and slid down along the near-vertical fault line. Somehow, the mountain above had held together, now forming the cavern's ceiling. Apollo guessed the stresses on that ceiling must be colossal, and he suspected the cavern's lifespan was limited.

Apollo and Bronson stayed down in the cavern for over an hour. Apollo knew the battalion should be there, and he was surprised no medical personnel had come down. He hoped there was not a problem. Bronson had chased all the Sughi people out of the cavern. Normally, Apollo would have left too, but two of the six peace-nerds were quite alert, to the point that Apollo could converse with them. Apollo was afraid that if they were left alone, they would have no idea how to get out of the cavern and end up terrified and lost deep in the mountain. Plus... it gave Apollo more time alone with Bronson.

Apollo had given Bronson the option of leaving so he would not end up in camp when the Olam battalion arrived. But Bronson asked, "Will you cover for me like I've covered for you?"

Apollo was thrilled at that. Of course he would. Hopefully, this meant good things for the future.

They waited another ten minutes. "My guys should be here," he said to Bronson. But they were too deep in the ground to talk to the comm network. One of them would have to physically go up and check.

"Do you want me to go up top, maybe to bring them down?" Bronson asked.

"They'll fight you as soon as they see you," said Apollo.

"I know. I can take the hits. Then I'll tell them to get down here."

Apollo knew that could work, and Bronson was the type of guy to pull it off. "Okay," said Apollo. Mostly, we need medical people down here. And a few soldiers."

Bronson left. But two minutes later, he was back. This time with Myke, who was in a panic. "They took her!" Myke exclaimed. "She's gone. We can't find her!"

"Who?"

"Torith! She's gone!"

Apollo was confused.

"They took her? Gone? How? I thought you and Tamir were protecting her!"

"We were. But it was a set-up!"

A sickening feeling flushed through Apollo.

"They planned it. As soon as you went underground, they attacked."

Apollo still did not get it. Myke, Tamir, and Torith could have easily fought their way out of any attack. They had practiced this many times.

"You guys planned this!" Myke was now in Bronson's face and yelling at him. "This was all a setup! Where's Torith!"

Apollo was still trying to understand. "But the battalion? It's here? How could they—"

"It all happened before the battalion got here," said Myke, turning back to Apollo. "Sughi sent his best. At least twenty of them. They flatlined Tamir and they tried to flatline me. I was able to get away, but as soon as I got clear and tried to help Torith, they were all over me.

Apollo was having a hard time with Myke's explanation because Tamir, Myke and Torith could easily handle twenty strong soldiers.

"But, Myke, nobody can stop you."

"These were Sughi's best," Myke said. "His personal guard."

Apollo had never heard of Sughi exposing himself by letting go of his personal guard.

"First, the squadrons attacked Tamir and me. We were mopping them up, but then Sughi's best came right up out of the ground. They must have been waiting right there all of the time. There were at least ten of them on me, and I finally had to take a dive into the ground to shake them. Tamir got manhandled. Then all the strong ones went to Torith and blew her whole system. She went to zero. Then they did the same to Sasha."

Apollo was confused. "Sasha, too?"

Myke continued, "I was recharged and back in the fight quickly, but they were already moving Torith away. Tamir recharged, too. We both went after her, but some of Sughi's guard were watching their back and slowed us down. It was all too much, Apollo. They got away."

"Did you know about this?" Apollo demanded of Bronson.

"No, sir," Bronson answered. "I doubt any of us lower ranks knew. They don't trust us."

"Tell me that again," challenged Apollo, and Apollo moved right inside Bronson. "Tell me!"

Normally, Apollo's move was a fight move, but Bronson showed healthy self-control, and he said plainly and clearly to Apollo, while Apollo read him, that he knew nothing about it.

Apollo believed him.

"Who is looking for Torith?"

"Almost everyone," answered Myke. Most of the battalion took off in the direction they took her. Hundreds of soldiers."

"Okay, we're going to look for Torith," Apollo said to Bronson. "You stay here and take care of these people, and we'll send down a medical team. If soldiers come—"

"Don't worry about what the soldiers do to me," interrupted Bronson. "Go. I can handle it, sir."

"Let's go, Myke."

Things were unresolved with Bronson, but Torith was the first priority, and in less than a minute, Apollo and Myke were at the surface. They found the battalion commander, who said they were doing everything they could to find Torith. He had sent hundreds of soldiers off in the direction the Sughis had taken her. "All of my good trackers went. And my best people, regardless of their normal assignments. Only the medical people were held back."

Myke and Apollo called up Tamir on a comm. Tamir was out helping to find Torith, but Apollo wanted him to come back. "We need you hacking and data tracking," said Apollo. Tamir had been beaten up pretty hard, but he was recovering.

"Go scorched-earth," Apollo ordered. "Carpet-bomb their servers. Ruin their routers. DDoS them to a full stop. Call in your entire brain trust!"

"I'm on it, boss," Tamir answered.

Then Apollo said to Myke, "Give me a minute, Myke. I need privacy."

"I know why. But hurry! We need to go!"

Myke moved away, and Apollo called up a B-Channel com and reached out to his high-placed Sughi source, Malta.

"I had nothing to do with this," she said. "It must have been Sughi himself running the op. It caught everybody off guard."

"Help me on this, Malta. Please."

"Apollo, you know I'm jealous of Torith's relationship with you. But you also know I'll do my best." Then she said, "Apollo, you know why Sughi did this, right?

Apollo had a suspicion.

"It wasn't to go after Torith," Malta explained. "It was to go after you. The whole thing was a setup to get you out of the normal fight. You're too strong, Apollo. They want you taken out. Sughi Command regularly complains to your command that it's not fair. You should be a Mentor and not out on the field. If you had become a Mentor, Torith would be safe right now."

There were many things wrong with what Malta had told him, but now was not the time to discuss it. "Please, Malta," he said. "Please. I need your help."

After the conversation with Malta, Myke and Apollo took off to go help with the search. Apollo knew he had made bad decisions today. He thought his team was invincible, and Torith was now paying for the misjudgment. Overconfidence had beaten him.

Apollo, Myke, Tamir, and most of the battalion hunted for Torith for weeks. They did not find her. No trace. Tamir and his brain trust also found nothing. No leads. No sources. Zero.

55

Search for Torith

The desperate hunt for Torith changed into an intense and prolonged operation that consumed Apollo, Myke, Tamir, and several special teams under Reemo's direction. Malta had been right. This definitely had taken Apollo out of the normal fight. Sughi's side got what they wanted. They were brutal, devious, and, in this case, effective.

There were many search missions looking for Torith. A command center had been established, and Apollo, Tamir, and Myke spent most of their time there when not out hammering on Sughi positions. The team hung in there strong, but it was a dark time for all of them. Over the weeks, Apollo felt himself slipping into a deep, emotional exhaustion.

Apollo could not forgive himself for the mistakes he made in Deer Canyon. He had gone into the operation worried about Torith, and yet he took his focus off her, thinking everything was fine. If he had stayed with Torith until the battalion arrived, Sughi's people could not have beaten them. Myke and Tamir were strong. So was Torith. But Apollo was stronger. Sughi's people could not have won over all of them.

His failures that day showed that he had a lot to learn about strategy and leadership. Sughi's team had planned and executed their Deer Canyon trap perfectly. Had the sequence of events happened differently, he never would have felt comfortable enough to leave Torith. All he had to do was wait an hour! Having Sasha assure him of Torith's safety and introducing him to Bronson, who was so straight up, were both smart moves to put Apollo at ease. Sughi had to know Apollo would want to pull Bronson aside and recruit him. Apollo's desire to do the "right" thing was effectively used against him.

"I feel so stupid," Apollo said to Myke and Tamir.

"You were," said Myke. "And I warned you." Myke did not hold back. "So did mega-brain," Myke added, looking at Tamir. "He warned you, too!"

Apollo was resigned to the criticism. He deserved it. These were his closest friends, and he only wanted their straight advice.

About twenty-four exhausting hours after Torith was first taken, Apollo had the idea of calling Sasha on a comm. To his surprise, she answered. He was too tired to yell at her. All he could do was plead. "She's your sister, Sasha. How could you do that? She would never do that to you!"

To Apollo's surprise, she claimed she did not know the kidnapping was going to happen. "Remember, Apollo, they blew my circuits, too—my own team!" She knew Olam's side would try a rescue operation, but she did not know it would involve Torith. She assumed the rescue would be a regular attack by one of Olam's battalions and not one where Apollo's team came in first. "I was told to keep my people at Deer Canyon as long as I could. I did not know they planned the whole thing to take you out."

"But how did they know Torith would be there? They pre-planned her kidnapping."

Sasha said she did not know. "You might have a leak," Sasha said.

Apollo had no idea if she was speculating or knew something. But he was surprised at how openly she, an enemy commander, was talking to him. She explained, however, that she had been told to tell Apollo everything. "They want you to know they planned it and that you were manipulated, Apollo."

"So, what are you doing to get your sister back?" Apollo demanded.

"I've asked, but they are totally shutting me out... except they are assuring me they are not hurting her like they did you. Remember, Apollo. It's you they are after, not Torith."

Apollo hated the thought that they had captured Torith to hurt him. "How can you say they aren't hurting her? She's strong. She'll beat the ghost of anyone who tries to hold her. They'll have to hurt her to hold her."

"No... not true. I'm sure they are keeping her circuitry at a minimum charge. They have to do that. But they assure me they are not torturing her when she starts to come out of it. All they are doing is keeping her close to zero. It's not like the way they treated you, Apollo. When you were taken, they were trying to hurt you. They would charge you up so they could torture you. They wanted to put you through as much pain as possible."

Now was not the time for Apollo to try to explain to Sasha how he had been able to embrace the darkness and use it to protect himself against their weeks and months of attempted torture. It was something he still only partially understood. He also knew it was a gift that most ghosts did not have.

Apollo asked if Sasha would talk to Mom about it.

Sasha refused. "Of course not, Apollo. I know what Megantha will say. If she won't help you find Torith, there's no way she'll tell me where she is."

"But why not at least ask?"

At this, Sasha scoffed. "Don't you see, Apollo? Mom and Dad aren't going to tell you, and they won't tell me either. That's what I detest about your side. You have all the power. Mom claims to be all-loving, and she could free Torith in two seconds. But instead, she'll let Torith suffer because of some freedom of choice thing. It's two-faced and absolutely ridiculous."

Apollo was confident that any decision by Megantha or Olam would be right, even if he could not understand it. It was about agency. But even so, Apollo was frustrated and felt angry. Right now, he did not like agency.

"You know," Sasha said. "You had better be prepared for a very different Torith if they ever release her."

Apollo knew where this was going.

"Torith might come out of this totally changed."

"She's too feisty to let Sughi win," Apollo said.

"Yes, but that same feistiness is going to make her mad that nobody was allowed to save her. She's going to be torn up about that. It might be enough for her to tell all of you to shove it."

Apollo did not want to contemplate that. "How long do you think they'll keep her?" Apollo asked.

"They are never giving her back, Apollo. Don't you see? The only way you'll get her back is for you to switch sides, and we all know that will never happen."

"What if I let them have me? I've been tortured before. I can handle it. Tell them I'll give myself up." Apollo really meant this.

"Normally, I'd say they might bite on that offer, Apollo. But you sooo beat Sughi at his own game last time, they'll never let you do it again. That's the big irony here. Your previous victory now means a long purgatory for the woman you love."

Apollo was taken aback and could not respond. He fell silent and defeated. He was empty, and there was nothing he could say. And... yes, he knew he did *love* Torith.

A minute passed. Then two. Sasha said nothing more. Finally, she cut the connection, and Apollo's comm went blank. His heart and mind were blank, too.

56

Frustration

Six months passed. Apollo spent hours pleading for Torith's release. Not begging or throwing tantrums. Not like a child. But he tried to work it out with Megantha and Olam. They could have released Torith immediately. However, as expected, they would not do it. Through these sessions, Apollo knew they loved him, but they would not provide reasoning for not releasing Torith other than saying it was the right thing. It was incredibly frustrating, and it was the kind of thing that drove people to Sughi's side. Apollo talked to them about that, and they said it was all part of the process to see what people are really made of. Their answers were not comforting.

Apollo also asked for their help in being a better team leader. Apollo had more success with this approach. He did not get "no's." Instead, he was always encouraged to build his skills, and they said they would help. Also, he was told to keep asking for help. Olam and Megantha told him to talk with them every day. "We love you, son. Keep talking to us and keep asking for help."

Apollo asked both Tamir and Myke to have the same kinds of conversations with Olam and Megantha. Apollo knew that Tamir did, with pretty much the same results. Myke, on the other hand, could not get himself to talk with any Quasars. He did, however, regularly talk with Reemo, who said he would talk to Olam for him.

Reemo did not know where Torith was, but he was powerful enough that he could have gone out himself and found her. Reemo... and any Mentor like him... had the power to singularly plow through any Sughi command or any set of Sughi soldiers. He could cause enough havoc that Sughi's side would have to give up Torith. It might take several weeks or months, but eventually, he would find her. "But that's not my job," Reemo said to Apollo. "My job is to help you find her, not to find her myself."

Apollo struggled with Reemo's stance, like he did with that of Mom and Dad. Myke was angry about it. Tamir expressed his opinion to Reemo by shaking his head and saying, "Good luck explaining that to Torith—if we ever get her back."

Sughi had really done a number on Apollo by taking Torith. Not only had it pulled Apollo and his team out of their normal, tremendously effective operational status, but it had driven a wedge between Apollo and Reemo, and between Apollo and his parents. Apollo had always been a good son. Right now, he was a grumpy son, and it was difficult for Apollo to keep himself and his teammates in the right frame of mind. It would be so much easier if they could find Torith and do some serious Sughi ghost smashing in the process.

One good thing came out of the catastrophic Deer Canyon operation. Apollo had been able to bring the soldier named Bronson back to Olam's side. Surprisingly, Sasha had helped with this process. She told Apollo she knew Bronson would be happier with Apollo, and she finally ordered Bronson to go. "He's conflicted," Sasha said. "There's still too much Olam in him to be with us. You take him."

Apollo wondered if Sasha would be in trouble with her command for kicking out a good soldier. But Sasha explained, "We're like you, Apollo. We don't want people who don't want to be here. Yes, we fight people to get them to listen. Yes, we force them to hear our side. But in the end, all we're doing is helping people figure out who they really are." Apollo had heard this kind of talk from people on Sughi's side in the past. He always thought it was nothing more than one thread in their web of manipulations. They were too brutal in their attempts to force their views. How could Sasha say that with a straight face? But when Sasha said it about Bronson, it seemed like the truth.

Reemo agreed that Bronson could be brought onto Apollo's team. This was only after Apollo had Myke and Tamir's okay. Tamir did a deep data dive on Bronson and came up with no red flags. There did not seem to be any chance that Bronson was actually a spy. Just as important, both Tamir and Myke had spent time with Bronson, even melting into his brain while asking him questions, looking for any sign of deceit. The mere fact that Bronson allowed that level of probing was a good sign.

"He has done some bad stuff in the past," Myke and Tamir told Apollo. "That's why he thought he should be fighting on Sughi's side. He thinks he's not good enough for Olam."

"We can straighten him out on that," Apollo said. "So, you guys think he's the real thing? Not a Sughi plant?"

"He's what he says he is. Take him," Myke said.

"I agree," said Tamir.

That's how Bronson was given the green light. Having him on the team would mean a change in the way they operated. Before, with Torith on the team, all four of them were very much independent power units, and each could be dispatched into a rough situation where they risked being confronted by many of the enemy. They were each strong enough to handle it. But the team could not use Bronson like that. He was an excellent soldier, but not one to be put up against ten or twenty Sughi fighters. Apollo explained clearly to Bronson that often, he would be left off missions and that he would be a lower-ranked subordinate to Myke and Tamir. Like Apollo, they could order him around. Bronson was okay with that.

Tamir started calling him "Bronny," and Myke picked up on it, too. Bronson called everybody "sir," and that was a good move on his part.

Bronson was not technical on a level anywhere near that of Tamir, but he had basic tech skills, and he had a mountain of patience needed to comb through piles of detail. That trait would come in handy.

57

Tamir and Bronson

It was standard procedure for Summa's planet-wide network to record the geographic locations of network logins and logoffs. This was public information, and intelligence personnel on both sides regularly analyzed location patterns for important activity, such as troop movements or the concentration of high-ranking personnel.

Olam and Sughi soldiers were taught to log off the network well before arriving at the scene of any important battle or operation. This helped maintain the secrecy of the location. Apollo and Myke had B-Channels, which automatically hid their locations, but most did not have that advantage.

Tamir had improved on existing logon/logoff analysis tools, and he applied these improvements against the activity of many Sughi targets. He and Bronson spent hours poring over that data, looking for clues that might lead to Torith.

At one point, Bronson said that maybe the thing to analyze was the dead zones and not the places where there was logon and logoff activity. This was not a new idea to Tamir, but Bronson's bringing it up made Tamir think about it another way. Perhaps it wasn't the dead zones themselves so much as the patterns surrounding them. Tamir explained that to Bronson, and they both went to work.

Tamir had tracked down some of the identities of the strong Sughi soldiers who had been the attackers at Deer

Canyon. All their logons and logoffs since the day they took Torith were input as part of the data being analyzed.

"What about before?" Bronson asked.

"Before?"

"Yes. Before they took her. They had to do some advance planning. Maybe they were going to the place where they planned to hold her."

Tamir was surprised he had not thought of that. It was perfectly logical, and so, for some Sughi targets, they also collected activity for a month before Torith was taken.

It was a big project, and helping Tamir and Bronson was a room full of analysts. The data was endless and seemed to amount to nothing more than an incomprehensible swarm of dots all over the map of Summa.

The analysis concentrated on terrain within a five-hundred-mile radius of Deer Canyon. Most likely, Torith was trapped in that circle—somewhere. She would not be on the surface, but instead deep in the ground, and too deep for network sensors to detect her ghost DNA.

Tamir and Bronson hashed through many data analysis ideas. Apollo watched their brainstorms, and it was an interesting process. Tamir's mega-mind could come up with endless ideas, some of which were very complicated. Bronson's more basic mental skills could not keep up with the sophisticated analytics, but he could ask Tamir clarification questions that were amazingly on point, and this helped Tamir bring his research processes down to a more practical level. Bronson kept Tamir grounded.

As Apollo observed Tamir and Bronson interact, he could see why Bronson had been a good squad leader. In battle, there is always information overload. Bronson did not have the mental bandwidth to analyze large amounts of data, but he had a gift of seeing what was most important and ignoring the less critical. This was vitally useful in the fog of war. Had Bronson been leading the team the day Torith was kidnapped, he probably would not have made the mistakes Apollo made.

Also, Bronson could maintain concentration on a problem for hours. This was good because sometimes the outputs from Tamir's data runs required extensive manual review. Bronson was also adept at managing analysts who were assigned to help. He was patient, and he had a way of clearly explaining what needed to be done. He could talk on their level, whereas Tamir's brain was running too high and fast for that.

Months after Tamir and Bronson teamed up, they reached out to Apollo on a comm and said they had found something. They seemed very excited. Apollo quickly arranged a meeting with Reemo and the whole team. Two other Mentors came too. One of these was Savana, Torith's Mentor. She had been very involved in working with the teams looking for Torith. The third Mentor was named Shayne, but everyone called him "Staff." It had something to do with a former military, naval assignment. He was Bronson's Mentor, and he also acted as a roving, on-site Mentor, providing support and encouragement to those working to find Torith.

Tamir said what he found was too sensitive for anyone else to be there, and the many analysts who had been helping with the case were not invited.

They assembled in a conference room, and Reemo asked, "Show us what you found."

"A pattern that makes sense," answered Tamir. "Finally... one that is logical... logons and logoffs that may point to Torith."

Tamir then explained how the right combination of data analysis and filtering, set against statistical averaging and some basic geometry, showed arcing patterns of logoffs and logons.

"Take Sughi Soldier A, for example. Say he regularly travels to and from Torith's location. He knows he needs to be off his comm well before he gets there, so he makes it a habit of logging off about two hundred miles out. Then, when he leaves, he logs back on. Again, he does so about two hundred miles away. After he has done that a few times, there is a definite pattern showing where Torith might be."

As Tamir explained, he also plotted points on an electronic board in the front of the room. He plotted a series of X's for logons and logoffs, and then he drew lines through what would be the averages of these plotted X's. The lines were arcing, curved lines. He did these arcs in blue. Then he drew extensions of these arcs in red, continuing the arcing lines all the way around so that the blue sections became parts of big circles.

Tamir went on to explain that if you plot similar patterns for multiple soldiers, you end up with a series of circles. Then, you overlap these circles and plot the center of each circle. Tamir did this on the board, showing six circles of different sizes, and plotting on X in the center of each. Then he erased all the circles, leaving only the X's showing the center point of each of the erased circles.

"That's where we'll find Torith," he said confidently. "We came up with a circular area that has a diameter of about ten miles."

This circle plotting was not the genius part. Instead, it had been the long, tedious analysis Tamir and Bronson had done to come up with the right Sughi soldiers to plot, and where in the Summa world the plotted activity might be relevant.

"But, Tamir," asked Apollo. "You tried that same kind of analysis when I was kidnapped. You said it didn't work. Why do you think it's working this time?"

"Two reasons," said Tamir. "For one, Bronson thought of looking at data for the month prior to when Torith was kidnapped. Our targets were not as careful then, and they gave us better plot patterns. Secondly, the area where we think Torith might be is remote. Nobody goes there without a specific reason. Whereas you, Apollo, they had you in an area where there was a lot of surface traffic. Also, you were not far from Sughi City, which was full of Sughi fighters. There was so much traffic, it made it impossible to come up with logical conclusions."

The meeting room had a large conference table. The surface of this table was like many of the briefing tables in the building, and it could be controlled with a comm. Reemo used one to change the surface of the table into a three-dimensional surface map of Summa. Tamir then adjusted the map to expand and show only the area where Torith might be. The map was as detailed as it would be if a ghost overflew the area in person.

The entire surface of the ten-mile-diameter target area was covered with thick pine forests, interspersed with rocky mountain peaks and a few mountain lakes. Other than the peaks, the terrain was not rough, and it averaged six to nine thousand feet in elevation. Neither the lakes nor the peaks were distinguishable. There were no large rock formations, no deep canyons, and no spectacular cliffs. Also, there were no cities or towns or any signs of ghost habitation. It was a good place to hide Torith because you could fly over it a hundred times and not remember any of the terrain's specifics. The area was about 250 miles northeast of Deer Canyon, where Torith had originally been kidnapped.

Given the thick forest, even a battalion would need a week to effectively grid search the area. But it was not the surface they needed to search. Instead, it was the area under this surface, down in Summa's crust, a thousand feet down, or more. Here, they would need taggers, and it would take twenty to thirty taggers weeks or months to search it. They would have to work through it, taking fifty-foot slices of Summa's underworld at a time. It would be impossible to do that without alerting Sughi's side, giving them the opportunity to move Torith before Apollo's people could find her.

"This could all be a set-up," Myke said. "Sughi knows we have a Tamir. They might try to use Tamir's brain against us. Maybe they've been purposefully logging on and off just to have us chasing our tails, burning resources."

Myke's point was valid. To confirm the conclusions of Tamir and Bronson's work, the team needed to come up with a strategy that was stealthy. A lot of ideas were thrown around. Apollo noticed that when it came to ideas, Reemo and the other Mentors were not saying much. That was typical because they wanted the team to figure it out. But then Apollo noticed that Reemo and Savana were looking at each other. It was one of those knowing looks, and Apollo understood what that meant.

"Wait, wait, wait…" Apollo said, standing and holding up his hands. Now, he had everyone's attention. "Are you having fun, Reemo?" Apollo asked, teasing but also probing. "You and Savana? You're both looking pretty smug."

Reemo tried to play innocent, but he knew he'd been caught.

Apollo turned to his team. "They know the answer. Look at their faces. And they think we should know it, too."

Mentors, being Mentors, were supposedly far superior in ability to Apollo and his crew. While that was true, they were, nevertheless, Summa Ghosts. They were not aliens, and one Summa Ghost could read another.

"Yes," said Myke. "I see it too. They know!"

At that, Staff, the other Mentor, started chiding both Reemo and Savana. He scolded them in fun. "You mean you know?" His voice was full of friendly sarcasm. "You are Apollo's Mentor, Reemo. And you, Savana... Torith's!" And you're not helping them?"

Reemo gave in. He took the floor at the head of the room and looked around. He rubbed his chin like he was having some new, enlightening thought, stalling for fun and effect. "I'll give you a hint," he said. "A hint at how I'd search the target area covertly." He waited and then said, "I would not have you or any of us do the search."

The room was silent, filled with looks of confusion.

Finally, Tamir responded. "Not us? So... do you mean a network search? Won't they know?"

"Not a network search," Reemo said.

Apollo and his team looked at each other, still confused.

"Animals," hinted Reemo.

"Animals?" Myke asked, a funny look on his face.

The team was blank.

"Can I track animals?" Tamir asked. "I don't see how?"

"Not any animals," Staff interrupted. "Apollo's animals."

Apollo's brain shot into high gear. The answer flashed to him, but Tamir beat him to it.

"Apollo's wolves!" exclaimed Tamir.

"Glacier and Fjord!" said Apollo.

"Right!" exclaimed Reemo. "Good job, boys!"

What an idea! And it was a plan that made Apollo thrilled. *Thrilled, thrilled, thrilled!* he thought loudly to himself. The rest of the team liked the plan, too, but for Apollo, it involved a badly needed blast of joy.

The plan involved Apollo's wolves, Glacier and Fjord. They would be tasked to search the ten-mile forest area under which Torith might be held. The wolves would only be searching the surface. There surely was a standard place where the Sughi soldiers stopped and entered the ground. The wolves could find that spot. They would smell it out. They never had to be there when soldiers came or left. Their noses could tell if anyone had been there in the last two or three days—maybe longer. It also would not matter if the Sughi soldiers saw them. Wolves could be part of the habitat. They could search openly. Then, once Apollo and his team knew where the soldiers were going in, they could flood that specific area with taggers and their best fighters. They should be able to rescue Torith before the Sughis could move her.

There was a lot more discussion of the plan and whether it could work. Apollo pushed for it, although he knew he was biased, and he told the team he was. The chance to see Glacier and Fjord again was a burst of euphoria.

One potential hiccup was that it required the help of the owner of the wolves. This was the Forza named Lionah, the Forza who had visited Apollo several times while he was healing in the Sub-Summa sanctuary. She is the one who had once been one of Myke's students back when Myke was a Mentor.

In today's team meeting, it was decided that Myke should be the one to approach Lionah for help. Myke was uncomfortable with that. Given his past, he did not want to talk to anyone higher than a Mentor. He had not spoken with Lionah for many years.

"But, Myke," Savana said. "I know Lionah. I know how much she cares about you."

"I let her down," Myke said.

"No, you didn't," Savana responded. "She has the utmost respect for how you handled things with her. When you decided you could no longer be a Mentor, you never used your power the wrong way. You told her straight up why you had to step down. It was total class, Myke."

Myke shrugged.

"And Myke, she's told me how much she admires you because you never abdicated your responsibilities. You only stopped handling them when you told them you were out. It was totally honorable."

Bronson leaned over to Apollo with a quizzical look on his face and whispered, "Abdicated?"

Savana picked up on that. "What I meant was that Myke never failed to do what he was supposed to do as a Mentor—even when he no longer believed." Then, turning back to Myke, "You hung in there out of respect for your students. She knows that."

There was more discussion. Finally, Myke reluctantly agreed to approach Lionah.

"Tomorrow?" Apollo asked, thinking that Myke might need a day to gear up.

"No," said Myke. "Today. I'll do it today. For Torith."

Myke was true to his word, and he asked Lionah that afternoon. She gave the plan her full support. The team was thrilled, especially Apollo, who could not wait to see Glacier and Fjord again.

58

Reunion

Lionah talked with Apollo and said she was going to have him transported to the Sub-Summa sanctuary, where he would meet up with Glacier and Fjord and be there for two or three days. "That will give you some time to re-establish your relationship with the wolves." Then she told Apollo to lead both Glacier and Fjord to that cave—the one that was a portal to the surface. "If you can't find it, ask Glacier to help you," she told Apollo. "He knows where it is."

"How can I explain that to him?" Apollo asked.

"You'll figure it out," she told him.

Her comment was dismissive, and it surprised Apollo. *You'll figure it out,* he thought to himself. *What does that mean?*

Lionah continued, "Call me on a B-Channel when you get out. You'll be close to Sughi City when you exit. You'll need to keep a low profile until I can spring you back to your side of Planet Summa. It's important that the Sughis do not see you with the wolves."

Apollo asked her how he would convince Glacier and Fjord to go into the transport cave. They clearly had not wanted anything to do with the cave the last time he was there.

"It'll be different this time," Lionah said without further explanation. She again seemed dismissive of his questions, leaving Apollo wondering.

After his conversation with Lionah, Apollo debriefed with the team, explaining he would be back in a few days with the wolves.

Myke, Tamir, and Bronson said they would do everything they could to get things ready, although there really wasn't much for them to do since it would be up to the wolves to find the right spot. Tamir and Bronson would continue to monitor the Sughi data they were collecting, looking for more clues on Torith's location.

At the end of the debrief, Tamir brought up something new. "One more thing," he said. "It may be nothing, but there has been a change in the patterns of two of the Sughi fighters we think are assigned to keep Torith captive."

Apollo didn't understand. "Change?"

"Yes. As we know, the captors seem to be running shifts where two will arrive at Torith's location at about the same time, and then the same two will leave close to the same time. Normally, the pairs arrive from different directions, and they depart in separate ways, as if they are work associates but not friends. But these two Sughis are different. They come together for the same shift, and they leave together. It wasn't like that at first, but it's been that way for the past several weeks."

Bronson added, "We also think that, while they are there, others are coming and going too."

"Why is that important?" Apollo asked.

"It's kind of weird because the others seem to be hiding the fact that they are going there."

"Hiding?" Apollo didn't understand. All the Sughis going there were trying to hide their movements. So, what was the big deal?

"Hiding it from everyone, not just us," Bronson said.

Tamir explained further, "Yes. We think they might be going in with the two regulars but trying to keep it hidden from Sughi's side—and us, of course."

"That definitely is strange," Myke said. How many of these extras are there?"

"Twenty to fifty," Tamir said. "We can't tell. The data is limited."

"I understand what you are saying," said Apollo. "But why would they do that? Why would a bunch of Sughis be going to see Torith? Do you think they're having a torture show or something?" Apollo was worried.

"It's a total mystery," Tamir answered. "We're not even sure we are right. But it seems to be that way." Tamir looked at Bronson, who nodded in agreement.

"We need to end her capture soon!" said Apollo.

"Roger that," Myke agreed. "You'd better hurry up with those wolves, Apollo. We need them pronto."

Tamir then changed the subject by asking, "Apollo, how are the wolves going to understand what to do?"

"I think Lionah is going to talk to them," Apollo answered. "But she did not explain that to me." Then, turning to Reemo, Apollo asked, "Can you talk to the wolves, Reemo? Do you have that kind of power?"

"I would have to ask for it, Apollo, just like you'll have to."

"Oh, I've tried talking to them. Come, Go, Stay, Good Boy. That's about as far as I ever got."

"That's not what I'm saying, Apollo," said Reemo. "You need to ask for more."

"Me?" replied Apollo, surprised. "Me?"

"Yes, you, Apollo." Reemo locked eyes with Apollo. Apollo was beginning to understand.

"Oh, boy," muttered Tamir. "Apollo, don't you understand?"

Apollo looked at him, and Tamir said, "He's saying the gift is yours, Apollo. But you have to ask. You're gonna be a wolf-talker!"

There was no such thing as a "wolf-talker." They all knew that. But they also knew there was such a thing as gifts from Olam. Tamir considered his technical abilities a gift. Myke admitted that his tagging ability was probably one, and Apollo knew Olam had given him unusual power for fighting, and for resisting Sughi's darkness.

Apollo now understood why Lionah had been dismissive of his earlier questions about Glacier.

"Wolf-talker," Apollo muttered. "That's crazy stuff." Then he looked at Reemo. "Okay, I get it. I'll ask them. Megantha and Olam." Apollo shook his head in amazement at the thought of such a gift. *Wow!*

ᐊ◊ᐅᐊ◊ᐅᐊ◊ᐅᐊ◊ᐅ

Lionah sprang Apollo to Sub-Summa. Apollo had asked her to not tell the wolves he was coming. He did not want them waiting for him, and he hoped to surprise them. But he was also not sure where they would be. "Do they keep the same patterns?" he had asked her.

"You'll find them," she had said with a confident tone. "Use your gift and work through Glacier."

Now that Apollo found himself back in Sub-Summa, there was a comfort and familiarity he had missed. This truly was a protected place of healing. No Sughi soldier could bring his darkness here. What a gift it was to return and be strong this time, not deeply broken and in need of extensive repair.

When springing Apollo to Sub-Summa, Lionah had chosen to bring him to the same meadow where he had first arrived years ago. Apollo immediately knew where he was, and he was awash in memories. Despite his request not to be met by the wolves, he looked to where he had seen them the first time he arrived. He half expected them to be there and waiting for him at the edge of the meadow, near the tree line. But, no. There were no wolves, and he could not help but feel disappointed.

Apollo's ghost breathed in the beauty of Sub-Summa. He loved the aspen and pine from which this meadow clearing was carved.

Apollo left the ground and rose to an altitude of about five hundred feet. He then started his search for Glacier and Fjord. *Think like a wolf,* he pressed himself. *Think like Glacier.*

Olam told Apollo he now had the ability to share thoughts with a wolf, especially with Glacier. "You'll have to work on developing it, my son. Many of my children love animals and feel a deep affinity towards them, like your sister Celti, but few will have the ability to communicate with them like you'll have with your wolves." Then Olam paused and seemed to muse to himself. "Oh, how I wish I could give this same gift to your sister," he said. "I love her so much."

Apollo had asked Olam if the capability would continue with him when he was a Blood. "Oh, yes, my boy. It will be there. But it will be buried. You'll have to find it and then work to develop it."

Apollo scanned the terrain from altitude, looking for the beasts. At the same time, Apollo continued to replay the conversation he'd had with Olam about his wolf gift. "It's a rare ability," Olam had told him. "Use it well."

It was morning in Sub-Summa. Apollo hoped he would be lucky and spot the wolves out in the open. This was the time of day when they were the most active. He wanted to see them before they knew he was there. He remembered the first night he had spent with them, years ago, when he was in his early reconstruction stages. He remembered how Lionah had come that night, and how she had enjoyed sneaking up on the wolves, not revealing her location, to watch their excitement as their keen senses knew she was somewhere near.

Apollo searched out the meeting place under the thick canopy of trees where Lionah had met them the first night. The wolves were not there, and Apollo went back to altitude and headed over to the valley with the beaver pond. No wolves. Next, he checked the flat outcropping on the side of the mountain above a lake. This was the place he had played with the wolves, howling with them at Sub-Summa's moon. No luck.

Apollo continued to be flooded with memories, and he continued to search. Then, he had an idea that made him both sad and hopeful. Could it be that Glacier was waiting for him? Maybe he had been waiting all this time? And if so, wouldn't he wait at the last place they saw each other?

If that really were the case, it saddened Apollo to think of the years Glacier may have waited for him to return. Could this be true? He wanted Glacier to miss him, like Apollo missed Glacier, but not so deeply that it drove the animal's daily actions. It was too heartbreaking to think the wolf may have been physically waiting all this time. Had Glacier been frequently checking the open field and the cave area where Apollo had been taken away? *Please, no!* hoped Apollo. That was a level of sadness he hoped his friend had not endured. It would have been better for Glacier to have forgotten him than to miss him on such a deep level.

Before today's arrival, Apollo had wondered if he would remember the layout of Sub-Summa well enough to find the place from which he'd been sent to the surface. The problem was that he had only been there once. He remembered that he and the wolves had been working their way through an expansive, mostly flat forest with thick trees. They had come upon a clearing with a rock wall at the other end. That wall rose several hundred feet, and at the base of the wall was the cave that had "portaled" Apollo to the surface. Apollo remembered how Glacier would not go anywhere near the cave.

Apollo covered extensive terrain from altitude, searching in a rough grid pattern. He could not find the clearing with the rock wall and cave at the bottom. He was frustrated. Time was important. He had to get on with the plan to save Torith. Maybe he had been selfish in wanting to find the wolves on his own. It was time to ask for help, and he asked Olam. As soon as he did, the clear thought came to him. *Use your gift!*

At that thought, Apollo felt foolish. *They are giving me everything. I have the tools. Why can't I see that?*

Apollo landed on a rocky peak that was isolated and high enough to give him a view for many miles. The weather was calm, with only a light, halting breeze. Apollo could see many of the areas he had already searched.

Apollo then calmed his ghost and tried to clear his mind. It took a few minutes. Some ghosts were very good at meditation and mental control. Apollo was less patient with his mind, but he tried. To help calm himself, he let his ghost sink into the rock of the mountain peak, going in up to his chest. Becoming part of the rock was a psychological experience. It helped him feel more settled, wrapped, and protected.

His mind continued to race. Would he really be able to talk to Glacier? And would he understand what Glacier said back?

This would not be the first time Apollo had tried to talk with animals. Apollo and his older sister, Celti, had tried it many times when they were kids. Celti would try to get into the brains of dogs, horses, cows, and even those of frogs, lizards, or fish. But she and Apollo found that when they mind-melted with any animal, it was always beyond weird. They could sense a little of their emotions, but the rest was gibberish. Sometimes, he could tell he had accessed their hearing, but the sound interpretation was so different that it made no sense to him. It was the same with their vision. Apollo could see light and dark, and there were some colors, but the way it transmitted through the animals' brains was so different that Apollo could not get it to make any sense. Celti said she could tell what they were thinking. Apollo suspected it was more wishful thinking than reality.

Apollo again tried to settle his thoughts, concentrating only on Glacier. *How do I use the gift Olam gave me?* He attempted to see in his mind's eye where Glacier might be, but this process only brought fog.

I probably have to be right there with him, Apollo thought. *Not miles away on top of some mountain.* He mulled that over, but then he had another idea. *Me trying to see where he's at isn't the gift. That's not what Olam gave me.*

Apollo switched his focus. Rather than attempting to see Glacier from the outside, he tried to be inside Glacier, seeing what Glacier was looking at through his eyes. *Can I do that from a distance?*

Apollo tried that perspective. To his amazement, it began to work. His vision became double-tracked. One track was his own clear and understandable vision. The other was much less clear, but it was there, and it was not his. It had to be Glacier's.

Not only was Apollo seeing some of what Glacier saw, he also had a sense of what Glacier was thinking. Concepts, not detailed thoughts.

Apollo could tell that Glacier was relaxed and half asleep. Glacier's vision was fixed and blurry, not scanning or looking around. It looked like Glacier was half-focused on some trees. Glacier's view did not include Fjord, but Apollo knew Fjord was close to Glacier because Glacier knew it. Apollo could feel Glacier's security that his friend was nearby.

Apollo could not tell where Glacier was. He needed Glacier to look around. He tried to pass a thought to Glacier. *Stand up!*

To Apollo's amazement, Glacier stood up. Apollo could tell he did so. He could feel Glacier's brain register the stress on his legs and frame as he stood up. Apollo could feel the solidity and electrical currents in the ground through Glacier's paws.

Look around, Apollo thought to Glacier. *Look hard and concentrate. What is nearby?*

The feed from Glacier's vision improved considerably, and Glacier started to look around. Apollo saw Fjord, and Glacier looked away from the trees and toward the more expansive scenery that had been behind him. It did not take long, and soon, Apollo knew right where the wolves were. The two of them had been resting under some trees at the edge of a rock outcropping near the shoreline of a small lake. This lake was in the same valley as the beaver pond, but it was farther up. The water in this lake was especially clear. Apollo had flown over this area earlier in the day, but he had missed seeing the wolves because they had been partly hidden under the trees.

Apollo wondered what Glacier was thinking. Could he sense Apollo was in his brain? Did he know it was Apollo? These were things Apollo hoped to understand better.

Apollo blasted off the mountain peak at full speed and arrived at the mountain lake within minutes. He descended from flight elevation, moving off to the side and out of Glacier's view, and then approached through the tree tops, making it impossible for Glacier or Fjord to see him.

Apollo slid into the trunk of a thick pine tree near Glacier, but twenty feet above him. He pushed his eye forward just enough to look down at the dogs, knowing there was little chance they could find him.

Glacier and Fjord were both at full attention, nosing the air, looking around for the presence they knew had arrived. Apollo wondered if Glacier understood it was him.

Apollo spent a wonderful, long, full minute watching his friends. *They saved me once,* he thought to himself. *And they are going to save me again.*

Glacier snorted and did a little prance, holding his ground but circling on the spot to look in all directions. He looked excited.

"Look up," Apollo tried thinking to Glacier. Amazingly, Glacier looked up. "More right," said Apollo to Glacier. Apollo was sure Glacier did not know the terms "right" or "left," so Apollo thought of the direction compared to where Glacier was looking. To Apollo's delight, Glacier shifted his focus more to the right.

Incredible, thought Apollo. *Absolutely incredible! What a gift!*

Apollo slipped out of the tree and called to Glacier, who burst into a joyous dance. Apollo came down and interwove himself with the two wolves. Fjord was thrilled, and Glacier was ecstatic. Apollo had not been this happy since his last days with these friends years ago. Apollo attempted to speak to Glacier in his mind, and Glacier seemed to understand—not completely—but much more than before. Apollo also found that he could communicate the same way with Fjord. His gift was for all wolves, although it seemed especially strong with Glacier.

The communication was not in words. Apollo might express words to Glacier, but it was the concepts these words formed in Apollo's brain that were transmitted to Glacier. And the concepts had to be on Glacier's level. No calculus for the wolf. *Heck! No calculus for me, either!*

The reverse was true for Apollo. Whatever wolf language Glacier and Fjord might have between them was incomprehensible to Apollo. Instead, it was concepts that came through to Apollo. The wolves did not have to speak the concepts, but they needed to think them specifically for Apollo to receive anything.

Apollo knew that what he would ask of Glacier and Fjord would be hard for them. It would require a big change from the sheltered lives they lived here in Sub-Summa. He would take them to a place where the whole world was at war. There was so much hate. Ghosts might try to hurt or abuse the wolves. Everything was going to be far from perfect.

As Apollo basked in the tribal love and affection of these two beasts, he questioned what he had done. What right did he have to take these beautiful creatures out of paradise and into rough seas? He thought he loved Glacier. And yet he was now going to show his love by making Glacier's life much more perilous. Glacier and Fjord would no longer enjoy this protected Eden.

"I want to free Torith," he said to himself. "We need to save her and get her back!" But at what cost?

Apollo looked at the wonderful beasts and fell silent. As he did, Mr. Doubt and Mrs. Guilt joined Apollo. They looked Apollo squarely in the face, and then they wrapped themselves around his soul with their powerful, immobilizing embrace. He let them in. His actions had given them squatters' rights, at least for now.

"What have I done?" he uttered to himself. "What have I done?"

59

Reconnect in Sub-Summa

After their joyous reunion, Apollo, Glacier, and Fjord spent
the rest of the afternoon wandering through Sub-Summa.
Apollo's only goal for the day was to reestablish himself
with the animals and build lines of communication. Where
they went did not matter.

Like before, most of the time, Glacier was up front
but taking directional cues from Apollo. Fjord acted as a
rover, sometimes positioning with Glacier or Apollo, but
most of the time taking up a rear guard.

Apollo started them in a direction that he thought
would lead them closer to the cave, although he was still
unsure of its location. They worked their way up the side of a
mildly sloped canyon that had a mixture of trees and
boulders at the bottom, thinning to lighter vegetation and
alpine ground cover towards the top. Once on top, they
followed the ridgeline, paralleling the valley bottom. They
did this for several miles, then they left the ridgeline and
descended into a more rugged valley on the other side.

Hours later, they stopped for the night. Once he and
the wolves had settled in and were resting, Apollo thought
back to his months of darkness and torture by the Sughis. He
thought about the gift Olam had given him. The one he had
only come to understand later. The one giving him the
strength to embrace the darkness and withstand the Sughi
abuse. The one that also allowed him to innately and

undeniably reject the darkness B. Z. Sughi had attempted to force on him.

Now, in the middle of the night, he watched the comforting auras of his two sleeping friends, and he contrasted his present self with the broken one he had arrived with before. He was strong now, bordering on too strong.

Reemo and others had spoken to Apollo about the need for him to advance and become a Mentor. "It's time for you to be a teacher, Apollo, and not a fighter. You have too much power. You are interfering with the agency of the Sughi warriors whom you battle."

Apollo had heard this in various forms from those above him. He knew his time as a warrior was coming to an end. He wondered if he would ever feel more alive than he did when in full battle, hammering on twenty Sughi soldiers at once, feeling them strain under his might, sensing their every fear, weakness, and desire as he purged through them and discharged them to nothing. It was a heady feeling and a power that he knew, if not controlled, could turn against him. It soon would be time to gain even more power as a Mentor, like Reemo. That greater power could only be used to teach and help others. It was not meant to be unleashed directly on the Sughis themselves, at least not yet.

"Boring," Apollo said to himself, but he also knew it was right. It was the next step in his path, and one he would need to take soon. He hoped he could adjust.

The next morning, Apollo and his companions continued their wandering. Apollo felt less at ease today because of what he had to do. Apollo waited until the afternoon when he stopped near a small waterfall. There, a medium-sized creek cascaded down a series of uneven, rocky steps into a catch pool. Then, the water gathered itself before winding down a gentle, sunlit canyon.

Like the water, it was time for Apollo to gather himself. He needed to enlist Glacier and Fjord's help. In doing so, he would be asking them to leave this wonderful place.

Apollo knew the wolves saw him as their leader. They would follow him, and that made him responsible for their well-being. He was sad to think of them having to leave Sub-Summa for the Sughi-infested world above. He knew they would only partially understand why they had to leave. He also knew they would fully trust him. It was that trust that scared Apollo because he did not want to let them down. Torith trusted him, and look what had happened to her.

He asked Glacier to lead them to the place with the open meadow and the cave. This was the place where Apollo had disappeared.

When Apollo made that request, Glacier's whole demeanor shrank. Apollo had asked to go to the cave of sadness. The wolf's heart was breaking. Apollo was going away again. Apollo could feel the weight in Glacier's heart.

But Apollo explained that it was different this time. Glacier and Fjord were to go with him. "I need your help in another place. We need to find my friend."

Glacier perked up.

"She is a friend like Fjord is a friend. She is a strong friend. She is in trouble. We need to find her. She is lost." Apollo tried to wrap his words in conscious, idea-filled thoughts. The wolves could not understand the words themselves.

Glacier seemed to understand, at least partially. Layers of sadness lifted from him, replaced with purpose and anticipation.

Apollo asked Glacier how far the cave of sadness was. Glacier's response was not in hours or days, but more

of a general concept of time. As best Apollo could tell, it
might take them a half-day to get there, the way they
traveled, along the ground as if they were physical beings
and not ghosts.

Apollo told them they would leave for the cave of
sadness tomorrow morning. "We will all go in together,"
Apollo emphasized. "We go to help an important friend. We
won't be sad."

That night, the other two wolves joined them. These
were the same two who were sometimes with them before.
The younger of the two was older now. They both greeted
Apollo warmly. Apollo loved spending the night surrounded
by the auras of these four sleeping wolf ghosts. The night
was quiet except for an occasional wisp of wind that rustled
the tops of the pines. Apollo knew this was a magical night
and the final night of innocence for Glacier and Fjord. It was
a night to savor. He felt bad for the two wolves who would
be left behind. He considered taking them, too. After all, he
was breaking up a family. But Apollo decided against it.
Lionah would take care of them. And Sub-Summa was huge.
Hopefully, there were other wolves they could join.

The next morning, Apollo had another mental
exchange with Glacier and Fjord. The wolves did not want to
go into the cave, but they were going to do what he told them
to do. He tried again to explain that he needed their help in
another place. Then, he attempted to explain the concept of
rescuing someone who was being hurt. That seemed murky
to the wolves, so Apollo simplified it. "There are some bad
people whom you need to help me find. We need to fight
them." That was more black and white, and Glacier and
Fjord could understand that. They were wolves and
inherently programmed to fight, even if there had been
nothing to fight here in the Sub-Summa.

"Okay, we'll go" was the thought stream Apollo sensed coming from the beasts, and it was reinforced by looks of loyalty and determination on their faces. Then they transmitted thoughts Apollo had not considered. "We want to work. We want to help. We want to do something important."

Apollo was surprised and taken aback by this response. It brought a whole new dimension to his relationship with them. These magnificent animals wanted to be on a team. They wanted to contribute. Their pack mentality demanded it.

"Yes, you will help," Apollo said and transmitted. "Your help is important."

Glacier and Fjord seemed satisfied with that, and the three of them soon left the other two wolves. Apollo did not sense any form of permanent goodbye from Glacier and Fjord to the other two. He opted not to make a big deal out of their separation.

Travel to the cave had started mid-morning. By late afternoon, they were at the edge of the clearing opposite the cave. Apollo brought the wolves close and looked both in the eyes, staying back a few feet so they would maintain eye lock with him. "We are on an important mission," he conveyed. "We are strong. We go together!"

Glacier let out an audible, guttural "yelp" in agreement, and both wolves bristled with energy.

"Okay," Apollo said. "Here we go," and he started across the clearing. This time, Glacier did not lead, but he and Fjord stayed close, right behind Apollo.

At the mouth of the cave, Apollo stopped, got down on their level, and told them how much he loved them. He could feel their loyalty and love flow back.

All three entered the cave.

Seconds later, Apollo, Glacier, and Fjord were transported to the surface of Summa. They had been portaled to an open, grassy field, and Apollo immediately moved them into some nearby trees. Apollo knew they could not be far from Sughi City, and he was following Lionah's directions to keep the wolves out of sight.

Apollo then called for a comm and pulled up his B-Channel. He reached out to Lionah. Ten minutes later, she sprang them to a lake on the other side of Summa. This lake was about twenty miles south of the area where the wolves would be needed to search for Torith.

Apollo doubted that the wolves had a sense of how far they had traveled, but he could see that they knew they were in a different place. Here, like Sub-Summa, was wolf country, with vast pine forests, sparkling lakes, and a latitude north enough that wolves might be expected. However, this environment was more complete, with fish in the waters, crayfish hiding along riverbanks, leeches and worms in the shallows, and an occasional turtle basking in the sun.

The wolves immediately began investigating. There was much more here for their tremendous senses to process.

A lot more—both good and bad, thought Apollo.

Apollo told them to "stay close by."

Glacier transmitted that he understood.

Then Apollo brought up a comm, pulled up a B-Channel, and called Myke.

Myke responded quickly, apparently waiting for Apollo's call. "I'm leaving in about five minutes, Apollo," Myke said. Then, with an urgent tone, he added, "There have been changes. We need to find Torith as soon as possible!"

Myke's comment alarmed Apollo.

Myke said he would explain when he got there. Myke was a faster traveler than most ghosts, but he was no Forza.

He had to travel the distance physically. He could not spring himself.

It took Myke four hours to get to Apollo.

60

Wolves at Work

Myke arrived where Apollo was waiting with the wolves. Apollo wanted updates. But Myke explained that they needed to get going as soon as possible. "Things are worse than before," he said to Apollo. "We need to go."

Apollo hesitated, not understanding.

"I'll explain everything after you send the wolves out hunting," Myke said. "We'll have plenty of time to talk then. Come on, A.P.," Myke insisted. "Let's move!"

What Myke was saying made Apollo afraid for Torith. Apollo trusted Myke's judgment, so he skipped the delays and hastily introduced the wolves to Myke, making it clear that Myke was part of the pack. Glacier and Fjord got it, sniffing Myke and then accepting him. "He fights with us," Apollo conveyed to them. "Now we need to hurry."

The four of them then headed out in the direction of the search area. Myke had started to fly up and go to altitude, but Apollo corrected him. "The wolves don't fly," Apollo told Myke. "Treat them like land animals... like they are Bloods."

Although the wolves would not fly, their progress with Myke and Apollo over the ground was much faster than it would have been had they been real, physical Bloods. Instead, as ghost wolves, they could go up and down steep slopes with ease, and thick brush posed no problems because they transitioned right through it. They also were not subject to injury and could travel with little rest.

It only took them an hour to cover the twenty miles to the edge of the search area. As they approached, Apollo slowed them down and took more care to stay in cover. The last thing they wanted was to come in and be spotted by a random Sughi. The wolves could be in the open, but Myke and Apollo had to be in stealth mode.

Arriving at the search area's border, they found some high ground with decent cover, and then Apollo took on the challenge of trying to tell the wolves what was expected of them.

"Good luck, wolf-talker," Myke said to Apollo with a slight tease. "This'll be interesting."

Apollo did his best to explain that the wolves were to search the entire area in front of them. They were looking for any people, or anywhere people had been. "Come back here tonight," he told them. I'll be here waiting for you."

Apollo was not sure how much specific direction to provide. He doubted he could convey instructions to use a grid search pattern, or to stay within five miles, or to come right back as soon as they found someone. But the wolves would naturally want to return to him at night, so he left it at that. He hoped he would be able to put himself into Glacier's mind and see what he was doing during his search. Hopefully, he could steer Glacier when needed. Apollo suspected that the extremely powerful noses and senses of these wolves would make up for the lack of a scientific, methodical search. Maybe they'd be lucky. The wolves might hit pay dirt on their first day.

Apollo sent the wolves on their way, out on the search. Then he and Myke talked.

"Are they really going to know what to do?" Myke asked.

"I'll give them a few hours, and then I'll try to get into Glacier's head to see what's going on," Apollo responded.

"You can talk to Glacier remotely?" Myke asked.

"It seems that I can share thoughts with him. And I can see what he sees. Not clearly, but somewhat. Enough to get a sense of where he is or what he's doing."

"Wow!" said Myke. "That's amazing!"

Apollo thought it amazing, too, but he needed the conversation to switch to Torith. "What's this about Torith? What changed?"

"Yes... well... remember how the brain team thought a bunch of Sughis might be going to see her?"

"Yes, something like twenty... or more... maybe fifty, right?"

"Bronson said it might be as many as fifty—but they really didn't know."

"Okay."

"Well, the day after you left to go get the wolves, I received a call." Myke hesitated, looking Apollo in the eyes for effect. "Secret Sauce. She called me."

"You?" Apollo was surprised. "Secret Sauce" was the nickname Tamir had given to Apollo's well-placed source in Sughi's camp. Tamir, Myke, and Torith all knew the source had to be Malta, but the team never mentioned her name. The fact that she was talking to Apollo could not get out, not even to Olam's side. So, they referred to her with the nickname, and they rarely spoke of her at all. "Why?" Apollo asked. "I mean, I don't care that she called you, but she detests you, Myke."

"Detests... yes... that is for sure," said Myke.

Apollo knew why Malta disliked Myke so much. During the time that Apollo was kidnapped, Malta had helped to search for him. She had even provided some of her soldiers to help. That was more than five years ago, and a very different time when there still was some civility between the warring sides. Malta had made it clear to her Sughi chain of command that it had been wrong to take Apollo. They denied any involvement, blaming it on the rogues who they said were out of their control. That position gave Malta the freedom to use her formal chain of command to help rescue Apollo. At the same time, Myke was also trying to find Apollo, and Myke was brutal. He single-handedly decimated Sughi platoon after Sughi platoon, trying to find someone on their side who could tell him where Apollo was being held. His scorched-earth approach was too heavy-handed, and Malta thought it only served to further motivate those holding Apollo, feeding their hatred and resolve.

"I know she can't stand me," Myke said. "But since you were off grid, she said she had to talk to somebody right then."

Apollo had zero problems with Malta talking to Myke. It was not an ego thing. It was the mere fact that she would reach out to Myke that surprised him.

"What did she want?" Apollo asked.

"Before she would tell me anything, she made a big deal out of saying that nobody could know she had called. You could know, but nobody else."

Malta was taking a big risk every time she supplied information. If the Sughis knew, they'd hunt her and harass her so hard she'd have to come over to Olam's side or go into deep hiding. She would lose all the prestige and power she had built for herself in the Sughi command structure.

"I assured her that only you would know," Myke continued. "Then she said that hundreds of Sughis were going to see Torith... every day."

"Every day?" repeated Apollo.

"Yes, but she said she didn't know why. She had learned about it from one of her sources, but there was little additional information."

Apollo had previously asked Malta many times if she could tell him where the Sughis were keeping Torith. She had assured him she was trying to figure it out, but that it was tightly held information her sources had not cracked. Apollo never knew if he should believe her.

"Apollo... there was almost a panic in her voice," Myke said. "As if she cares for Torith or something. I thought she didn't like Torith."

Apollo knew that Malta's feelings about Torith had more to do with how Malta felt about Apollo. But now was not the time to explain it.

"Then Malta told me where she thought we should try to look for Torith."

"Really? She always told me she did not know."

"Correct, but with all the people going to see Torith, her sources had figured it out, and we're right on," said Myke. "She said she only had a general idea of where we should search, but from her description, Tamir and Bronson did a bang-up job of nailing down the right search zone. Your wolves should be able to find her."

"Does she know we're already looking for Torith here?" Apollo asked.

"No."

Good, thought Apollo. *We must be in the right place.*

"And she doesn't know anything about the wolves," said Myke.

Another 'good,' thought Apollo. Then he asked, "So... you don't think it was a trick? Maybe one where she was probing for what we are doing?"

"Not at all," Myke said. "She was careful calling me. She had my cousin log in on her comm, and Malta called from that one."

"Your cousin?" Apollo asked.

"Do you remember my cousin? Darcie? The one in Sughi City? She took us to the Anti-Blood building ...?"

Apollo remembered Darcie well. "Yes, Darcie. She was great," Apollo said.

Myke continued, "Darcie and I still talk sometimes. So, comm sessions between us would be logged by Sughi intelligence as routine."

Apollo thought it surprising that Malta would go to all the effort of seeking out Darcie for a call to Myke. She must have thought the information was vital, and that made Apollo more concerned for Torith. Apollo could only hope the wolves would find Torith soon.

"If Malta figured out where they have Torith, I'm afraid Sughi Command will think we figured it out, too, and they'll move Torith before we get to her."

Apollo and Myke waited for about two hours, giving the wolves time to start exploring, and then Apollo began concentrating on being inside Glacier's mind. Would the wolves stay on task and really hunt? Or would their train of thought wander? Maybe they were lounging under a tree, taking a siesta?

As Apollo concentrated, he started to feel movement, and he could tell it was Glacier's gait. The wolves were clearly on the move. Then, more importantly, he was able to receive enough of Glacier's thought sequence to sense that

Glacier clearly was on the hunt. Looking for human ghosts. Find human ghosts. Keeping looking. Hunt and search.

"They're definitely still on task," Apollo said to Myke. "They are amazing beasts."

"True," said Myke. "But, Apollo, the way you talk with them is even more amazing. I'm frankly surprised Olam gave you a gift like that. I mean, yes, you're the good boy, but still... I don't think any ghosts have that gift."

"I know," Apollo answered. "It makes me nervous."

"It would make me nervous, too," Myke said. "Olam is going to want something in return. Are you ready for that?"

Apollo knew what Myke was referring to. It had to do with Apollo becoming a Mentor. Reemo, Megantha, and Olam were all starting to push for that. Apollo was hesitant. "What was it like for you, Myke? Being a Mentor? Was it really that bad?"

"For me, it was," Myke said. "It was way too much responsibility. All the people I was helping to advance and train. They needed so much love from me. I'm just not that way. You are. You're a good person, Apollo. You can coddle all those people. I can't. It went against my grain. I thought I could grow into it, but more and more, I resented it."

"But, Myke, why would they make you a Mentor if you weren't ready for it?"

"I think it was so I could learn my limits. Now, I don't have to wonder. Being a Mentor is not for me."

Apollo analyzed. "So, you stepped down. That makes some sense, but why did you go over to Sughi's side?"

"I wanted to fight," said Myke. "I needed to counterbalance where I had been. Going to Sughi's side was a total break, and I could use that side to go to war. I was fighting myself more than fighting your side. But I didn't want Olam's side trying to talk me back into being a Mentor. I needed a clear break."

"Then you met me," said Apollo. "In battle. The perfect place."

"Yes. The 'perfect place' is right. And you saved me, Apollo. You brought me back. And now they know who I am: on Olam's side, but not a good boy like you. I'll never progress like you will, Apollo. But at least I'll be a Blood, and I hope I can be a Blood warrior too—for the good guys—even if I, myself, won't be a good person."

Apollo's conversation with this best of friends made him both happy and sad. Myke was the real thing, strong and fighting for the good side. It seems he had made peace with who he was. Apollo also knew there was no telling at this point what Myke's life as a Blood would be. He was determined to think of himself as not a nice person. But despite that, he was working hard for the good guys. How could he not be a nice person when his every waking moment, for months, had been dedicated to saving Torith? He might be grumpy, direct, and abrasive. He might not have the best veneer. But... really? Apollo had nothing but love and respect for Myke, whatever flaws there might be.

The friends fell silent. It was mostly a waiting game now. They needed to stay off any communications, which was a good excuse not to message anyone or deal with the endless administrative requests from Diamond Command.

Apollo spent the next several hours carefully wandering in the local area, trying to always stay in good cover so any random Sughis would not see him. Myke did the same. Like the wolves, they were looking for Sughis. Unlike the wolves, who could openly cover vast amounts of terrain, Apollo and Myke stayed hidden and close by.

Apollo worked his way to lower, flatter ground where there was an edge to the pine forest. Beyond that was a grassy meadow with two deer. They were real deer, not ghosts. They were physical, and their heads were down. They were grazing, and Apollo could hear them pull the grass from the soil, bite it off with their incisors, grind it up with their molars, and swallow it. *That'll be me someday, stuffing my face with physical food. Hopefully, it will be something better than grass. I wonder what it's like to feel hungry?*

Apollo knew the deer could not see him since they were physical, and he was a ghost. Most animals on Summa were ghosts, like Apollo, but Olam, Megantha, and the others had put a few Blood animals on the planet for everyone's enjoyment.

Apollo watched the deer carefully and remained hidden. Since they were a bit of an anomaly, anybody else who found them might spend time watching them, too. Apollo moved back from the clearing and began working his way around it, staying well-concealed within the trees.

The weather in the area was starting to deteriorate. There were traces of far-off mountain lightning, and dark clouds were headed their way. Apollo knew there might be rain. He began working his way back to the higher terrain from which he had dispatched the wolves. He met with Myke, who, like Apollo, had not seen any Sughis.

Apollo wanted the wolves to start back, and he tried to push a thought to Glacier that it was time to return. He also tried to see what Glacier was seeing. Apollo found that the wolves were approaching one of several small lakes in the area.

Apollo's memory was not complete enough to know which lake the wolves were near, but he hoped the fourleggers could find their way back soon. "Hurry!" he conveyed to Glacier.

61

Lightning

The weather was worsening. Strong convective activity built in the area. Moisture-laden air was forced aloft, releasing its water as droplets. These churned and fell, creating friction that discharged as lightning—a lot of it.

Electricity, and especially lightning, was one of the few physical phenomena on Summa that could flatten a ghost. Suddenly, there was a crack from a bolt of lightning several miles from Apollo. The lightning had come from the direction where Apollo estimated the wolves might be. Apollo saw the flash from his eyes, and he also saw it from Glacier's. From Glacier's perspective, it had been in front of him, to his right, and across the lake, whose shoreline the wolves were skirting.

"Maybe we'd better get underground," said Myke. Apollo and Myke knew they would be safe fifty to a hundred feet under the ground.

Apollo was worried for the wolves, and he could feel fear inside Glacier. There was no serious weather or lightning inside Sub-Summa, where the wolves had spent all their lives. They had never seen anything like this storm. Close lightning was a scary thing for any person or animal, but it was especially scary the first time in a new environment. Apollo could feel Glacier wanting to stop and hide somewhere. "Keep coming!" Apollo ordered. "Keep coming!" To Apollo's surprise, he sensed something deep inside Glacier that rallied and forced him forward, despite his fears. Apollo realized that Glacier could feel Apollo's fears, too. Glacier was determined to protect Apollo from the terrifying electrical monsters. *Amazing!* thought Apollo. *He's terrified, and he still wants to help me!*

Flash/Boom... Flash/Boom. Powerful twin bolts of lightning exploded in the air, close to Apollo. This time, the lightning's power knocked Apollo unconscious. When he came to, the rain was flooding from the sky. It was hard for him to think clearly. He was not sure how long he had been out. His whole frame hurt from the overwhelming charges. He looked over at where Myke had been. He, too, had been knocked down by the lightning. He was still lights out and had no aura. His menapses were blown, circuits destroyed.

Apollo knew he would fully recover, and so would Myke. If the wolves had been knocked out, they also would recover, but they would be terrified.

Myke came to and said he was going underground for protection.

Apollo wanted to go down, too, but he also wanted to reach Glacier, and he fought to reach Glacier's mind. There was no connection. He could not project himself. He was too discombobulated and weak to connect. He could not help his friends. Apollo felt terrible.

The angry black sky continued to dump heavy, pelting rain. Apollo regretted bringing the wolves here. This was not their fight, and he was using them as pawns. The pre-human ghosts were the problem, not these magnificent beasts. Only the pre-humans should suffer. The beasts had done nothing wrong. Apollo had been selfish, pulling them from their sanctuary into this stupid war. *I was selfish, selfish!* Apollo knew what he had to do—or what he had to ask Lionah to do. "Send them back to Sub-Summa," he would ask her. "Please!" he would beg her. "It's not their fight. I was wrong." Apollo's mind was fog-filled from the lightning, but it was clear what he had to tell Lionah. *I made a huge mistake!*

Apollo slumped on the wet ground. Through the pouring rain, a far-off look could be seen on his face. "It's like Torith had said," he mumbled, shaking his head. "Sometimes, I am a stupid man."

Another bolt of lightning hit the ground. It was closer than the last ones. It knocked Apollo unconscious again. This time, he was out for hours. Sometimes, while he was out, he dreamt of his months of dark captivity by the Sughis. Then, he dreamt of wonderful, bright, healing days in Sub-Summa. And there were long periods where he dreamt of nothing, oblivious to the rain pounding all around him.

Finally, Apollo's mind started to gel. He was waking up, his menapses self-repairing, and he was coming back to Summa Firma.

Apollo began to feel strong presences around him, protecting him and willing him back to consciousness. *I must have been rescued,* he thought.

As Apollo's vision focused, he could see that the rain had stopped. The sun had set, but there still was some daylight, revealing scattered, non-threatening clouds. The violent storm had passed.

Then, to Apollo's amazement, he realized he was tightly flanked by Glacier and Fjord. They were both buttressed up against him, partially intermixed with him. From their projections, they were clearly there to protect him. He could feel their power coursing through him, recharging him.

"They've been there for hours," Myke said. "At first, I thought it was because they were scared. But you should have seen the way they would react to the lightning. Glacier especially. They would growl and snap at it as if they could force it away. They were scared to death, but it was also clear they would fight it to the end to save you."

Apollo got up and hugged the wolves. *What incredible protectors. I might be a stupid man, but I am a favored one, too!*

Glacier and Fjord returned Apollo's affection but seemed exhausted. Apollo told them both to get some rest. He could protect them now. Apollo felt their relief, and he stayed right with them. It was their time to recover.

"How are you feeling, Myke?" Apollo asked. "You were hammered, too."

"I hate lightning," Myke said. "All forms of it."

"But... Myke? When you were a Mentor... your lightning? That too? You hated that?"

"Yes. That, too."

Apollo was surprised. Lightning was a specific power given to every Mentor. Myke would have had it. The power was the ability to blast a lightning charge. With practice, a Mentor could channel it in a precise path. But even without practice, they could blast it in all directions—up, down, and sideways—all at the same time. In doing so, it would flatten any regular ghost within twenty to fifty yards. Olam gave this power to Mentors to make them completely immune to any Sughi attack. Most Mentors never had to use it. Simply knowing every Mentor had it was protection enough.

"Why, Myke? Did you ever use yours?"

"I used it once," Myke said.

"Tell me more."

"I'm not proud of it. I should have fought them. There was a squad of ten with an annoying squad leader. I lost patience and blasted them all. It was vengeful and not warranted." Myke went silent and looked at the dirt. "I was far from perfect as a Mentor. It's good that Olam pulled the blast power from me. I never deserved it."

62

The Portal

Apollo's plans to ask Lionah to send Glacier and Fjord back to the protected world of Sub-Summa had been crystal clear during the storm. His whole motivation for wanting them home was to protect them from a war that was not theirs. But his thoughts on that had changed entirely when he saw how intently they had tried to protect him. They were terrified of the lightning and thunder. But instead of following their instincts and hiding, their primary focus had been on Apollo, not themselves!

This changed Apollo's thinking. The wolves now knew they had a purpose. Their lives were fuller, and they were content to be up to their canines in this struggle for the right. As he exchanged thoughts with Glacier, Glacier said he and Fjord wanted to be part of the fight. They wanted to be with Apollo, whatever pain it might bring. In his own way, Glacier helped Apollo understand he was happier in the top world, away from the protective Sub-Summa, whatever forms of pain and confusion it might hold. Apollo could see the wolves' lives were much more complete, even if it meant fear, pain, and potential loss. They did not want Sub-Summa's artificial, protected world.

Because of this, Apollo never asked Lionah to remove the wolves. Instead, he continued to task them with searching for Torith, which they did wholeheartedly, thrilled to have work and meaning.

The wolves' dedication finally paid off, even though their persistence took more days than expected. It was not until day four of searching that there was a break.

After the first two days of searching, Myke had gone back to Sughi Command. Apollo moved his base camp to an area that was more centralized to the target search zone. The area had no lake or distinctive features, other than the forest being thick and protective from wandering eyes. Apollo could not see more than a hundred yards in any direction, but he also could not be spotted from any direction, including from the air, because of the density of the pine tree cover.

The wolves' sense of direction was amazing, and they seemed to have no problem returning to Apollo every four hours for rest and directions. Apollo took to waiting for them high in a tree in case they were followed.

Since the storm, there had been several sessions of light rain, but the air had been calm, and the rain clouds never stayed long.

On the morning of the fourth day, Apollo instructed Glacier to search southeast of base camp. Apollo tried to convey a back-and-forth, sector-by-sector grid pattern to Glacier. The wolf definitely wanted to do whatever Apollo said, but it was not clear how well he understood. Apollo then watched Glacier and Fjord move off in the southeast direction. They soon arrived at a small lake, which they had circled and searched before, and then they continued on.

Apollo had moved up into the tree to stay out of sight, and he occasionally checked into Glacier's mind for a status. The wolves were definitely on the move, but it seemed random.

Apollo let Myke know there had been no change. Then he went back to waiting. He wished he could be out searching with the wolves, but it was more important to stay out of sight. He was bored.

It had been several hours, and Apollo was about to start concentrating on Glacier's mind when he was surprised to sense that Glacier was reaching out to him. Apollo connected, and he saw that Glacier was looking at two Sughis. It was a man and a woman, and they looked like soldiers. Glacier's view was partially obstructed by foliage and several pines, which meant Glacier was staying hidden. *Good boy,* thought Apollo. "Keep out of sight."

Glacier was too far to hear what the Sughis were saying, but it looked like a casual conversation, and they did not seem to be looking around. From what Apollo could tell, the Sughis were in a small clearing at the top of a hill no higher than a house. The clearing would be noticeable from the air but not distinctive. Apollo knew there probably were other landmarks nearby that a Sughi could use to find this clearing, assuming it was the portal to where they were keeping Torith.

Maintaining a mind link with Glacier was taxing, and Apollo asked him to stay where he was. Apollo had a sense of the distance Glacier had traveled to be where he was now. He could approach and then reconnect. He would have to move carefully, staying in the treetops for his best cover. Before heading out, he comm'd Myke on the B-Channel that the wolves had found something. Per their prearranged plans, Myke would go in person to tell Tamir and Bronson. Depending on what else Apollo and the wolves found, Myke would then go, in person, to a pre-arranged Olam battalion commander who would put his command into an on-deck training status, making it much more responsive if needed for quick deployment.

Apollo spent the next hour carefully working his way toward Glacier and Fjord. He soon passed the same lake they had circumvented earlier. After that, Apollo could only guess at direction and distance, so he moved conservatively and then stopped in good cover for a mind check with Glacier.

The wolves had moved a little but seemed to be in the same area. They were still in cover, and Apollo could not sense anything through Glacier indicating that any Sughis had spotted the wolves. Glacier did not seem to be tracking any Sughis, and Glacier said the two had gone up into the sky. How long ago that happened was unclear.

Apollo asked the wolves to back away from the spot and start towards base camp. They did so, and Apollo periodically checked in with what Glacier was seeing. After about ten minutes, they came to a stream that was down in a narrow, steep ravine. They could have easily transitioned over it, but instead, they found the log of a large tree that had fallen across the ravine, and they crossed there. There was an actual trail in that area leading to the log. Physical, Blood animals were using the log too, hence the trail.

After the log, the wolves climbed up a steep slope and topped out on a rocky ridgeline from which they had a commanding view. Through Glacier's eye, Apollo could see where the wolves were, and he maneuvered to them in about ten minutes. Then, he had the wolves lead him back to the place where they had seen the Sughis. There, they set up where the wolves had last watched before, and they waited.

Three hours went by. Nothing. Apollo was tempted to have the wolves leave cover and go over to where they had seen the Sughis. How many Sughi scents would they find over there? Just two? That would not be encouraging.

Or would there be the scents of many Sughis? If that were the case, it would mean a jackpot and the portal to Torith.

Apollo left the wolves and went into the tops of the trees, looking for landmarks. How were the Sughis finding this place? They could not navigate by comm without revealing their position. So, they had to come in by land navigation, through the observation of terrain features. And it had to be easy so that any Sughi could do it. As Apollo looked around, nothing stood out. No nearby cliffs, rock formations, or lakes. Maybe he had to be higher to see it, but he dared not leave cover and go to altitude. Instead, he went back down.

Now, it had been four hours, and still, there was no sign of any Sughis. Apollo sent the wolves over to have them sniff around. From what he could read in Glacier's mind, it seemed like Glacier was only detecting two people. So, this could not be the portal to Torith's prison. Apollo was disappointed. The search had already gone on so long!

Apollo B-Channeled Myke with a quick summary. It was all very frustrating. Still, they had to be close.

Apollo took the wolves back to the log that crossed the ravine. He explained to them that this was the new base camp, and that they were to hunt all around it looking for Sughis. Apollo explained that they were to search nearby and never go too far. They did not understand distance factors like feet or miles, so he had to visualize in his mind how far from the new base camp they should be searching. The wolves were eager to get going. Apollo was amazed at how much they wanted to please and help. He hoped they understood and sent them off, suggesting they follow the stream up the ravine for a while before branching out.

Soon after the wolves left, Myke messaged Apollo, saying they had been able to ID the two soldiers the wolves had found. They were on one of the teams that had been holding Torith from the beginning. "You are close, Apollo." Myke signed off.

Apollo was debating going out to search for himself when he heard voices. He pushed himself down into the dirt for cover, and a dozen Sughis flew by. They were under the treetops, apparently trying to hide their movements. Apollo watched as they seemed to follow the ravine with the stream in it. They went in the same direction that Apollo had sent the wolves. Soon, they were out of sight in the thick forest.

Apollo reached out to Glacier and found Glacier looking at a large group of Sughis. Many of them did not appear to be soldiers. The Sughis, in turn, were looking at the wolves. Like most pre-humans, these Sughis thought that seeing wolves in the wild was a wonderful thing.

Apollo told Glacier to try to stay away from the Sughis, but that he and Fjord did not have to hide from them. "They are not part of the pack!" Apollo emphasized. "Watch what they do."

Glacier and Fjord were at the edge of thick trees. In front of them, where the Sughis were gathering, it was more open. The trees were spaced enough that sunlight came through, and there was patchy grass on the ground.

In the middle of the cleared area, one distinctive tree stood out. It was an enormous pine tree, or it had been. This tree was split in two, blown apart by lightning. The split went from the top of the tree, three-quarters of the way down, the wood mangled, burned, and splintered from the electrical force. The two parts of the split sagged away from each other, V-shaped. Some of the branches of each of the two parts had been blown off. The brutal lightning strike must have happened within the past year because the tree, albeit terribly damaged, was still clinging to life. A few twisted branches showed small amounts of green.

Apollo was no lightning expert, but he knew that a healthy pine tree in good soil would have large quantities of moisture in its trunk. If hit by lightning, all that moisture could superheat and blow the tree apart. That is probably what happened here. Apollo wondered why the tree had been so big in the first place. It was a lot taller and bulkier than the ones around it. Maybe there was something in the ground where the tree was growing that made it different. Maybe it had to do with why the Sughis were gathered here. Maybe whatever was in the ground was also what attracted the lightning to the tree. Tamir could figure it out after they rescued Torith. He would be fascinated by it all.

It was tiring for Apollo to keep the concentration required to see through Glacier's eyes. His efforts, however, were soon rewarded. He watched as Glacier and Fjord observed the group of Sughis. One by one, they started to disappear into the ground. They all went in at the base of the lightning-stricken tree. Soon, every visible Sughi was gone. There must have been fifty to eighty of them.

We found the portal to Torith!

Apollo told the wolves to wait, and he came in person to the area. Approaching as close as he could while still in good cover, he pulled up a comm and logged in via his B-Channel. Then he used the comm to plot a lat/long fix, marking exactly where he was. He transmitted the location to Myke, telling Myke the actual portal was within about fifty yards of the fix where there was a huge tree blown apart by lightning. Anybody with Apollo's coordinates would be able to find the tree on arrival.

Myke acknowledged, and Apollo logged off, not wanting to be on any longer than needed. Apollo then moved back with the wolves. It was crucial to stay hidden until help arrived. If the Sughis were smart, they would be doing regular patrols.

They should be able to free Torith within just a few hours. Finally!

Apollo dared not think of what they had been doing to her all this time. Horrible things, he was sure.

If I were a Mentor, he thought, *I could go in the portal now, by myself, and easily free her. There might be a thousand Sughis, and I could fry all of them!* And yet, as Apollo thought this, he knew that if he were a Mentor, he could not use his power that way. If so, Reemo or Lionah would have found Torith and freed her months ago. He was glad he was not a Mentor today. He wanted to enjoy extracting payment from Torith's captors for what they had done to her. Better yet, he'd be doing it with his good friends, Myke and Tamir, who would be here soon.

63

Going In

Tamir and Myke arrived as fast as they could, and Apollo moved them all, including the wolves, a short distance away to some thicker trees for better concealment.

"Part of the battalion will be here an hour after we go in," Tamir said. "Two companies of three hundred soldiers each. The three remaining companies will be about thirty minutes behind them."

Apollo understood why the battalion would not arrive all at once. It was all part of the plan to catch Sughi command off guard. The battalion's five companies were each maneuvering separately and not in ways that made it look like they were headed toward the portal. The maneuvering put them in full readiness. Two of the companies were working an arc that kept them equidistant from the portal, but the other three were slowly moving in directions away from the portal, hopefully to throw the Sughis off.

The attack plan called for Apollo's team to go in, find Torith, and make sure she was not moved. As soon as Apollo's team went in, the companies would all race for the portal. Sughi Command would see this and scramble all available soldiers. But Diamond Command did not think Sughi had enough fighters in the area to take on Apollo's team and the battalion's five companies.

"They may have a plan to draw you off, Apollo," Myke said. "Like last time at Deer Canyon."

Apollo and Tamir both knew Myke could be right. Sughi always had to have a plan to deal with Apollo. He was a big factor in any battle.

"We have to stay together this time. You can't go off trying to save people," Myke continued. "Stick to the plan." Myke was stating the obvious and not being tactful about it.

"I know, Myke," Apollo said. "I learned from Deer Canyon, okay?" Apollo held a steady gaze into Myke's eyes.

Myke backed off.

Myke, Tamir, and Apollo planned to wait an hour, and then they would attack.

Apollo took the extra time to formally introduce Tamir to the wolves, who were bristling with excitement. They could tell something was happening, and Apollo could feel Glacier trying to read his mind. Glacier and Fjord knew a fight was coming. A big fight.

Tamir had taken the time to study how to communicate with the wolves. He had read up on topics such as mannerisms, body language, tones of speech, eye contact, and how to treat Apollo in front of them. The wolves considered Apollo the pack leader and expected other pack members to treat Apollo the same way.

Tamir's efforts seemed to work because Glacier and Fjord both warmed up to Tamir quickly, especially after Apollo consciously assured them that Tamir was part of the pack, just like Myke.

Apollo had tried to come up with a way he could use the wolves in the fight. The problem was that the plan called for Apollo to be underground during the crucial phase, and the wolves had never been underground. He could not expect them to fight there. Apollo also did not think he could leave the wolves up on the surface, where there was sure to be a lot of fighting. They would not understand who to fight and who to protect. So, Apollo told Glacier to go back to the former base camp, the one where Apollo had been knocked out by lightning. "Stay away from everybody," he told the wolves.

Glacier did not want to leave. Apollo could tell he wanted to fight, and he especially wanted to protect Apollo. If there had been more time, Apollo might have been able to figure out another solution. But there was no option. He ordered Glacier and Fjord to go. Heads down and confused, they left. These were powerful, willing warriors being told to go away. The image of their dejected departure would hang permanently in Apollo's mind.

Apollo and his team had waited an hour. It was time to attack. Tamir pulled up a comm and contacted the battalion commander. "Can we go in now?" Tamir asked.

"Yes," was the response. "First, I need that final fix."

Tamir rushed over to the broken tree and used the comm to give the commander that precise location. "There you go, sir. This is the place."

"Roger that, Tamir," the commander responded. "Pound those ghostards to Hades. We're rushing your way now."

Tamir closed the comm and shooed it away.

"Ready?" Apollo asked Myke and Tamir.

Thumbs-up from Myke, and a "Yep" from Tamir.

Into the portal they went.

Apollo was first, and they felt their way down. They stayed very close to each other so they could talk. Only ten feet down, they found a comm. It was not transmitting, but it was lit up, full blast. Then they found another and another. The Sughis had made a comm trail.

Fifty feet down, they met their first Sughi. He was a
lone sentry, and they knocked him unconscious before he
could send out an alert. Continuing on, they found more
sentries, sometimes two or three of them together. The
powerful threesome took them out with minimal effort.

Now they were deep enough that the network could
not find them, even if they had attempted to log in. Their
negative altitude, and everything below it, was sub-network.

The first ten to twenty feet down from the surface
had been rich, moist, mineral-laden soil. Apollo now
understood why the lightning tree had grown so big. After
that, they moved through one or two thousand feet of rock,
gravel, and sand.

They were still tracking a comm trail, and Summa's
crust became denser, eventually turning into solid rock. The
temperature was increasing. Continuing straight down
several hundred more feet, they broke through into a large
cavern.

How did the Sughis ever find this place? Apollo
asked himself. It was not on any map at Diamond Command.

Apollo assumed the cavern they found had been
formed by tectonic activity or the movement of large
sections of rock. The floor of the cavern was sloped about
fifteen degrees from one side to the other, and it was covered
with rocks and boulders layered with fine grit. The high-
ceilinged cavern was at least fifty yards wide and well over a
hundred yards long. The ceiling was interspersed with
hanging stalactites. On the floor, corresponding stalagmites
reached up toward their descending brothers. Together, they
implied eons of mineral-laden drips, though the cavern now
seemed dry.

Apollo, Tamir, and Myke hid in the shadows of one of the corners of the ceiling. Surveying the cavern, they could see that it was well lit by many comms.

They were in the back of the cavern, where it was a little darker. They expected to be discovered any second, and there was no time to waste. They had to find Torith. The front of the cavern was more lit up and had more activity. They advanced along the ceiling towards the front of the cavern.

Surprisingly, they still had not been spotted, and Apollo could not see any Sughis in the back half of the cavern. Everybody appeared to be up front. There did not seem to be any active security down here, which did not make sense.

As the threesome approached the front, Apollo could see a large group of people—maybe a hundred—who had arranged themselves in concentric circles, all surrounding one person in the middle.

All of this continued to make no sense. There was nothing aggressive, protective, or hostile about the hundred circled people. Most of them were clearly not soldiers. Some were children. Others were young adults, too young to be fighters. Almost all of them looked happy.

Apollo wondered if he, Myke, and Tamir were in the wrong place. *Is this some kind of club, or friends, or family group?* If so, he had made a colossal tactical error in calling in the troops. *But what about the sentries? Wasn't that military?* It was confusing, and Apollo could tell Myke and Tamir were also confused.

Apollo's team was close to the circled Sughis. Surely, somebody in the group had spotted them by now, but none of them called out an alert. They were totally focused on the person in the middle, and they looked perfectly at peace.

Apollo had not noticed it at first, but now he realized the comms were doing more than providing light. They were also playing music. It was not the militaristic music he would have expected. Instead, it was calm and soothing. The music contrasted strongly with Apollo's "tear-them-up-and-fight" mentality. He was geared up for a maelstrom, wanting to relieve months of frustration.

The person in the middle of the circled Sughis was clearly their leader. It was a female, and she was facing away. She was on a rock that made her higher than most of the others. She now turned and calmly faced Apollo and his team. Apollo was floored.

"Holy Summa!" Tamir gasped.

"Mercy!" exclaimed Myke.

The woman on the rock was Torith!

64

Power Up

"Hello, Apollo... and Tamir... and Myke," Torith said to them, with a deliberate, calm, grace-filled confidence they had never seen before. "I knew you were coming today. I've missed you, and I'm happy to see you!"

Apollo couldn't believe it. Torith was in no way the victim they were expecting. Here she was, fully awake and one hundred percent in control. She was powerful, and she was beautiful.

Some of the Sughis who were in the circles surrounding Torith looked over at the threesome, but their looks were not ones of concern or hostility. It was as if Apollo and his fighters meant nothing to them.

Apollo tried to absorb it all as he scrambled to switch gears. Torith clearly was not being held captive by anyone. As he looked further, he could see that the Sughis surrounding her were drawing strength from her. She, in turn, had extended many filaments of herself into the rock. These strands were pulling power out of Summa herself, which Torith was transferring to those around her.

"Look at her," Myke said to Apollo. "She's a Mentor!"

Apollo knew that Mentors rarely showed their power. But here, Torith's power as a Mentor was on full display. Apollo could feel the energy Torith was drawing straight from the bowels of Summa, redistributing it to those with her.

Apollo, Tamir, and Myke had paused at the outer perimeter of the group. Torith had not said anything more, but she was looking at them, smiling, while also continuing to feed the many around her.

"What do we do now?" Myke asked Apollo. "She doesn't need our help."

"The battalion is going to be here soon. Hundreds of ramped-up soldiers are going to be pouring into this cavern soon. Torith needs to get these Sughis out of here," said Apollo.

Apollo went forward, over the crowd, to speak with Torith. She was not the person he knew before. Normally, he would have given her a friendly ghost hug, but instead, he held back out of respect.

Torith did not hesitate. She rose and came right to him. She gave him a powerful hug. Then she pulled back and looked him in the eyes. "I know what you've been through trying to find me, Apollo."

"Tori... Torith ..."

"And I know this is confusing."

"Yes, why ..."

"There is a lot I need to tell you. And I will. After I was kidnapped, I was tortured like you, Apollo. They lied to you about that. But then, I was able to reverse things. I powered up, and Olam gave me the chance to save these ghosts." She looked at the hundred as she said this. "I'm taking them to a safe place on Olam's side. We are leaving now."

All Apollo could ask was, "How?"

"I'll explain later. But you have hundreds of soldiers coming... right?"

"Yes... soon... hundreds... a thousand."

"A thousand won't be enough, Apollo. Tell Diamond Command to bring many more. Ten thousand if you can."

This was more confusion for Apollo. He knew Sughi had nowhere near that many soldiers in the area. Why did Olam's side need so many?

"It's going to be a world-sized battle. The broken lightning tree up top will be ground zero. You're going to be in the fight you were expecting, Apollo. Myke and Tamir will, too. A lot more of a fight than you planned."

"My wolves?" Apollo asked. "Can they stay protected?"

"No. They fight with you. Lionah is already talking with them, teaching them how to fight and which side to fight for."

There was a pause. Apollo did not know what to say. He did not want to leave her. She was magnificent.

Torith continued pushing energy into those around her. "They are going to need it," she said. Then, back to Apollo, her tone changed. It became warmer and more personal. "Apollo," she said, "I know how much you were hurting. I know you searched and searched and begged Olam, Megantha, and Reemo for help. I know you have put your wolves in harm's way, and I know you have fought lightning to find me. I know you would never stop until you found me." Then she paused and said. "I know you love me, Apollo. I love you, too." She looked at him, her brown and aqua aura glowing. "Do you understand?"

For years, Apollo had always been the strong one with Torith and his peers. Now, he felt like a little boy and out of his league. He had nothing intelligent to say in response. He mumbled a pathetic, "I love you, too," his head spinning. Despite the weakness of his reply, he knew it was true. Torith would know it also.

"Now," she said, "remember how I feel about you. Because the battle you are walking into now will be like none other." She teared up. "I don't want you hurt, but you will be."

Torith then called Myke and Tamir over. "You are here to fight. You think it is over because I am safe."

Tamir and Myke did not respond. Hers was a statement, not a question.

"The fight is still coming," she said. "A battle like no other."

"Now?" asked Tamir.

"Right now," she responded. Then she ordered, "Come forward... all three of you. Come close."

They huddled up to her, her power radiating through them. "Olam is growing tired of this war with Sughi," she said to them quietly and with intensity. "He is unleashing his power, and he will end the war soon."

She let that sink in. Then she continued, "Olam knows you are my best friends. He has given me a gift that I am to pass to you."

The threesome did not understand what she was talking about.

She looked at the three of them intently. "You are already lions. Now, I am giving you the power to fight like a hundred lions. Use this gift with wisdom. But use it. That's why it's given to you!"

At that, she put her right hand on the forehead of Apollo. He felt the gift from Olam power through him. She did the same to Myke and Tamir.

"Now, go and save your army," she told them.

Apollo could feel himself change to the core. He looked at Tamir. "Can you feel it?"

"Yes," Tamir said. "It's like Summa herself is pushing power to me."

"Myke?" Apollo asked.

Apollo was surprised at Myke's response. He almost bowed to Torith, stopping himself because she was not deity, and the gift was not from her. "I know, Torith, you have felt like I'm too heavy-handed. You have disagreed with me many times on that. Why would you give me more power?"

"Olam wanted it, Myke. Have that confidence as you use it with wisdom. But use it!"

Myke backed off a few steps, clearly shaken with emotion and humility at the trust Olam and Torith had placed in him.

Torith then turned to Apollo and said quietly so only he could hear. "Only you can know this, Apollo. The hundred Sughis you see here—it was Malta who sent them to me. One by one, she found them and sent them."

Another surprise in an incredible string of surprises. Apollo shook his head in amazement.

"But, Apollo, even though Malta has helped to save these people, she won't save herself. After the battle, you need to go to her. She has to save herself, too!"

Apollo understood Torith's words, but he was having a hard time grasping them.

"Remember Malta!" Torith insisted.

Apollo solidified on that point. He would remember what Torith said, and he would sort her words out later.

Apollo was reeling from everything that had happened in the last two minutes.

Addressing Apollo, Myke, and Tamir, Torith said, "It's time for me to take these people to a safe place. And it's time for you three to go fight. You have the strength of a hundred lions, but you will also feel the pain of the same hundred. Strength, power, and pain like you have never experienced." She paused. "Now go, my lion friends! Be strong! Save our soldiers!"

Apollo, Tamir, and Myke watched as Torith gathered her one hundred and took them away, together as a group, sideways through the rock wall. She was staying away from the normal portal, guiding them somewhere where the people of Olam were in control. Apollo had no doubt that if Torith's group were attacked on the way, Torith would swat the attackers as if they were lumbering crane flies.

As the last of the departing Sughi converts left, the cavern was suddenly quiet and empty. Only Apollo's threesome remained. They eyed each other, and they eyed themselves. They were strong before; now, they were individually much stronger than they had been as a threesome. It was a heady feeling.

"Should we wait here or go up top?" Tamir asked.

Just then, an advance squad from the Olam battalion came down the chute. Their sergeant rushed over, ready to fight, but pulling up at attention, seeing that it was Apollo. The sergeant said that two Olam companies were minutes away. Apollo told the sergeant he needed to go back up and warn the battalion commander that thousands of Sughis were coming. It was going to be a huge battle. The commander needed to call for more help.

"You'd better go with him," Myke said. "The commander needs to hear it from you. From what Torith said, it's going to be a nightmare."

"Okay," Apollo said. "Have fun cleaning up down here. Hopefully, there are no more captives, but we need to check."

Apollo then followed the sergeant up the corridor, and when he reached the top, he called the battalion commander to tell him what Torith said.

"Intel shows only a few hundred Sughis are coming to the fight," the commander said.

"Torith said it will be many thousands. She is a Mentor now."

"A Mentor? Incredible! How did that happen?"

"I don't know, sir. But we saw and talked with her. I can assure you she has the juice. Ask your Mentor if you want. But, please, we need you to scramble at least two more battalions... immediately if possible."

"Hang on," said the commander. There was a pause. Twenty seconds later, he was back on. "Maramba! You are right, Apollo. My Mentor says the same thing. I'll call for more help."

More Olam fighters were arriving, expecting to immediately be in a battle, but right now, it was calm. Apollo raced between them and told them to expect a horde of angry Sughis any minute.

Despite Apollo's new power, he was scared. Scared of what he could do. Scared of what he would have to do. And scared of the pain that was coming for all of them.

Apollo tried to reach out to Glacier, but he did not have to. Glacier and Fjord came racing out of the woods. "Do you know who to fight?" he asked them.

"Lionah told us," they conveyed. "She also gave us the gift. The same one you have, pack leader. We are many wolves each."

At that, the sky darkened. Apollo thought it was thunderclouds, like the other day. But no, not this time. The sky was full of thousands of Sughis. There were hundreds of times more of them than Olam fighters. Only part of Diamond Command's first battalion had arrived.

"Fight right here," Apollo told Glacier and Fjord. "Right by this broken tree. I need to go get help."

With their new gifts, Apollo's communications channels with Glacier and Fjord were much clearer. The wolves understood that the tree was ground zero.

Apollo blasted down the portal, found Myke and Tamir, and told them of the approaching hordes, and all three raced back to the surface, where they found absolute mayhem.

The Sughi soldiers were endless in numbers, and each soldier was endless in his or her hate for Olam. Olam's soldiers were tremendously outnumbered. It was terrifying. Many of Diamond Command's troops had already been smashed into inert heaps of blown menapses.

Near the broken tree, however, it was a different story. The two wolves were viciously tearing into the psyche of the Sughis, who could do nothing to defend themselves against the maniacal canines. The wolves were everywhere. No Sughi soldier could get close to the portal without being torn apart by the wolves. Sughis near the tree had to retreat, only to be replaced by many more Sughis who either learned the same hard lesson or were quickly flatlined.

Myke and Tamir were stunned. "They have the same power you were given," Apollo yelled at them through the chaos.

Apollo repeated his instruction to the wolves to protect the portal, then he, Tamir, and Myke split up the battlefield and began blasting their own form of terror onto the throngs of hostile Sughis.

As Torith had warned, Apollo was tremendously powerful. He truly had the strength of a hundred lions. But he also had the combined pain all those lions would feel when attacked by many Sughis. The more he exploded on them, the more he felt their fighting back. The contrast was intense. There was so much more anguish, and yet he had the power to handle the ramped-up searing of his menapses.

This new state came at a high cost. It made Apollo want to give up and leave. Did the wolves feel the same? He had to know. He pushed hard and flattened an acre of Sughis. Then he raced over to Glacier.

"Are you okay?" Apollo queried. "What about the hurt?"

Glacier did not stop fighting. Neither did Fjord, who was right next to him. "I ignore it," was the message Glacier sent. "You need to, too, pack leader."

And from that, Apollo took some understanding. The pain was going to be there. It was part of the power. Apollo would ride the torment as he mowed over the Sughis. He could attack Sughis one by one, or ten by ten, and he would feel almost nothing. But when he used his real ability and started cutting them down in scores at a time, their combined hate and resistance was an intense torment he had never felt before.

Apollo could see that Olam's soldiers were overwhelmingly outnumbered. Normally, they would not have stood a chance. He began mopping the field, cutting down swathes of Sughis.

The evil legions kept coming, and after a time, thousands of Sughis became layered, inert, on the field of battle, ghost-dead. They were temporarily dead—the work of Apollo, Myke, Tamir, the wolves, and the many brave Olam soldiers.

Many Olam soldiers lay ghost-dead, too. They had fought bravely, often more bravely than Apollo. They faced the terrifying masses with no special powers—nothing beyond their own determination and will. Some of these soldiers were magnificent ghosts, holding their own against a dozen attackers by the sheer solidity of their convictions.

Seeing the determination of these fellow soldiers caused Apollo to forego all the pain and ramp himself up to full throttle. As he progressed through the power curve, he was dumbfounded by the amount of force Olam had given him. He realized he had only been administering the work of death at half speed. Faster and faster he went, able to work through opposing Sughis more and more at a time.

Then, more Olam soldiers arrived. The full battalion was here now, and companies from other battalions were arriving. The fury and frenzy of the first hours of the battle started to change. Apollo began to back off on purpose. The many Olam soldiers arriving needed Sughis to fight. They were geared up and had come all this way. It was right that they engage in battle.

Apollo went to both Myke and Tamir and asked them to slow down. Things had reversed. "Keep fighting," he told them. "But we no longer have to save the battlefield. Let the regulars do that. They need to feel it, like we have. Myke and Tamir understood.

Two hours later, the fighting part of the battle was over. Ghosts on both sides who had been knocked into oblivion were starting to recover. None were in a position to fight. Olam's recovering fighters were attended to. The Sughi fighters were also offered help. Most refused, but they also did not reengage. Thousands of fresh Diamond Command soldiers were ready to fight them if they did.

As "dead" Sughi commanders returned to consciousness, the Olam commanders would ask them to talk. Most were too full of hate and refused. They were allowed to leave. A few, however, agreed to stay for a post-battle parley. Some of those who stayed complained bitterly about Apollo and his team. They knew Apollo was strong, but they had never seen anything like today. "It's not fair," they said. "They should be Mentors and not on the battlefield. They are too strong!"

The Olam commanders were also surprised at Apollo and his team. They let Apollo address it. "Things are changing," Apollo said. "That is what I was told today. The power that you saw in my team was given to us today by Olam."

One of Olam's highest-ranking commanders on the field backed up what Apollo said. "My Mentor told me the same thing," he said. "Your command needs to check with Olam's Diamond Command. I'm sure your leaders are going to be told the same."

"Olam is tired of this war," Apollo added. "What you saw today is the beginning of the end. Olam has given you much time and freedom to make your choices. But the consequences are coming."

Apollo noticed that several of the Sughi commanders coming out of "death" were not saying anything, and they were also not leaving. Instead, they were hanging off to one side. "Go talk to those guys, Tamir," he said. "Take Fjord with you."

Apollo could see Tamir and Fjord go over to the Sughi group. Glacier came over to Apollo, flanking him.

"But the wolves," one of the complaining Sughi commanders said. "Now, Olam has animals fighting for you, too?"

Nobody answered the commander's question because the answer was obvious. The wolves had been a huge factor in the battle. They were terrifying and extremely efficient "killers."

Apollo noticed that Myke had also pulled aside a group of Sughi officers and line soldiers. There were at least thirty people in the group. It was not a fight. They were listening to him. Later, Myke told Apollo that many in the group wanted to defect to Olam, but they had friends and loved ones they were going to try to bring with them.

Tamir's conversation with his group had been much the same. Tamir told them to reach out to him personally when they needed to get out, and he would help them, each one of them individually.

The recovering dead from both sides were spread over a large battlefield, scattered between the trees of the forest. The Olam commanding officer sent soldiers to fan out among the dead of both sides to help them as they recovered. Sughi soldiers, when possible, were approached about switching to Olam's side. The fighting had turned to recruiting. A few switched, and they were corralled away and separated from the Sughis. Most Sughis, however, refused to change. They left, taking their hate with them, firmly entrenched in their bitter psychology, even when it must now be obvious that they could never win. Regardless of the consequences, they were determined to go down with the Sughi ship.

Today's battle became known as the Battle of Lightning Tree. Diamond Command never fully understood how the Sughis knew to flood the fight with over ten thousand soldiers. Apparently, Sughi Command had snuck them in over some time and kept them underground for days, waiting for the go signal. That was why Olam's intel analysts never knew there was so much of the enemy in the area.

Apollo wondered if, in fact, it had been Torith who had let Sughi Command know about the impending rescue. Maybe she told Malta about it, and maybe that was why Malta had called Myke in a panic. Maybe Torith did it because she knew about the gifts coming to Apollo and his team.

Apollo later asked Torith about it. She would not confirm his suspicions. What she said was, "Things worked out the way they were supposed to. That is all I can say."

Tamir and Myke left the battlefield and went home to Diamond Command. They needed to recover. Like Apollo, their incredible power had come at a high price. It was now important that they rest and internalize.

Apollo chose to stay in the forest with his wolves, where they felt more at home. They moved miles away from the battlefield to fresh ground. Here, they would rejuvenate away from anybody. It would be the three of them, as they had been in Sub-Summa.

Two nights later, Apollo and the wolves were still in the forest. Another violent electrical storm began thrashing the area. Normally, Apollo would have found a cave for the wolves or low ground to stay away from the lightning. But instead, the three of them did the exact opposite. There was no cowering tonight. Apollo, Glacier, and Fjord found high ground and stood near the highest tree. They dared the lightning to strike them. The wolves growled, howled, and snapped at it. Apollo concentrated and willed the lightning to them. The rain poured down, and then a powerful bolt of electricity slammed directly into the three of them, scorching everything around them. The rain vaporized to steam, the air exploded in thunder, and the rock cracked under their feet. Apollo's ears rang, and his whole ghost body tingled. But he and the wolves took the direct hit without harm. Such a change from the last storm! They were so much stronger than before.

Amazing! Apollo thought. *Absolutely amazing. What a gift!* He vowed to use it wisely, as Torith had instructed.

"Thank you, Olam," Apollo said, knowing his gratitude would be heard. "And thank you, Megantha." Then, looking at Glacier and Fjord, he said on their behalf, "The beasts thank you, too."

65

Sughi City RSC

Apollo and his wolves suddenly appeared in a park in the middle of Sughi City, not far from the primary Sughi command center. Apollo and the beasts had come from the other side of the planet. Lionah had sprung them. It was much too far to fly.

With the vastly increased amperage Apollo and the wolves had received from Torith… or … from Olam via Torith…, Apollo had been able to teach the wolves how to fly. They now understood that travel from point A to point B could be direct, through the air, and did not require passage via the ground. The wolves had become credentialed flyers, and they were much faster in flight than Apollo.

It had been six months since Apollo and the wolves had been given their power at the Battle of Lightning Tree. Per the instructions relayed by Torith, they had used the force in many battles. No Sughi army could stand against them. It was only after Apollo and the wolves stood up to the direct hit of the lightning bolt that Apollo truly understood the magnitude of what he had been given.

The war against Sughi had turned. It was clear on all fronts that Sughi would lose. Others, besides Apollo and his team, had been given the same kind of power. They were unstoppable by any Sughi formation.

Apollo admired the patience and wisdom of Olam in conducting the war. Olam could have ended it at any time.

Instead, he applied steadily increasing pressure, always giving his prejudiced children the chance to change. Olam wanted them back, but only if they made the decision to come back. Olam did not demand one hundred percent acceptance. Voicing and discussing concerns were fine. But there were limits. Fighting the plan was too much. Fair or not, now was the time to be in or out.

Apollo could see people in the park staring at him and the wolves. They would be shocked to see them there—right in the middle of Sughi City. Apollo saw multiple comms appear, and he was sure reports were flooding into the nearby Sughi command center. There would be tremendous fear that an attack was coming.

Apollo saw two Intels arrive in a panic. They warily approached Apollo. Glacier blocked their access, and they cowered, shaking. "We're not soldiers!" one of them blurted out. "Please don't fight us."

"We're not here for a fight," Apollo answered. "We're going to Sughi Command."

"Why?" the Intels asked, worried.

Apollo was not going to give them any more information. Instead, he said, "The two of you need to switch sides. You're out of time. Figure it out!"

Apollo knew he was wasting his time telling the Intels to change. Their minds were set, and if not, they certainly were not going to change from his one snide comment. It would be tough for any Sughi to switch, especially Intels, who were trusted and well-placed. It meant severing close relationships, often with family, and surely with close friends. It meant having many of the people in those relationships hate you. It meant leaving them behind and being branded as a traitor. It was no small thing to ask someone to switch, and very few would. But time was running out. The time for diplomacy was ending.

Apollo and the wolves headed for Sughi Command. Two teens, a boy and a girl, stepped in front of Apollo. They wanted to see the wolves. Apollo was surprised they were not afraid. Maybe they did not realize Apollo was the enemy. Apollo gave the teens time for a short greeting, which the wolves tolerated well. Then, Glacier gave Apollo a look, and the three of them moved on.

The command center was as impressive this time as it had been six years ago, back when Apollo saw it for the first time. That was when he came here with Myke. Like so many of the impressive buildings and surroundings in Sughi City, the Forza named Pacifica had been the center's main builder and architect, with Megantha's help. Apollo had yet to meet Pacifica, which he regretted. He wanted to tell her how much he loved her work. Apollo wondered if the Sughis could internalize any appreciation for her work. *Maybe not,* Apollo thought. Because she stands with Olam, they might not allow cross-over admiration. Apollo hoped some could feel and see the magnificence of her architectural prowess.

Apollo, Glacier, and Fjord passed between two of the forty-nine massive stone columns surrounding the command center's entrance. Like all ghosts, Apollo knew the significance of forty-nine. It was built into every ghost's core structure—billions of seven-by-seven clusters of subatomic menapses, endlessly and intricately networked.

The columns held up the solid rock ceiling over the entrance area. This entrance was at ground level. It was circular and about one hundred yards in diameter. There were no internal columns or walls, which meant the seven-times-seven were bearing an enormous weight. As impressive as the columns were, even more impressive was the engineering Pacifica had built into the ceiling, held in place by the columns. It was a round disk of solid rock, one hundred yards across. How could this massive rock span that distance and not break? Her engineering secrets were enclosed in the rock itself. *Another reason I hope to meet Pacifica,* he thought. *I'd better have Tamir with me when I do. He'll understand her explanation of how she solved this structural challenge.*

The columns gave the structure a coliseum-like feel, with this top, ground layer being an enormous, rock-covered foyer. Below the foyer, underground, were both Sughi Command and the Regional Server Complex, or RSC. Apollo's destination was the RSC.

The floor of the entryway was covered in stone tiles. There was nothing else on the entire ground level except for a round administration desk right in the middle.

Apollo remembered all this from his first visit. What he did not remember, and what he was surprised to see today, was the composition of the floor itself. The stone of the floor was solid, but it looked like an oscillating liquid that was several inches deep. It had a see-through, clear, light-blue look to it. There were waves of light passing through it in rushing water-like patterns. Apollo knew there was no natural stone like this on Summa. Pacifica had recomposed the stone to give it its current properties. The floor was mesmerizing and beautiful, and Apollo wondered why he had not noticed it last time. *Maybe the floor lighting could be turned off, or maybe it had been a different color?*

Apollo and the wolves approached the administration desk. Four Sughis were manning it today, and they looked terrified. They likely had been alerted to Apollo's presence, and they would know they had no ability to stop him.

"We are here to see Gerard in the RSC," Apollo said, trying to strike a tone that was firm but not overbearing. Gerard was the Forza who protected the RSC from the Sughis.

The last time Apollo was here, both Olam and Sughi personnel were at the desk because this was the control point for both Sughi Command and the RSC. Now that the war had escalated, only Sughi people were present. Gerard and his RSC network engineers entered the RSC via a different entryway to avoid conflicts.

Apollo knew he was messing with the Sughis by entering the RSC through this no longer used front door. He watched them scramble because they did not know what to do.

"Sir... we... we... you... y... you can't go in this way," one of the Sughis managed to get out.

"Last time I did," Apollo answered with calm authority.

"Yes... but... no... sir. Not anymore."

"Please call Gerard and tell him Apollo is here," Apollo instructed the attendant.

"We don't do—"

"Do you have the number?" Apollo interrupted.

"Yes, but—"

"Then call him!" Apollo was more insistent.

"Sir, we're not supposed to—"

"Otherwise, I'm going to have to go in unannounced. That would be rude, right?"

"Yes, sir, but ..." The attendant looked over at his other three admin desk mates, apparently wanting their guidance. They were of no help.

Apollo looked at Fjord and head-motioned to the desk. Fjord jumped up on the desk, his canines now mere feet from the attendant.

"That's Fjord," Apollo said. "He really wants to meet Gerard."

Then Glacier also helped himself to the desktop, and he started walking the round structure's circumference. Apollo did not have to look around to know that every Sughi in the foyer was watching this scene.

"They won't hurt you," Apollo said, enjoying the moment. "Now... Gerard? Please?"

The attendant used his comm to make a call the control desk had not made in a long time. Soon, Gerard was on the screen.

"Wolfman is here?" Gerard could be heard asking. "Great! Please send him down!"

To the visible relief of the attendants, Apollo and his wolves passed without further issue and descended the chute into an underground foyer that separated Sughi Command and the RSC. As they arrived, Sughi soldiers were pouring into the space from the Command side. They looked hastily summoned, tense and uncertain, ordered into a fight they did not understand.

Apollo held up his hand. "Stay back!" he ordered. "We're here for the RSC."

No soldier showed any interest in challenging Apollo.

Then, the main door to the RSC opened, and Gerard walked out, an amused look on his face as he calmly assessed the ruckus. "Apollo!" he exclaimed, sporting a broad, warm smile. "You came with your wolves! Please come in, come in!"

Apollo followed Gerard into the RSC, with Glacier and Fjord close behind. The door shut behind them, disconnecting them from all the Sughi drama in the foyer.

Several of Gerard's network engineers rushed over, glad to see a friendly soldier. They were well-protected by Gerard, but to see an actual hands-on fighter was exciting for them. Of course, the wolves were a huge hit, too.

"I'm Viola," one of the networkers said. "My big sister—house sister—is Lionah."

Apollo was thrilled. "Then you know these wolves are really your sister's?" Apollo said.

"Yours now," Viola countered. "But, yes, hers before. She has told me all about you."

Apollo turned to Gerard. "Do you mind, sir, if Viola handles the wolves while we talk?"

Gerard looked over at Viola, who was giving her boss a big "Yes, please."

"Sure," Gerard said. "But first, let me tell you something about Viola." Viola looked embarrassed, and Gerard continued. "The Battle of Lightning Tree, Apollo. You guys had one battalion assigned to that fight, right?"

"Yes," Apollo said, wondering where this was going.

"But you really needed many more soldiers than the one battalion."

"A lot more. And luckily, they showed up."

"Ah, yes," said Gerard. "But didn't it seem like they showed up quicker than expected? I mean, it takes a lot of time to rally a battalion."

During the battle, Apollo remembered being surprised at how fast Diamond Command had been able to bring so many soldiers. "It did seem quick," Apollo said.

"Well," Gerard said, "you can thank her for that." Gerard was pointing at Viola.

Apollo looked at Viola. "Tell me, please. It sounds like you saved us."

"No, not saved," she said. "Helped. You see, I have an algorithm. Once in a while, it pays off. And when it does, I feed the info to the Intel Division."

Apollo liked this Viola. "And?"

"The algorithm monitors comm traffic, just like many programs do. Mine is different because it does not focus on location, time of day, or who is talking to whom. People like your Tamir are already doing all that. Instead, mine looks at the quality of the connection and the connection speed. It alerts when there is a significant change, especially when that change applies to a group of people."

"I get it," Apollo said. "Yes, now I see. All those Sughi soldiers were waiting, hiding underground. They all would have had degraded communications." Apollo looked at her. "Am I correct?"

"Bingo, smart boy," she said.

"Smart girl," Apollo emphasized back. "My friend Tamir would like to meet you!"

"Oh, I know Tamir," she said. "I would have called him with the info, but he was out, busy saving the world with you."

There was a brief silence as Apollo and Viola looked at each other. She was undeniably attractive. But before it became weird, Apollo said, "Okay, so… Viola, can you teach Glacier some network engineering? Maybe how you fight Sughi DDOS attacks or something?"

"Sure thing, wolf boy," she said. "Come on, Glacier… you too, Fjord. Let me show you handsome beasts around."

Glacier and Fjord looked at Apollo, who told them to go with Viola. They seemed happy to do so, and it was clear they would be in good hands.

Apollo wished Tamir were with him. Usually, he wanted Tamir's company for his brain. But this time, it was for Tamir's heart. Viola and Tamir would make each other happy.

66

Gerard

Apollo and Gerard went into a side briefing room. The door shut, and Gerard started, "Look, I know Torith is probably your person. But, Apollo, that Viola is a special one."

"Maybe better for Tamir than me," Apollo said, deflecting any matchmaking.

"Has Olam promised you anything related to Torith?" Gerard asked.

"Only that we'll be on the same earth at the same time. It's up to us to find each other."

Gerard was thinking. "That's going to be hard, Apollo. You know that."

"I know."

"We're not going to have clear insight on anything," Gerard said.

"We?" asked Apollo.

"Yes, we. I have to go through it, too, my boy. I'll be as clueless as you."

Apollo found himself taken aback at Gerard's comment. Forzas were so powerful here on Summa. It was hard to think of them as regulars in the future when they became Bloods.

"Do you think you'll remember each other? You and Torith?" Gerard asked.

"No promise on that either. I can only hope that if we meet, we'll know there is a connection."

Gerard nodded his head up and down. "Maybe Torith won't like you, Apollo. Or more likely, she'll meet somebody before she meets you. It could be that you and Torith will only be friends."

Apollo paused, thinking. "Well, then, maybe I'll be lucky enough to find Viola, although she's really best for my friend, Tamir. Unless you find her first." Apollo gave Gerard a wink.

Gerard smiled. "There will be a lot to sort out. The whole Blood life is crazy. Sapienti is going to be busy."

"Busy talking to people who don't want to listen to him," said Apollo. "I hope I'm attuned enough to hear him."

"I hope you have someone who will teach you to listen to him."

"Good point," Apollo responded. Sapienti isn't exactly a hit-you-over-the-head kind of guy. He's easy to ignore."

Gerard was quiet for a moment, and then he said, "I hope I'll hear Sapienti, too."

They both went back into silence, contemplating it all. Then, Gerard asked, "Shall we get down to business? The real reason you are here?"

Apollo's aura rippled with a quiet reset. "Yes. Malta."

"Ah, yes," Gerard said, knowingly. "Malta. The enigma."

"To put it mildly," Apollo said.

"She's done a lot of good, Apollo, as you know. I'm sure that's why you are here."

"Yes. A lot of good—and plenty of bad. But, yes, so much good."

"You're running out of time with her," Gerard said.

"I know. I think I'm a lot more worried about it than she is. I need to try her one more time. Is she here today?" As Apollo asked, he pointed through the wall toward the adjacent Sughi Command.

"I fixed it so she would be, Apollo," Gerard said. "I made up some mandatory command meeting for the big brass, and I had one of the techs shove it into their calendaring system."

Apollo did a little head shake. "So, you can force them to go to meetings... but you can't force them to save themselves?" Apollo asked, teasing.

"I do what I can." Gerard grinned.

"Do you think we can get her over here, on this side of the wall? Just to talk? Would you allow her in here?"

"As long as you stay right with her, Apollo. I'm fine with it. But you'll have to talk her into coming over."

"Yes, of course," Apollo said. "Knowing Malta, she'll be happy to be my prisoner."

Gerard chuckled. "I think you're right on that one."

Apollo and Gerard talked more, and then Gerard took Apollo over to one of the engineers who could help raise Malta on a comm. The engineer masked the call to make it look like it was coming from a comm inside Sughi Command. Spoofing the caller ID was easy for the engineer.

The engineer had Apollo sit out of his comm's camera view, and then he made the call. Malta answered. The engineer spoke to her first, posing as a lower-ranking Sughi officer and making sure she was alone.

"Yes, I'm alone," she said, clearly annoyed at this sub-life form demanding her attention.

The engineer then gave the comm to Apollo. With his face now showing on her screen, he said, "So... how is my favorite Sughi?"

Malta froze and then smiled. "Apollo!" she exclaimed. "Wh… why are you calling me this way?"

Malta's question was expected. Malta was Apollo's well-placed source in Sughi Command. They normally went to extra effort to be sure each side did not know they were talking. Today was different.

"This is a social visit," Apollo said. "I'm here to see you."

"Here?" she asked, confused.

"Yes, here. In the RSC next door. I'm surprised you haven't heard. I made a pretty big stir walking in the front door."

"Oh, that was you? I heard there was an alert."

"Yep. And I'm over here with Gerard. My wolves are here with me. They want to meet you."

Apollo knew Malta would be happy to see him, but his being here in person was a whole different thing. He watched as she calculated her logistics. Then she said, "Great. Will Gerard let me in? I've always wanted time in the RSC."

"Yes. You can come over, but won't your Command—"

"Forget about them," Malta interrupted. "They know I have a history with you. Can I come over now? Through the front door?"

Apollo had wanted to talk face-to-face with Malta, and he hoped it would be here in the RSC, but he thought she would want to sneak in the back, not come over right in front of everybody. She would be on camera, and her whole world would know.

"Yes, great. See you at the front door," Apollo responded. Then he closed the comm and gave it to the engineer, thanking him. He also announced loudly that a high-ranking Sughi was being let in the front door. That was unusual, and it had their attention.

"I approved it," Gerard told his staff. "Apollo will escort her."

67

Malta's Choice

Apollo headed towards the door. He could see through a camera that Malta was walking up. There was also a Sughi security team in the sub foyer between the two centers. Malta was motioning them to back up, which they did, warily. It was Apollo they were afraid of, and they knew he was on the other side of the door.

Apollo opened the door, and Malta came right for him, giving him a huge ghost hug. She clearly wanted the Sughi security team to see that, and then the door to the RSC shut. Apollo looked at her, not sure of her strategy, but confident she was messing with her own people.

"I always keep them guessing," she said, thumbing towards where the team had been. Then she stepped back and gave Apollo a look over. "So, this is the new Super-Apollo," she said. "There's no stopping you anymore, is there?"

Malta then took a look around and openly feigned amazement. "W-o-o-o-w-w-w! And this is the famous RSC. We've been trying to attack this place for years, and here you let me walk right in. Maybe not the smartest move, my friend," she toyed. "I am one of the evil ones. And you are letting me defile your sacred space!"

Gerard came over to greet her. Malta visibly had to buck herself up to be around him. His piercing power was such a contrast to what she normally experienced with her own leaders. The presence of a Forza was hard for her to tolerate. Gerard would have known this, and he was quick. "I just want to say welcome, Malta. Thank you for coming."

Malta could only shake her head, and Gerard backed off. He did not want to torment her.

Malta pulsed. "Mercy! I forgot how that feels," she said. "I can tell you've changed, Apollo. But still… you're normal. I can be around you. That Forza almost shut me down."

"He meant no harm." Then Apollo walked Malta into the same conference room he had been in earlier with Gerard. "I want to talk with you, obviously. But do you want to meet the wolves first?"

To Apollo's surprise, Malta seemed ambivalent about the wolves. "If you want," she said. "I mostly want to see you."

Just then, Viola brought the wolves to the door, expecting that Apollo would want them. Apollo had her bring them in. Malta greeted them more out of courtesy than warmth. There was also a palpable coolness between Viola and Malta. If the two women were cats, the claws would be out. Apollo said nothing about it, but he was slightly amused. *Holy Summation!* He thought. *Look at these two!* "Thank you, Viola," Apollo said. "Would you mind keeping the wolves for a while?"

Viola left with the wolves, and the tension in the room immediately dissipated. It was Apollo's turn to toy with Malta, and he made a low but audible cat screeching sound.

"I'm jealous of them all," Malta said. "Especially Torith. I know she's going to have you."

Apollo had not planned this tactic because it was unfair and cheap, but he could not resist. "What if Olam promised you that you and I would be together on an earth somewhere? Would you come back to our side?"

"You think a lot of yourself, don't you, Super-Boy?" Despite her words, Malta made it clear in her tone that she was having fun with him.

Apollo wisely said nothing. The ball was still in her court.

"I would be a terrible wife to you, Apollo. Yes, I would love you to death, but I'm not a good person. I would be good to you, but not good to your family, friends, or people you work with. And I'd be vicious with any woman you had to deal with. You would be miserable with me, and I know it."

What Malta said was surprising. Not because of the content, but because she stated it so plainly.

"I'm better off going to your earth as a ghost, like I am now."

"But don't you want to feel the air and the sun and hold a child in your arms and—for me—pet your dog or wolf? As a ghost, you can't do any of that. You're missing so much."

Malta looked Apollo in the eyes. "Apollo, I don't want all the bad that comes with being physical. I don't want to forget what happened here on Summa, and I don't want to forget this conversation we are having right now. I don't want to forget our friendship, and I don't want to forget how much I love you. You'll forget it, and you'll forget all your time here. You'll have no idea who you really are, Apollo. You won't know all the good you've done. You'll forget all your battles. You won't remember meeting your wolves. You'll forget the day you and your wolves fought lightning and won! You'll forget me, and you'll forget Torith and

Tamir and Myke. All of that will be gone. Forgotten. That's terrible, and it's sad!"

"Yes, but Olam says I'll remember it later. The day will come when all of my memories will be restored."

"Okay," Malta said. "I'm sure Olam is telling the truth. And how will you feel that day? Will that be a happy day?"

Apollo had always assumed it would be.

But Malta said, "No, Apollo. It will be a terrible day for most people. Maybe not for you... since I think you'll be good no matter what. But what about regular people? What about all the people who will mess it up badly on their earths? How are they going to feel when they remember everything?"

Apollo listened.

"They'll wish they were me, Apollo. They are going to be floored, stunned, and heartbroken. They're going to wish they never were Bloods on any earth!"

Apollo still listened. He agreed with much of the picture she was painting. He also knew he did not need to argue any points with her. This was Malta. She was well-versed on all sides of the arguments.

"I chose to stay a ghost. I'll be a Summa Ghost forever, Apollo. Not here on Summa, but on some earth."

Malta stopped her speech and fell silent. She looked dejected.

Apollo waited and then said, "You helped a lot of people come over to Olam, Malta. All those people you sent to Torith while she was captive... that was amazing."

Malta remained dejected but joked, "Pretty good of me, even if I am a jealous witch."

"Yes, and you saved Torith herself. You got them to stop torturing her."

"Yes. That was mostly for you, Apollo. And because I hate my Sughi management so much. They deserve to lose this war. They never should have kidnapped Torith… or you."

"Have you met Sughi himself?" Apollo asked.

"Eeuuww, no!" she spat. "He gives me the creeps. People line up to greet him. I never do." Then Malta smiled, returning to her happier self. "You sure did a number on that pretty-boy slug-face," she said, her eyes sparkling with mischief. "He really thought he had you."

"Isn't he going to retaliate against you for coming over here to see me?"

"Well… on that… I'm hoping you'll do me a favor."

"What?"

"Now that I've been in here long enough to send my side into a tizzy, can we continue talking outside? Right under their noses? Can we go to a park or something? I want them to see me with you and your wolves."

"Yes, of course, Malta. I came here for you. But why?"

"They are afraid of you, Apollo. They're freaking out over there knowing you are here. They already know you and I have some history, but if they see me hanging out with you now… now that you are so strong, they're going to be afraid of me too. They won't come after me because they'll be afraid of you."

"Okay, let's go," Apollo said. "There are some things I still need to ask you. We can do it at the park."

Apollo took Malta with him while he said goodbye to Gerard. Then they found Viola, who was playing hide-and-seek with the wolves in the server room. "I'll tell Tamir to call you," he said to her.

"Fine. You can call me too, Apollo."

That was awkward with Malta right there.

"For computer help, of course," she added.

Apollo avoided any eye contact with Malta while also trying to yes-acknowledge Viola. He then gave Viola a business-like goodbye and left with Malta and the wolves.

While heading toward the main door of the RSC, Malta looked over at him, shook her head, and pretended to gag.

"Not my fault, Malta," Apollo said defensively. "She's trying to help."

Malta scrunched up her nose and morphed her face into an evil cat face. It was hilarious.

Apollo, Malta, and the wolves were soon at the main door to the RSC. It opened, and they went into the sub-lobby. Two squads of Sughis were there, ordered by some higher-up to maintain an Apollo watch.

"We're going out," Malta told the soldiers. "Tell your commander I'm taking the threat with me." At that, Malta, Apollo, and the wolves went up the chute to the main foyer on ground level. The four staffers at the desk were still on duty. Again, they froze. Malta authenticated by showing her face to a comm, and she said she was signing everybody out. Then, to mess with the staff, she asked, "Where are the wolf sign-ins?" She looked at one admin who could only stammer.

"We... don't... didn't... there aren't—"

"You mean they didn't sign in?" she demanded. Malta was not a small-time manager. They would know she had juice, and they would dread any conflict with her.

Malta eyed all four of them. "No wolf log?"

"No. No, ma'am. We don't have one for animals."

Malta said nothing and held all four of their stares. She had a scowl on her face. Finally, she said, "We're leaving." She started to walk away, and Apollo's team moved with her. None of them looked back.

"I love being mean," Apollo. "I know it's wrong, but I love it!"

"Wolf log?" Apollo asked. "That's a new one."

Malta flashed her evil cat face again, then she switched it to a mischievous smile.

68

Same Earth as You

Apollo and Malta went to the park where Apollo had arrived with the wolves. A crowd gathered but kept its distance. Apollo told Glacier and Fjord to greet any children who dared approach but to stay close. At one point, two Intels came over, wanting information. Malta sternly shooed them away. A squad of soldiers also came too close. Glacier and Fjord quickly raced to the soldiers and forced them back. The only ghosts given access were children.

Apollo and Malta talked about a lot of things, including growing up in school, kids they had known, surfing at the canyon, and other common ground.

To Apollo, Malta's purple beauty and personality were as intoxicating as ever. Dangerous, powerful, with an evil streak, but also attractive and impossibly fascinating.

Malta then asked Apollo if he would ask Olam for something.

"Of course, Malta. You should ask him yourself, but what do you want?"

"When I'm kicked out of Summa, I want to be sent to the same earth as you, the one where you go as a Blood."

"I won't have any idea who you are or that you even exist," Apollo said. "I won't be able to see ghosts."

"I know," Malta said.

"And I won't remember you."

"I know that, too," she responded. "But, don't you see: I'll be able to see you... and Torith. I want to protect both of you."

"How? You'll be a ghost."

"The same way you protected those people from the pirates, Apollo. You had some influence. Enough to kill that boss pirate!"

Apollo remembered.

"And enough to save the little girl."

Apollo hoped to meet Marika someday. Megantha had told him he would.

"Look. Olam is kicking us out of Summa. We're the bad people. He's sending us to the same earths you good guys are going to."

"I know."

"That's why I want to stay a ghost. I want to fight the ghosts who mess with good people like you. And you know me, Apollo. I like to be mean. I'll be mean to the Bloods who are mean. Not to the good ones."

Apollo absorbed.

"I love vengeance," she said. "Olam says vengeance is his. True vengeance probably is. But when I'm on an earth, and I see a Blood hurting others, I'm going to do everything I can to avenge them. Like you did, Apollo, with the pirates."

It was weird for Apollo to think that in the future, when he was a Blood, Malta might be near him, helping him. She was a Sughi.

"There will be plenty of Sughi ghosts who will want to have a piece of you in your next life, Apollo. I know you'll be strong against them, but I want to be with you, fighting those ghost-turds off, even if you have no idea of the battle going on around you."

Malta and Apollo continued to talk. Eventually, Glacier and Fjord were bored and wanted to leave. They were done with entertaining children, and they came over to Apollo. "Let's go," Glacier conveyed.

Apollo never could convince Malta to switch sides. He promised he would ask Olam to grant Malta her wish— that she go to Apollo's earth.

The last thing Malta said to Apollo was how much she looked forward to a day, long in the future, well after his time being tested as a Blood, when Apollo would again remember his time on Summa and his friend, Malta. "Please come find me," she begged him. It may be hundreds of years from now, and who knows where I will have been relegated to by then. But please look for me so we can be friends again."

Apollo promised her he would.

Apollo left her in the park. Her purple aura looked dim and spent as she sat there and watched them go. Apollo thought she might be crying. He was.

Apollo knew he would not see or remember her for a long time, many years.

It broke his heart.

69

Emptiness

After leaving Malta, Apollo took the wolves and headed for a dense forest of beech and sugar maple one hundred miles to the south. He wanted time alone.

While en route, Apollo noticed two Intels following from several hundred yards back. Apollo asked Fjord to rush them, and the Sughis scattered.

When Apollo and the wolves arrived at the forest, Apollo picked an area where the beech and maple trees formed an especially thick canopy. He wanted to be hidden because he did not want to be bothered. Under the thick overhead, he found an opening tightly surrounded by branches and trees. Here, it was quiet, seemingly remote, with subdued lighting. The only sound was a tiny, sparrow-like bird, flitting in the maze of branches above.

Apollo B-Channeled Myke.

"I have the information you need," Myke said. "Tamir gave it to me. But first, Reemo wants to talk."

Reemo came on the comm and said, "I'm sorry about Malta, Apollo. I know her decision hurts you deeply."

"Yeah… it's a rough one," Apollo answered, dejected. There was silence, and then Apollo told Reemo about Malta's request to go to the same earth as Apollo. "What do you think about that, Reemo?"

"It's up to you. Olam will probably allow it if that's what you want."

"She says she's going to try to protect me. Is that possible?"

"It's a total role reversal," Reemo said. "As you know, most of the Sughis kicked out of Summa will want the worst for you. But, yes, just like you had some effect on the pirates, she might be able to protect you... a little. Mostly, I think she'll be able to take on the ghosts who try to bother you."

Apollo pondered.

"Talk to Megantha or Olam about Malta," said Reemo. "I'm sure they'll approve it if you decide it's best."

Apollo and Reemo talked some more, and then they ended. The last thing Reemo did was wish Apollo good luck with Shumaker. "I hope you can bring him back," Reemo said. "You're going there now... correct?"

"In the morning," Apollo said.

Apollo then spoke with Myke, who had updated details from Tamir on where Shumaker was thought to be hiding. If Shumaker came over to Olam's side, he would be protected. But so far, he had refused to be with Olam. He also refused to support the radical views of Sughi's people. Because of that, he was on his own, and he had gone into deep hiding, trying to stay away from everybody.

Apollo remembered the day he and Myke spent with Shumaker. It was one of their first days in Sughi City. Myke's cousin, Darcie, had taken them to meet him. At the time, the Sughis held Shumaker on a pedestal as a special recruiter for Sughi's position. They protected him with a security detail. But since then, with the radicalization of everything on Sughi's side, the moderate and well-reasoned views of Shumaker were considered much too tolerant. The Sughis had demanded that Shumaker radicalize his position, which he refused to do. His security detail was pulled, and they started harassing him. Finally, he had to hide.

Malta was angry at her management over Shumaker. "Another reason why I hate those putards," Malta once told Apollo. "Shumaker was our best recruiter. He had good ideas. Now, they can't hear anything outside their radical rants. Idiots!"

Sughi's people were hunting hard for Shumaker, and they had developed limited information about his whereabouts. Malta feigned interest in the search and found out what the Intels knew. She then passed the information directly to Tamir, who had also been hunting for Shumaker at Apollo's request. With what Malta supplied, Tamir was able to figure out how to find him. It was the final results of Tamir's analysis that Myke passed to Apollo today.

I hope the Shum' will talk with me, Apollo thought to himself. *Time is scarce.*

Apollo spent the rest of the day lying low in the forest, tucked beneath the trees. He wanted time to mourn the loss of his friend, Malta. The emptiness of losing her required special treatment. He wanted to bask in the pain, let it wash through him. He would not push it aside. Instead, he wanted it to imprint on the core network of his inner and eternal ghost.

Apollo truly hoped Malta would be happy with her decision to remain a ghost.

Do I love Malta? he asked himself.

The answer was complicated—and always would be. He knew he would never choose to be with her. But love her? That answer was probably a yes.

It was hard to think Malta might be there, in his Blood world, watching him and trying to help him. He would be totally oblivious to her presence and have no memory of her. It was tragic, and it would be many years before he saw her again. Olam's plan was brutal.

70

High Altitude

Early the next morning, Apollo left his hardwood tree sanctuary and headed south with his furry beasts. Their destination was a total contrast to the beautiful tree haven where they had spent the night. They had over a thousand miles to travel, and they kicked it into gear.

They were headed for the Sing-Sing Desert, most of which consisted of boring, nondescript terrain. Nobody lived in the Sing-Sing because it was a vast nothingness consisting of thousands of square miles of low, rocky hills, sporadically decorated with sage and colorless, stunted vegetation. The Sing-Sing was no place to take a majestic wolf, much less two of them.

To make the journey, Apollo climbed with the wolves to an extremely high altitude. He estimated he was up around fifty thousand feet. He wanted the altitude for multiple reasons. One was to help him find the Sing-Sing. From this height, he would see the desert from a much greater distance.

A second reason was the positively charged electricity in the air. At this altitude, there was a lot more of it, which would help keep him and the wolves charged in flight.

But the most important reason was because, at this high altitude, they stood almost no chance of running into anybody. Apollo did not want Sughi Command to know where he was going. He did not want some random Sughi reporting having seen a flyer with two ghost wolves headed south. The Sughis would know it was him, and they would wonder why he was headed in the direction of the Sing-Sing.

Four hours into the journey, Apollo was nearing exhaustion. The increased electricity at their altitude had helped, but it had not charged them as fast as they were draining. The wolves also looked tired, and Glacier was sending question marks to Apollo's brain. Normally, it would be time to land and charge up.

"Up ahead," Apollo conveyed to Glacier. "See those clouds? They will take care of us." Apollo hoped Glacier understood, and the threesome pushed forward on what little energy they had left.

Soon, they arrived at the tops of a series of monstrous atmospheric canyons formed by huge cumulonimbus clouds, boiling with energy-filled static electricity. Apollo chose the darkest wall and dove straight in. The circuits of Apollo, Glacier, and Fjord gulped in the raw electricity, recharging them instantaneously.

Apollo would never have dared such a move before. The lightning in the clouds would have blown his and the wolves' menapses, sending them into the black. But now, the three had the amped-up circuitry to handle any charge.

Their journey continued, batteries full.

An hour later, with the thunder clouds well behind them, they were in clear air. Apollo noticed that the horizon off to their right had become indistinct. It was not possible to see where the ground ended and the sky started. Apollo suspected that it might be the desert. The nothingness of the terrain, combined with desert dust in the air, might produce that type of washed-out horizon.

Apollo was right, and an hour later, he and the wolves were in a rapid descent, headed for the desert floor. The first half of their effort to find Shumaker had been a success. They had found the Sing-Sing. Now, the challenge was to find Shumaker in this enormous wasteland. To do that, Apollo and the wolves would have to wait for dark.

Apollo spent the rest of the afternoon exploring with the wolves. The terrain was incredibly boring, as he'd been told it would be. He wondered how any Blood mammal could live here. It looked challenging for even the most hardened desert dwellers, such as lizards and scorpions. *Small, tough insects might be okay,* he thought, *if nocturnal.*

Apollo also spent time explaining to Glacier and Fjord the importance of their trip to the Sing-Sing. They seemed to understand that they were looking for an important friend of Apollo. Apollo said they were trying to rescue him—a concept the wolves had not been able to assimilate with their first assignment—to help find Torith. The wolves seemed to better understand the rescue notion with Shumaker. Apollo hoped Shumaker would consider it a rescue mission, too.

During their afternoon exploring, Apollo went underground a few times, hoping to find something more interesting in the deep. When he did, the wolves stayed on top. They wanted nothing to do with underground forays. For the canines, flying had become a resounding "Yes!" but tunneling was an equally resounding "No!"

Apollo limited his in-ground explorations to depths of only several hundred feet, not wanting to be gone from the wolves for too long. Once, about three hundred feet down, he found an underground aquifer. In the dark, he had no way of estimating the amount of water it held, but there was much more than he would have expected. Thousands of gallons.

Perhaps hundreds of times that much. Everything else was nothing more than rock, clay, gravel, and lifeless dirt.

71

Sing-Sing Night Search

Apollo and the wolves were happy when the sun went down. The boring, brown desert floor evolved into a deep, vibrant black. Above the floor was an exquisite, star-filled sky. The Sing-Sing's ugliness by day was replaced with a magnificent night. Apollo was mesmerized by the celestial display of infinity. Apollo remembered enough of his astronomy to know that many of the stars were actually galaxies. Olam and Megantha had endless worlds, endless power to know every ghost in those worlds, and endless ability to navigate the space and time continuum of it all. It was impossible for his linear mind to understand.

As Apollo and Glacier looked at the sky, Apollo said, "Our earth is out there. The one Olam is sending us to. We'll be there together, Glacier."

Fjord was looking at Apollo.

"I hope you're there with us, too, Fjord. I think you will be."

As Apollo conveyed these thoughts to his friends, he noticed that both of their soft auras brightened. *One reason why I like the night so much,* Apollo thought.

Prominent in the night sky were two bright stars. They looked like they were close together. From Summa, they appeared equal in size, as if they were twins. Apollo knew they were radically different in size, but the larger one was many more light-years away. They were at about a forty-five-degree angle to Apollo's position on Summa. Atmospheric scintillation caused them to give off multi-colored twinkles. These night twins were known as the "Axis" because they were directly in line with Summa's axis. They remained a constant north as the stars in the rest of the sky rotated around them, from east to west.

Apollo waited until it was fully dark. The moon would not come up for three or four hours. Now was the time to go hunting, while the desert floor was pitch black. He needed the help of Glacier and Fjord's keen eyesight. "We're looking for burning underground," he told them, trying to think of a better explanation. "Like there is a red fire in the ground." Apollo said it would not be bright, and it would be hard to see, so they needed to watch carefully.

Tamir had explained that deep under parts of the Sing-Sing's desert were big lava tubes left over from massive underground lava flows. The heat and force of these flows plowed tunnels through horizontal layers of relatively soft rock deep under the desert. In some cases, after the tremendous forces of the lava had done their job, the lava flow stopped, and the flow in the tube moved on, leaving huge, empty underground tubes. These tubes were thousands of feet underground, with no indication of their existence on the surface. Shumaker was living in one of those tubes. He was sub-network and impossible to find—unless you knew the navigation code, which Apollo thought he did.

Tamir explained, "Five miles straight west of Shumaker's hideout is a place in the desert where, at night, you can see the glow of lava deep underground. There are some fissures in the ground that have opened up all the way to the surface. Their openings are not big, and they do not form any significant landmarks. The only way to see them is at night, from the glow of the lava." Then Tamir emphasized a point, "The glow is faint. It's not like you can go to some high altitude, scan the whole desert, and pick it out. Nope. You have to be right on it. Five hundred feet up, at most, and seeing it from just the right angle."

"But there is a trick," Tamir said. "One part of the fissure is relatively bright and long when viewed from a specific angle. If you hunt by flying patterns that match that angle, you'll have a much easier time seeing it."

"Fly your search pattern in parallel tracks. They need to be at 030 degrees when going northeast, and 210 when going southwest."

Tamir had also said the open fissure was somewhere near the middle of the desert, but that was all he knew. The middle of the desert was an enormous area. Apollo had a big job ahead of him. Unless he was lucky, it would be a long night with no guarantee of success.

Apollo took Glacier and Fjord, and they started their first run. He guessed at a 030 heading, based on Axis's position of straight north or zero degrees. Off they went, trying to stay at roughly five hundred feet in the dark night, scanning the ground for the fissure. Ten minutes later, Apollo sidestepped to the east and came back at an estimated heading of 210, putting Axis over his right shoulder. After a half dozen passes, he and the wolves became more accustomed to the flight and heading patterns. They picked up speed and covered more territory. It was hard, tedious work.

Three hours later, Apollo still had not seen anything. They had covered many square miles of desert floor. To the east, the sky was showing some light, which would be the moon. Once it was up, their chances of seeing the fissure against a less than pitch-black desert floor would be greatly diminished. Apollo was getting tired, and he could tell the wolves' concentration was waning. "Hang in there, boys," he encouraged them. "We need to push a little more."

Ten minutes later, Glacier yelped, and the three of them stopped midair. Apollo saw nothing. Glacier again yelped, and Apollo looked harder. Then he saw it. It was amazingly faint. He never would have seen it on his own, but there it was, a soft glow that had to be what they were looking for. The three of them headed to the surface. Now they were directly above a fissure, and down inside, there was the remote glow of very deep lava. This had to be the place.

"Thank you," Apollo directed to Olam and Megantha. He was not sure if they had helped in tonight's search. All Apollo knew was that he would have missed it without Glacier's help. *Does Sapienti talk to Glacier?* Apollo was not sure, and he was surprised that he did not know the answer. *Why wouldn't Sapienti talk to him?*

"When it gets light," Apollo said to the wolves, "we'll go find Shumaker." In the interim, it was time to rest.

Apollo and the wolves settled in and soon were gifted with the moon's rise. Apollo thought back to times when he and the wolves had howled at the moon together for fun and sport. That was a different time, carefree in Sub-Summa. Apollo again wondered if he had done the right thing, bringing these powerful beasts out of their sanctuary. He had pushed them into the heart of the war against Sughi. *People problems, not wolf problems, and yet they have to fight. Not fair.*

Just after sunup, Apollo had been dozing and was surprised to be awakened by the faint rustling of a horned toad moving over the sandy clay near him. It was a "real" horned toad in that it was a Blood, not a ghost. Of course, even though it was real, it was not a real "toad." It actually was a lizard with a toad name. A lizard blessed with a beautiful and intricate pattern of aggressive-looking horns all over its body, making it look like a small, cuddly, horned monster.

Apollo knew this beautiful reptile would be oblivious to Apollo and the wolves. Apollo pointed it out to Glacier, who came over for a sniff. They all watched it as it moved across the broken and sandy clay, looking right through them for "real" threats, and probably "real" food. *Amazing,* Apollo thought. *That little guy has a thousand times more effect on the physical world than I do. He moves the sand and tiny pieces of clay. He leaves a trail. I can't do any of that.*

It was time to find Shumaker. Apollo thought the horned toad was a good omen and hoped their final step in the search process would be successful. "Let's go, guys," he said to the wolves. He climbed to about five hundred feet and picked out a far-off landmark straight to the east. That was his line of flight, and he did his best to head straight for it while flying an estimated five miles. If his navigation was correct, Tamir said he would see a small, indistinct canyon opening onto a flat section of terrain about as big as the playground of a children's grade school. In that flat section, there would be seven stunted and shabby-looking yucca plants. Yucca plants were not uncommon in the Sing-Sing, but they were by no means omnipresent, and Tamir said they should be distinct enough to tell Apollo he was in the right place.

Tamir was right. Within minutes, he and the wolves were in the flat with the yuccas. The rest would be easy. Supposedly, two thousand feet below these yucca plants was a huge cavern, carved and burned out by underground lava flows. That was where he would find Shumaker.

Apollo explained to Glacier and Fjord that he needed to go underground, and that he might be gone for hours. "I'll call you when I'm out."

Glacier and Fjord were used to waiting for Apollo. They would be fine. They had no interest in going underground. He thought he might be able to force them, saying he needed protection, but there was no need for that.

72

Shumaker's Choice

Apollo started his descent, and he found the cavern several minutes later. Tamir had said it would be easy to find, and it was. It was enormous—and beautiful. The cavern was lit with twenty or thirty comms. Their projected light was refracting through thousands of crystals embedded in the ceiling, walls, floor, and rock formations. It was spectacular and mesmerizing. The beauty of the refracted light was as beautiful as this desert's incredible night sky. It was as if the after-dark heavens had been rolled up and spread over the rock surfaces inside this cavern. No wonder Shumaker had wanted to keep this place hidden. If Summa's general population knew, the cavern would be overrun with ghost gawkers.

"Hello, Apollo," Shumaker said calmly. "I was hoping you could find me."

Apollo had fully expected Shumaker to be there and did not turn to look at him. Instead, he continued to stare at the beauty. "You have a wonderful home here," Apollo said. "How did you find this heaven?"

"A Mentor helped me, Apollo. The same Mentor who told me you were coming. He's my older house brother, and he watches out for me."

Apollo was not surprised, and he continued to absorb the incredibility of what he was seeing. "You know, then, that we will protect you," Apollo said.

"Of course, from the Sughis, but you can't protect me from myself."

At that, Apollo unlocked from the spectacular view and looked at Shumaker. Apollo moved towards him and embraced him as much as he could, sensing the soul of this wonderful man. "It's good to see you, my friend."

The last time, years ago, when Apollo and Myke had been with Shumaker, Shumaker was the phenomenon. Now it was a role reversal. Shumaker was no less of a person, but Apollo was the super force.

Apollo looked around, searching the cave. "Were you able to bring Bucky?"

"Yes. To the desert. But he's like your wolves. He wants nothing to do with coming underground. He stays on top."

Bucky was the myna bird who hung out with Apollo, Myke, and Shumaker all day the last time they were together. He had adopted Shumaker, and Apollo was glad to hear they were still close.

Apollo continued to absorb the wonders of Shumaker's underground hideaway. "Maybe I'll stay here with you for a while."

"You know you're welcome, but neither one of us is going to be here long."

"I'm sorry you're looking at eviction," said Apollo.

"You are, too. We're all Summa short-timers. Olam is booting all of us."

"Well, if we're both getting thrown out, you may as well get thrown my way. Yes?"

Shumaker avoided the question. "Come on. Let's go meet your wolves." At that, Shumaker started up.

Apollo took another look around and then followed Shumaker. Two thousand feet later, they both exited onto the desert floor near the yucca trees. Glacier and Fjord were not in sight, but Apollo mentally connected with Glacier, asking him to come over. "They're coming," Apollo said.

"I can't do that with Bucky," Shumaker said. "No animal-talker gift for me. Not like what they gave you. Can you also talk to birds?"

"Only wolves," Apollo said.

"What did your Mentor say about the cave?" Apollo asked. "Can you stay there until the end?"

"Yes. Until I'm banished."

"Why not come over to Olam's side? We're getting banished too, but we move forward."

Shumaker was silent, then said, "I fought against it for so long, Apollo. With all the damage I did—all the people I pulled away from Olam—I'm amazed that my brother would let me live here protected in this paradise."

"There was nothing malicious about what you did. You only wanted to do the right thing."

Shumaker did not respond.

"When you're on an earth somewhere, I hope you'll be able to find a good place to hide. The Sughis there are going to hate you there like they do here."

"They hate you, too, Apollo. And even if you have your wolves, you'll be a regular person like everyone else. None of the firepower you have now."

"Yes, but I'll be a Blood. They can't do much to me unless I let them. You, on the other hand... you'll still be a ghost. You'll have to fight with them, just like you do here."

Silence from Shumaker.

"Unless, of course, you come over and become a Blood."

Apollo could tell Shumaker was struggling.

"So, I go back on everything I preached for years to protect myself? That way, I won't have to fight with Sughis for eternity?"

"It's not a compromise of your principles. You have the right to change your mind. It's different now. The debate is over. It's Olam's way or the boot."

Shumaker said nothing.

"Look. Don't you see? There are many things I would change about Olam's plan if I could. I would limit what bad people could do, like you would. But the Quasars all say, no."

Glacier and Fjord came over a small rise. Amazingly, Bucky was right with them. Somehow, they all knew they were on the same team.

"Well, look at that," Apollo said, now switching his tone and teasing Shumaker. "Bucky gets it. He knows where he should be."

"It's a sign," Shumaker said, with a hint of mockery, looking at the sky.

The wolves immediately liked Shumaker. They liked Bucky, too. Bucky reciprocated and decided his spot for the day was on top of Glacier's head.

"How's Bucky doing here?" Apollo asked. "He's more of a tropical bird, isn't he?"

"I spend a lot of time with him above ground," Shumaker explained. "It's amazing how much life is here when you take the time to look for it."

Apollo told him about the horned toad.

"By far one of the most beautiful creatures on Summa. I don't know who made them. Maybe Olam. But the style is more Mom, Megantha."

Apollo and Shumaker spoke for hours on many topics. Later in their conversation, Apollo pointed out how differently he and Shumaker processed things. "I'm very much a surface guy," Apollo said. "You can see that. I'm rarely conflicted, even when I know I could be. But you... you're like my friend Tamir. You look at everything five layers deep."

Shumaker chuckled. "It's my curse, Apollo. I'm constantly at war with myself."

"You don't come across that way. There's an outward calm and wisdom."

"It's a mask," Shumaker said.

"Well, it works. You convinced hundreds, thousands, of people to follow you."

"Yes, and I deserve to pay for that."

"So, does that mean you think you were wrong?"

"The only thing I'm sure of, Apollo, is that it was wrong of me to try to convince people to side with Sughi. I'm a horrible person for having done that. I ruined many people with my pretend wisdom."

Apollo was surprised at Shumaker's demeanor. It was clear he thought he was responsible for stopping the progression of all those people. Many kind souls would crumple under the weight of such realization. But Shumaker stood there and took it. Fully accepting it.

"If I switch sides and go back to Olam," Shumaker said, "how can I live with myself? I dragged all those people away, and now I go back? And I go on to be a Blood? They are left to their misery, and I simply forget about them? I go into blissful forgetfulness? How can that be right... or fair? I need to pay for what I did."

"So, for you, going back to Olam and then on to an earth as a Blood is the easy way out?"

"Yes. And wrong."

"They made their own choice," Apollo countered. "Each one of them. They chose to listen to you, but they deliberately chose to reject Olam."

Shumaker was silent.

"In my one-level, simple brain, you may have done wrong. But I also think you are only responsible for yourself. You are not responsible for their decision to follow Sughi. It's not your fault that they'll always be ghosts, and only ghosts. They are their own masters."

Shumaker said nothing. Apollo knew Shumaker was not hearing anything new, and Apollo did not try to present it as if it were.

Apollo and Shumaker spent the rest of the day together. There was no more substantive talk of Olam, Sughi, and Bloods. Instead, Apollo wanted to enjoy being with this man who, technically, was an enemy, but who was one of the people on Summa whom Apollo liked the most.

Shumaker took Apollo back down to his cavern and showed him some of the most exquisite crystals. "When I have to go, I will miss this place deeply. I don't want to forget it."

After more exploration of the cavern, they returned to the surface and wandered in the local desert. Shumaker showed Apollo small insects that lived in the yucca. There was a hillside with almost constant shade where sand beetles were nesting. Then Shumaker took him to a low rock overhang under which Apollo and Shumaker could see the yellow eye of a banded gecko. He was burrowed way back underneath in a dark corner. "He hunts at night," Shumaker said. "Bucky and I follow him around for fun. He's a Blood, and he has no idea we exist."

"I love the desert," Shumaker said. "Its nothingness conceals a wonderful vastness."

Apollo had planned to leave once it was night and Axis was in view. He wanted the reference for navigation. But, like last night, this second night in the desert gifted an equally magnificent, star-filled sky. Apollo decided to stay until morning. He listened as Shumaker talked about the constellations, faraway galaxies, and the endless earths he and Apollo both knew were out there. "Your earth will have wolves, Apollo. That's for sure."

"Olam is not vindictive," said Apollo. "I think yours will have myna birds... and horned toads. Regardless of whether you go as a ghost or as a Blood."

In the morning, Apollo left Shumaker and Bucky. Glacier and Fjord projected that they were sad to leave them. Apollo hoped Shumaker could forgive himself. "I need you on my earth with me," Apollo had said to him. "I need your guidance. I'm going to be lost."

As Apollo and the wolves rose to altitude, high above the desert, Apollo already missed Shumaker. The plainness of the Sing-Sing desert passed below them, its living secrets hidden from the unobservant.

Apollo knew he would soon be a Blood and forget everything, Shumaker included. Like his feelings about Malta, this broke Apollo's heart. Apollo understood better why Malta refused to switch. She did not want to forget. Apollo thought of the beautiful horned toad he had seen with the wolves. He would forget that enchanting little monster.

Olam's plan was brutal.

73

Celti

Time was short, and Apollo wanted one more try with his older sister, Celti. She had left Olam many years ago, refusing to be part of a plan that would lead to so much harm to animals. She loved animals more than people. Apollo hoped Glacier and Fjord would be the ace needed to save her. Apollo alone could not.

Celti was not hiding. She was easy to find. Rather than tell her he was coming, Apollo showed up unannounced—with the beasts, of course. Apollo had been tempted to recruit Bucky for the visit, too, but he decided Bucky was better off sticking tight to Shumaker. Maybe Bucky's presence could help Shumaker save himself.

For years, Celti had lived in a small community of Sughis who were peaceful animal lovers. For the most part, they had escaped the aggressive, radical Sughi side that was now the norm. They stayed in their little hamlet, off the radar, and they made no waves. Nobody had any interest in fighting with them, and the community had been given a pass from most of the violence.

"Hello, big sister," Apollo said, seeing her. She was living in a small house Megantha had built for her. It was filled with various species of ghost animals. She had convinced these animals to leave their normal environments and come stay with her. There were birds, rabbits, one deer, several pigs, multiple dogs, and even some fish. It was amazing, and Apollo knew Celti was happy, at least for now.

Celti greeted Apollo with reserve. She knew why he was there, but she could not hold back when Glacier and Fjord fully embraced her. Apollo had told them to bury her with affection, and they were happy to do so. These wolves—so strong and capable in battle—were also formidable contenders in the "I love you" arena.

"Can you really talk to them?" Her face was lit up with energy.

"Not just *to* them. I can talk *with* them." Apollo let that sink in. "It has to be concepts on their level. They know, for example, how much I love you, sis."

"I heard Mom and Dad gave you a gift." She hung her head slightly, clearly jealous, and not hiding it. "You are lucky, my brother. But you always were the good one."

"Celti, you are not bad," Apollo countered.

Her tone changed, now more authoritative. "Do you make the wolves fight?" She was the older sister, and she had the right to demand answers from her little brother.

"They saved me, Celti, after I was kidnapped. They helped put me back together."

"I know, Apollo. You've told me. I'm so sorry that happened to you." Then she continued to look at him. He had not answered her question.

"Yes," Apollo finally said. "They fight with me. We are a team."

"You are using them." Her voice was flat.

Apollo messaged Glacier to nuzzle into Celti. He did, and she softened.

"They want a job. They want to be needed, and they want to protect me."

Apollo told Celti about the first lightning storm with the wolves. "It was terrifying for them, Celti. They had never seen lightning before. But all they cared about was me."

Apollo could see some of Celti's coolness melt away. She sat on the ground with Glacier. Fjord did his part too, standing right next to her, his eyes locked on hers, only inches away. Celti was in heaven. Then, two of Celti's pigs came over and rolled on the ground right into Celti and Glacier. Apollo was surprised at that. He thought they would be afraid of the wolves.

"Those pigs are goofballs," Celti said with a laugh. "They'll be eaten on day one when they are Bloods. They have zero sense of self-preservation."

Apollo did not want to hardball his approach with Celti. However, he made it clear to her that if she stayed on Sughi's side, she would always be a ghost.

"I know all that," she said.

"But I don't understand, Celti. You won't be able to help any animals as a ghost."

Celti did not respond.

"You can't stay here. You know that."

"I can't forgive Mom and Dad."

"Don't think about it that way, Celti. If you come over, then when you're sent to an earth, you'll be able to help all kinds of suffering Blood animals."

Celti sighed.

"Stay a ghost, and all you'll be able to do is watch. That will be pure hell for you, Celti."

"But it's people who are bad, not animals. There is no reason why they have to suffer," she said.

"I know, but you can't change that. The plan is the plan. Like it or not. I don't want to see animals suffer, either."

Apollo did not push more. This might be the last time he saw his sister for many years. He wanted to relish the time with her. He loved her.

Apollo stayed with Celti for several days. The wolves smothered her with affection the whole time. Several hours before he planned to leave, he left the house and went to a nearby patch of woods for a talk with Megantha. She came to him in person as soon as he called.

"I've tried, Mom. I don't know what else to do."

Megantha sat with Apollo and gave him a physical hug.

"Can I talk to her?" she asked him.

It was a funny question because she did not need his permission for anything.

"Of course. Yes, if you think it will help."

"What do you think, Apollo?"

This, too, was a funny question. She would already know what he was thinking.

"I don't know, Mom. Yes, please do. We have to try everything. She's still angry with you, but we're out of time. Aren't we?"

"You're definitely out of time, Apollo. You're going to be a Blood soon, son. Very soon. And you'll do great."

"With Glacier... yes? Can Fjord come with me, too?"

"Of course. You will have both, and you will have the gift of communicating with them and all wolves. You have earned that."

Then Apollo had an idea, and he was about to ask Megantha about it when she stopped him by putting her hand over his mouth. He could feel the warm solidity of her fingers. Then, looking at him, her diamond eyes shining all colors, she said, "Let's go talk with your sister."

At that, Megantha started out of the woods and moved towards Celti's house. It was late in the day, and Megantha powered up, showing light everywhere. She was coming in full guns, illuminating the entire neighborhood. Sughis came out of their houses to see. Celti did too, meeting Megantha and Apollo in Celti's front yard.

Glacier and Fjord came right over to Megantha. Apollo watched their fur lie down and spring back as Megantha ran her hand over their heads, necks, and backs. She squeezed their skulls affectionately. The ghost skin on their skulls compressed as she put her hand on their heads. Their ears moved as she rubbed deep behind them. Glacier rolled his eyes back in ecstasy. Apollo wished he could touch them like she could. He would love to manhandle and wrestle with them. He knew the time would come—soon, apparently—when he could do that.

"Thank you for taking care of my boy," Megantha said to the canines. "Both of you are his forever, and he is yours."

Celti had not yet hugged her mother, but now they were locked eye to eye. Despite Celti's resentment, it was impossible to be face-to-face and angry with the magnificent being that was her mother. Still, Celti resisted stepping forward. The brief standoff was broken by the two goofball pigs who came tumbling out of the house, eager to greet Megantha. She reached down and picked up both of them. They licked her face and squealed with delight.

Celti still refused to hug her mother. It was becoming ridiculous. Apollo could hardly hold his tongue.

Megantha stepped back, a squirmy pig in each of her arms, both held tightly, running back style. "Let's go into the house and talk," she said.

The whole group, animals and all, moved into the house. Megantha dimmed her powerful aura. The show for the neighbors was over. She put the pigs down, and then she took Apollo and Celti both by a hand and sat down with them on the floor. She was cross-legged, firmly on the ground. Apollo and Celti adjusted to match her position, but their ghosts were partly in the ground itself, not physically on the ground.

"Do you believe in perfection, Celti?" she asked.

"Mom, I don't think your plan is perfect." Celti looked down, and her words were a borderline mumble.

"Do you think I can do anything?"

Head still down, Celti mumbled a "Yes."

"So, all powerful, but not all perfect?"

"Something like that. I mean… no. I think the plan could be perfect. If you wanted it to be."

"Do you think I want to hurt the animals?" Megantha asked.

"I think you can figure out a way to do it, so they are not hurt so much. People are bad. Animals aren't!"

"Are there different ways to be perfect?"

"Of course," Celti said. "The pigs are as perfect as the wolves, only different."

"Right. Good. So, maybe there is a perfect plan that involves less pain for animals?"

"Yes… yes!" Celti said. "There has to be!"

"Is that what you'll do when it's your chance?"

Celti did not answer, and Apollo knew why. The only way Celti would ever have the chance to set up her own plan would be if she advanced, and that meant joining her mother, giving Sughi's side the heave-ho, and moving on to be a Blood. Failing to do that, she'd forever remain a ghost.

The three of them were silent for a full minute. Apollo looked at the wolves. They sensed tension. Apollo told them to sit right next to Celti, which they did. Celti's mood softened.

Apollo's idea from before came to him again. As soon as it did, he saw that Megantha was looking at him. She gave him a slight nod, and he knew the idea had come from her. She was giving him the green light, and she hinted an imperceptible, almost mischievous smile. As a bonus, she threw in an ever-so-slight raising of one eyebrow.

"Mom," Apollo said, then pausing.

Celti looked up.

Apollo continued, "Mom, you've given me gifts. You gave me the wolves. And you gave Myke and me the gift of being on that pirate ship." Apollo paused. "That pirate thing was a rough gift, but a gift nonetheless."

"Yes, Apollo. It was all for your good."

"Well, why not give a gift to Celti?"

Celti looked at her brother and mother, wondering where this was going.

"I love your sister, but she has rejected me," said Megantha. "You were given the gifts because you've always been with me, Apollo."

Celti hung her head. The defiance seemed to be draining from her.

"The gifts are mine, correct?"

"Of course."

Celti was watching. Light was pouring in. She started to see where this was going.

"Then, if they are mine, are they also mine to give to my sister?"

Megantha looked at her son. Pride and love beamed from her face. She was going to speak, but Celti interrupted.

"No, Apollo… no. That is too much. Not the wolves. I could not take them. They love you so much. I can feel the way they love you."

Apollo and Megantha said nothing.

Celti started to panic. It was not fair. Her brother should have the wolves. She loved them, too, but they were his. "No… Apollo… no!"

Celti turned towards Megantha. "Please, Mom. No. They are Apollo's. I don't deserve them. Please. My little brother. He should not have to pay because of what I do. Please… no!"

Celti moved towards her mother and took hold of both of her hands. "Please, Mom. I could never forgive myself. Please do not do this to him." Celti's eyes started to tear.

Megantha fixed her eyes on Celti for several moments, then she turned towards Apollo. "Is that what you want to do, son?"

"I will give them to you, of course. To save you, Celti. The wolves saved me. Now they can save you."

Celti shook her head. "No! No!"

"But that's not what I was thinking." Apollo looked at Megantha and then at Celti. "It's my other gift I was thinking of giving."

Megantha, of course, knew what Apollo was referring to. Apollo watched as Celti tried to understand. She looked relieved that her brother would not have to give up his wolves. Then her face went blank—a question mark. "What?" She shook her head inquisitively. "Not the wolves? Then what are you talking about?"

"Talking," said Apollo. "I'm talking about… talking."

Celti looked back and forth between her mother and Apollo. "What?"

"Talking to the wolves. That gift, Celti. Leave Glacier and Fjord to me. But if Megantha lets me give you the talking gift, you'll have all the wolves you want. Here and on your earth!"

Celti looked at Apollo. Surprise and joy overwhelmed her. Then she looked at Megantha, who nodded, yes. At that, Celti crumpled into her mother's lap. "I could talk to wolves?" she asked. "Really? Me?" She started to cry.

"You understand, my love. You don't deserve this gift. But Apollo does, and he can share it with you."

Megantha had said *share*. Not *give*. Both Apollo and Celti picked up on that.

Celti bolted up. "Share?" asked Celti. Share? Not give?"

Megantha looked at Apollo. "You were willing to give it. But how about if you and your sister share it?"

"Yes," Celti said, a pleading tone in her voice. "Yes, share it. Please let Apollo keep it, too. He has wolves already! He needs to talk with them. Please!"

"You're sharing," Megantha said to Apollo. "Which means you both have it. It also means, my daughter, that if you come back, you and Apollo will share a special bond on your earth."

Apollo was thrilled. He had been more than willing to give the gift away to save Celti, but his mother had made it all even better. And now, maybe he could be with Celti, too. On an earth with wolves. Wolves, they could talk with. How incredible was that?

Apollo was silent for several minutes, as was Megantha. Celti was making noise. She was sobbing softly, overwhelmed with remorse and joy.

"I don't deserve this, Mom," Celti said. "You know I don't."

"Correct," Megantha said. "But Apollo does. He loves you so much. You and he can be together. You'll be a special force on your earth. Wolf people."

The small family group said nothing. Apollo and Celti were soaking in the wonder they both felt. Celti remained crumpled in her mother's lap. Glacier and Fjord flanked them tightly.

74

The Mordax

Apollo never felt closer to Celti and his mother than he did that night. It was a wonderful way to end his time on Summa.

Megantha left Celti's house about an hour later.

Before Megantha left, she told Apollo and Celti that Apollo's time on Summa was up. "You are going to your earth tonight," she explained.

Celti was told she would go to Apollo's earth, too, in a few years. "You'll be the younger sister this time. It will be his turn to boss you around and grill you with questions."

Celti agreed to take care of the wolves until she was sent away. After that, Lionah would send the wolves back to the Sub-Summa, where they would be safe. Later, when Apollo and Celti were old enough, the wolves would be sent to them as Bloods.

As Megantha was leaving, she asked Apollo to walk with her. Outside, and away from Celti, she became quite serious, and then sorrowful.

"What's wrong, Mom?"

"It's your older brother, Dramos. He's been given a terrible task."

Apollo wondered what she meant.

"I've chosen to tell you this now, Apollo. Not before, because I did not want to burden you."

Megantha faced Apollo and took him by his two hands, holding each separately. She looked Apollo in the eyes. She was tearful.

"Son, I want you to know this before you move on. You'll forget it while you're a Blood, but you'll remember it later."

Apollo shook his head in the affirmative, understanding.

"You know Dramos is strong."

"He's an animal, Mom. I've always wanted him to fight with us."

"Yes. Diamond Command has always insisted that he fight elsewhere. The two of you together are too much. But I fear for him, Apollo. Olam has given him a tool I'm afraid will destroy him."

"A tool?"

"It's too powerful. Too personal."

"My wolves are powerful."

"Yes, they are. But they are their own entities. Your brother's tool is powerful in a much different way."

Apollo did not understand. He searched his mother's face. Her piercing eyes saw so much. Through those eyes, Apollo could glimpse the eternities.

"Mom?"

She sighed and looked to be in pain. It was almost as if she were drawing strength from Apollo. He had never felt this before. It frightened him.

"Apollo, what if you could fight with a piece of me, or a piece of your father?"

Apollo did not understand.

"A piece you could hold in your hand. A sharp piece, and you could hold it like I can hold you?"

Apollo tried to visualize such a tool. "Sharp?"

"Yes."

"But I can hold it? Like a sword?"

"Yes. A short sword. More like a long knife. Like no object on Summa. You are a ghost. Normally, you cannot hold anything."

Apollo continued to imagine what such a tool would be like. "Like a sharp piece of a Quasar. One I can grasp? Can it cut?"

"Yes," she said, and Apollo could see more fear in her eyes. Her grip on his hands tightened.

"Cut anything? Ghost or Blood alike?"

"Yes."

"Can it cut rocks? And trees?"

"Yes. It cuts right through them all. It is unstoppable."

Apollo could only begin to understand how a ghost could use such a tool. In battle it would be devastatingly powerful. With it, he could cut open the doors to a Sughi command center, sever its data and power lines. The possibilities for destruction were endless.

"But, Mom. Dramos is strong and good. Do you fear he would use the tool unwisely?"

"Mordax," she said. "It's called the Mordax."

"Mordax," repeated Apollo.

"How big is it?"

"Its length is from your wrist to your elbow, handle, blade, and all."

"Colors?"

"White until you pick it up. Then it becomes part of you. It takes on your aura. For you, it would be a glowing blue."

Apollo had many questions, but his concern was more for Megantha. "But, Mom, Olam gave it to Dramos. Why would he do that if you disagree?"

"You know I love your father, Apollo. But it does not mean we always agree. I wanted Dramos to have lightning, like a Mentor. Not the Mordax. It is too personal and deadly. You can feel it in your hand as it cuts another ghost apart. You feel the carnage of the blade. You could easily use it to torture another ghost."

"Cut another ghost apart? Permanently?" asked Apollo.

"Not permanently, but the ghost body is rendered unusable. If you cut through its neck, the head and body remain together, but the connection is severed. It does not heal and restore for days. Cut an arm, and that arm is useless to the ghost until the severed line heals. Cut through something physical, like a tree, and the cut is permanent."

"Why is that worse than lightning, Mom? Lightning could take out fifty ghosts."

"It's not the power, Apollo. It's the way the power is used. The Mordax requires the warrior to be up close and personal. Dramos can feel every cut."

Apollo was starting to understand. When he fought Sughi ghosts, there was opposition. He could feel the enemy fighting back on the same terms. It was all under confines they both understood. But what if he simply sliced the enemy apart? No fight. No resistance, and nothing the enemy could do? And for each one, he'd have to be up close, looking them in their hateful eyes, and "whoop," slice right through their torso in one full sweep, severing the ghost from shoulder to hip, leaving him or her in a diced-up heap on the battlefield.

"Dramos feels the blade tearing and cutting," Megantha said. "If he comes to love that feeling—if he craves it—it will destroy him. And he'll go over to Sughi."

"He'll never go to Sughi, Mom. Not Dramos."

"Then he'll destroy himself. His conscience will crush him. He may self-destruct. He knows he has to use the tool to save others—and he will. But it might ruin him." She looked up and away. "I begged Olam not to do this."

"Can you send Dramos to my earth. With me? Send him now! Please!"

"Oh, how I wish I could, Apollo. You are lucky and blessed to be going now. It's only becoming worse on Summa. You are being spared the terror and horror that must come before the end. But Dramos is destined to stay through it all. He must walk through Summa's final hell. He is key to Diamond Command's ultimate plans."

Apollo loved his brother so much. He realized the pain he had been through as a warrior was nothing compared to what his older brother would have to endure. "Mom… you say I am leaving tonight. Can I say goodbye to my brother?"

"I will tell him, Apollo, my boy. But your time here on Summa is over."

Megantha gave Apollo a wonderful last and final hug.

"Dad will get it right with Dramos," Apollo said to her.

"I know," she said, her eyes locked on his. "Goodbye for now, my strong boy. I love you."

75

Olam's Plan is Brutal

Continuation from Chapter 2. Back on Planet Kodiak,
Present Day, Perseus Arm of the Milky Way ...

Malta, the purple ghost, watched Apollo as he greeted the wolves she knew to be Glacier and Fjord. No longer ghost wolves on Summa, the beasts had been brought to Apollo on Kodiak. They were physical, deadly, and powerful.

Malta wondered what the wolves remembered, if anything, of Summa. Had their memories been wiped clean, like those of Apollo and all Blood humans? She did not know. But regardless of what the animals remembered, they obviously knew and loved Apollo. And Malta could see that Apollo knew they were his.

Apollo stood and walked into camp. He told Myke and Tamir not to get up, and Apollo sat down with them, cross-legged.

Glacier and Fjord followed Apollo into camp. The animals were intimidating, weighing at least 150 pounds each.

"The Great Spirit gave me a gift," Apollo told his friends. "These wolves are mine. And I can talk with them."

Tamir and Myke were frozen. Both beasts came over to them and smelled them. Tamir reached out his hand. To Tamir's amazement, Fjord sat on his rear and gave Tamir a paw. An enormous paw. Tamir began petting Fjord.

Myke was less affectionate, but soon he, too, was at ease.

"What about the rest of the pack?" Tamir asked.

"I think they are with us. Not like these two who are mine. But the pack knows we are on the same team."

"Good job," Apollo, Myke said. "The Sky Spirit... I always knew he favored you."

Glacier and Fjord had settled comfortably on the ground. Glacier was close to Apollo but away from the fire. Fjord took up a protective position, close to Myke and Tamir, facing into the night, as if standing sentry.

"There's more," Apollo said. "Sister moon has the gift, too."

Tamir needed clarification. "Sister Moon?" he asked, pointing to the sky.

"No," answered Apollo. "My sister. Celti. I think the other wolves are going to save her."

Tamir's mouth dropped open.

Malta was surprised at how quickly and easily Glacier and Fjord adopted the boys. Their pack mentality was strong, and she could see that Glacier and Fjord considered Tamir and Myke part of the pack. She wondered if Sapienti had been talking to them, helping them understand and remember Apollo. *Does Sapienti talk to animals?* She wondered. *Probably, yes.*

Malta thought back to that last time in Sughi City when Apollo came with Glacier and Fjord to see her. She missed Apollo terribly.

Malta hoped for a night soon when she could better connect with Apollo in his dreams. Better yet, she had spoken with ghosts on the planet who said they had experienced times when a human had been able to see them. It only lasted for short periods, sometimes only seconds.

Something would fall into sync with the physical and ghost realm, allowing humans to briefly see the other side. Some humans found it terrifying. Others had more understanding and were fascinated. Malta was not sure what caused the change in alignment that allowed them to see the ghost realm. Some thought it was a quickening, but she thought it was more random, and not so much related to a person's goodness, badness or abilities. All she knew was that, occasionally, the one-way veil between her world and the human world would break down, allowing humans to see ghosts like her. *Too bad,* she thought. *Think of the havoc I could reap if they actually knew I was here!*

Malta wondered if Olam would ever grant Apollo the ability to see her. Malta suspected that, if Apollo asked for it, the Sky Spirit might grant it. Apollo was heavily favored, as he should be, given his life on Summa. However, Malta knew Apollo would never ask for the gift because he would not have any reason to ask. He had no memory of Malta, and it would not occur to him to ask for such a thing. The thought made her heart heavy.

Malta watched the boys and the wolves. Their fire was getting low. Tamir put more wood on the flames and then went back to sleep. The rest of the camp also tried to rest. Glacier moved close to Apollo, helping him stay warm.

Malta left the boys and the two wolves, and she headed out into the black night. She was at Celti's camp five minutes later. Unlike the sleepy calm she'd left at the boys' camp, this camp was in turmoil. Everyone was awake, fully dressed, and tense.

They, too, had made contact with wolves. But unlike the bond between human and wolf in the boys' camp, the clan's camp was surrounded by the remainder of Glacier's pack. In the dark, Malta could see the auras of the wolves, circling beyond the camp's perimeter. There were twelve of them. Most of the time, the wolves stayed out of sight, unseen to the humans. On cue, they would howl and yelp in unison— a tactic, Malta suspected, was meant to rattle the herd. All it would take is one person to panic and run, and the wolves would have their meal.

There were twenty men and only twelve wolves. These large wolves would no doubt win a full-on frontal attack, but they would suffer injury and loss. Instead, the wolves bided their time and continued to project terror and intimidation.

Malta heard the clan warriors talking. They had encountered wolves many times, and individual clan members had been killed and eaten by wolves. But the clan had never been hunted like this, in a persistent, organized fashion, encircled by night.

The clan pulled members and prisoners into a tight, defensive square. Each corner of the square had a fire. Psychologically, it was a defensible fort. Malta could see, however, that they did not have enough wood gathered to keep all four fires burning through the night. And there was no way to go out into the night to get more. The wolves owned everything beyond the immediate perimeter.

The clan's prisoners looked as frightened as the clansmen. Malta saw, however, that Celti was calm. Torith had locked herself to Celti, and Torith looked calm, too. The other girls were terrified, some of them in tears.

The wood was running low, and it was hours before sunrise. Malta heard the clansman talk that they might have to sacrifice one or two of the women. Maybe if they left them for the wolves, the rest of them could get away.

Malta wished Lucen and his gang were here right now. She would fully support and assist them in attacking the mentality of several of these clansmen. Some were weak souls who would crumble if subjected to a ghost raid. These were the types of people who had no inner structure— humans the ghosts could drive crazy. With Lucen's help, she would ramp up one of the warriors into a state of crazed terror, maybe even causing him to charge into the night. That would give the wolves meat for their efforts, and it would create super-fear in the living.

Where is that weasel Lucen when you need him? Malta thought.

But Malta then saw that Celti had another plan. A much better one. Malta watched Celti get to her feet and stand outside the fire perimeter, facing into the night. No guard tried to stop her.

Malta sensed the connection she knew was there between the girl and the wolves.

"Untie me!" Celti demanded.

No warrior moved. "Sit down," Flat Nose said. "You are not the one we will sacrifice."

Celti remained facing the night. Suddenly, she let out a blood-curdling wolf howl. In sync, the entire wolf pack responded.

The warriors were stunned. What was this girl?

"Untie me!" Celti demanded a second time. "Or you will all die. Untie me now!"

Torith got to her feet and went over to Celti. "Me too!" Torith demanded. "Untie me!"

"Now! Both of us!" Celti again demanded. The wolves on the perimeter howled, as if accentuating her demand.

At that, the warrior leader threw his knife at the feet of the girls. Torith used it to cut Celti free, and then she cut herself free.

Celti held out her hand for the knife, which Torith gave to her. To everyone's surprise, Celti walked the knife over to the clan leader whose name was Caleb.

Standing in front of Caleb, Celti pointed the knife at each clansman, counting them off. Then she said, "Your people killed four of my people. You also killed the girl by leaving her to the wolves. That is five."

Celti handed the knife back to Caleb. "You will use this knife. Five of you must die. A life for a life."

Pointing at Flat Nose, Celti said, "He killed my uncle. He dies. The other four… you pick."

The moment was surreal and confusing, and Malta could tell the leader did not know what to make of it. Flat Nose half-smirked, but fear showed on his face, too. Who was this wolf girl?

Celti walked back to Torith. "The wolves tell me my brother is close. Let's go." Celti took Torith by the arm, and the two of them walked beyond the fires into the night. Before disappearing into the darkness, Celti turned back and said, "Do your duty, Caleb. Flat Nose and four more. Or my wolves will take all of you!"

Celti took several more steps with Torith towards the night. Then she stopped and belted out a mournful, penetrating howl. No normal human could generate such a noise. There was no doubt she was part wolf.

The wolf pack responded. Two wolves rushed to flank Celti and Torith. They faced the camp, snarling and showing their fangs as they backed into the darkness, protecting the departing girls. The wolves and girls disappeared into the black.

Once out of sight, Celti wolf howled again, to which the pack forcefully responded. Clearly, she was in charge. The clan had brought Celti to her base of power.

Flat Nose swore. The smirk was gone, and his face only showed fear.

Malta watched Caleb, the leader, as he looked down at the knife in his hand. He was stunned and dejected. Malta could see the terrible choice Celti had thrust on him. There was only one way for him to save his warriors. Five lives must be sacrificed for the lives he had taken. It was fair. Horribly fair.

"Amazing," uttered Malta. "Olam's plan is brutal!"

About the Author

Chris Nelson was an FBI Agent for 26 years, including ten years as an FBI pilot. He is married with four children. He has a finance degree and an MBA. He was an internal auditor for a large oil and gas company, an investigator for a major international bank, and a licensed private investigator. He comes from a close family of ten children. In his youth, he lived in Geneva, Switzerland, and Southern Italy.

Planet Summa Lexicon

Terms unique to the culture and world of Summa.

- **Fikabean** *(noun)* – Low-level, childish insult.
- **Forza** *(noun)* – Third level in the Puissance. Forzas are very powerful.
- **Kutard** *(noun)* – Hard-core adult profane insult.
- **Mordax** *(noun)* – Powerful, blade weapon Olam gave to Dramos, Apollo's older brother.
- **Maramba!** *(interjection)* – Harmless expression of surprise, similar in tone to "Wow!" or the Spanish expression "¡Ay caramba!"
- **Menapses** *(noun, plural)* – Self-repairing and self-multiplying connection hubs or circuits that support the billions of energy and light pathways of a Summa ghost's subatomic essence.
- **Mentor** *(noun)* – Second level in the Puissance.
- **Pitner** *(noun)* – Harsh, adult-level insult—profane and extreme, equivalent to any culture's strongest curse words.
- **Putard** *(noun)* – An insult used by the character Malta. It is a morphed version of the harsher word, kutard.
- **Puissance** *(noun)* – Power of the Quasars distributed on varying levels to Summa Ghosts. Lowest level is SunStar. Next is Mentor. Then Forza. Highest is Quasar.
- **Quasar** *(noun)* – Highest level in the Puissance.
- **SunStar** *(noun)* – Lowest level in the Puissance.
- **Wiffle Boy** *(noun)* – An insult that is not particularly harsh.

No ghosts were harmed in the making of this book.

Olam's plan is brutal.